His heart could be captured—but his passion could never be tamed....

TOUCH
of the
WOLF

"A vivid, talented writer with a
spa...

D0049890

SUSAN KRINARD

Author of *Body and Soul* and *Prince of Shadows*

BANTAM BOOKS

US $5.99 / $8.99 CAN

ISBN 0-553-58018-3

9 780553 580181

50599

CAUGHT BETWEEN TWO WORLDS

Braden's kiss was nothing like his brother's.

It was nothing like Cassidy had imagined a kiss would be, a mere touching of mouth to mouth. This one left her breathless and amazed and exhilarated. It raged through her blood the way he said the Change would do, sent heat surging into parts of her body she'd only begun to discover.

She'd been afraid when she'd undressed, though she knew he couldn't see her—afraid she could never match Braden's perfection. Her first glimpse of his nakedness had inspired awe and a host of other feelings she couldn't name.

Braden kissed her, and she smoldered; she caught fire; she burned to ashes and was born again. He initiated her into a mystery she couldn't wait to possess.

"*Touch of the Wolf* is Susan Krinard at her best. [It is] a fascinating tale of beasts and beauties, love and betrayal, werewolves and humans, men and women. . . . Susan Krinard is a vivid, talented writer with a sparkling imagination, and *Touch of the Wolf* is full of wonderful surprises."
—Anne Stuart

"*Touch of the Wolf* is a mystical, enthralling read, brimming with lyrical prose, powerful emotions, dark secrets, and shattering sensuality. Susan Krinard brings the world of the werewolf to life in a riveting and believable way."
—Eugenia Riley

"Bantam star Susan Krinard returns to her werewolf roots to spin an absolutely thrilling tale of a young American girl whose inexpressible yearnings lead her back to England and into the heart of a man who has sworn never to love again. . . . A compelling, unforgettable romance of two lonely people who finally discover that love holds all the answers."
—*Romantic Times*

Also by Susan Krinard

touch of the WOLF

SUSAN KRINARD

BANTAM BOOKS

New York   Toronto   London   Sydney   Auckland

TOUCH OF THE WOLF
A Bantam Book / October 1999

ISBN 0-553-58018-3

Published simultaneously in the United States and Canada

Bantam Books are published by Bantam Books, a division of Random House,
Inc. Its trademark, consisting of the words "Bantam Books" and the portrayal of
a rooster, is Registered in U.S. Patent and Trademark Office and in other countries. Marca Registrada. Bantam Books, 1540 Broadway, New York, New York
10036.

This book is dedicated to my dear and loyal friend, Rose-Marie Froemming, who's always there for me.

My deepest gratitude to B. L. Carter and Eugenia Riley for their generous contributions of time and support during the writing of this manuscript.

Special thanks to Felicíta Reid, Jesús Arantes, and Ana Isabel Samuels for their help with the Spanish language.

touch of the
WOLF

prologue

Northumberland, England, 1860

Braden stood in the broad shadow of his grandfather, Tiberius Forster, earl of Greyburn, and gazed about the Great Hall into thirty pairs of eyes. Eyes that, like his, seemed human but were not. Watchful eyes: fierce, ever alert, weighing every other man and woman who waited in silence for the earl to speak. Even now, at this ninth great meeting of the families, the delegates never forgot what they were.

Loups-garous. Werewolves. A breed apart from mankind, but living among humanity. A race that would have faced extinction if not for the earl of Greyburn's great Cause.

Braden had been told the story so many times that he knew it by heart. Tiberius had spent his youth searching for his scattered people—in Europe, Russia, Asia, America. His special gifts let him sense them wherever they survived—among the aristocracy and elite of their homelands, more likely than not; more rarely among the common folk, hiding what they were.

The hiding was always necessary. It was a world of humans, and humans far outnumbered the wolf-kind. Yet the *loups-garous* had intermarried with humans and ceased to breed true.

Tiberius knew that their people would die out, fade to nothing in a matter of years or decades—inevitably—unless the blood bred true again. Unless those purest of lineage and power were joined to others equally pure.

There was only one way it could be done. Boundaries must be set aside; old national rivalries, old hatreds forgotten. The *loups-garous* must come together, must make a great pact to preserve their race. Tiberius had cajoled, threatened, pleaded, argued, and used his considerable power to bend others to his will.

And they had come, to this stronghold in the inner heart of Northumberland, where the Greyburn Forsters had held their land for hundreds of years—Forsters who shared a surname with humans but were so much more. That first Convocation in 1820 had been fraught with peril and suspicion, but in the end the *loups-garous* had chosen their salvation. The first marriage contracts had been negotiated, bloodlines traced for the new records.

So it had been now for forty years, twice each decade. But this was Braden's first meeting; at fourteen he had learned to Change, and was at last worthy of taking part in the Cause.

He stared under drawn brows at the Russian delegate, the father of the girl who had been promised to Braden at this very meeting. A great landowner, this prince, who ruled a virtual kingdom of serfs in his distant country. The Russian blood was strong yet, and when joined to the ancient British strain . . .

Braden shook his head. It was too much to consider here, in this forbidding place with its banners and cold stone. He looked instead at the other delegates, memo-rizing faces: dour Scots from Highland and Lowland; French aristocrats, who with their powers had survived the purging of the nobility in their land; the wary Austri-ans and Prussians; the small conclaves of proud Spanish and Italians from warmer climes, where their people clung to the mountains; Norsemen who crossed the sea to land again on shores where once their ancestors had raided and conquered.

There was a handful of guests from more exotic lands, who had come but reluctantly: an Indian prince, a sheikh from the deserts, the last survivor of a venerable clan in Nippon. Only their nonhuman blood bound them to the others.

And then there were the Americans. They fiercely guarded their independence and looked askance at the British nobleman who claimed leadership of all who ran as wolves and men. But they, too, recognized Grand-father's warning, and so they had arrived at Greyburn—to talk, debate, hammer out compromise.

Today, the ninth gathering of the families was at an end. The delegates would scatter for five more years, but new contracts were set in place, and there would be an-other generation of children born to carry on the revived bloodlines. Just as the first contract had bound Braden's late father to Angela Gévaudan of the old French blood. Angela had dutifully borne the Greyburn heir three chil-dren: Braden, Quentin, and Rowena. Each would, in turn, marry as the great Cause dictated; and their children would follow suit, on into the future when the *loups-garous* would become the powerful, fearless people they were meant to be. . . .

"Boy."

Braden jerked out of his thoughts and stared up at his

grandfather. A glance from Tiberius could freeze any other man, human or werewolf, and it had always reduced Braden's knees to jelly.

But Braden had learned to Change, and fear had turned to respect. "Sir?"

Tiberius cuffed him lightly and pushed him toward the massive wooden doors. "Go. I have final words for the others, but I shall speak with you later." He dismissed Braden with a jerk of his shoulder, and Braden saw that all the strangers' eyes, cool and assessing, were on *him* this time. The delegates knew Braden was to inherit the earldom and his grandfather's great purpose. They watched him for any sign of weakness.

I shall be strong, like Grandfather, Braden thought. *One day they will all respect me.* He stood tall and marched from the room, closing the heavy carved double doors behind him.

"Well?" hissed a voice as he passed into the entrance hall. Quentin's eyes were bright with curiosity and mischief. "Was it as exciting as you thought it would be? Did you get to talk, or did they even notice you were there? What did you think about the one with the funny—"

Braden snatched at his brother's arm. "Not here," he whispered. He glanced at Rowena who stood, as always, at Quentin's elbow, and herded the twins down the entrance hall to the front doors. A footman hurried forward to open the doors, and then they were out in the fading sunlight. Once they were alone and beyond the high shield of rhododendrons across the lawn, Braden fixed his sternest gaze on his younger brother and used his deeper voice to best advantage.

"You were spying," he accused. "You had no right to be there. If Grandfather caught you—"

Quentin laughed. Nothing ever frightened him—no

threat of punishment, no prospect of dire consequences. He was, as Maman had said before her death, impossible.

"Do you think it's just a game?" Braden asked. "What Grandfather has done to save our people—"

"I know, I know." Quentin rolled his eyes. "You're so deadly serious. What's the use of being able to Change if it's never any fun? When I make the passage, I shall enjoy it."

Rowena curled her small fingers around her twin brother's arm. "I shall not," she said. "I wish I never had to Change at all."

"You don't have a choice," Braden said, more harshly than he'd intended. "We all have to do as we're told, or there won't be any of us left." His voice softened. "Anyway, when you can Change, you'll find out, Ro. It's amazing . . ." He shivered. "Poor humans. I almost feel sorry for them."

"Not me," Rowena began. "If I could, I would—"

But her words were quickly drowned out by Quentin's. "I know you can't wait to become leader when Grandfather dies," he said to Braden, his grin belying his words. "But he's not nearly ready to stick his spoon in the wall, so you may as well resign yourself to a few more years of playing second fiddle."

Braden stiffened. "When I am leader, you'll have to do what I say."

Quentin snapped into a mock salute. "Yes, my lord. But not quite yet." He gave a yelp as Braden grabbed for him, and suddenly there was a chase in progress, half in earnest and half in play. They tumbled onto the lawn, Quentin nearly holding his own in spite of his lesser years. Rowena hopped a little as if she'd join in, but she was far too proud of her new frock to dirty it, and her twelve-year-old's dignity was too fragile to compromise.

At last Braden had Quentin pinned. "Promise me," he said breathlessly, "promise me that you'll obey me when I'm leader."

There was no surrender in Quentin's eyes, and his smile didn't waver. "Are you afraid I shall do what Grandfather's brother and sister did, and spoil your Cause?"

Braden knew that story by heart as well. "They were both traitors. Great-Aunt Grace married a human instead of the mate chosen for her. And Great-Uncle William broke his word. He went to live in America, but he never sent his children back to England. Now he's dead, and we've lost his bloodline—"

"Bloodlines. You talk just like Tiberius."

"And you talk like a child, because you don't understand."

"Just because the families who come here are *loups-garous* like us doesn't mean they're worthy. Like that Russian girl—"

"What about her?" Quentin bent lower, showing his teeth.

"You like her, don't you? I saw the way you looked at her. Just because Grandfather's arranged it so you have to marry her in a few years. But she and her father have something wrong with them. I saw him hit a stableboy and call him a serf, and that girl is wicked and vain. She said when she comes to live here, everyone will have to do as *she* says."

Braden tried to picture that delicate, exotic face spouting such threats. Surely not. Milena had smiled at him, made him think she liked him, too. . . .

"I don't believe you," he said.

"Maybe not now. But I don't think she will find Greyburn at all to her taste."

The tone of his voice put Braden immediately on alert. Quentin's exaggerated, too-innocent expression was one Braden had seen many times—just before his younger brother pulled a prank on some hapless and unsuspecting victim. They weren't dangerous, his little tricks, and never mean-spirited. Except on those very rare occasions when he didn't like the recipient. . . .

"What did you do?" Braden demanded, grabbing Quentin's collar.

Quentin only grinned more broadly, but Braden hadn't long to wait for an answer. There was a shriek from somewhere inside the house, loud enough for nonhuman ears to hear even through the thick walls. Braden let Quentin up and gave him a shake.

"If you hurt her—"

"Remember those flowers in the garden that made her sneeze? I just made sure she had plenty to decorate her room." Quentin cocked his head. "She won't look very pretty with a runny nose."

Braden closed his eyes. "Why, Quentin? Do you know what Grandfather will do to you when he finds out?"

Quentin knew. He'd been punished before. But he'd never played a trick on one of the family delegates.

"You had best go to the wood for a while," Braden said, shoving Quentin away. "Ro, you as well."

Rowena, at least, had the wits to be frightened. She tugged at her twin's arm. "Come, Quentin!"

Quentin stood his ground. "You'll peach on me anyway, so why should I bother—"

Braden snarled and charged at Quentin. "Get out of here!"

Under any other circumstances, Braden might have been pleased at how quickly Quentin obeyed. The power of Braden's will was growing, and he could feel it coursing through his veins like the magic of the Change itself.

But he was nothing against the earl. He swallowed and walked back to the house, reaching the broad steps just as Grandfather came charging out. His white hair was on end, his eyes blazing, and such was his fury that Braden expected to be knocked from his feet.

But Tiberius stopped short, fists balled at his sides.

"Quentin," he growled. "Where is he?"

"I don't know," Braden said. "He was—"

"Do you realize what he has done? The count's daughter has been insulted, and the count himself—" Grandfather's will bore down on Braden like a stifling weight of water, making it nearly impossible for him to breathe. "The Russians have threatened to break the marriage contract. Because of that boy, the alliance itself is at risk. Tell me where he is."

For a moment Braden wavered. Quentin had to learn. But Grandfather's way of teaching was harsh at the best of times; in his current temper he might do far worse than administer a beating.

"I apologize, sir," Braden said. "I don't know."

There was something far more menacing about Grandfather's sudden stillness than in his short-lived rage. "Do you think to betray me as well?" he said quietly. "No. I would kill you first."

Braden shivered in spite of himself. He'd been raised from leading strings to believe that nothing mattered more than the Cause, that all else must be sacrificed to it. He had seen that principle at work in his grandfather's marriage to the woman he had chosen for her pure blood, and again with Maman and Father.

But Tiberius would not kill the carrier of the very blood he was fighting to preserve. At least not the body. But there were other things to lose. . . .

Abruptly Grandfather took Braden's arm in a hard grip and dragged him into the house. The Russian count stood waiting at the foot of the grand staircase, his eyes silvery slits. Grandfather stopped before him, and some silent communication passed between lord and lord, the kind that Braden was only beginning to comprehend. Wills clashed, and it was the count who broke away first.

"Go to my rooms," Tiberius ordered his grandson, and Braden didn't hesitate to obey. He could buy Quentin more time, and Grandfather would lose the first edge of his anger. He started up the stairs that led to the landing and corridors that ran the length of the first floor through the family and guest wings. A small group of the delegates and their mates stood watching with wary curiosity from the guest wing, but they melted aside as Grandfather reached the landing. Human servants retreated with equal discretion.

Grandfather's suite was a place for which Braden had never borne much affection. Here punishments were meted out, lectures given. And here the weight of the Cause was overwhelming.

Ancient armor stood against the wall, shields and weapons surviving from a more savage age. The Forster blood went much further back than this house had existed, though the names Braden's ancestors carried had changed with the centuries. There was nothing of gentleness in the room. It was icy, for Tiberius denied anything that hinted of a human weakness. The *loups-garous* did not suffer from mere cold.

Grandfather sat down in his hard-backed chair. "Stand where you are, and listen," he said. "I had believed you were old enough to understand. I was mistaken. I shall make it clear to you again. Quentin is only worth to me whatever children he can sire. Rowena is the same. But you—of you I expect far more."

Braden lifted his chin. "I know my duty."

"No." Tiberius pounded his fist on the carved arm of the chair. "But you will, before I am done with you. Your father was worse than useless, but your blood is strong. You will not betray me in the end." He stood up and walked to the old mullioned window that looked over the park. His voice dropped to a rasping whisper. "I've been betrayed twice before. My dear sister eloped with a human before her marriage to the man I had chosen for her could take place. She rejected the ways of our people. And William's daughter Edith ran off with some American peasant, a human named Holt. William and Fenella have been dead these five years, and Edith and Holt and their two offspring have taken up residence in some forsaken wilderness to the far west of America."

"But if you know where they are—" Braden began.

"As of a year ago, yes. If they survive, they will be found and brought back. That shall be your charge when you come of age. Bring them back and force them to—" He stopped, breathing hard. "There will be no more betrayals."

The passion and anguish in Tiberius's voice was very real and utterly unexpected, and it struck at Braden's heart as nothing else might have done. Grandfather had spent his life trying to save a race, and his own siblings had turned their backs on him. Only his innate power had kept the other werewolves cooperative when they had cause to doubt his strength and authority, even over his own family.

The *loups-garous* respected strength. But loyalty to family was burned into their very souls, and so a brother's and sister's rebellions were wounds that would not heal. Braden could not imagine Quentin and Rowena doing that to him. Never.

He crept across the worn carpet to his grandfather's side. "I won't do what they did," he promised. "I won't let the Cause die."

Grandfather looked at him, and it was as if he'd never slipped to reveal a single moment of vulnerability. "When I'm finished with you, you will have no other purpose.

You will live for the Cause, as I have. Nothing else will matter to you. Do you understand?"

Braden couldn't speak. Grandfather's stare held him like the mantraps set in the woods to catch human poachers, and his tongue was leaden.

"You will not lie to me again. Today you will track down your brother and bring him to me. Then you shall administer the punishment the count himself selects. Go."

Behind those words lay no room for negotiation, no latitude for compassion or mercy. The lesson was meant not for Quentin, but for Braden himself. It would be fashioned so as never to be forgotten.

Braden turned and left the room, his mind a blank. He followed the landing to a door that led into several twisting, narrow corridors, hidden stairs, and a back entrance used by the servants. There he paused, scenting the evening; autumn was coming, and he could smell hay and heather and sheep and the smooth-flowing waters of the river below the great sloping park.

He discarded his clothes behind the shrubbery along the wall and Changed with a single thought. On four legs he ran through the gardens, past the open park and into the wood an ancestor had begun and Tiberius had nurtured, until now it was far greater than any private wood in northern England.

As he ran, leaping the burn and dodging pine and oak and ash, he ignored the spoor of rabbit and fox and all the other small creatures that shared the wood. There was only one he hunted. And soon enough he found the familiar scent. But it was Rowena who met him, her eyes very wide and her face pale. Her skirt was muddied, her hair snarled with twigs and leaves.

"What will they do to him?" she whispered.

Braden Changed, and Rowena quickly looked away.

Her modesty had always been exaggerated, but Braden had no time for her almost-human sensibilities.

"Where is he?" he asked.

"Did you come to get him?"

"I came to tell him to stay in the woods." Braden wrapped his arms around his chest, though he hardly felt the chill in the air. "Grandfather told me to bring him back. The count is to decide his punishment. But if Quentin stays away until the Russians leave, maybe it won't be so bad."

Rowena bit her lip. "You'll get into trouble if you don't bring him back."

Braden shrugged. "I know Quentin can find somewhere to hide for a few days. When you see Quentin, tell him—"

"You can tell me yourself." Quentin emerged from behind a thick stand of trees, his habitual smile nowhere in evidence. "I'm no coward. It's my fault. I'll come back with you."

"No." Braden glared at his younger brother, working his will. "You're not as strong as I am, and Grandfather has never liked you. But you owe me for this, Quentin. Don't forget that you owe me."

Quentin clenched and unclenched his fists. "I won't forget."

Braden glanced at Rowena. "You'd better come back. Just don't go near Grandfather for a while. The delegates will be leaving soon, and things will be back to normal."

Normal. As normal as they ever were at Greyburn.

"I'll come to check on you, if I can," Braden said to Quentin. "But stay out of trouble, for once."

They stared at each other. Rowena wept soundlessly. After a moment Quentin took a step backward, and then another, until he had vanished behind the trees again.

Later Braden would talk to Rowena, try to comfort her

if she'd let him. But she'd always been closer to Quentin, and the separation would be difficult for her. He repeated his command that she return to the house, and then Changed once more.

His run home was not so swift nor certain. He knew what would come when he admitted his failure to Tiberius. The pain he could bear, but the humiliation and his grandfather's scorn would cut far more keenly than the whip.

But he would bear it without flinching, to prove his strength. To show he could not be broken. He would be worthy to carry on the work of the Cause.

I will, Grandfather, he promised. *I will make our people strong again. Nothing will stop me, ever.*

Within half a mile of the house he angled away and ran to the top of Rook Knowe. From here he could look down into the valley, across the small fields and isolated cottages and beyond to row upon row of heather-clad, treeless hills marching into the distance. This was his country; he loved it as he loved Greyburn, its hardy human tenants, the bleakness of a landscape that had been never been wholly tamed.

Yes, he would devote himself to the Cause. But he, unlike Tiberius, would find room in his life for other things. For family affection. For the beauty of moor and wood and burn. For the possibility of love in an arranged marriage. For an ideal not driven by anger and bitterness.

I'll do my duty, Lord Greyburn. But I'll do it my way, not yours.

Braden believed with all his heart that it was a promise he could keep forever.

Sierra Nevada Mountains, California

Cassidy pushed the door open with her foot, ignoring the frightful groan it made, and let the armful of branches and kindling fall to the ground near the fireplace. She paused to catch her breath, wiping dirty hands on her equally dirty pants. Dry, brown leaves swirled into the house before she could shut the door, joining those already piled in the corners of the tiny cabin.

Mother had died when the first leaves began to fall, and now the trees were halfway bare. Cassidy went to the larder and looked at the few bags and canisters that remained of the cabin's stores. It wasn't a lot of food, even for her, with winter coming on. And she wasn't a hunter like her mother, or a big, strong man like Father had been before he went away. Not even Morgan was here to help find more food before the snows came.

"You're a strong girl," Mother had said in the weeks before she died. *"You have the true Forster blood, God help me. The blood I wanted to forget—"*

Cassidy closed her eyes and crouched by the fireplace, snapping a brittle piece of kindling between her hands. She had memorized almost everything Mother said to her those last few weeks, because it was important. Mother had known there was something wrong with her, and so she'd tried to explain things that would help Cassidy afterward.

Most of it Cassidy knew: how to build fires, cook simple meals like biscuits and what she called "mush," soften the dried meat stored for winter. She knew where to find the best water and where the berries grew, how to judge the weather and keep warm in the snow.

But Mother hadn't told her how to be so alone.

Leaving the wood where it lay, Cassidy left the cabin and trudged to the small hill behind the house. The mountains were high and sharp all around. The sky looked like a lake thrown upside down. Trees shivered in the wind.

There was nothing here to show when or where Edith Holt had died. Cassidy had done what Mother wanted her to do. They had spent their last night together away from the cabin, in a quiet tree-shaded hollow Mother loved, where she often went to Change. *"Give me to the wild,"* she'd said, while her eyes closed and her breath became quieter and quieter. *"Let me lie here. Do not come back, Cassidy."*

She hadn't gone back, not after she'd cried all the tears inside her, and kissed Mother's forehead, and pushed up some of the pine needles and fallen branches and leaves about the still body. She'd known Mother wouldn't be cold, but it helped a little to do it anyway.

The sky and trees and mountains had been just like today when Father left, nearly a year ago. Cassidy never knew why he went away, though Mother tried to explain. Something about silver, and money, and things that hadn't meant much to Cassidy then, when she was only six. All she knew was that she missed him, and Morgan when he left just after the snowmelt to find Father.

Father wasn't like Mother. He couldn't Change. He couldn't become a beautiful, perfect wolf who could run like the wind and vanish like a shadow.

Morgan was. He'd learned to Change just before he left. He wasn't afraid of anything.

But he'd never come back. Neither of them had. And Mother was never the same after that.

Cassidy sat on the bare ground and listened. Sometimes she thought she could still hear Mother's howl, echoing through the valley. Father would come in from the pasture, and Morgan from the field, and they'd all go to greet her when she ran from the woods, her skin gleaming and her hair loose, with a rabbit or a pair of grouse for dinner.

"Someday," Mother promised, *"you'll be like me. Like Morgan. You, too, will Change."* And even when she was only six, Cassidy had dreamed of that day.

But there was no one left now to show her how to Change. She had only this body that was too small and too weak. Clumsy, not graceful like her Mother's.

If she were able to Change, maybe it would be easier. She would stop being so sad. She would know the secrets that Mother hadn't had time to teach her. In a way, she would be closer to Mother than ever.

She sniffed and scrubbed her face. *"You're such a baby,"* Morgan used to say when she cried. She'd been mad at him then, but now she wanted him back. She wanted him back so bad it hurt inside.

But she couldn't cry anymore. She had to start the fire before it got dark, not even so much for the warmth as the comfort it brought. And she was hungry, always hungry.

The door to the cabin was still partly open, letting in the chill. She pushed her body against it to close it firmly from inside and went to the fireplace. Carefully she arranged the kindling, adding to it bits of paper Father had left in neat stacks about the cabin. Very few of them remained, because she would never burn the few books on the shelf in the corner. Before Mother died, Cassidy had been learning to read. She'd been good at it. Some of the books were too hard for her, but she kept trying, the way Mother and Father would have wanted.

And because the books and their words were like magic carpets to carry her away.

She picked up one of the last pieces of paper and was about to feed it into the small flame when she felt the difference in it. It was not just one big yellowing sheet with lots of small writing—newspaper, Father called it—but an envelope with an address on the front. An address in the city, the place called San Francisco, miles and miles away.

The address was in Mother's writing.

Cassidy lifted the envelope to her nose. It still smelled

like Mother. She opened the envelope slowly with a chipped fingernail and unfolded the sheet inside. One by one she picked out the words, crisscrossing the brittle paper in wavery lines.

My Dear Isabelle,

I pray that you receive this letter in time. Even as I write these words, I know that my hours remaining on earth are few, and it is my hope that this page will be in your hands before I depart.

Take a deep breath, my friend, and do not grieve. I have known for months that I am close to death, but I have tried to fight it for Cassidy's sake. Forgive me my brevity.

Last year—only months after you left us—Aaron went to the Nevada mines. He never returned. Morgan followed, and he too has vanished. I can learn nothing of them. I know in my heart that Aaron is dead, and my soul has gone with him. It is the way of our kind when the bond is very deep.

No, my dear friend, I could not burden you with this—not when I know you felt so indebted to us for those happy years you spent here. There was never any debt between us, Isabelle. But now I must ask you to help me.

I have made what provisions I can for Cassidy, but there is none in these mountains I trust. None but you. Please come with all haste and take Cassidy to your heart and home. I do not care about your past, as you care nothing for my nature. We are sisters in all but blood.

I have enclosed papers which reveal the names of those kin in England my own dear mother wished to forget. They are people of wealth and rank. I wished never to go against my Mother's desires, but they are

*family. They are my kind. Cassidy must know them if
she is to understand herself and her gifts.*

    *I know you have no wish to face England ever
again, but I have no other choice but to ask your help.
If you can bring yourself to so great a sacrifice, take my
child to those who can give her what no human being
can. I will pray with my last breath that this decision is
the right one, and that Cassidy will find happiness and
belonging as my mother and father never could.*

    Come, oh come in haste, my dear friend.

The letter ended with the last words trailing off, as if
Mother had been too tired to finish. Her name at the bottom was a scribble.

Cassidy pressed the open sheet to her face. Isabelle. She
remembered Isabelle, hazily, as a bright face and sweeping
skirt, laughing with Mother or taking a moment to play
with a little girl. Aunt Isabelle. Yes, Mother had talked
about her, and smiled when she did . . . before Father left.

This was a letter, and it was supposed to go to Aunt
Isabelle, who had moved away to San Francisco when
Cassidy was hardly more than a baby. Cassidy knew about
letters, and how Mother used to go down to town some-
times to mail them. But this one had never left the cabin.
Maybe Mother had forgotten, or was too sick.

Some of the letter was confusing, but Cassidy understood enough. Mother had wanted Isabelle to come here
and take Cassidy to a place called England, where there
were—she paused to puzzle out the words again. "... *kin in
England my own dear mother wished to forget . . . family . . .
my kind.*"

Family. *Loups-garous,* like Mother. That was the word
for people who could Change.

Cassidy found the other papers Mother had talked
about and looked at the short list of names.

Forster. Mother had mentioned that name before, too. *Forster blood.* It didn't mean anything to Cassidy, nor did words like "earl" and "Greyburn" and "Northumberland." But they all had to do with family. Belonging. Never being alone again. Knowing all the secrets that made someone safe for always.

Not always. Mother was dead. But somewhere there were people like her. People to go to . . . if she could find Isabelle.

Cassidy rocked back on her heels and stared into the feeble flame catching on the wood. San Francisco was a very long ways away, she knew. Would Isabelle be glad to see her?

A lump formed in Cassidy's throat. To feel someone's arms around her, and hear loving words, a voice saying everything was going to be all right again . . .

From outside the cabin a horse whinnied.

Cassidy jumped to her feet. There weren't any horses here anymore, not since the mare was stolen.

All the hair on her head seemed to stand on end, and her legs felt wobbly. *Father.* Father, come home. Or Morgan. Or both of them. Come to take her away.

She jammed the letter into her pocket, rushed to the door, tripped over the threshold, and flung herself onto the narrow porch. The man was just getting down from his horse, but Cassidy knew at once that the smells weren't right. Not Father, or Morgan. A stranger.

"Hello?" the man called.

Cassidy froze very still, like a rabbit. The man saw her anyway, and started toward her.

"Is this the Holts' cabin? Is your papa at home, child?"

He knew her last name. Maybe he knew her Father. She stepped forward and stopped herself at the edge of the porch. "My father is gone," she said, trying to sound grown-up. She met the stranger's eyes. They were nested in a web of wrinkles and his skin was very tan. There was something about his face . . .

He frowned. "What is your name?"

"Cassidy," she said. "Cassidy Holt."

The man's shoulders sagged. "Then I've come to the right place." His gaze swept the cabin and returned to Cassidy. "When will your father return?"

She bit her lip, because she was afraid she might blubber. "He went away and never came back."

The stranger pulled his hat from wiry gray hair and held it in his hands. "How long ago?"

"When I was only six," she said. "Then Morgan left, and Mother . . ." The words wanted to pour out, because there had been no one to listen until now. But she bit harder on her lip and stared at the man's booted feet, worn and caked with red mountain dirt.

"You must be about seven," the man said. "Where is your mother?"

Cassidy caught her breath on a sob and jumped off the porch and into the stranger's arms. He took a startled step back and closed his arms around her, just long enough to set her on her feet again. He held her away with his hands on her shoulders. She hugged herself instead.

"She's dead," she whispered.

The man made a harsh sound under his breath, took her by the wrist, and pulled her after him up to the cabin door. He pushed it open, looked inside, and shut it again.

"Damn you, Aaron. You've left me to clean up after you one last time."

Cassidy stared up at his face. He was angry now, but there was no one to be angry at. Except her.

Abruptly he crouched before her. "Listen to me, child. You will have to come with me." He didn't talk as if he wanted her to go with him. "I can't leave you here, whatever your mother—" He shook his head. "You are kin."

Kin. Family. "You are . . . my family?" she asked with an almost painful twinge of hope.

"Your uncle Jonas," he said, rising again. "Your father's brother. I came to California for other reasons, but it seems I'm to have the care of you, like it or not." He went into the cabin again, leaving her on the porch, and returned a few moments later with a bundle tied out of an old blanket. "These are little better than rags, but they'll have to do." He looked her over again. "Dear Lord, child, alone here for God knows how long—it's a wonder you're still alive." His face darkened. "But why am I surprised?"

She didn't understand him except that there was something here he didn't like. For a long time he simply stared at her. "God send that you are more Aaron's child than hers. We'll stay in town tonight."

"San Francisco?" Cassidy asked.

He snorted. "We're going east, child, not west. To New Mexico. I have a farm there. You'll have enough to eat, and work to keep you busy. Your aunt will see to that." He held out his hand. "Come—you'll ride behind me."

Cassidy realized then that he meant he wanted to leave right now—that she was to go with this stranger who was family but didn't really want her. She looked wildly about and dashed into the cabin, to the few worn books on the shelf. She found another blanket and made an unsteady pile of books in the center of it, then added what little food she could carry.

When she returned to her uncle, he frowned. "What is this?" He slipped the uneven knot at the top of the bundle. "Books? I have no room—"

"I can't go with you," she said. "I have to go find Isabelle."

"I know no Isabelle."

"My mother's friend." She dug in her pocket and

pulled out the letter, smoothing it against her chest. "Mother wrote to her—"

Uncle Jonas took the paper from her hand. After a moment he crushed it in his fist and let it fall to the ground. Cassidy bent to pick it, but Uncle Jonas ground it under his foot until it was little more than pulp. Swallowing the hard lump in her throat, Cassidy closed her eyes and recalled every line of the letter, so that she would never forget.

"You have no need of your *mother's* friends," Jonas said.

"But my mother's family, in Eng-land," she said, pronouncing out the word carefully. "She said that they could help me."

"Forget about them."

"But . . . can you teach me how to Change, Uncle Jonas?"

His head snapped up. "We will not speak of this further. *They* have nothing to do with us. You will not mention this Change again."

She fell silent under the harshness of his words. She'd already guessed that Uncle Jonas, like Father, wasn't a *loup-garou*. There was something different about the smell, the feeling she got when she touched someone who could Change. But Jonas didn't want to talk about it. Something made him afraid.

Cassidy wasn't afraid. Even if Uncle Jonas wouldn't talk about it, there must be someone who would. Someone who understood and could explain the gift she'd been promised before Mother died.

"Don't worry about me," she said. "You don't have to take care of me. Isabelle—"

Without another word he wrapped his big hand around her wrist and pulled her toward his horse. She had just enough time to grab her books. He tied the bundle to the saddle and mounted, scowling all the while. He was strong enough to pull her up behind him, though she had to scramble to find a seat amid the pack and bundles secured behind the cantle.

Jonas kicked his horse into motion, and she grabbed his coat and held on. He didn't look back once as they rode away from the cabin, away from everything Cassidy had ever known. She twisted her neck and shoulders to look as long as she could, as if there were someone still in the cabin who could say good-bye. Then they rounded a curve and passed behind a stand of pines, and the cabin was gone.

The ground was a long way away. If she jumped off, she wouldn't have her books and food. She couldn't leave the books, not even to find Isabelle.

She was too small, now, to do what Mother wanted. But the time would come when she was big enough, and strong enough, to go to San Francisco. Then Isabelle would take her to England, and she would be with family again. Family who could love and want her and teach her how to be *loup-garou*. No matter what happened in New Mexico with Uncle Jonas, she would never lose that dream.

I promise, Mother, she prayed silently. *I'll never forget.*

one

London, England, 1875

Cassidy opened her eyes to unfamiliar darkness and held very still, listening for sounds of lapping water and the rumble of the steamer.

But the smells were not of brine and sea air, and the noise was nothing so peaceful as the sea. She lay very still and retraced in her mind the long road that had brought her here, to the hotel in Victoria Station and the heavy stench of a London night.

It had all been like a dream from the moment she'd left the ranch where she'd spent the last fifteen years of her life—left behind a place that had never been home and people who were glad to see her go. Her father's kin, who could never understand or accept her, because within her ran Edith Holt's wild blood.

The blood of those she'd come so far to find.

She thought back to the long trek westward from New Mexico Territory to California, rationing out what little money she'd scrimped and saved for herself over the years.

She had been immersed in a flood of alien sensations from the moment she boarded the crowded coach in Las Cruces. Her narrow experience of the world—a world of sagebrush and creosote and mesquite, desert heat and cattle and adobe—had been forever changed by the time she reached the train in Colorado. Not even her carefully preserved books of poetry and tales of romantic adventure could prepare her for what she found in the bustling railroad towns, nor could she imagine anything else so vast and daunting.

Until she reached San Francisco, and searched out the address she had memorized so long ago. Only instinct and stubborn determination had led her through the maze of streets and buildings to find the one person in all the world who could help her.

Isabelle Smith, her mother's friend, who had made the rest of this journey possible. And now they were both in London—a place bigger than San Francisco, bigger even than New York, which Isabelle had said was America's greatest city. Immense, seething, impossible to escape even in sleep.

Cassidy sat up and looked at the dim square of the window. It must be near midnight, and yet the constant din and clamor from the streets below had hardly lessened. If she went to the window, she'd see the carriages rattling up and down the cobbled street, on their way to and from places with names like Belgravia and Mayfair.

It was "the Season," Isabelle had explained, a time of parties and constant activity in this fashionable part of London. The people in the neighborhood were wealthy or titled or important in some way. It was the sort of place where the earl of Greyburn might live.

The earl. A lord, like knights in the old stories—a kind of man unlike any Cassidy had met in all her life. He would be powerful, and noble, and far too grand for the likes of Cassidy Holt.

But he was a Forster. He was on the list Cassidy had memorized when she was seven years old. He was family.

And tomorrow they would find him. But tomorrow was already today. The long years of waiting were over.

She swung her legs to the floor and glanced across the darkened room to the matching bed where Isabelle slept. Her delicate face—surely as beautiful as that of the Blessed Damozel in Rossetti's poem—was soft with sleep, and Cassidy felt a rush of affection and gratitude. Isabelle had been Mother's friend, and now she was Cassidy's. She was a real lady, just like those who rode in the carriages below. And she had been born in England. She, too, had come home.

Home.

Cassidy crept to the window and pushed it open, sifting the thick fog for a single familiar scent. There was a place of growing things in the midst of this endless city: they called it Hyde Park, and she could smell it, along with the other cramped, walled-in spaces the English made for their gardens. Far stronger were the odors of horse dung, and smoke, and the tang of stale water from the great river to the south. As far as she could see were buildings like ugly square cliffs above deep, noisy arroyos, marching row upon row until they were lost in the endless haze and darkness.

She wondered how anyone could bear to live among those cold canyons. The hotel walls seemed to close in around her, and she remembered with longing, the clean, austere beauty of the desert, unfenced and untamed.

But in New Mexico she had been alone.

A shiver of anticipation caught hold of her like an unseen

hand at the back of her neck. They were waiting for her, out there. She could feel them. A silent call hung in the heavy damp air, half-remembered like the soft cadence of her mother's voice. The voice of the *loups-garous*. The language Cassidy yearned to make her own.

Isabelle had taught her something of city ways on the journey to England; here, a young woman didn't travel alone. Isabelle would never approve of the thoughts that raced through Cassidy's mind.

But Isabelle was fast asleep, and Cassidy knew how to move quietly. At night she could walk unseen, undisturbed by the throngs of people who made the streets impassable by daylight.

She could follow the call. She had to.

She hesitated in choosing her clothes; there was the plain broadcloth traveling dress Isabelle had bought her, but she couldn't move freely in it. Her calico dress— the only one she'd owned on the ranch, saved for special occasions—wasn't the kind of armor she needed to venture forth into the unknown.

She murmured a quiet apology to her sleeping friend and pulled on the denim trousers and old shirt she'd hidden from Isabelle's critical eye. Isabelle had made her give up the battered work hat; she tucked her hair on top of her head and tied it back as best she could with a bit of ribbon Isabelle had left on the dressing table.

It wasn't difficult slipping out the door and past the few people in the hall—hotel staff and guests about late-night business. She found a side staircase and followed her nose to a narrow door far from the grand main entrance.

In a few minutes she was out in a small alley. It was very dim and heaped with refuse, but she found her way to the main street, pausing at the corner. A row of streetlamps illuminated the way for passing carriages and made her choices clear.

To the north was the odor of grass and trees and water, to the south the great river called Thames. It was much broader than the Rio Grande, she'd heard, but no farmers worked its banks in London.

Somewhere, starting on this very street, lay the path to her future. In New Mexico she'd been able to trail a rabbit over miles of scrub and desert. All she needed was a sign, a track in this trackless place, to show her the way.

She closed her eyes and wished with all her heart.

The answer came as a thin, elusive wisp of scent that grew steadily more distinct, rising above the heavier odors like the cry of a hawk in a thunderstorm.

She could not have explained how this one scent, so unlike any she'd encountered before, made her heart pound and her breath come short. It was extraordinary, like a flower blooming out of season in the desert. Unique. Compelling. And yet . . .

She *knew* it. It was the dream made form. It was life. It was herself.

And as she stood frozen in amazement, the scent began to drift away, fading beyond her reach.

She stepped into the street and caught the trailing end as if it were a rope snatched from her hand by a cranky maverick. North; it was leading her north, and the source was not far ahead.

She could not lose it. She was the best trailer and tracker on her uncle's ranch; none of the other *vaqueros* even came close to her skill. Under the sallow glow of the streetlamps she followed the scent at a run, barely aware of passersby, unnoticed because she wished to be.

The one she sought was unmistakable. When she found him, she knew.

He walked by himself, head down and gaze bent on the street ahead as if he expected all obstacles to melt from his path. He was tall, and broad-shouldered; he wore a coat and hat and carried a cane, and his stride was sharp and purposeful.

Cassidy had seen men of every kind on her roundabout journey to London. Tall men, short men, handsome and plain, high and low, rich and poor, gentle and cruel. But always as human as the people she'd known in New Mexico.

He was something else altogether.

It didn't matter that she couldn't see his face and didn't even know his name. The need within her was strong; it was a wild thing in itself, the part of her that longed for awakening. It was too powerful to resist. She had no choice but to follow this man, this familiar stranger, as she would follow her destiny.

He was entering a wide square, with neatly clipped lawns and hedges and isolated trees and rows of grand houses, all very much alike, on every side.

The wealth of fine carriages and handsomely dressed people told Cassidy who lived in these houses. It seemed right that her stranger should belong among them. He walked up the steps to the entrance of one of the houses, and after a moment the door opened and he stepped inside.

Cassidy crouched behind a shrub and rubbed her palms on the worn knees of her trousers. The poets spoke about things like fate and destiny. Maybe they had something to do with why she was here, at this place and time.

Isabelle would be horrified at her situation, if she knew. But Cassidy couldn't turn back now. She was working up the nerve to cross the street when a carriage drew up in front of the house, a sleek vehicle with spirited horses and a driver and a uniformed man who leaped down as the carriage came to a stop. Her stranger emerged from the house again, and the uniformed man held the carriage door open for him.

By the time the coach moved away Cassidy had already made her decision. She let the coach gain a little distance ahead, and then ran after it. She could run for miles, if she had to. A slight drizzle had begun, a wetness that soaked her clothes and skin. She barely felt it.

The coach followed a curving street out of the square and moved onto a wider lane, flanked on one side by iron-fenced gardens. Cassidy remembered Isabelle pointing it out to her as Buckingham Palace, belonging to the queen of England. But the carriage moved past, to a busy inter-section that took all of Cassidy's concentration to negoti-ate. Then they were alongside Hyde Park, the biggest open space Cassidy had seen in London, and turning east on a narrower street, once more boxed in by rows of tightly packed houses.

It was more difficult to hide herself here. There were many carriages, people getting in and out, entering the houses and leaving them amid bursts of laughter and faint music. The house where her stranger's carriage stopped was the busiest of all, brilliant with light, guarded by costumed men who bowed to the guests as they came to the door.

Once Cassidy had thought her aunt's and uncle's friends and acquaintances attending their frequent parties very splendid in their fancy storebought clothes. Cassidy had often watched those gatherings, to which she was never invited, through the windows of her uncle's adobe hacienda, and envied the *ricos* inside. She knew that she, in her patched and dusty work clothes, would never be one of them.

The people here moved as if they wore such rich and gorgeous clothes every day, as if they'd never known the feel of dirt under their bare feet or mended a hole in a pair of stockings.

Not one of them was as magnificent as her gentleman.

He stepped out of his carriage and paused, head lifted, and she saw his face in lamplight.

He matched the promise of his scent in every way. His bearing was that of a king, his dark clothing perfectly tailored over a sleek, strong body.

His face was breathtakingly handsome. Under his hat a single lock of gray hair draped down across dark, imposing brows. His mouth was mobile, his nose long but not too big, his chin square and strong.

But it was his eyes that arrested her. They were green, the rich color of life like the desert after a good rain, slightly tilted above high cheekbones. They had the power to pierce the darkness, and if he were to turn and look her way . . .

"Tyger! Tyger! burning bright," she quoted silently. That was the image that came into her mind. He burned very bright indeed. His nostrils flared as if to scent the air, a hunter about to spring. Authority and power radiated from him like heat from desert earth, flowed like a spring that would never run dry—a spring with the gift to restore life at the end of a long and perilous search; a magical well that could answer all her questions.

In New Mexico, when the questions and unfulfilled needs had become almost too much to bear, she would run far out into the desert and stand under the moon and howl until her throat was raw. She felt like howling now, so she bit her lip and sank deeper into the shadows. But caution could not still the excitement that convinced her that she knew this stranger as well as herself—that if she dared walk into the light he would open his arms and carry her off to his magic kingdom. . . .

He turned away from her, unseeing, and walked up the stairs of the house. He spoke to the costumed men, who bowed low and ushered him in. The remaining man looked right and left and followed, leaving the doorway deserted.

Cassidy knelt beside the scant cover of a low iron fence and glanced toward the street. There was a lull in the comings and goings of carriages and people; the guardians at the door were absent. She dashed up the steps, paused at the door, drew in a breath, and pulled it open.

The grand hallway she entered was empty, but she felt that was only a temporary condition. Those costumed men were sure to return. She could hear music plainly now, and many voices echoing down the wide staircase that rose to the second floor. It was obvious where her stranger had gone.

She couldn't see any other way to follow but go up those same stairs. At least her shoes were new and wouldn't dirty the polished perfection of the marble steps. Cassidy pressed herself to the banister and hurried up the stairs, listening for the shout that would bring her adventure to a humiliating stop.

But she made it to the top of the stairs unseen. She had a feeling that there should have been more people on the landing; a sense of anticipation hung in the air, and it came most of all from the open doorway across from the stairs. That was where the music and voices were loudest, and where the two costumed men lingered, looking into the room but not entering. A woman in a black dress and white cap joined them, whispering excitedly.

Something was about to happen. Cassidy abandoned caution and moved up behind the spectators in the doorway. The scents of close-packed bodies and perfumes and flowers were overpowering, yet she knew her stranger had passed this way only moments before. The woman with the cap glanced at her in surprise, but Cassidy smiled and met her gaze, and the woman's attention slid away.

Cassidy crouched and found a clear view into the room between two pairs of white-stockinged legs.

The first thing she noticed was the vast number of people, squashed into every part of the room, between potted plants and artificial columns and in every corner. The music came from the far end, emerging from behind a row of shrubs; the players were nearly invisible.

Then she saw her gentleman. He stood just inside the door, minus his overcoat and hat, very still. His hair, she saw, was not gray at all, but a salt-and-pepper mingling of black and white. As she watched, he seemed to sweep the room with his gaze, fixing at last on one particular spot just out of Cassidy's sight.

That was when it became very quiet. The hum of voices and the laughter trailed off as heads in the room turned, one by one, toward Cassidy's gentleman. The hush itself had a life of its own, ominous and stern. Someone tittered and was cut off instantly. The music died with a whimper.

It was because of her stranger. *Tyger, Tyger, burning bright.* They were staring at him, a sea of pale faces above gorgeous costumes, the lustrous colors of the ladies and blacks of the gentlemen. They stared as if they had never seen him before.

Her gentleman began to move. He walked forward, slowly, with a grace and authority as much a natural part of him as his brilliant eyes. Magically the crowd parted in his path like so many half-wild calves dodging a *vaquero* with a branding iron.

Cassidy craned her neck to see the object of her gentleman's interest. A small cluster of women were gathered in the far corner of the room, so bunched together that Cassidy couldn't tell one pale, rich dress from another.

But one of the women was subtly different from her companions, and Cassidy knew she was the object of the stranger's interest. The lady was a few years older than Cassidy, with a slender figure and a striking if not beautiful face crowned by golden hair. Her white, nearly bare shoulders gleamed in the soft light as if she had stepped out of the pages of one of Aunt Harriet's fashion magazines.

Just as Cassidy's gentleman was about to reach her, an older and much stouter woman intercepted him. She spoke in a low, pleasant voice pitched for him alone, but her body in its heavy gown all but shouted fear. Cassidy's gentleman hesitated for only a few seconds, murmuring a short string of words to the older woman. She fell back, visibly shaken.

Abruptly the young blond woman stepped away from her friends, chin high and back very straight. Cassidy's gentleman met her in a circle of silence, and they stood face-to-face, alike only in the air of absolute control that each possessed.

"Rowena," Cassidy's gentleman said, his voice deep and assured, as smooth as velvet and cold as a desert night in winter. "It's time to come home."

The lady didn't answer, but her face might have been carved like the statues Cassidy had seen in the hall. Without haste she turned back to her friends, touched hands and spoke with the faintest of smiles. Then she returned to Cassidy's gentleman, who offered his arm. She took it, barely resting her gloved hand on his sleeve.

The silence lasted until they were halfway back across the room, and then the murmurs started up again, hushed whispers that gradually gained volume as the ladies and gentlemen flowed back into the empty space.

"Blimey! I'd never o' believed it. The earl 'imself, 'ere, givin' 'em all a fright. And the lady—"

Cassidy remembered the men standing above her just as they stepped hastily back out of the doorway. The one who'd spoken stumbled over her before she could scramble aside, and he stared down in blank amazement.

" 'Ere, now, who're you? What're you doing in 'ere?"

He made a grab for her, but she shook him off and sprinted for the stairway. On the way down she passed several other soberly dressed men and women, but none of them were fast enough to stop her.

She flung herself out the door and pelted down the stairs, looking for a place to hide. She found a sunken alley to either side of the stairs, partly surrounded by an iron railing. She braced herself and jumped, landed on her feet, and backed into a shadowed alcove.

But her pursuer must have been otherwise occupied. After a moment Cassidy heard voices, and she knew her gentleman was leaving the house in company with the lady. She angled for a better view and watched them make their way to the waiting carriage.

She lingered in hiding until the doors to carriage and house were safely shut, and the carriage had started off. Then she sprinted after the carriage as she had done before, praying that the man clinging to the rear platform behind the wheels didn't notice, and that no one else would try to stop her.

But even as she ran, her thoughts kept returning to the way her gentleman had looked among all those proud and fancy folk, the way he'd dominated the room just by standing there.

And who was the lady he'd claimed so boldly? She was a match for him in every way, splendid and proud. Not a tigress to his Tyger, but . . . a Snow Queen, cool and regal.

Cassidy shivered in her wet clothes. It wasn't too late to stop and make her way back to the hotel. The carriage was retracing its path to her gentleman's house; what would she do there? Follow him inside?

Yes, a rich inner voice sang out, vibrating in her blood and bones. *Yes.*

Still she hung back as the carriage turned into the square and stopped before the gentleman's house. She was safely hidden behind a shrub across the lane before the Tyger and his lady were on the front steps. They were bowed through the door by the costumed man who'd accompanied the coachman, and then Cassidy was alone in the London night.

She knew what Isabelle would say at this moment. She had an idea of what was proper, and how things were or were not done among these folk. She knew she was only a drab, skinny girl wearing boy's clothes, a scraggly desert mouse in a nest of elegant tropical birds. But her inner voice was not to be denied. It was her mother's legacy; it was her destiny.

"Ask me no more," she whispered, "thy fate and mine are seal'd: I strove against the stream and all in vain: Let the great river take me to the main: No more, dear love, for at a touch I yield. . . ."

She was getting to her feet when powerful fingers seized her arm and swung her in a circle.

She gazed up into the face of her Tyger. His green eyes were mere slits, his face grim and forbidding.

"Who are you?" he demanded, the velvet stripped from his voice. "You've been following me."

She was mute, gone from startled to sizzling in his presence. "I—"

He jerked her closer, nostrils flaring. "You're one of us," he said. His mouth twitched, and he lifted his free hand to touch her face. "Impossible. I would have known—"

It was all Cassidy could do to keep her feet as his fingers traced her jaw, her cheek, her ear. She had the crazy thought that maybe she was back in the hotel, and this was a dream, cruelly unreal. She was afraid, yet fear was the smallest part of the emotions that set her whole body trembling. She was speechless, struggling to pull from memory a line of poetry or fragment of some fanciful story that would explain her reaction to his touch—the incomprehensible joy of feeling him only a heartbeat away, freeing all those half-familiar and somehow terrible needs that she'd never dared let loose. . . .

"You're one of us," he repeated, and there might have been wonder in his words if not for their harshness. His grip tightened, and his breath stirred the flyaway tendrils of her hair. *"Who are you?"*

"C-Cassidy," she whispered.

He gazed at her with that piercing stare, green eyes like her aunt's treasured emerald. "Cassidy who?"

"Holt," she choked out. "From America. Cassidy Holt."

She was so lost in him that she saw every subtle change in his expression: the relaxing of his mouth, the parting of his lips, the softly withdrawn breath, the way the line between his dark brows smoothed out. His hand fell to grip her other arm, and he held her as if he would devour her like the Tyger he was.

"Cassidy . . . Holt," he said. "You're alive."

two

Braden had known he was being followed ever since he'd walked into Lower Belgrave Street.

He'd identified his stalker as female by her scent, and that she was *loup-garou* the moment he touched her. That in itself was a miracle—had he still believed in miracles. He'd been certain he knew every man or woman of the blood in England, and most beyond this island's shores.

But never in his wildest imaginings—had he allowed himself such frivolities—would he have guessed whom he held in his arms.

Cassidy Holt . . . Edith's daughter, granddaughter of his great uncle William Forster . . . was alive.

He flashed back to that day eight years ago when Tiberius Forster, on his dying breath, had charged his grandson and heir with the task of finding the lost Forster branch in America and restoring it to the Cause. Braden had been little more than a callow boy then, madly in love with his young bride and preoccupied with new responsibilities as earl and master of the Cause. But he had done his duty. He'd sent agents to America to trace the wandering path of William Forster's daughter, Edith, and her human mate—pursued them all the way to California.

Where the trail ended in death. Edith Holt's death, and the apparent disappearance of her husband and their two half-human children. Braden had accepted and dismissed his agents' reports without question, for of what importance was the fate of distant, mixed-blood relations when the rest of the world lay in the palm of his hand, the perfect mate shared his bed, and the Cause was his to shape and bring to triumph?

Only later, much later, had he realized what had been lost when he'd failed to continue the search—after he had paid the price of his arrogance, and learned just how little he did control. After he understood, personally and bitterly, how precious and rare good *loup-garou* blood could be. Because of him, twice over, the Cause had been irrevocably damaged.

Yet a miracle had occurred here tonight on his very doorstep. He had not looked for it. He had not earned it. One of Edith Holt's vanished offspring had come to London like a promise of redemption. Come directly to him.

A handful of years ago he might have laughed for sheer amazement. He didn't laugh now. He absorbed the reality of the girl's presence, felt shock settle into a grim and sardonic sense of triumph.

Do you see, Grandfather? he asked silently, though he had no more faith that the old tyrant could hear him than he believed in genuine miracles.

The girl in his hold was very still. He could feel her stare, as physical a sensation as the electric tension that sparked through her body and into his.

"You're like my mother," she said. Her voice was low and husky, accented with the distinct American drawl, but it held all the breathless excitement of a child's. "You're *loup-garou*."

Hope traced a long-unused path in his heart, and he pushed it aside. "Of course," he said impatiently. "How did you find me?"

"I . . . I caught your scent, at the hotel near the train station. I followed you."

He remembered when he'd passed by Victoria Station an hour ago, snatching a few moments for a private walk before confronting Rowena at the Leebrooks'.

Was it possible? Could this girl's blood be so strong, her gifts so pure that she could distinguish the unfamiliar scent of a fellow *loup-garou* from the morass of stink and stench that was London?

But London was also all eyes and ears, and he had no intention of carrying on this singular conversation in public. He tugged on her arm, pulling her toward the house. "Come. You may explain the rest inside. . . ."

She was tall, though not as tall as he, and surprisingly strong when she dug in her heels and refused to move another step.

"But I don't even know your name!"

He half stumbled on the lowest step of the staircase and swung to face her. She had recognized what he was, but hadn't known who she followed? Without questioning the impulse, he reached out to touch her face again, felt her flinch and then accept his exploration as she had before.

This time he moved more slowly, tracing each contour and line, stroking the softness of her skin. Before he had been driven by urgency; now he took in the details one by one.

Distinct features. Stubborn chin, wide mouth, slightly upturned nose. The typically tilted eyes of the Forsters, bred true. Thick, slightly curling hair barely confined by a loose ribbon. He paused at her lips, running the tip of his finger along the seam. They were tender, sweetly curved.

Her lips parted, and her tongue darted out in a nervous gesture to touch his fingertip.

He withdrew his hand and clenched it at his side. "Why have you come to London?"

"To find my family. My mother's kin. They live here, in England." Her voice lifted eagerly. "Maybe you know them. They're called the Forsters, and one of them's a lord. He probably lives right—" She tensed as if in sudden realization, and then began to laugh in a joyful burst of sound.

"It's you, isn't it?" she said. "You *are* my family!"

A smile tugged at his mouth, as if her childlike happiness were infectious. He mastered the impulse and bowed stiffly. "Your cousin, Braden Forster."

Cassidy Holt stepped away, her footfalls beating out a soggy little dance on the wet lawn. By God, she *was* a child. A child just barely of age, but old enough. Yes, old enough to play her essential role. She could not possibly conceive of how important she was.

"Isabelle won't believe it," she said. "I found you." Without warning or the least bit of modesty she hurled herself at Braden, closing her slender arms around him, pressing her face to his coat.

"I found you," she repeated.

Braden held himself utterly still. Her scent enveloped him: wildflowers and unfamiliar greenery, sharp and pungent, cattle and dust and sunlight not yet overwhelmed by the damp and smoke and dirt of London. With great care he disengaged her arms from about him and placed her hands at her sides.

"Young woman," he said. "What are you wearing?"

"What? Oh . . . these are from the ranch." Her silence burned with embarrassment. "I have a dress, but—"

"How fortunate." Yet perhaps her choice of clothing—

if choice it was—had been an intelligent one. Unlikely that passersby would have perceived her as female. He raised his head to listen for any intrusion on their privacy, but they were alone in the square for the time being. All of fashionable London, it seemed, was at the Leebrook party.

"Where was this ranch?" he asked.

"In New Mexico. I went to live there with my uncle when I was seven, after my mother died." Her voice softened. "But she wanted me to come here, to you. To the Forsters. She wrote to Isabelle, to ask for her help, but the letter was never sent. My Uncle Jonas came for me, and I couldn't leave—not for a long time, until I—"

"You came to England alone?"

"Oh, no. Isabelle came with me—we just arrived yesterday. Isabelle is a fine lady, my mother's good friend. *My* friend. She's the one who told me where I might be able to find you." She blew out her breath. "I left her at the hotel. I guess she'll be mighty worried by now, if she's awake—"

"And what possessed you to leave your hotel in the middle of the night?"

"I felt . . . I heard something calling me." He felt her move closer, stop, hold herself still. "Ever since Mother died, I've been waiting for this." She swallowed audibly. "My uncle and aunt never understood. They didn't want me, no matter how hard I worked. They were always afraid."

Because they were human, as Edith Holt's mate was human. Braden heard the pain behind Cassidy's words, and knew there was more to the story than she was willing to share. He could imagine well enough. She'd been left an orphan, taken in by people who had denied her very nature.

Pity was an indulgence he rejected—from others, or for them. There was no self-pity in Cassidy Holt.

"*You* were calling me," she said. "Calling me home. And now I'm here."

His immediate instinct was to reject her claim. He had not even known she was alive, let alone in London. She mistook her own keen ability for recognizing her own kind, uncommon even among *loups-garous*, for some mystical summons.

Why not let her believe? He should encourage her ingenuous simplicity, her sense of destiny, her peculiar but absolute trust in him. In these few brief minutes he'd learned little enough about her, but already he was grateful to the uncle who'd kept her hidden away out of fear. She'd clearly grown up ignorant of the greater world and its myriad complications—propriety, social distinctions, temptations, and hidden dangers—with her innocence remarkably intact.

All to the good. Such naïveté would make her biddable, easily shaped to the role required of her.

And yet she'd come across the sea to find relations she'd never met and walked the night streets of a foreign city alone, this child from the backwaters of an outlandish country, this paradoxical offspring of the rebel Forsters. Her gifts were unmistakable, her common sense sound. As *loup-garou* she was safe from most ordinary harm, but she had the wisdom not to run as a wolf in an unfamiliar world.

She was innocent and canny at once, an unexpected combination. And she had been restored to him. To the Cause.

He could not afford to forget that she was more than merely some valuable article lost through his carelessness and fortuitously recovered. Far more. He vividly recalled the feel of her skin, her hair, her mouth under his fingertips and felt the first stirrings of a deeper interest touched by an emotion he couldn't define: almost intimate, personal, altogether separate from his concern for her part in the Cause.

Too personal. Treacherous. Forbidden.

"You . . . do want me, don't you?" Cassidy asked. "I won't be any trouble. I can work—I know cattle, and sheep, a little cooking and sewing. If you'll just give me a chance . . ."

His throat acquired a peculiar knot. "The Greyburn Forsters are not servants, cousin. You're among your own kind now." He took her arm in a rigid grip and steered her toward the house. "I'll send a man to the hotel for your things. You may write a note to this Isabelle informing her that you are safely with your family, and that her services are no longer required."

This time she allowed him to lead her as far as the front steps before she jerked him to a stop. "I *asked* Isabelle to come with me. She's English—"

"But she is human, is she not?"

The question seemed to startle her. "Yes. But she knew everything about my mother. She was never afraid."

It was no surprise that Edith Holt had chosen humans as friends, just as she'd chosen one as a mate. She, like her parents, had turned her back on her blood and heritage.

Cassidy had not. But she understood nothing of what lay in her future, or how much rested on her slender shoulders. She must learn, and accept.

"You do want me, don't you?" In one simple question she'd revealed her greatest vulnerability, what she hungered for above all else, what she had never known among her father's people. Something only he could provide.

Belonging. Family. Acceptance. He could grant or withhold what she had come so far to find.

"There is no place for Isabelle where we're going," he

said. "We shall remain in London only a few more days, and then—"

"We're leaving London?"

He took her hand—warm, fingers slender but strong and roughened with work—and removed it from his sleeve. "To Greyburn, the heart of our family and our blood. You do wish to join your family?" He hardly paused for her affirmation. "Then you may begin by doing as you're told. You know nothing of our ways. Rowena will take you in hand and see that you get proper clothing—"

"Rowena? Is she the lady you brought back from the party?"

It was unfortunate that she'd witnessed that little scene: Rowena's veiled mutiny, the defiance that masqueraded as feminine obedience to her brother's will. He would tolerate no further opposition—not from her or from anyone who scorned the Cause. There was no time for the indulgence of childish whims—

"Is she your wife?" Cassidy asked.

Startlement broke his anger. "My wife?" The word emerged as a curse. "No. She is my sister and your cousin, Lady Rowena Forster. You'll meet her tomorrow." He ascended the stairs and opened the door. "Come."

She obeyed, this time, without argument. Aynsley appeared in the hall, and Braden had him send a footman for the housekeeper and a blanket. Cassidy would require dry clothing and a bed prepared for her, possibly food as well. The rest could be settled at Greyburn.

Everything would be settled, once and for all, at Greyburn.

He led Cassidy into the library and pulled a chair up to the fire. "Sit," he ordered. She did so, her intent silence suggesting that she was fully engaged in observing her surroundings.

Mrs. Fairbairn appeared and Braden gave her the necessary instructions. He could feel her curiosity, but she knew better than to linger and stare at the unexpected female guest.

"Was that your mother?" Cassidy said.

Cassidy Holt had an unwelcome habit of asking astonishing questions. "That," he said, "was the housekeeper, Mrs. Fairbairn."

"Oh. She looks very nice."

"She is an efficient servant." He unfolded the blanket Fairbairn had given him and shook it out. "You're soaked through, cousin. Wrap yourself in this. Mrs. Fairbairn will have the maids prepare your room."

Cassidy sprang up from the chair, dodging the offered blanket. "Please don't go to any trouble. I can sleep anywhere. Right here would be fine."

"I trust you had a room of your own at your uncle's ranch."

"Oh, yes," she said, "but I often slept out in the desert with the *vaqueros*. I don't need anything special."

He tried to picture her bedding down among a rough lot of human males, but his imagination balked at the idea of it. What kind of life had she led since the death of her parents? She dressed as a boy with little self-consciousness, and she spoke her mind without any sense of decorum.

Yet he knew she was untouched. He would swear to that on the Cause itself. There was nothing hidden about her, no dark secrets or dangerous complexities; she was as obvious as heather on the moors.

"How you lived in America is unimportant," he told her. "Here you will have a room of your own, and a maid will see to your needs. Have you dined this evening?"

"*Ay Dios!* I don't think I could swallow a bite."

Doubtless that was some American oath learned from

the ranch hands, those *vaqueros* of hers. Braden was momentarily distracted at the thought of Rowena's reaction to such language and behavior. Rowena believed that she could turn her back on her werewolf blood by playing the perfect lady, as if the two identities were incompatible.

Braden knew better. The werewolf kind had been natural aristocrats since the beginning of history. They rose easily to positions of power. They were superior to ordinary men in every respect, and that superiority was evident in all they did.

Of course there were exceptions. There were *loups-garous* who broke the unwritten rules by which werewolves had coexisted with man for centuries. They were criminals, to be cast out and punished.

But they were rare. Rowena's refusal of her heritage was worse than foolish, it was madness. The Greyburn Forsters lived in a world of order and control, a perfect balance between wolf and man.

Whatever Cassidy's upbringing, she must learn to adjust to Forster ways. She would never enter human society—Braden wouldn't make that mistake again—but discipline and duty would temper her immoderate behavior.

Braden draped the neglected blanket over the back of the chair and sent a footman to check on the housekeeper's progress. Even now, when Cassidy was quiet, absorbed in her thoughts, he was disturbingly aware of her.

And why not? Her arrival had changed everything. Quentin was long overdue for a mate. What better choice for him than William Forster's American granddaughter?

Cassidy interrupted his thoughts with a whisper of off-key song, her scent enveloping him like a shaft of sunlight. For a single mad instant, his mind was filled with an impossible image: this artless girl at *his* side, not Quentin's; *his* mate, taken in the name of the Cause, sharing his bed, lending him light without shadow and a taste of simple happiness. . . .

He ruthlessly shut off that thought. His part in the Cause had been settled three years past, and it did not include mating again. That path was forever closed. He'd proven himself unworthy because of unpardonable imperfections, and he could serve the Cause only if he held to his vow.

It was the duty of others to produce heirs to carry on the blood. Quentin's time had come. And Quentin would be here tomorrow.

"This is such a grand room," Cassidy said at his shoulder. "So many books. Are they all yours?" She moved away again. "I collect poetry, but I haven't seen this one." Pages ruffled.

> "With thee conversing, I forget all time,
> All seasons, and their change; all please alike.
> Sweet is the breath of morn, her rising sweet,
> With charm—"

"Stop."

The book thumped back into place on the shelf. "I'm sorry," Cassidy said. "I shouldn't have touched your books."

Braden unclenched his fists and let out his breath. "They were my mother's," he said. "She died when I was a boy."

"She must have been beautiful," Cassidy said. "You must have loved her very much."

All at once she'd gone from backward child to earnest comforter, as if she had a right to impose her assumptions and naive solace on him. He turned his back on her, letting the force of his will convey the displeasure he could not express in words.

She must have felt it; she was far too sensitive not to. But instead of retreating, she drew closer still.

"I don't know much about my mother's side of the family," she said, very low. "I want to learn. About what you did when you were a boy, and what it was like to grow up—with people who understood."

People who understood. He stepped away from her sharply. "You will learn," he said. "You are a Forster now. The past is gone, Cousin. Remember that."

"I will." Her voice was humble but far from submissive, filled with an unfamiliar warmth. "All I've ever wanted is right here. You'll never be sorry you took me in."

No, he would never be sorry. But what he wanted or felt was irrelevant to the Cause. What any of them wanted or felt was irrelevant.

One of the maids came to the library then, sparing him further speculation.

"Cousin," he said, "this maid will show you to your room. Let her know if there's anything more you require."

She didn't move. "Don't you think you could call me Cassidy?"

"Very well . . . Cassidy. You may retire."

"And what should I call you?" she asked.

"You may call me Greyburn."

"Greyburn," she said in her American drawl. "It's a different kind of name. Like mine."

He was in no mood to explain his title, of which she plainly remained ignorant. Time enough for that in the morning, when his mind was clear. "Go to your room, Cassidy."

"I'm grateful, Greyburn—truly I am. But first I have to talk to Isabelle." Her voice grew serious. "She's the best friend I've ever had, and I can't just leave her this way."

So much for her assurances of obedience. But she never had promised that, had she?

"I'll be back as soon as I can," she said. The warmth of her breath on his skin gave him an instant's warning, and then her soft lips pressed his cheek. He flinched.

"Cassidy," he said sharply.

But she was already out the door.

three

The hansom driver didn't so much as raise his eyebrows when Isabelle announced her destination. Perhaps he believed she lived in the haunts of the very rich, though few respectable women would travel alone at such a time of night. Or perhaps he had other, less savory theories.

Isabelle didn't care. When she'd awakened well after midnight to find Cassidy gone from her bed in their hotel room, she could think of only one place to turn for help in finding the girl. The earl of Greyburn might reasonably be expected to use his influence to find Cassidy, once he realized that she was his cousin.

The sound of hoofbeats on cobblestones had an oddly soothing effect, but Isabelle didn't allow herself to relax. Soon she would be among people far less honest than those she had dealt with in San Francisco.

Werewolf aristocrats. Surely a most dangerous combination.

It was difficult not to panic at the thought of taking them on—she, who had fallen so low.

She looked out the cab window and saw a woman alone under the light of a streetlamp, lingering in the chill as if she were waiting for someone. Her clothing was far from fine, though relatively clean, and it was obvious that she was not a resident of Belgravia.

Isabelle had little difficulty in guessing the woman's profession. In the dim light she'd seemed pretty, still untouched by despair and illness. Perhaps she had been born for better things. Perhaps she, too, had once been betrayed, left with no choices at all.

Choices. Isabelle had believed herself beyond the possibility of change in her life when Cassidy had turned up on her doorstep in San Francisco, a slender figure dressed in dusty denim trousers and an oversized shirt, scuffed boots, pack, bandanna, and battered hat. At first glance Isabelle had mistaken her for a boy—until she'd tugged the hat from her head and long hair, thick and black, tumbled loose about her shoulders.

A girl, to be sure. Tall she was, but there was no mistaking the curve of generous hips beneath the cinched waist of the jeans, nor the bosom only partially disguised by the baggy shirt. The face was strong but delicate; it might have been attractive under the smudges of dirt. Striking, at the very least.

"Isabelle?" the girl said, the hat clutched between her work-roughened hands. "I'm Cassidy. Cassidy Holt, Edith's daughter."

Isabelle could still recall the shock of that moment. *Edith's daughter.* A three-year-old child when Isabelle last saw her; she'd never expected to meet any of the Holts again. Never in her wildest dreams had she imagined that Edith's youngest child would come to find her.

She could see Edith in the girl's eyes, so wide and gray. But it was not that which arrested Isabelle's attention. There was something that radiated from the girl, an undefinable purity such as Isabelle hadn't seen in many years.

Without any notion of the hidden doors she opened,

Isabelle had welcomed Cassidy into her modest home. The girl had dropped her heavy pack, then flung herself into Isabelle's arms.

Isabelle smiled, remembering. She might have been taken aback at such exuberant affection from a stranger if it hadn't been so reminiscent of Edith. Wild and charismatic Edith, who'd been possessed of so great a power . . .

But Edith was dead, and her husband and son had vanished. Cassidy was an orphan, raised by her father's relations. She had come to her mother's dearest friend for help.

Help in finding her mother's people in England. It was all in a letter Cassidy had memorized when she was seven years old. A letter meant for Isabelle but never sent.

Forgive me, Edith, Isabelle thought. *I owed you so much, but I couldn't help you when you needed me most.*

How many times had she apologized in her mind, and then answered herself the same way: *What would you have done? Raised a young child in the kind of life you lived?*

Even that was no answer. *You could have taken her home. To England.*

England, to which Isabelle had sworn she'd never return. Fifteen years ago she could not have done it. But when Cassidy came, everything changed.

Cassidy had already journeyed unescorted through hundreds of miles of rough country, by coach and rail, shielded by her shining innocence. There was no trace of worldliness in her words, her face; in spite of the loss of her parents at so young an age, she hadn't learned bitterness or cynicism. Not of the kind Isabelle knew so well.

But no amount of hope or courage would see her safely across the sea and into an alien world filled with a thousand obstacles and pitfalls waiting for the uninitiated.

Isabelle was a graduate of that hard school. There was no question of letting Edith's daughter walk into the dragon's nest alone.

Escorting Cassidy to England was a way of repaying an old debt. Cassidy's mother had been her one true friend during a very bad time—and, oddly enough, it seemed that experience hadn't entirely steeled Isabelle's heart to the gentler emotions.

So here she was, chasing Cassidy across one of the largest cities in the world and praying for the goodwill of a certain Lord Greyburn.

Would he see through her own brazen masquerade?

She scoffed at herself. Why should any of them remember her? She'd meant nothing, counted for nothing in their world. Let them accept Cassidy; that was all she asked. Let her kin be less like men and more like beasts, if those beasts were like Edith Holt. . . .

The hansom jolted to a stop. The driver appeared at the door and opened it, his sleepy face still blank of curiosity.

"Here we are, ma'am."

The square, like so many of its kind, was gated to keep public carriages from its hallowed streets. The driver had gone as far as he could. She paid him, smoothed her skirt, and started along the pavement. She kept her gaze straight ahead, ignoring the magnificent facades of the houses on all sides of the square, until she reached her destination.

A young, liveried footman, far more inquisitive than the hansom driver, answered her knock. She'd no sooner finished giving her name than the startled footman pressed back against the door to make way for the denim-clad figure who skidded to a stop at the threshold.

"Isabelle!" Cassidy said, grinning from ear to ear. "I found him!"

Isabelle swallowed her shock. Why should she be surprised? She assumed a practiced smile and held Cassidy's offered hands.

"I see that you have," she said. "But I do wish you had told me—"

The sound of masculine throat-clearing echoed in the hall. A tall, neatly dressed man, presumably the butler, arrived on the scene, too late to prevent the disruption to his household. The footman sidled up to the butler and whispered in his ear.

"Mrs. Smith?" the butler said, his voice prim with disapproval. "If you will wait in the hall, I shall inquire to see if Lord Greyburn—"

"You may go, Aynsley."

The man who interrupted walked into the hall, tall and dark as he stepped from the shadows. Isabelle knew immediately who he must be.

And she was definitely not prepared for the earl of Greyburn. She had dreaded this moment, but she hadn't counted on the stunning impact of the earl's inhuman nature.

The man who stared at her was tall, muscular in his tailored evening clothes, compelling in his simple presence. He would draw all eyes wherever he went; he would be obeyed without question. Isabelle felt as if she were in the lair of a hungry predator who was duly considering whether or not she would make a satisfying meal.

No, indeed. He was not even as interested as that. He regarded her as he might an inferior creature, hardly worth the bother.

And she had helped Cassidy find . . . this. But Cassidy was not afraid, and met Greyburn's gaze with steady candor. Whatever had passed here in the previous hour had done her no harm.

Yet.

"I beg your pardon, Lord Greyburn," Isabelle said, inclining her head slightly. "I am Mrs. Isabelle Smith. I accompanied Miss Holt to England, and only a short time ago discovered that she had left our hotel. I had come so late in hope of obtaining your help in finding her, but I see that my concern was unnecessary. We had intended to call at an appropriate hour tomorrow, to make Miss Holt known to—"

He raised his hand in a dismissive gesture. "My cousin has told me of you," he said. "She has explained how she came to be here. As it happens, we had believed our American relations lost to us. Her arrival was most fortuitous."

So Cassidy was not unwelcome, at least. That put one of her worries to rest. But the earl's face was without expression, handsome as it was, and his slanted green eyes were curiously opaque, as if he were preoccupied by his own thoughts.

"It seems I owe you thanks for escorting my cousin to England," he said. He walked toward Isabelle, each motion impeccably smooth and graceful, and stopped before she could become alarmed at his proximity. "I shall see that you are properly compensated for your inconvenience and expenses on her behalf. Now that she is with us, she shall have no further need of your services."

Isabelle had been prepared to swallow her defiance and hatred for Cassidy's sake, no matter how provoked. She would be worse than a fool to provoke this man. But even as Cassidy stepped forward to speak, Isabelle pushed her back and met the earl's icy gaze.

"You will forgive my blunt speaking, Lord Greyburn, but Miss Holt knows nothing of England or English ways. Her mother was a dear friend—"

"Then you know what I am."

He didn't have to make open threats to start her shivering with the most primitive kind of fear. "Yes. As I knew Edith. And Cassidy, who wanted nothing more than to find others like her mother."

The earl cocked his head, a deceptively boyish gesture that somehow hinted at menace. "And you are not afraid."

"Edith was kind to me, always. She was a remarkable woman."

"And she told you there were others like her?"

"She told me of the Greyburn Forsters, and—" She bit back her desire to tell the earl how much Edith had not wanted her children to know their English kin. "I always knew, yes."

"Then you have been privileged." He moved again, this time to circle around her. Cassidy gripped her hand, as if she would protect her friend from one of her own.

"I would never abuse that privilege," Isabelle said, refusing to turn. "I understood the need for secrecy. I still do."

"Admirable."

He sounded anything but admiring. She had the bizarre conviction that he could somehow . . . *know* what she was. What she'd been in the years since she'd left England in disgrace.

"I am the only connection Cassidy has to her parents," Isabelle said cautiously. "I . . . care about her. If you would only allow me to stay with her, for a while . . ."

"I doubt that you would be at ease among us, Mrs. Smith," he said, and now there was no mistaking the warning in his voice. "My cousin belongs here; you do not. I will arrange—"

"No," Cassidy said suddenly. "She came because of me. This is her country. She's home."

Home. Isabelle looked bleakly at the earl and almost wished he would refuse to let her stay.

Lord Greyburn turned on Cassidy with a frown—the first genuine emotion he'd shown since Isabelle's arrival. Cassidy gazed back, entirely unintimidated. That fearless innocence was one of Cassidy's unique gifts, and she used it, quite unconsciously, as the earl used the strength of his will. For the first time Isabelle wondered which would prevail. The scene put her in mind of David and Goliath.

She knew the end of that story. Did Lord Greyburn?

"Isabelle is the finest lady I ever met," Cassidy said. "And she's also my friend. If you make her leave, I'll go with her."

It was a reckless statement indeed from a girl so desperate to reunite with her own people, her own kind. But she didn't waver. The earl was rigid, doubtless amazed that a country cousin dared speak so to him.

But he fell before her, just like Goliath. "Cassidy," he said, "I wish to speak to Mrs. Smith alone."

"You won't send her away?"

"I shall naturally consult with you before taking any action." His words were heavy with irony, but Cassidy gave him her brilliant smile and started toward him. He took a single step back.

"Aynsley," he said. "See that Miss Holt is escorted to her room, and send the maid to attend her."

Cassidy turned to Isabelle, squeezing her hand. "Don't worry," she said. "Everything will be all right."

Isabelle almost believed her. *Perhaps you won't have everything quite your own way, my lord.*

He glared at her as if he'd read her thoughts—though as far as she knew, that particular power was beyond even his kind. But he swiftly resumed his pose of indifference, his eyes hooding in apparent boredom.

"It seems my cousin can't do without your presence, Mrs. Smith," he said. "You may stay . . . on sufferance. If that offends you, you are free to go. She has no need of a governess—"

"And I want no recompense for helping a friend," she said, meeting his gaze. "I was the one who told her of you, Lord Greyburn, when you were but a name on a piece of paper. I hoped that you would be . . . what Cassidy wished."

"And am I, Mrs. Smith?"

"We have only just met, Lord Greyburn."

They stared at each other. At last Lord Greyburn tilted his head, his smile without humor. "Very well, Mrs. Smith. Perhaps you'd like to join your . . . friend in inspecting the guest room. I'll see that another is made up for you, and send a footman for your luggage."

Isabelle's victory was precarious at best, and well she knew it. "Thank you, my lord. I am most grateful for your kind courtesy."

They understood each other, for the time being. Lord Greyburn turned away and spoke to the butler, who summoned a footman. Another maid appeared to conduct Isabelle down the hall and to the stairs that led to the bedchambers on the second and third floors. The house was very fine, but it had the feel of a place often left vacant. Hollow, somehow, and very cold.

She followed the maid to a door at the end of the third-floor hallway. Cassidy opened the door before the maid could knock, and she grabbed Isabelle's hand and pulled her inside.

The room was plainly furnished but comfortable enough. A steaming jug of water stood beside the wash-stand, clean towels were laid out, and someone had located a soft cambric nightgown for Cassidy's use. The maid waited quietly until Isabelle nodded dismissal, then the girl bobbed a curtsy and left them alone.

"Can you believe it, Isabelle?" Cassidy said. "I'm here.

I'm actually here." She all but danced across to the bed, fingered the nightgown with its lace trim and spotless white fabric, and grinned.

Isabelle sat in the chair nearest the bed. "I may know what to believe if you'll tell me how you came to be here."

Cassidy sobered, but the sparkle remained in her eyes. "I know I shouldn't have run off without you. . . ."

"In the middle of the night—" Isabelle added.

"But I felt someone calling me, and . . ."

Isabelle listened to Cassidy's breakneck explanation with growing wonder and forgot her intended remonstration. Clearly there was yet another facet of the *loup-garou* nature she knew nothing about. Werewolves . . . calling to one another, without voices. Even without conscious awareness, apparently, for Cassidy claimed that Lord Greyburn had been surprised to see her.

Surprised . . . and pleased. If so, Lord Greyburn had a peculiar way of expressing pleasure. Nevertheless, he had already made a place for Cassidy here—almost too easily—whatever his motives might be.

There was no question of Cassidy's happiness.

"You remember what we talked about in San Francisco," Cassidy said with a wistful earnestness. "I always knew I'd have to search for the kin who could show me how to be like my mother. Now I'll learn everything she wasn't able to teach me." She leaned forward on the edge of the bed. "I could never explain the reason why I finally left the ranch. Something in here"—she touched her breast—"told me it was time to go. And now I know it was real. It was meant to happen." She closed her eyes. "The first time I saw his face, I thought he was exactly like Blake's poem about the Tyger. He's everything I ever dreamed of becoming. And he wants me, Isabelle. He wants me."

Isabelle kept her expression carefully neutral. Had it

happened so quickly, then? Had the girl already developed an infatuation for this forbidding and austere man—who wasn't even human?

He was dangerous, and Isabelle had no doubt that he could hurt Cassidy deeply with no effort at all. What did the earl of Greyburn intend for his innocent cousin?

Cassidy wouldn't listen to warnings now. She was among her own. She was sure she'd found her home.

And therein lay the danger. With the earl of Greyburn as her teacher, what might she become?

The late storm began quietly, with a spattering of raindrops on the library window. Braden sat stiffly in his chair facing the fire, stabbing at the embers with a poker. A damp, chill wind forced its way through the tiniest gaps in the walls like a housebreaker bent on plunder. When the rain began to beat out a punishing rhythm and the first crash of thunder rattled the glass, he thrust so hard that a charred log toppled over with an angry crack.

The glare of lightning didn't reach him, but he felt it, streaking through his bones and speeding the motion of his heart. White light filled his head. He threw down the poker and stood up too rapidly, pushing the chair into the table beside it.

The next sound he heard was the crash of something fragile hitting the floor. One of Rowena's delicate figurines, no doubt.

Telford appeared in the doorway. "Is there anything you wish, my lord?"

Braden sat down again, ignoring the consequences of his ill-timed movement. He'd dismissed his valet hours ago; typical of the man that he would stubbornly disobey orders and remain on duty while his master sat out the storm.

"Go to bed, Telford," he said. "I know my way up to my own room."

Telford took a few steps into the library and paused. "A book, my lord? The *Origin of Species*, perhaps?"

Braden shook his head. The valet was one of the few Greyburn servants who would take the liberty of even such mild disobedience. Braden permitted it; without Telford, there would be occasions when he was truly helpless in spite of his keen senses and instincts.

Those senses tracked the valet as he moved across the room and knelt beside the shattered objet d'art.

"Was it valuable?" Braden asked.

"A rather unattractive object, my lord, and thus of little consequence. I cannot imagine where it originated."

Rowena would hardly appreciate such a comment. Telford was a connoisseur of beautiful things—beauty Braden could no longer appreciate.

Thunder vibrated the window. Braden pulled his attention away from the storm and deliberately leaned his head back against the chair.

"Leave it, Telford. I wish your opinion on another matter."

"At your service, my lord."

"You observed the young lady who just arrived—my cousin, Miss Holt."

"Yes, my lord."

"Describe her to me."

Telford cleared his throat. "She is . . . American, my lord?"

"Yes."

"Then perhaps . . . one mustn't consider English standards when offering an opinion—which is, of course, entirely irrelevant to the—"

Braden turned his face toward Telford. "Do you find her hideous?"

The valet's scent announced his unease as decidedly as a shout. He wouldn't lie to Braden. Few humans lied successfully to a *loup-garou*. "She is . . . unusual, my lord."

"How?"

"If you will permit plain speaking, she is a . . ." He coughed again. "A ragamuffin, my lord."

The corner of Braden's mouth twitched. "And apart from her conduct and clothing?"

"Her hair is very thick and black, my lord, and curling. It falls to the middle of her back."

He could still feel the lush weight of it. "And her figure. Is it well-formed?"

"It was somewhat difficult to tell. She is quite tall."

"Her eyes?"

"Nondescript. Her skin is rather . . . tan, my lord."

That would certainly be a mark against her in Telford's view—and Rowena's. "She lived in a warm climate," he said, and wondered why he defended her to his own valet. "I take it you find her less than beautiful?"

"I would never presume."

Braden remembered tracing her features, feeling the strength and stubbornness in them. So she wasn't a beauty. Her looks were of no significance—least of all to him.

The storm was fading now, the thunder more distant. Lightning no longer burned inside his skull. His heart beat at a normal pace, and the chill had been replaced by an unaccountable warmth.

He dismissed Telford, rose, and started for his room. When he reached the third floor, he found himself stopping dead in the hallway, as if he'd encountered an unexpected wall.

No wall, but something far more ethereal. Sagebrush and sunlight, cattle and cactus. Cassidy, asleep in the guest room. He could hear her steady breathing through the door, the deep sleep of exhaustion. Or unalloyed innocence.

Only minutes ago he had almost regretted that he could not see her face as Telford saw it—meet the gaze of those "nondescript" eyes, no doubt as full of contradictions as the girl herself.

But his impediment was a blessing. It was an effective defense against intrusive emotion, an invisible protection from the dangers of intimacy, a shield neither human nor werewolf could penetrate. Least of all Cassidy Holt.

He turned away and walked slowly to his room.

four

M iss?"
      Sunlight flowed like honey across the bed, and
Cassidy finally opened her eyes. She'd been awake since
well before dawn, basking in the knowledge that she
was home.

Home. But this was not the tiny room off the kitchen
at the ranch, crowded by her lumpy bed, three-legged
chair, and the tilted shelves holding her precious books.
There were no cows to be milked, cattle to be worked,
weeds to be pulled.

Some minutes ago she'd heard the door open and the
maid creep in, but the feather tick was marvelously comfortable. She cracked open one eye and saw her books
neatly lined up on the dressing table like old friends ready
to greet her—the only possessions, besides her calico dress
and the clothes on her back and a little saved money, that
she'd brought from New Mexico.

The maid returned from opening the curtains and
shutters and went to stand, absolutely still, by the door.
Cassidy thought she'd stand there forever unless she was
told not to.

It was very difficult to think of people as servants; though the Holts had men and women working for them on the ranch, they weren't anything like the humble, invisible people who came and went at Greyburn's behest.

Greyburn. She sat up with a burst of anticipation, warmth flooding her body. That word was only a title, not a name; it revealed his power, but not his heart. Not who he was inside. Today she'd find out what his real name was. She planned to know everything about him.

Cassidy stretched, flung off the bedclothes, and grinned at the maid. She curtsied deeply.

"I hope I didn't disturb you, miss," she whispered.

"Not me. I've been lazy this morning." Cassidy swung her legs over the side of the bed and planted her bare feet on the floor. The room was cool, but not cold enough for a fire; the fireplace was shiny clean and empty of ashes.

"I've brought up hot water, miss," the maid said, her brown eyes downcast. "Her ladyship's maid will be comin' with your clothes. I am to tell you that breakfast is served in the morning room at precisely nine o'clock."

Precisely. That seemed the kind of way Lord Greyburn would want things done. "Thank you so much . . . what is your name, anyway?"

The maid flushed red above the high collar of her print dress and dropped another curtsy. "I must go, miss. Please ring if you need anything." She bobbed again and fled the room, bumping the doorknob in her haste.

Cassidy grimaced. She must have done something wrong to scare the girl that way. How could she frighten anyone?

But the Holts had always been scared, ever since they'd taken her in. She hadn't known it for years and years. They kept her from meeting guests at the ranch, sent her out with the cattle—anywhere she'd be away from them.

Only when she began to feel the deeper changes within herself, impossible to ignore, had she realized how much of their coldness to her was out of fear.

These servants were also afraid. Of Greyburn, most of all.

Cassidy examined the washstand and the new stack of clean towels, already replaced from last night. The cambric of the nightgown felt luxurious against her skin, and she almost didn't want to take it off. She had so much to learn, but she had to—because she wanted Greyburn to find her worthy. To smile at her. To teach her to be like him.

For he was the epitome of everything she wanted to be. Confident, strong, complete in himself, knowing fully who he was and where he belonged. His inner power seemed to rub off on her when she was with him. She was beginning to believe that nothing could be more wonderful than staying by his side.

If he would allow it. If she proved herself deserving of his attention, his friendship.

Yes. That was what she wanted most of all.

Someone knocked on the door. She hurried to answer, expecting Lady Rowena's maid.

But it was Isabelle who marched into the room, a bundle of clothes draped neatly over her arm.

"I intercepted Lady Rowena's maid," Isabelle said briskly, closing the door. "I thought you might like my company this morning. Everything must seem very strange to you." She laid out Cassidy's best dress and her new underthings on the bed. Although Cassidy had thought them almost too fancy when they bought the items in San Francisco, she couldn't help but compare them to the gorgeous gowns she'd seen last night at the party.

But what would she do in a grand lady's dress, anyway?

At least Greyburn would see her wearing something besides old trousers and a secondhand work shirt.

"Did you sleep well?" she asked Isabelle.

"Well enough." Isabelle's tone was neutral, as if she didn't really want to talk about herself. Maybe her head was as full of thoughts as Cassidy's. She smoothed out the dress a second time. "And you?"

Cassidy answered with a smile and began to wash her face and neck. "The maid said breakfast is ready at nine, 'precisely.' "

Isabelle came up behind her with a brush and began to untangle Cassidy's hair. "Then we must get started, beginning with this," she said, working through a snarl. "Your hair is so lovely when it's properly cared for."

"I've never really known how to fix it up. Maybe you can help me?"

"I'll do my best. Lady Rowena's maid will doubtless be more skilled at such matters, but for this morning . . ." She moved out of sight and came back with a box full of clips and hairpins. Her frowning reflection moved behind Cassidy's as she tried various ways of piling hair on top of Cassidy's head.

When she was finished, Cassidy's face didn't look much different than it did when she had her hair pulled back under a hat for working cattle. But her hair seemed fuller, shinier, and more feminine than she'd ever seen it. Cassidy grinned experimentally.

No, that wasn't right. The ladies at the party hadn't shown all their teeth like that. She experimented with different faces, ending with a slightly pursed simper that looked silly at best.

"Do you think I smile too much, Isabelle? Greyburn never smiles. I must be doing it wrong for England." She turned in her seat. "Can you show me, Isabelle? I need to know how to be more like them."

Isabelle didn't answer at once but turned away, standing for some moments with her back to the washstand. "You are fine just as you are, Cassidy. Never try to alter yourself for someone else's sake. Not even Lord Greyburn's."

The silence that followed was heavy with an uneasy feeling that made Cassidy's skin shiver. She reached up to Isabelle.

"Something's wrong, Isabelle." She frowned, trying to define the feelings she sensed. "You're not happy here."

"Nonsense." Isabelle patted her hand. "I was merely suggesting that you should not rely on anyone else for your happiness or worth."

She walked to the bed and held up Cassidy's gown. "Come. It's almost nine, and I suspect the earl will wish us to be prompt."

"I think you're right." Cassidy bit back another smile, changed into her clean underthings and let Isabelle help her into the dress.

She felt nearly as grand as a real lady when they left the room and started for the staircase. Halfway down they met a small, dapper man in neat clothing who bowed to them both and introduced himself as Telford, Lord Greyburn's valet. He regarded Cassidy with polite but piercing interest, and then excused himself with another bow and went on his way. Cassidy was left feeling as though she'd been judged, and she wasn't sure if it had gone in her favor.

The morning room was on the ground floor—what Americans would call the first floor, Isabelle explained. They had special rooms for everything in England, it seemed.

The room was bright with sunlight streaming through a single large lead glass window facing the street. A table sat in the center of the room; a footman and the dignified butler, Aynsley, stood at attention beside a side table covered with silver dishes and trays. The smell of food was overpowering.

Greyburn was already there. He turned as they entered, his face expressionless.

"Good morning," Cassidy said, standing very straight in her dress.

Greyburn seemed not to notice any change in her at all. "Good morning," he said. "I trust you were comfortable in your room?"

"Yes . . . thank you. The bed was—"

He cut her off with a gesture toward the table. Isabelle touched her arm and drew her away. Aynsley moved up to seat first Isabelle and then Cassidy, who kept as still as she possibly could for fear of upsetting the elegant place settings at the table or the vase of fresh flowers in the center.

Greyburn remained standing, his face turned toward the open door. Cassidy realized that the tension she felt was only partially her own; Greyburn was waiting for something.

Twice she tried to start a conversation, and each time her words went unanswered. After five minutes of stillness that made her feel ready to jump out of her skin, someone else entered the room. She was dressed much more simply than she'd been the night before, but there was no mistaking her identity.

Lady Rowena Forster was awe-inspiring. Cassidy watched her float across the room in her bustled frock, her steps so fastidious that she seemed graceful even in a skirt that hugged her knees so closely.

"We are gratified," Greyburn said, "that you honored us with your presence this morning, Rowena."

Rowena faced Greyburn with an identical lack of expression and made an exaggerated curtsy. "Is that the *royal* we, Greyburn? Oh, do forgive me. I see our cousin is here. I should be remiss indeed if I fail to make her welcome after such a long journey."

Greyburn formally introduced them, as if they weren't kin at all. Rowena dipped her head in acknowledgment, but her eyes were cold. They were a striking light brown with gilded highlights, complementing her beautifully coifed golden hair.

Cassidy stood up and made an awkward half-bow, nearly upsetting her chair. "I'm very pleased to meet you, Rowena," she said. "I hope we can be friends."

Rowena's perfectly arched brow lifted. "You are our cousin," she said. "From one of the wilder parts of America, I believe? How fortunate that you were able to find us." Her gaze flicked sideways to Greyburn. "I hope that you will be given a proper opportunity to enjoy our city." She allowed Aynsley to seat her and became absorbed in studying the flower arrangement. Cassidy sat down again, feeling as clumsy as an hour-old calf.

Greyburn's dark brows drew together, but he seated himself without a word. Aynsley moved to the side table and placed toasted bread, some kind of egg, and a thin slice of meat on a china plate and carried it to Rowena.

Cassidy's stomach chose that moment to growl. She clapped her hands across her waist. "Sorry."

"I do apologize, Cousin," Rowena said. "Aynsley should have served you first. I trust you'll appreciate our English fare. I hesitate to disappoint you, but we have no buffalo this season, nor . . . I believe it is called . . . jerky?"

"Rowena." Greyburn threw his sister a look sharp enough to rival the thorns on a prickly pear. He turned his gaze on Cassidy, and something like a smile touched his mouth. "Aynsley, please provide Miss Holt with a selection and let her sample what we have. Cousin"—he seemed to have forgotten his promise to call her Cassidy—"please taste whatever appeals to you and ignore what does not. You'll become adjusted to our dining customs in time."

From Greyburn, it was an unexpected kindness. Cassidy smiled at him, but he had already risen and was filling his own plate as Aynsley did the same for her.

The food was plentiful and more varied than Cassidy had ever seen, including several kinds of meat and fowl, breads, muffins, rolls, eggs, and even fish. She sampled everything, including the tea and chocolate the footman provided. Once or twice she caught Rowena observing her with that arched brow, as if she disapproved of Cassidy's appetite. Rowena didn't eat enough to feed a humming-bird. Maybe that was what made her so graceful—and so stern.

But it was Greyburn's opinion Cassidy was concerned about. He didn't so much as glance at her.

"It's very good," Cassidy said to ease the labored silence. "At home we have Mercedes's special beans and the best tortillas you ever tasted. They melt in your mouth. Though Aunt Harriet thought Mercedes's regular food wasn't grand enough to serve to guests—" She faltered in embarrassment. "*Caramba!* I didn't mean all this fancy food isn't delicious—"

Greyburn set down his fork, and the weight of his attention settled on Cassidy. It was like basking in the full heat of the sun—you could only look at the ball of fire for a short while, and then your eyes began to hurt and you had to run into the shade.

"This is your home now," he said. "You are one of us."

He might as well have told her she was beautiful. But he looked away again, as if he'd forgotten her existence.

"Cassidy," Rowena said. "Such a very . . . American name. Or is it Irish?"

"I was named after my father's friend."

"I see. And your dress—it's quite American also, isn't it? Very quaint. Very . . . appropriate for life on a ranch, I should think."

"I didn't wear this on the ranch. It would have been ruined in two days. The cattle—" She bit her lip and looked at her plate. She couldn't admit she had never owned a decent dress on the ranch.

Rowena leaned forward. "How fascinating. You drove cattle on the ranch? I'm afraid our pastimes are somewhat different here in England. But I'm certain we can find some entertainment that will suit you." She took a sip of her tea. "And clothing appropriate to a Greyburn Forster—since you are 'one of us.' "

Chair legs scraped the floor as Greyburn rose. "I'm glad you are so concerned about Cassidy's well-being, Rowena. She has come to us with very little, and has need of a woman's help in selecting suitable clothing. I'm putting you in charge of helping her purchase the first items for her wardrobe—this afternoon."

Not by look or word did Rowena react, but Cassidy knew that in some way Greyburn had won a round in the hidden battle with his sister—using Cassidy as a weapon.

"Thank you, Greyburn," Cassidy said, getting to her feet, "but Isabelle can help me. I still have some money—"

"You shall have all you require to assemble a proper wardrobe—including adequate funds and my sister's help." He turned to Rowena. "You will consider Miss Holt's best interests—no expense to be spared."

"Of course," Rowena said. "She will need a great deal if she is to be presented this Season—"

"You know very well that she won't be presented. We're leaving for Greyburn in a matter of days."

Rowena stood, almost jerky in her motions, and

looked directly at Cassidy. "Perhaps it is fortuitous for you, my dear. I'm afraid you might have found the Season a little bewildering when you're accustomed to the society of cattle drovers and men in bearskin overcoats."

Cassidy lifted her chin and smiled. "I never knew anyone with a bearskin overcoat—"

"I believe," Isabelle said, "that Cassidy and I are finished. May we go examine the piano I noticed in your drawing room?" She took Cassidy's arm and urged her away from the table. Cassidy went willingly, glad she wouldn't witness whatever was to happen between brother and sister. It felt a lot like a stampede coming just around the bend.

Sooner or later she'd figure out what was going on, and how she could help. She very much wanted to help, as the Holts had never let her.

This was her family.

But she gave up that mission for the moment and followed Isabelle to the room with the cabinet grand piano. Isabelle sat down to play some pretty tune, and Cassidy set herself to wait. She'd always been good at waiting, but something was changing inside her, and she felt as if a lot more than the tension in the morning room was going to fire off soon. She planned to be ready when it happened.

"Did you enjoy yourself, Rowena?"

Braden stood over her, no longer hiding his anger. "I had thought you prided yourself on your refinement, yet you baited the child when she clearly didn't even understand your insults. When did you become so cruel?"

"Cruel?" Rowena laughed, a harsh sound reserved only for him. "If I have been cruel, I certainly learned it from an excellent teacher."

Braden brought his hand down hard on the table. "Whatever quarrel you have with me, it has nothing to do with our cousin. She is a member of our family, and you will treat her as such. You will also guide her in adapting to our ways.

"And when did you ever care about the comfort of others . . . Braden?" She used his name as if it were a weapon designed to cause pain. "You don't usually trouble yourself about your family. Or is it because our newly discovered cousin is important to the Cause?" She breathed a laugh. "Yes, of course. The long-lost Forster blood. Does she have any idea of her role in your fine breeding program?"

Braden didn't so much as raise his hand. He had never struck his sister. He didn't have to resort to physical measures to make her feel his displeasure.

Rowena flinched away from him, conceding his power. Though she denied the wolf within her, her instincts recognized his dominance.

"I allowed you to remain with Lady Beatrice in London last year for one more season," he said, "in spite of her family's betrayal of the Cause. I summoned you home after the Little Season, and you didn't return. So I came for you. Your future mate will be attending the Convocation in two weeks. You will be there to greet him."

"Another American." She retreated around the table in a hissing rustle of skirts. "Do you suppose he has ever bathed?"

"You may like him or not, as you choose. But you will bear him children to strengthen the blood. He was selected as the best of the American candidates."

"Perhaps, if I am very fortunate, he may be capable of writing his name and reading a child's primer."

"He needs neither skill to sire your children."

He could feel her disgust at his blunt words. The *loups-garous* had always been an earthy people, accustomed to the realities of nature. But, over centuries, the veneer of civilization had weakened that ancient understanding. Rowena was living proof of the disintegration of their people.

If only some former leader had had the wisdom to guide the werewolf kind to some pristine wilderness, far from the defilement of men, they would not have lost so much.

But too many had fallen under the spell of power that came so easily, that made a life of luxury and dominance over others simple to possess.

Rowena wanted still more, and infinitely less. She wished to be human.

"And who do you plan to mate with our little American cousin?" she asked, her voice thick and tight. "You seem rather fond of her already, Greyburn. But that is impossible. You were incapable of caring for Milena, and she was a thousand times more—" She caught her breath. "But no. Milena was too much for you and your Cause, and too little. Perhaps Miss Cassidy Holt is more to your taste. Malleable. Unpolished. Closer to . . . *nature*." The word was filled with contempt. "I feel pity for her if she is destined to suffer Milena's fate."

Braden heard her from a distance, as if his private shield extended to sound as well as sight. "You need have no fear of that, sister. I shall not take another mate." He showed the tips of his teeth. "But your intemperate language proves that you cannot control the very impulses you scorn. I suggest you address your own defects before you complain of others'."

He sensed the way her spine stiffened in affront. "You are right, elder brother. I shall do as you say. But I promise I will not become a beast. I shall never again run on four legs and howl at the moon. I will die first—just like Milena."

And she spun and walked away, her steps for once not

dainty and confined but awkwardly long for the binding skirts she wore. At the last minute she turned, her train whipping about her ankles.

"I pity *you*, Braden. You have nothing but your Cause to live for. You will end up like Grandfather. Is it really worth the price?"

After she was gone, Braden sat down in the nearest chair, draining his mind of all emotion. He could scarcely remember a childhood when he and Quentin and Rowena had played and fought and laughed together, before the Cause had woven them into its inevitable pattern. Even then Rowena had wanted to be like Lady Beatrice Sayers' daughter, Alice—carrying the werewolf blood but living as human.

If Rowena hated him, so be it. It was a price he'd long been willing to pay—to alienate his family for the sake of their race. He would continue to pay that price willingly. Just as his grandfather had done.

He was not lonely. There was no room for loneliness in the life he had built. As long as he led the Convocation and oversaw the Cause, he had work enough to drive every other distraction from his life.

The coming Convocation would be the greatest challenge. There hadn't been a meeting of the werewolves since his accident. The others must have no doubt at all that he was still leader. Still the strongest. Still the one to guide the Cause to ultimate success.

After a while he rose and summoned Aynsley, to whom he gave explicit instructions regarding the coachman and footmen who were to accompany Lady Rowena and Miss Holt on a shopping trip to Bond Street. Rowena would be given no chance to slip away. And the impressionable Cassidy would be shepherded from one shop to another in minimal contact with the chaos that was London during the Season.

Soon enough they'd all be far from here. Safe, at Grey-burn, where there were no temptations to lure and debase. He'd sensed the shock and excitement of the ladies and gentlemen at Lady Beatrice's party last night, felt their stares like so many loosed arrows, heard their whispers. Once he'd walked among them, for Milena's sake. Did the rumors surrounding Milena's death make him an object of dread and loathing? So be it. He welcomed his reputation. Let the humans avoid him. And let the other *loups-garous* of England and Europe beware.

He went upstairs for a few words with Telford, then set about arranging certain business matters that needed attention before he left London. The Greyburn Forster fortune continued to grow because he, like his ancestors, was unashamed of the taint of commercial income.

He knew when Rowena and Isabelle and Cassidy left the house, two hours after breakfast. He continued to work until he could no longer concentrate, and then took his accustomed place in the library to wait.

Much later that afternoon there was a stir at the front door. Braden rose with a rare frisson of anticipation, assuming the ladies' return. His inner picture of Cassidy, formed by touch and Telford's description, could not quite be reconciled with the image of a bustled gown and a host of women's furbelows. Would she lose that scent of desert and wildflowers forever?

But she had not lost it. It preceded her as she and Rowena marched into the house, trailed by package-laden footmen. . . .

And someone else, a man whose laughter rang in the hall as if all the world were one great, satirical joke.

Quentin.

Braden walked into the hall. Rowena was quiet enough; her very silence held bitterness. Quentin's laughter came to a sudden halt.

"Greyburn," Cassidy said, her young voice strained with the fatigue of too much excitement. "We bought so many clothes. And when we were coming back, we met your brother—"

"Quentin," Braden said. "How was Paris?"

"Amusing, as always. Never fear, I found time to carry out your little errands. But what has happened in my absence, Grey? I find that we have not one but two lovely ladies in residence, and one of them a charming and exotic stranger from a faraway land."

Cassidy gave a husky laugh. Braden stiffened. "Rowena, perhaps you and the ladies would care to rest before dinner."

Rowena took his cue readily enough. Cassidy's curiosity was as evident to Braden as her unique scent, but she allowed herself to be herded upstairs by her cousin, the scuffing of her shoes betraying her reluctance. Different shoes, he noted—not the ungainly ones she'd worn when she arrived. Rowena had indeed seen to the necessities, as he'd known she would.

"Your timing is excellent, Quentin," Braden said, gesturing his brother into the library. "We are to leave for Greyburn within the next few days."

Quentin threw himself into a chair. "Such a warm welcome. Have you anything to drink? No, of course not. Yes, yes, I know—a filthy human habit, but one does acquire a taste."

"Kindly try not to poison yourself just yet," Braden said.

"Ah. I surmise that you have plans for me, brother. Dare I inquire? Or should I flee to China while I have the chance?"

"You won't run, Quentin."

"How well you know me, brother. Running requires far too much effort." The chair creaked as he settled deeper. "But before the unpleasant truths unfold, tell me about our fair cousin. Rowena told me she's the long-lost granddaughter of Great-Uncle William. A virtual savage, from Rowena's description. I thought she looked rather fetching in that plain little dress."

Braden could imagine the sparkle in Quentin's cinnamon eyes, the ever-present laughter playing about his mouth. A man for the ladies, was Quentin—like the prince, to whose set he belonged. But he had noticed Cassidy, and there was no disdain in his voice.

All to the good. Yes, surely all to the good.

"I'm delighted that you find her pleasing," Braden said. "You'll have the chance to get to know her much better in the coming weeks."

Quentin's breathing changed. He hardly moved, but Braden had learned how to read silences as well as others interpreted the most obvious alterations in expression.

"So," Quentin said. "That's the scheme you have in mind. One wayward brother, one conveniently restored lost cousin, and . . . *voilà*. A perfect match."

Perfect. Yes. "Are you surprised, Quentin? You knew the day would come. Cassidy is an orphan with no other kin of our kind. This way she will remain within the protection of our family, and the Forster blood will be reunited."

Quentin knew too much to ask, as Rowena had done, why Braden didn't consider Cassidy for himself. He rose and strode across the floor. The door opened; there was a brief exchange between Quentin and Aynsley, and a few moments later a footman returned with something that reeked distinctly of alcohol.

"Don't blame Aynsley," Quentin said. "I brought it back from Paris. Excellent stuff." He dismissed the footman and poured for himself. "You won't deny me my small pleasures at such a pivotal juncture in an otherwise inconsequential existence."

It was said lightly, but Braden heard the self-mockery behind the words. In human society, a younger son in the peerage was all too often a financial burden who must make his own way in some respectable career. But aside from his few years in the army, Quentin had only one occupation laid out for him: mate of the *loup-garou* bride selected for him, sire to offspring of the pure werewolf blood.

There had always been an understanding between Quentin and Braden. Until the day came that he must surrender his freedom, Quentin could live as he chose. As long as he did not endanger his life through the sins of excess and idleness, as long as he fathered no bastard half-werewolf children, he was kept on a very loose rein. Even his service in India had been carefully arranged so as not to place him in significant danger.

If Quentin was bitter, he didn't let that emotion bother him overmuch. He knew how unimportant his feelings were. He'd accepted the bargain, lived for pleasure on the unlimited funds his brother provided, and carried out the occasional errand in the Greyburn interests.

Now his freedom was at an end.

"Cassidy Holt," Braden said, "has no conception of your pastimes. You will behave with discretion in her presence and suppress any habits which might distress her."

Quentin sighed and set down his glass. "Is she such a fragile flower, then? She scarcely looks it. The prince is fond of these American girls, you know. Loves them for their lack of pretense and their frightful honesty."

"She has much to learn, and you will help teach her."

"The skills I know won't be of much use to her at Greyburn," Quentin said, pouring himself another drink. "Except the single one that's indispensable. I'll endeavor to make that . . . as painless as possible."

Braden rose from his chair and gripped the arm. "She

must have time to adjust to our ways, our life. For now you will make yourself agreeable—"

"Oh, I should think that'll be easy enough. She is a pretty girl, in an American sort of way. In fact—"

Into the gap left by Quentin's unfinished sentence came the rustle of skirts and twin sets of footfalls. One of them belonged to the widow Mrs. Smith. The other was Cassidy's. Slower than it had been before, more decorous, but indisputably hers.

"Please pardon the interruption," Mrs. Smith said, "but Cassidy was so anxious to show you her purchases, Lord Greyburn, after all your generosity. . . ."

The footfalls stilled. Quentin whistled under his breath.

"Cousin," he said. "May I say that you look absolutely enchanting." He moved across the room, and Braden could imagine him suavely bowing over Cassidy's hand. Playing his habitual role to the hilt. Charming his mate-to-be with no effort at all.

"Thank you, Cousin," Cassidy said with that throaty little rasp of excitement. "It must be this dress. I've never had one like it before."

"Call me Quentin, please. And the gown merely enhances your natural beauty—Cassidy, if I may?"

Cassidy laughed, the startled sound of a girl at her coming-out encountering the practiced charm of a man-about-town. "The back drags like a fish's tail. It's so close around the legs, I feel like a roped heifer. I can barely breathe. But Rowena said that everyone in London wears all this so tight—" She broke off, as if she'd suddenly guessed the impropriety of discussing feminine garments with the opposite sex. Silk whispered as she turned. "I wouldn't have known what to do without Rowena and Isabelle's help," she said. "Do you like it?"

Braden heard the subtle difference in her voice and

knew she was addressing him. He felt her unseen gaze as he might feel the sun come out from behind a cloud.

She wanted his approval. She wanted smooth compliments from him, the sort that came so easily to Quentin. She still hadn't guessed.

Would Telford find Cassidy beautiful now, in her London gown selected by Rowena's faultless taste? Did a change of clothing strip away the roughness, the awkwardness, the naïveté of the trouser-clad American girl who'd washed up on his doorstep?

"The dress is . . . most appropriate," he said. "Rowena chose well."

"Oh, dash it." Quentin said. "Forgive me, ladies. Brother, I have an urgent letter from Gévaudan, regarding the Convocation. He told me to deliver it to you immediately. I'd completely forgotten." Paper rustled in his hands. "Here it is."

Braden reached for the letter. The marquis de Gévaudan, his maternal grandfather, had not written in many years. Perhaps the marquis was planning to attend the Convocation in spite of his poor health—

The sheet of paper grazed Braden's fingers and then was snatched away. "Oh, how clumsy of me," Quentin said. "I've dropped it."

There was a moment's pause. Braden stepped forward impatiently. "Kindly retrieve it, Quentin."

"Let me," Cassidy said. He heard her kneel to pick up the paper.

"Thank you," he said, holding out his hand.

She hesitated. "But this is—"

"If you please." She handed it to him, and he glanced down. "I'll read it later."

"How can you read a picture?" Cassidy asked.

Mrs. Smith gasped softly. Gripped by suspicion, Braden felt the surface of the paper.

It was not marked with the usual impressions of writing. The lines engraved on the surface were softer, larger, more random, forming shapes instead of letters.

The betrayal caught him unaware, like a piece of furniture left just a little out of place to trip him up in a familiar room.

"A rather nice likeness of Cassidy, don't you think?" Quentin said. "I did the sketch in the carriage on the way here."

A sketch. Quentin had deliberately tricked him, and let the paper fall so that Cassidy and Mrs. Smith could see its contents. See, as he could not, that it wasn't a letter at all.

He opened his hand and let the paper drift to the carpet.

"My brother," he said, "knows perfectly well that I cannot judge the accuracy of the portrait. His demonstration is hardly subtle, but it is effective." He looked directly toward Cassidy. "You see, I am blind."

five

At first Cassidy was certain he was joking.

She smoothed the gathered front of her skirt and smiled uncertainly, her heart still racing from the day's countless new experiences. She'd gone out with Rowena into London's damp, alien canyons to find new clothes, as Greyburn had ordered. She had taken Rowena's cool advice, let herself be turned about and pinned and measured like a doll by the women in the shops, one after another. She'd been bombarded by deafening noise, dazed by crowds of people the likes of which she'd never seen, ushered directly from shop to carriage and carriage to shop, shown a dizzying array of gloves and hats and parasols, talked over as if she had no mind of her own, pinched and pulled into a ready-made dress that made it impossible to walk with more than the shortest stride. She had stared at herself in the mirror and not known who looked back out of the glass.

It would be worth it, she'd thought, to see the look in Greyburn's eyes when he glimpsed the lady she'd miraculously become.

The look in his eyes.

"Greyburn?" she said.

He didn't answer, showed no reaction except for the briefest of glances at his brother. His gaze was fixed on her, unwavering, as if he could read her most secret thoughts.

But there was something wrong with his stare. And Quentin Forster, with his merry, open face and easy manners—so unlike Greyburn's—wasn't smiling. It was the first time in the hour since Rowena had introduced them that he'd been serious.

Without thinking she took a step forward and lifted her hand toward Greyburn's face.

He caught her wrist in midair, and she almost laughed aloud with relief. But then Quentin moved with uncanny swiftness, his hand descending between them like a barricade, inches from Greyburn's eyes. Cassidy flinched; Greyburn didn't so much as blink. By the time he reacted, releasing her and pushing Quentin's arm aside, she understood.

Her Tyger was blind.

He couldn't see the sketch Quentin had done of her, or the dress he had complimented, or her smiles, or her attempts to tame her unruly hair. She might have been fooled for days before she discovered the truth.

For the earl of Greyburn carried out a perfect masquerade. He moved easily, naturally, with the confidence of a man in control of his surroundings. He never hung back or stumbled. He looked at her when he spoke; he had found his sister unerringly in a room full of people; he had known Cassidy was following him from the very beginning.

Yet from the moment he caught her outside his house, she'd been invisible to him.

No. Not invisible. When they'd first met, he'd touched her face—not once, but twice. She remembered how it felt, how she'd thought that she would melt under the caress of his fingertips. She hadn't questioned his reasons for the intimacy, or the way her body had tingled at his touch. She had wanted it to go on forever.

But there hadn't been anything personal in what he'd done. It was only his way of looking at her. No more than that.

He wasn't looking at her now. He stood with his arms at his sides, unmoved by her shock. He had shut her out.

Isabelle, unruffled, stepped forward, smiling at Quentin.

"I know we've only just been introduced, Mr. Forster," she said, "but I understand you spent some time in India, and I should be fascinated to learn more of your life there." She looped her arm through Cassidy's. "I'm sure that Cassidy would as well. If you will excuse us, Lord Greyburn?"

"It would be my pleasure," Quentin said. He glanced at his brother, but Cassidy noticed that he was careful to keep his distance. "Tea in the drawing room, perhaps?"

Smoothly he and Isabelle trapped Cassidy between them, herding her toward the door. They were afraid, both of them, though they tried not to show it. Greyburn's stillness was as biting as the coldest desert night.

And as lonely.

Cassidy slipped her arm free of Isabelle's and turned away from the door.

"May I stay?" she asked.

Not even blindness could rob Greyburn's gaze of its power. He looked toward Quentin, who hesitated only an instant before escorting Isabelle from the room. The door shut with a barely audible click.

"Please sit down," Greyburn said. It was a command. She found the nearest chair and obeyed, but he remained standing. Listening. Waiting.

"I'm sorry," she said softly. "I didn't know—"

"Save your condolences." He turned and walked toward the side table where a bottle and fancy glasses rested on a silver tray. Unerringly he poured a strong-smelling liquid into one of the glasses, raised it to his mouth, curled his lip in disgust and set the glass down again, all without spilling a single drop.

"Yes, I am blind," he said. "I have been for three years. I find it to be a very minor inconvenience." He stalked away from the side table and moved to the window, shoving aside the drapes. Early-evening sunlight bathed his face, redrawing its strong lines in shadowed relief. "I do not know the color of your dress, but I know it is made of satin and silk. It has a train of modest length. Your hat is adorned with an ostrich feather, and was purchased from Rowena's favorite milliner. The woman's perfume is unmistakable."

Cassidy remembered being overwhelmed by that perfume when Rowena had led her into the shop. It was scarcely noticeable now, but Greyburn smelled it. He hadn't touched her dress, but he knew what it was made of. He had heard the sound the fabric made when she moved.

"A human without sight would be helpless," he said. "We *loups-garous* have senses far greater than theirs. I require no man's pity."

Least of all hers, even if she'd dared. And yet . . . She closed her eyes, plunging herself into the darkness he must live with every day. Never to see the blue sky, or the way the morning light painted the mountains, or the bright blossoms of the prickly pear, or the stars at night. Never to be able to pick up a book and read words that could carry you away when even the world's beauty wasn't enough.

How many people outside of the family knew of his

blindness? Surely not the fine folk at the party, who had dodged out of his path and whispered as he passed. In their own way, they, too, were blind.

But Rowena hadn't let on, nor any of the servants. Did they all believe, like Greyburn, that it didn't matter? Or were they simply afraid?

"You've just met Quentin," Greyburn said, not waiting for her to speak. "He has a peculiar sense of humor, but there's no real harm in him. You will come to . . . appreciate him, Cassidy."

She wanted to believe that, with all her heart. But Quentin had deliberately tricked Greyburn. Rowena was cold and rude every time she spoke to him. It was almost as if they wanted to punish him.

Punish him . . . for what?

"Why?" she said. "Why did you hide it from me? Did you think I would care?"

Only a slight jerk of his chin betrayed a reaction before he looked at her with that implacable calm. "I lead this family," he said, "as I rule the Convocation. All else is irrelevant."

But it wasn't, not if it hurt people—the people she wanted so badly to love. Braden looked unapproachable, proud, untouched by emotion, especially fear or sorrow. He refused to let his blindness cripple him.

He was her Tyger still, but he was so alone.

"I have some very nice books of poetry," she offered, watching his face for the slightest softening. "I can read to you. I'd like to—"

"Telford provides that service."

She rose from the chair to face him. "Isn't there anything I can—"

"I have managed to survive thus far without your personal intervention, Cousin. I believe I shall continue to do so."

It was a dismissal, but she wasn't quite ready to leave. "Cassidy," she said. "My name is Cassidy. Are you afraid to tell me *your* real name?"

He paused in the act of pulling shut the drapes, turning back to her with a rare half smile that all too quickly vanished. "You're a stubborn child, Cassidy Holt. My name is Braden."

Braden. It was strong, like him, but gentle—a reluctant gift, but a gift just the same.

"Braden," she repeated softly. "Thank you."

With a noiseless, unhesitant stride he crossed the room. His hand lifted, paused, brushed her cheek like a moth's wing.

Then he tilted his head in an attitude of sudden vigilance and reached past her to open the door. "Mrs. Smith," he said, "would you care to come in?"

Isabelle stood just beyond the doorway, her hands clasped at her waist and her eyes very wide. "I was just coming to see—" She stopped, her usual poise failing her. "If I might—"

"I wish to speak to you in any case, Mrs. Smith," he said, "regarding the trip to Northumberland. Quentin will be happy to entertain Cassidy in the drawing room."

Isabelle shot Cassidy a quick look and obediently followed Braden back into the library. He didn't speak to Cassidy again before he closed the door behind them.

She was tempted to linger by the door and listen, as Isabelle had obviously been doing, but she knew she wouldn't get any more answers that way.

And there was still Quentin Forster.

The drawing room was just down the hallway from the library on the same floor. Like all the other chambers in the Greyburn household, the drawing room was sparsely furnished in a way very different from the stifling, overcrowded rooms of the hotel. It was very clean and formal, and just yesterday Cassidy had been half-afraid to walk on the spotless carpet or sit on the grand furniture.

Quentin was there, as Braden had promised. He was seated at the piano, idly plunking the keys and lost in his own thoughts. She paused in the doorway to study his face. It was so completely unlike Braden's in every way that she might never have guessed they were brothers.

Strange enough to think that Rowena was Quentin's twin sister. He'd popped out of the boiling London throng, just as Rowena was following Cassidy and Isabelle into the carriage at the end of their shopping expedition, and swept Rowena off her feet. Rowena's expression had gone in an instant from severe to radiant, and Cassidy watched in amazement as the two heads bent together with evident delight.

Introductions had been rapid and informal. The Honorable Quentin Forster had been born in the same hour as Rowena, but the resemblance between them ended with their devotion to each other. Where Rowena's hair was golden, Quentin's was a rich chestnut; Rowena's eyes were the palest brown, and Quentin's were almost the russet of his hair. Where she was slender and graceful, he was lean and broad-shouldered.

Although Rowena had quickly regained her dignity, he'd kept the brash mischievousness of a little boy who'd just run off with the pie left cooling on the windowsill. He hadn't stopped teasing and telling jokes all the way back to the house in Belgrave Square.

Yet he had played a deliberate trick on his brother in the library. . . .

The piano gave a loud, discordant protest as Quentin slapped his hand down on the keys.

"There you are!" he said, pushing to his feet. "I see you've emerged from the lion's den unscathed. I suppose he has the delightful Mrs. Smith in his clutches now?" He strolled across the room and offered his arm. "I'd rescue her myself, but I'm afraid I'd only make matters worse."

Cassidy sat in the chair he offered and met his lazy, good-natured gaze. "If you thought he would be angry because you played a trick on him," she said, "why did you do it?"

He blinked and gave a bark of laughter. "Ah, that astonishing American frankness. It hits you right between the eyes." He staggered back several steps and collapsed into his chair. "What a refreshing breath of desert air you are, Cousin."

If he was making fun of her, she didn't really mind. He was easy to laugh with, and she liked to laugh. But she kept remembering the uneasiness that hung in the library, when Braden was caught in his brother's trap, and Quentin was afraid.

He was serious now, and the look sat as uneasily on his face as a smile did on Braden's. He lost his pose of indolence and shifted restlessly in his chair.

"You didn't know Braden was blind," he said, statement rather than question. "He's become very good at hiding it. Maybe you were a test, being one of us. But it won't work at the Convocation."

Convocation. Braden, too, had used that word. But she wouldn't be distracted from what she'd come to learn. "Did you want to hurt him?" she asked.

"Hurt him?" He sprang up and paced halfway across the room. "Hurt my brother? It isn't possible, I assure you." He turned to her again. "No, Cassidy. Nothing of the kind. I thought he intended to deceive you, and I didn't think it was fair. You had a right to know. You're one of the family now, aren't you?"

"I want to be."

"Then there shouldn't be secrets among us." He came back to stand before her chair. "Braden is proud. He doesn't like to believe he has any weaknesses. He won't accept that he needs anyone for any reason, and that is his downfall."

She shivered at the unexpected intensity in Quentin's eyes. Wasn't that what she admired about Braden: his strength, his confidence, his certainty of who he was? Why, then, did it make her heart ache to hear that he didn't need anyone?

"But you wouldn't understand, would you?" Quentin murmured. "My brother deceives himself. I won't help him do it."

"Then you care about him."

The sharpness left Quentin's gaze, and he looked slightly bored. "He is my brother."

"He said I would like you."

The corner of Quentin's mouth twitched. "I hope you do, Cassidy. I'd like to be your friend."

She wanted that, too. Not only because he was her cousin, but because he could tell her more about Braden than anyone else except Rowena—and Rowena didn't talk at all.

"How did it happen?" she asked. "How did he become blind?"

Quentin turned on his heel and walked away again. "It was an accident. I was out of the country then—" He stopped, words and motion, and changed course for the piano. "I really don't know much about it." His agile fingers picked out an unfamiliar melody. "He doesn't generally confide in his little brother."

But Quentin knew more than he was admitting. He had to. Cassidy got up, wriggled in her dress as if she could loosen it like her old trousers, and went to join him.

"You've known him all your life," she said. "Since you were children."

"True. But Braden hasn't been a child in a very long

time." He began to sing, his voice lifting in a pleasant baritone. "For Lochaber no more, Lochaber no more, we'll may be return to Lochaber no more. . . ." He made a face and ended the mournful refrain with a dramatic bang on the keys. "I'm not in the mood for crying," he sang, "care's a silly calf; if to get fat you're trying, the only way's to laugh!" He winked at her and scooted over on the piano bench, patting it in invitation. "Do you play?"

She shook her head. "Aunt had a piano, but she never let me try it."

"I'd offer to teach you, but piano lessons are far too tedious for anyone over the age of ten." He reached inside his coat. "Eventually I'll ask what you think of England, and what your journey was like, and how you managed to turn up here after Braden gave up on our American relations. I have an idea that you may make things . . . quite a bit more interesting than they have been in ages."

"There's nothing very interesting about me."

"I beg to differ, Cousin. You Americans are like your country—not at all as common as you appear." He produced a deck of cards. "Are you familiar with poker? I learned it from an American railroad baron seeking investors in England. It is an unpretentious game, yet to play it well requires a certain faculty for deception."

She watched his hands fly as he shuffled the cards, almost too quickly for her to follow. "Are you good at it?" she asked.

"If I were to answer honestly," he said, "I might lose your high regard, and that I couldn't bear." He tapped the cards against the piano to straighten the deck and regarded her with twinkling eyes. "Still, it's a much more useful skill than playing the piano. Shall I teach you?"

Cassidy had seen men gambling on her uncle's ranch, the *vaqueros* playing poker or monte around the fire or in the bunkhouse after the day's chores were over. They'd laughed and seemed to enjoy themselves, but they would have been shocked if she asked to join them. No matter how much they respected her knack for working cattle, she wasn't one of them.

There was both mischief and warmth in Quentin's invitation, but she had an idea that Isabelle wouldn't approve—or Rowena, for that matter. "Is poker a game that ladies in England play?" she asked.

He coughed and swung off the bench. "Only the cleverest of them. Braden did ask me to see that you feel comfortable with us—"

"He did?"

"—and I do occasionally take my obligations seriously. When it suits me." He offered his hand. "Come along, Cousin. We have an hour or two before we march like good little soldiers into the dining room and pretend to enjoy sitting around the table while discussing how much rain is likely to fall tomorrow. Unless you have a better idea?"

She couldn't refuse, any more than she could hold Quentin's trick in the library against him. He led her to a group of upholstered chairs arranged around a small round table, and she listened with interest as he explained the cards and game to her with an easy humor that was infectious. He dealt the first hand and she followed his coaching, making her best attempt to mimic the exaggerated blank looks he put on when he tried to bluff her.

At first she was sure she'd never learn; he saw right through her time and again. But then she began to get the hang of it, and watched his face the way she'd watch a wily maverick to see which way he'd dodge next; sometimes the clue was no more than a twitch at the corner of his eye, but it was enough. She felt a sharp excitement when she won for the first time, and only the stiff poke of her corset in her ribs reminded her not to hoot in triumph. She settled for a broad grin instead.

Quentin threw down his hand and admitted defeat. "You're one of us, all right," he said. "Better than you have any right to be." His eyes narrowed. "I wonder if Braden has any idea what he's got in you, Cassidy Holt."

She flushed with pleasure. "Does he play poker, too?"

"Oh, yes. But not with cards."

He didn't explain himself but reshuffled the deck and gave her an expectant look. "I think you've already graduated to playing for stakes."

She glanced down at her dress. "I haven't got anything," she said. "Except the books I brought from New Mexico, and a little money—"

"You seem certain that I'll win," he said. "What if you beat me, Cassidy? What do you want?"

The obvious answer was on the tip of her tongue. She would ask him to tell her about Braden—his childhood, the things he cared about, his hopes and dreams—everything that crowded her thoughts whenever she was in his presence.

But she had a notion that Quentin would find some way to avoid answering questions about his brother. She bit her lip. "I want—" An image came unbidden into her mind, out of the dreamworld of her distant past. "I want to see you Change into a wolf."

Quentin froze, the cards suspended in his hands. After a moment he relaxed, as if she'd made a joke he'd only just understood.

"That's not much of a prize, Cassidy. I do it exactly the same way you do. We English aren't so different as all that, you know."

Heat rose in her cheeks. He thought . . . of course he thought *she* could Change, the way her mother had been able to. There was no reason he should think otherwise; she was one of them.

But she'd been too excited, too happy at finding Braden to tell him that she hoped her English family would teach her what her mother hadn't been able to. They must take it for granted, that ability she'd always felt was just beyond her reach. They would think her silly and ignorant because she didn't know how, just the same way Rowena found her lacking in the graces a lady should have.

"Of course, you were living with human relatives," Quentin said. "Your father's, I believe?"

She put on the "poker face" Quentin had taught her. "Yes."

"Well, you're here now, and you're unlikely to get rid of us even if you wanted to." He gave her a lopsided smile that didn't quite reach his eyes. "Very well. If you win, I shall Change for you. If *I* win . . ."

She held her breath. If he asked her to Change, she would be forced to admit she didn't know how. And she wasn't ready for that—not yet, when she was trying to do things right. When she was finally *wanted*.

"If I win," he said, "you shall owe me a favor which I'll redeem when I choose. Agreed?"

Her relief was so strong that she didn't hesitate. "Agreed."

They played another hand of five-card stud, but Cassidy's beginner's luck had run out. Quentin won easily, though he winked and clowned to take the sting out of his victories. They were still absorbed in the game when Aynsley appeared in the doorway, trailed by a maid and footman.

"Lord Greyburn wishes me to inform you, Mr. Forster, Miss Holt," he said, "that there will be no formal dinner this evening. The servants are engaged in preparing for the return to Northumberland. Meals shall be sent up to your rooms in an hour. Should you have any requests, please inform the maid or footman." He bowed. "Lord Greyburn also requests the honor of your company in the library, Mr. Forster, as soon as it is convenient."

Quentin set down his cards and shrugged elaborately. "So our fun comes to an end, alas. But it has been pleasant." He stood, bent over to lift her hand, and kissed her fingertips. "Most pleasant. I believe you have the makings of a true gamester, Cousin."

His words were flattering, but her skin didn't tingle or her heart pound when he kissed her—not as they did when Braden touched her in even the most impersonal way. She liked Quentin without reservation, but he felt very much like the brother she longed to have—the brother she'd lost long ago.

Quentin sighed and released her hand. "I'll be off to the lion's den," he said, "and you should rest, Cassidy. The maid will help you with the dress." He shuddered. "Rowena may take pleasure in being laced into a gown that fits like armor and weighs about as much, but I'm relieved that I'm only a gentleman. With any luck, you won't have to endure another day of shopping for at least a month."

Cassidy laughed, grateful for his attempts to put her at ease. Secretly, she thoroughly disliked the corset and binding skirts—she couldn't imagine walking a mile in the desert wearing them, let alone swinging a rope in pursuit of a balky calf—but she wasn't about to complain out loud. She owed Braden too much, and was even beholden to Rowena for her advice and guidance, however reluctantly given.

"Thank you," she said. "This was fun."

"And there's more to come, I assure you." He shared a sly wink with her, squared his shoulders, clicked his heels in a mockery of military precision, and marched toward the door.

Through the walls that delineated his solitary haven, down the echoing hall that had been empty of voices for so long, Braden heard them laughing.

He listened in spite of himself, wondering, not for the first time, if humans held the advantage with their duller senses. They weren't so likely to overhear what could all too easily bring them only vexation, sadness, and pain.

It wasn't pain he felt. Even vexation was too strong a word. He pushed annoyance to the back of his mind with an impatient shake of his head. He'd wanted Quentin to win Cassidy's liking and trust; Quentin was clearly succeeding, even more quickly than Braden hoped. Charm came easily to Quentin if he chose to use it. The whole fashionable world adored the laughing, gallant Quentin Forster.

Cassidy Holt would learn to adore him as well. It was the essential first step for what must follow. Quentin's small betrayal had done little enough harm to Braden, and she had neither shown undue pity nor questioned his leadership afterward.

That was fortunate indeed. If he couldn't convince a child of his competence, he'd have no hope with the delegates at the Convocation.

And he must. He was leader of the Cause. Its survival— the survival of the race itself—depended on him.

But not through the begetting of heirs of his body. That part of him was dead and beyond recovery.

A soft knock came on the door, and Quentin walked into the library. His steps lagged just enough to tell Braden that he was uneasy. As well he might be.

"I hear," Braden said, "that you and Cassidy have been enjoying yourselves."

"Immensely. She's a very amusing girl." He ambled to the sideboard, picked up the glass Braden had filled earlier, and took a small sip. "Perhaps the task you've set me won't be so laborious after all."

A slow, unwonted wave of hostility rolled through Braden's body. "And does that task include teaching her a gamester's tricks?"

"Ah, I see that Aynsley—or is it Telford?—has been making reports already." He took another, longer drink. "There's no harm in a bit of innocent fun, elder brother. She is an American, after all. Not as sheltered as our Englishwomen. Certainly nothing like Rowena." Glass rang on wood as Quentin set down his snifter. "Oh, but you're angry with me. You didn't really think you'd deceive her forever? Hardly sporting of you. And in any case"—he poured another measure from the decanter—"your embarrassment was only temporary. Little more than a mild irritation considering your undisputed power."

"And is it undisputed, Quentin?" Braden crossed the room to stand beside his brother, threateningly close. "Do you wish to challenge me?"

Quentin laughed around a mouthful of brandy. "Challenge you? Whatever put such an absurd idea into your head, elder brother? You know I haven't the skill, the courage, or the desire to take on your burdens. Even if I thought I were likely to survive such an unpleasant and thoroughly disagreeable contest. I know my limitations."

"Remember that, Quentin," Braden said, very softly. "Don't try me again."

"I shan't, I promise you. Arguments are so tedious." He reached for the decanter again, and Braden pulled it from his hand.

"No more of this. I want you sober and focused on your duty."

"Ah. I knew I couldn't escape my punishment." Quentin

dropped into the chair positioned before Braden's desk. "Speaking of my duty—have you told Cassidy just what you have in mind for her? The destiny you've undoubtedly planned down to the last detail, as you have for the rest of us?"

Braden sat stiffly at his desk, and stared toward his brother. "I have not told her. There's time enough for that when we reach Greyburn."

"A mere few weeks before the Convocation," Quentin remarked. "Do you think she'll be ready to face all those strangers?"

"She will be. You'll help see to it, Quentin. But you will not speak of her future. Is that clear?"

"Perfectly." Quentin yawned with more drama than authenticity. "And now I'm really quite fatigued. If I may be excused—"

"Have your valet pack your things. We're leaving tomorrow."

"So soon? I'd thought—"

"What the servants haven't finished by tomorrow they will send up later. I want us home."

Home. Braden closed his eyes, as if memory and imagination were somehow more vivid behind the veil of sleep and dreams. Every moment in London had been a kind of torture, an unnatural severance from the land he loved, burns and fells and lonely moors as much as part of him as the wolf he could not become in this endless cage of walls and machinery and civilization.

Would Cassidy feel the same? Would she love the north as he did? Or would she simply walk, unsuspecting, into yet another kind of cage?

Such mawkish thoughts were pointless. He dismissed Quentin with a lift of his hand, but Quentin couldn't leave without a final quip.

"I'm beginning to believe," he said, "that marrying little Cassidy Holt might be the making of me."

Braden laid his hands flat on the desk, concentrating on the velvet smoothness of the polished surface as if he could become as unfeeling and functional as the wood under his fingertips. "If she teaches you to care for something other than your own amusements," he said, "then I'll have much to thank her for."

"I suspect you'll have more to thank her for than that," Quentin murmured. "I wonder how long it'll take you to realize it?"

He slipped out the door before Braden could reply. Let Quentin play his verbal games; they were only words in the end.

Yet those words came back to haunt him as he summoned the servants one by one to give them their orders and arranged for the tickets to be purchased for tomorrow's journey. Yes, he had reason to be grateful for recovering Cassidy Holt. But when she was Quentin's mate, his only concern with her would be the *loup-garou* children she brought into the world.

Quentin's children.

He clenched his hands and sat immersed in his own private darkness deep into the night.

six

It was Cassidy's second time on an English train, her second journey into the unknown. She didn't know where she would end up or what her future held. No one seemed to want to talk about the days ahead—not Isabelle, lost in thoughts of her own, nor Rowena, beside Quentin in the opposite seat of the private compartment. Braden and his valet had a compartment to themselves, nearby but out of reach, and the remaining servants were in another part of the train entirely.

Yet as Cassidy watched the English landscape roll by, she was happier than she'd been since those dim, lost days with her parents and brother.

Greyburn was their home. *Braden's* home. She'd seen the change in his face when he spoke of it. Rowena didn't want to leave London, and Quentin seemed indifferent, but Braden was eager to return to a place he loved.

What Braden loved must be very special indeed.

The trip was too exciting to be tedious. Servants had packed food and drink, and the seats were padded; the hours flew by as the train made its way past the tranquil farmland of the south, through fens and wetlands of the east, north to Yorkshire with its sheep-covered hills and moors. The land grew more rugged as the train crossed into Durham and then followed the coast to Newcastle.

Newcastle was every bit as ugly as London; smoke belched from high stacks, streets were narrow and dirty, and there were too many people crushed into small spaces. The air stank of a hundred clashing scents Cassidy couldn't begin to name. She twisted her fingers together in the lap of her uncomfortably proper traveling dress and prayed Newscastle was not their destination.

But after a wait and some to-do of transferring luggage to another train at the Newcastle station, and settling with much bustle and unnecessary fuss into a new compartment, the Forster party was on its way again. Inland and west from Newcastle, away from the crowds and the noise and the stench. Into a country that gave way, as the train curved north from the Tyne River, to wilder hills, bare and windswept, sheltering tapered valleys where trees huddled along the winding paths of the creeks the northern English called "burns." Scattered farms stood lonely guard in the valley of the North Tyne, the river never entirely out of sight from the train window.

There was a peculiar similarity between this land and the one Cassidy had left behind in New Mexico. It wasn't in the color of the earth or in the unfamiliar trees or the look of the sky; here it was green, like the rest of England. The very air had moisture in it, and heavy clouds scudded ahead of the wind.

But like the desert, Northumberland was wild. Once the city was left behind, it was as if people were only a tiny part of a place too big to be fenced and gentled and broken. Oh, there were stone-fenced fields, and patches of farmland, and sheep and cattle. But Cassidy could see hills as majestic and bleak as the mountains in New

Mexico, where a person could run for miles and miles without meeting anyone.

"Ah," Quentin said, after hours of uncharacteristic silence. "Ulfington at last." He drew a pack of cards from inside his coat and began to shuffle them absently. "Not much farther now."

Cassidy craned her neck for a better view of the approaching town. The train slowed, lurching and puffing like an old horse summoning up its last energy to reach the barn.

Ulfington itself was a collection of buildings running along two intersecting streets, with a jumble of outlying cottages along the edges. Cassidy could just make out a few signs hung from doorways, the spire of a church, people and horses moving along the cobbled streets.

"There is where we get off," Quentin added. "There'll be carriages waiting to take us to Greyburn."

She turned to look at him. "It's not here?"

"Oh, no. Braden couldn't abide living so near a town full of humans—begging your pardon, Mrs. Smith— even if our ancestors had seen fit to build here."

Isabelle smiled at Quentin in acknowledgment but said nothing. She seemed to like Quentin well enough, and was respectfully cordial with Rowena. But since they'd left London, she'd become more and more withdrawn.

Was it because she wasn't one of them—not *loup-garou*? Braden paid no more attention to her than he did to the other servants, who were all human. Isabelle was going to a place that belonged to the *loups-garous* in a way London didn't. Did that make her afraid?

The train pulled to a stop. Quentin stretched as far as the cramped quarters would allow, and Rowena clutched her small valise and stared straight ahead. Isabelle touched Cassidy's arm.

"Well," she said, "you're almost at the end of your quest, Cassidy."

"It doesn't feel like an ending," she said. "It feels like a beginning."

Isabelle squeezed her hand and looked very sad. "I wish every happiness for you, my dear."

"I know." For the first time Cassidy really considered what Isabelle had left behind in America. She'd had a comfortable house there, pretty clothes, friends. Had she come to England only for Cassidy's sake, giving up a life she loved?

"Isabelle," she said softly, "do you wish you were back in America?"

For an instant Cassidy thought she was right. Naked longing crossed Isabelle's face. But then she straightened, smiled, and set about pinning Cassidy's new traveling hat on top of her wayward hair.

"I shall quite enjoy visiting a country house again," she said. "And I've never been to Northumberland."

Cassidy grinned and took Isabelle's hand as they followed Quentin and Rowena out of the compartment. Liveried footmen were already in attendance to help them down; Braden stood with his valet, speaking to a man who seemed to be in charge of a gorgeous carriage and a pair of handsome horses, drawn up beside the platform. A second, smaller carriage and a wagon were lined up behind.

"We'll go ahead in the brougham, and our luggage will be brought after," Quentin explained. His gaze scanned the village beyond the station. "It hasn't changed."

"Has it been a long time since you were home?" Cassidy asked. "You must be glad to be back."

"As the Bard so aptly put it, ' 'Tis ever common that men are merriest when they are from home.' "

But he was laughing, as usual, and Cassidy didn't believe him. He sauntered away from the platform, leaving Cassidy and Isabelle to wait alone. Rowena was nowhere to be seen.

"Oh, dear, my hat!"

A female voice lifted in alarm behind Cassidy, and she turned just in time to catch the windblown confection of feathers and artificial flowers as it fetched up against her skirt.

The owner of the hat came dashing up, blue eyes wide and blond curls askew. "Oh, thank you! I quite thought I'd lost it forever. This wind . . . I'd forgotten how it can be in the north."

Cassidy smiled and restored the hat to the young woman. She was about Cassidy's age, but much more petite and pretty, well-dressed and well-rounded in her fashionable gown. The young woman returned Cassidy's smile and began to pin her hat atop her curls. A servant, evidently her maid, came scurrying up behind her.

"See, Ann—I haven't lost it after all!" The young woman studied Cassidy with sparkling eyes. "I beg your pardon—you've rescued my hat, and you don't know me from Eve. My name is Emily—Emily Roddam from Stonehaugh. The squire of Stonehaugh is my father, and he's just called me back from France—but oh, what must you be thinking? I'm such a chatterbox!"

"I don't think so. My name's Cassidy Holt, and I'm on my way to Greyburn."

Emily's eyes grew wider still. "Greyburn! Truly? How fascinating! Stonehaugh is just over the hill from Greyburn, but we've never—that is—" She flushed.

"You live near Greyburn?" Cassidy prompted, leaning forward as if to share a secret. "I haven't been there. Have you?"

"Oh, no." Emily shivered dramatically. "When I was a

child, before Mama took me to Paris—I remember the stories. Our nurse told us that if we went over the hill to Greyburn land, the Gabriel hounds would come get us. But I daresay you'll think me foolish—"

"No. I've come all the way from America—"

"America? Your accent, of course. I met Americans in Paris. You're newly come to England?"

"Yes. The Forsters of Greyburn are my cousins."

"I see. . . . But truly, those old stories are foolish. I know that now. We just used to have such a delicious fright, you know. And the servants are all so superstitious!" She giggled. "Oh, but where are my manners! Are you here for the summer? Perhaps we can be friends. This is quite the end of the world, you know. I'd have rather stayed in London, but my father—well, he wanted me home, and with Mama gone—" She patted her hat. "I'm sure Papa would be glad to have you visit. If your cousins don't mind?"

It was almost too fast for Cassidy, but she felt warmed through by Emily's offer of friendship. She'd met few girls her own age at the ranch, and was close to none of them. To be liked for herself, just the way she was . . .

"I'd love to visit," she said.

Emily clapped her gloved hands. "Delightful. Do you ride?"

"I rode all the time in New Mexico."

"Then we shall both have someone to ride with. It's been ages since I saw the Wall. We can take a picnic. Oh, I know we shall become great friends!" She held out her hand, and Cassidy took it. They grinned at each other in perfect accord, and Cassidy thought she couldn't have had a better welcome to Northumberland than this. Everything was going to be perfect. She had Braden, and her other cousins, and Isabelle, and now Emily, her first real friend in England.

"Are you waiting for a ride to your house?" Cassidy asked. "If Stonehaugh is so close, maybe we could—"

"Cassidy."

Emily looked up as Braden's shadow fell over her. She took a step back, snatching at her skirts.

"The carriages are waiting," Braden said. He barely glanced at Emily, and his expression was icy. "Please excuse us."

Taken aback, Cassidy smiled reassuringly at Emily, who stared at Braden as if she'd seen a monster out of a childhood story. "I have to go now," Cassidy said. "I hope we meet again soon."

But Emily was mute, and her gaze fell on Cassidy with a look of mingled dismay and yearning. Someone called her name; with a little twitch of relief she bobbed a curtsy and fled with her maid along the platform toward a waiting carriage.

"Come," Braden said, taking Cassidy's arm. Isabelle fell in behind them, all but forgotten. Cassidy looked after Emily, but the young woman made no attempt to wave as her carriage moved off.

"That was Emily Roddam," she said by way of explanation, trying to make sense of Braden's rudeness. "She lives at Stonehaugh—"

"I know who she is. We'll speak of this later." He reached the end of the platform and stumbled at the edge; he caught himself instantly and turned toward the first of the Greyburn carriages.

Rowena and Quentin were already seated; Braden helped Cassidy in and let the footman assist Isabelle. He disappeared, and the carriage lurched into motion. Isabelle was gazing out the window, and Rowena was withdrawn, as she so often was. Only Quentin seemed in the mood for conversation.

"What did you think of Ulfington?" he asked.

"I don't know," she said honestly. "But I met Miss Roddam on the platform—"

"Ah. One of the older human families in the area," he said, emphasizing "human." "You must want to know more about our countryside."

Without waiting for her answer, he launched into a monologue about Ulfington and the road to Greyburn. She learned that Ulfington was the largest town for many miles around, a place where the local farmers and shepherds gathered in summer for their yearly agricultural fair. At Ulfington the North Tyne continued northwest to the Scottish border. The River Ulf fed into it from the north, a rougher and narrower valley winding toward the Cheviot Hills.

As he spoke, the narrow road paralleled the Ulf up the valley, passing more isolated farms at the foot of bare hills. There were no more villages, only handfuls of cottages clustered near pastures or fields of grain or grass. Once a small flock of sheep crossed the road on the way to the riverbank; the shepherd paused to touch his cap, his manner respectful but his face closed and wary.

At last they reached a fork in the road, where a still narrower lane led alongside a shining silver ribbon of water. A forest of trees formed a tunnel that all but enclosed the burn: Grey Burn, from which the Forster estate took its name.

More trees lined the roadside, in greater numbers than Cassidy had seen anywhere since they'd left the train station. "Our ancestors planted them," Quentin said. "Most of the forest here was cut down long ago, but the Greyburn Forsters could not live without their woods."

And the woods were lovely. They were deep and mysterious, calling to Cassidy in an unfamiliar voice, the distant echo of that compulsion within herself that she'd never learned how to follow.

The urge to open the carriage door, leap out onto the moist green earth, and fling herself among those trees was almost irresistible. She squeezed her eyes shut and tried not to listen to the voice of the woods, concentrated instead on the clop of the horses' hooves and the creak of the carriage and Quentin's tuneless whistle.

When she opened her eyes again, she saw Greyburn itself.

She'd been given no description of the estate beforehand, nothing on which to base her imaginings. It would have to be magnificent, grand, imposing like Braden himself. It must be worthy of his love.

It was all those things, and more. " 'The splendor falls on castle walls,' " Cassidy whispered. Greyburn wasn't a castle, not really, though there was a kind of ruined tower off to one side, and the main house itself, standing in the midst of a great sloping lawn and flanked by tall, stately trees, had an ancient look of stone and majesty. Chimneys and spires rose from a jumble of straight and sloping roofs at irregular intervals, and high windows gazed out from every wall like watchful eyes. It was big enough to satisfy anyone's idea of a palace fit for a mighty lord.

"It's a rather odd pile, I admit," Quentin said, leaning forward to follow her gaze. "Every earl of Greyburn has left his mark on it, but the original building was Elizabethan. My grandfather had a taste for the medieval, but he chose to add rather than alter. God forbid the sacrilege of symmetry. Braden has done relatively little. . . ." He paused and threw her an amused glance. "But I don't suppose that matters to you."

"It's wonderful," she said.

"This house and these lands are filled with legends. Most of them date back to the age of the Border Reivers, families of Scotland and England who fought over these lands and spent much of their time raiding each other."

He widened his eyes. "They say a ghost of one of those warriors still haunts the estate—Matthias, one of the first guardians of Greyburn. Perhaps you'll meet him one day."

A guardian ghost seemed just right for a place like this. "I hope I do," Cassidy said. "I want to know everything about Greyburn."

"Braden ought to appreciate your enthusiasm. I should warn you that you won't find many modern conveniences at Greyburn. My family prefers historical tradition to vulgar progress."

She couldn't believe that Greyburn lacked anything to make it perfect. When the carriage rattled to a halt on the curving drive in front of the steps leading to the wide front doors, she could barely wait to be helped down by the footman. She tripped over her skirts as her foot touched the ground, but it was a familiar hand that steadied her.

Braden released her arm as soon as she had her balance. His head was lifted and turned toward the great house, a kind of contentment in his face.

This was what it was like to come home. Home was more than a place; it was a way of feeling. It meant you belonged.

She wanted to belong here. She wanted Braden to turn toward her with that same aspect of quiet joy.

But he scarcely seemed to notice her. Quentin and Rowena and Isabelle had come to stand beside them, waiting on his lead. Assembled just below the steps were two neat double rows of men and women dressed in black and white: servants, far more than there'd been at the house in London, standing at attention.

One of the men came down the steps to greet Braden, bowing with impeccable dignity. Cassidy recognized Aynsley, who must have arrived at Greyburn ahead of them.

"Welcome home, Lord Greyburn," he said.

Braden walked up to the stairs, pausing before each servant with a brief word. Heads bobbed and curious eyes flickered toward Cassidy. She smiled at one maid in a smudged white apron, but the girl gave a soundless gasp and looked quickly away.

"This is my cousin, Miss Holt," Braden said to the servants. "She is to be regarded as one of the family." Almost as an afterthought, he nodded toward Isabelle. "Mrs. Smith, Miss Holt's companion."

A footman opened the front door and Braden offered his arm to Cassidy. Rowena swept up after them, and Quentin accompanied Isabelle into the house.

The entrance hall was lined by plain, heavy chairs, and the ceiling arched high overhead. A long carpet runner, its rich colors faded with years of wear, ran the length of the floor. A grand staircase with intricately carved newel posts climbed to a wide landing at the end of the hall, and more doorways led to rooms on either side.

Cassidy stared up at the ceiling and the large paintings visible on the wall above the first-floor landing. Braden left her to speak with Aynsley, his valet and the housekeeper, Mrs. Fairbairn, while the other servants silently filed past and disappeared within the house.

"It's most impressive, isn't it?" Isabelle said beside her, a catch in her voice.

"You've been in houses like this before."

"Yes. Once upon a time."

"It seems almost too grand for someone like me."

Isabelle glanced toward the others. "Appearances can be deceptive," she said. "Even such places hide their secrets. Never forget that, Cassidy."

The gravity of Isabelle's words caught Cassidy by surprise. She was about to ask for an explanation when a uniformed maid approached with a curtsy.

"Mrs. Smith?" she said: "Would you come with me? I'm to show you to your room."

"We'll talk again soon," Isabelle promised, and followed the maid to the grand staircase. Braden was still in conversation with Aynsley; Quentin had left the hall, and Rowena was already halfway up the stairs.

Suddenly feeling very much alone, Cassidy gazed about the hall. Isabelle's warning was clear in her thoughts, yet she didn't sense anything to fear. The smells of Greyburn seemed part of the walls themselves: wood, stone, leather, cloth, and dust overlaid by damp and the remote scents of cooking.

One of the side doors opposite caught her attention; it was huge and intricately carved, and she crossed the hall to study it more carefully. The images were of men fighting with swords, and horses galloping over rolling hills.

Unable to resist, Cassidy pushed open the heavy door.

Inside was a room completely unlike the hall and even more grand. The towering ceiling had a skeleton of heavy, bare beams, the floor was made of large stone squares, and there were a huge table and countless chairs at one end of the room, beside an immense fireplace. Banners and shields hung on the walls; Cassidy thought of knights in armor and deeds of daring long ago.

Additional carvings framed the fireplace, and Cassidy was inevitably drawn toward them. But the subjects here were different.

There were armored men, and horses, but among them ran lithe, furred shapes with bared fangs: wolves. Everywhere Cassidy looked she saw wolves, sometimes with humans and sometimes running alone.

And then she found the centerpiece, above the main part of the fireplace. It was almost too high up for her to see; she pulled up a chair and bunched her skirts to climb.

Two great wolves confronted each other, ears forward and tails high. Each perched on something that Cassidy thought at first were oddly shaped rocks. Then she made out the features, and saw the bodies of men, hands stretched out in supplication, pressed to the ground by the weight of the wolves.

"My grandfather commissioned those carvings."

Cassidy scrambled down from the chair and whirled to face Braden. He stood at the other end of the great room, but his voice carried pure and resonant across its length.

"The designs on the outside of the door were done in my great-great-grandfather's time," he said, walking toward her. "Do you perceive the contrast, Cassidy, between those within this room and those without?"

She guessed it was a test of her ability to observe and appreciate her new home, and she was determined not to fail. "The ones on the door don't have any wolves."

"That is correct." He passed her and stopped directly beneath the fireplace carvings. He was just tall enough to reach them; he ran his fingers over the wolves and their human captives. Gently, as if they were old and dear friends.

"My grandfather," he went on, "rebuilt this hall when he redesigned the house upon my great-grandfather's death. He increased the size of Greyburn by half again, but the Great Hall was his proudest achievement. This Gothic style was not fashionable in his day, but he wished to re-create an older time. A different way of life."

Cassidy looked up at the banners, the shields, the old weapons rusting high on the walls. " 'The sun came dazzling thro' the leaves,' " she quoted, " 'and flamed upon the brazen greaves of bold Sir Lancelot.' "

"Lancelot, if he ever existed, was human." He turned to face her, and he looked just as grim as he had in Ulfington, when he'd frightened Emily Roddam. "My grandfather built this for the *loups-garous*. For our kind alone, and those unquestioningly loyal to us."

Instinctively Cassidy glanced at the ominous carvings over the fireplace. As if he sensed her movement, Braden reached up to touch them again.

"All the carvings in this room but these were commissioned when my grandfather was young," he said. "This final panel was added when I was a boy. What do you see when you look at it, Cassidy?"

She shivered a little and said the first thing that came into her mind. "The wolves have conquered the people."

"Yes." He let his hand fall and moved to the table. "When he was young, my grandfather came to recognize that our race was dying, because too many of us over the generations had interbred with humans. We were losing the gifts which made us what we are—the very abilities that make us superior to ordinary men. For we are superior, Cassidy—that is something you must always remember."

This was the opportunity Cassidy had been waiting for—explanations to fill all the gaps in her knowledge, a chance to learn what Braden cared about, what he wanted. But his words chilled her, and all at once she saw the awesome vastness of Greyburn as something other than a fairy-tale castle or the stuff of romantic dreams.

"My grandfather had this final carving made when he realized how treacherous humans can be," Braden said, "when he knew that we can no longer afford to live among them as if we were equals. They outnumber us—they always have. But that is their only advantage."

Cassidy walked slowly to the table and pulled out a chair. It felt as heavy as a blacksmith's anvil. "I don't understand."

Passion blazed in his face then, a fierce conviction. "You will," he said. "You must. You will learn to think of Greyburn as your only home, we your only family. The rest of the world no longer matters."

The rest of the world. But he didn't mean only London or New Mexico or even all the places Cassidy had never seen. He meant people, too. People who weren't were-wolves like he was—or like Rowena, and Quentin, and Edith Holt.

Cassidy remembered Emily Roddam and her bubbling offer of friendship. It had felt so good to talk to someone who liked her just as she was, who wanted to know her better without judgment or expectations.

But Emily Roddam was not a Forster. She was not *loup-garou*. She'd been afraid of Braden, and he had wanted her to be afraid.

"At the train station," she said, "you didn't want me to talk to Emily Roddam."

"The Roddams are human. They have no part in our destiny."

Cassidy fisted her hands on the table. "She wanted to be my friend—"

"It was such friendships that nearly destroyed our kind, made us lose the very essence of what we are." He loomed over her, deadly serious. "Forget your past. Forget everything that made you less than what you were meant to be."

What she was meant to be. Most of her life she'd struggled with that question, bereft of the knowledge her mother would have passed on if she'd lived.

But this wasn't what she reckoned on. She'd thought that finding her family would be an adding, not a taking away.

"You hate humans," she said with sudden understanding.

"Hate them? No. But I acknowledge them for what

they are." His mouth tightened into a bitter half smile. "What was your life like among them?"

She remembered the look of distrust and fear in Uncle Jonas's eyes even when he was trying to be kind, and bad times with Aunt Harriet when he was away from the ranch. They never said what they were afraid of, never spoke of her mother, but they didn't let her forget that she was different, an unwelcome burden on their charity. A few of the *vaqueros* crossed themselves when she walked by, and she was sent out to the farthest ranges when guests came to the hacienda.

But there had been generosity, too. Mercedes the cook had always seen that she had enough to eat. Old Juan had praised her skill at finding lost cattle and helped order her precious books of poetry from the store in town.

And her father had been human. She hardly remembered him, but she had loved him. And he loved her. Had Braden forgotten that?

"Not everyone is the same," she said. "Some people are kind—"

"Most humans would hate and fear us, Cassidy, if we revealed ourselves. In times past, they often hunted us like animals. That is why so few know what we are."

"But Isabelle isn't afraid. She knows—"

"I allowed her to come here for your sake. She won't speak of what she's seen."

His certainty was ominous, like a great black thunderhead foretelling a summer storm. "The servants—they live here with you," she said.

"And they also know. But they are loyal to the family. They will never betray us."

She thought of the mute, anxious deference of the servants—all but Aynsley, who wrapped himself in a kind of stately detachment, and Braden's valet, whom she'd met on the stairs in London.

She frowned at her clenched hands on the table. "If we're so different from humans," she said, "then why do we live like them? Why did the werewolves marry them, and have children?"

If he knew she was speaking of her own parents, her own birth, he didn't show it. "We did it to survive," he said. "We thought that being like them would protect us. And there were less and less of our people to find each other. But now such ways have become a threat to our existence." His blind gaze was vehement, obsessed. "You are not like them, Cassidy. Your senses are keener, your reflexes faster. You can run tirelessly for a day, go without food for a week. You can hear sounds a human is deaf to, or locate a man by his scent over half a city. You are oblivious to cold and resistant to illness and pain. You are *loup-garou*."

She had never counted up her gifts the way he did now—not in so many words—but he was right. She was all those things, just as her mother had been. She should have felt glad, knowing how completely Braden accepted her.

But he spoke as if she were a collection of abilities, not a person. And she remembered the card game with Quentin, how she'd wondered what Braden would say when he learned she didn't know how to Change.

"Our duty," Braden said, "is to restore our blood to what it was in ancient days. It is the Cause to which I've devoted my life. You, too, are part of it."

Part of a cause that Braden cared about fervently, profoundly, that made his harsh, handsome face take on a radiant light of its own. He was finally giving her a chance to help him.

"How?" she asked. "How can I help?"

"Believe in the Cause, as I do." He spread his hands wide to encompass the room. "For more than fifty years, the last true *loup-garou* families of the world have met here, working to save our people. The next Convocation is in less than two weeks. You will be presented to the delegates, and take your place among us."

She tried to imagine this hall filled with men and women like Braden, all looking at her. Judging her, debating her worthiness. Braden was so sure she was worthy.

But she had to be what he wanted. She had to forget that part of her was human, or that she had human friends. That was the price she must pay to be one of them.

She got up from the table and walked around its massive length to stand beside him. A shiver rushed through her, from her toes to the very top of her head, just as it always did when he was near.

"This matters so much to you," she said.

"We're fighting for our lives." His attention focused on her—*her,* not some piece in a game she hadn't learned how to play. He caught her hands, held them in a grip that should have been numbing but made the blood pound in her temples and gather low in her belly. "Will you give yourself to the Cause, Cassidy?"

He *asked*—as if he wanted her not for his Cause, but for himself. Only part of her understood what that would mean, stirring within her like a seed in dry desert earth, waiting for the rains to make it blossom.

He was the rain, pouring over her, nourishing her with his touch, his scent, his strength.

And yet she had something he wanted—something only she could give.

"You need me,"she said. "You need *me.*"

His face was very close to hers, his lips parted, his green eyes as intense as if he'd never lost the gift of sight. His nostrils widened to take in her scent; suddenly he flinched away, letting her hands fall, and the light died in his eyes.

"The Cause needs you," he said, his voice stripped of

emotion. "As it needs everyone of the true blood. I know you will do your duty as a Forster and *loup-garou*."

A Forster, and a *loup-garou*. Not "Cassidy," or even "Cousin," but a pair of words that seemed utterly impersonal now. Words like "Cause" and "True Blood" and "Superior"—labels made to build walls between people. Slogans that hid dark places Cassidy didn't want to see.

Just as Braden didn't want to see *her*.

She hugged herself, aching and bewildered. "I'd like to go to my room now."

In answer he strode across the room and flung open the great doors. "A maid will show you up," he said. "I will send for you later."

Cassidy bowed her head and hurried from the Hall. A maid was waiting, as Braden had promised; Cassidy hardly noticed the young woman's curtsy. She had to get to her room, find the calico dress she'd brought from the ranch—clothing she could move in. She needed to think, and always she went into the wilderness when she was troubled as she was now.

In New Mexico she'd sought the desert. Here was no dry, open plain, but deep woods and moist hills beneath a foreign sky. The woods had called to her; she would go to them, and maybe they would answer the questions she didn't know how to ask.

The maid showed her to her room and came in behind her. On any other occasion, Cassidy would have been awed by the lavish chamber she'd been given, as she was by Greyburn itself. Her room at the London house had been small and plain; this one was fit for a princess. The wide bed was canopied and richly furnished, matched by elegant carved furniture, heavy patterned drapes, and rich carpet. A huge bathtub stood in front of the fireplace, where a modest fire took the faint chill off the room.

"There's a hot bath ready for you, miss, and your

clothes are in the wardrobe," the maid said. "I will prepare a gown—"

"My calico dress—do you know where they put it?"

The maid looked confused. The dress probably seemed like a rag compared to Cassidy's London collection. Cassidy found the wardrobe in the small adjoining dressing room and began to search. The calico had been hung in the very back, behind all the fancy clothes.

The small buttons of her traveling dress refused to give way to her clumsy efforts. "Can you help me with this?" she asked the maid. The girl came at once, undoing the long basque bodice, overskirt and underskirt, and then the corset, with expert fingers.

For the first time in many hours Cassidy could breathe freely. The maid helped her put on the calico dress, and stood back without comment as Cassidy tested her restored freedom. Cassidy unbuttoned her dainty, impractical boots and looked in vain for the shoes she'd worn to England. Someone had decided they weren't fit for a "superior" Forster.

She couldn't run in any of the London shoes. To feel the earth beneath her feet was exactly what she needed.

"You can go now," she told the maid. "I'll be fine. I just . . . want to be alone."

If the maid felt disapproval of Cassidy's appearance, she didn't dare show it. She curtsied again and went to the door. "If you need anything, miss, just ring."

Cassidy realized how uncomfortable she felt with that automatic deference, the knowledge that the girl's whole business was to wait on one person. But the maid wasn't to blame. Cassidy smiled and nodded her thanks, lingering in the room until the maid's footsteps faded away down the corridor.

Then she used all her senses to escape the house undetected. If Braden had been watching, she wouldn't have managed it. But the few human servants she smelled nearby didn't see her, because she didn't want them to. She discovered a door at the rear of the house and slipped through, into a garden lush with the scent of flowers.

A lingering twilight hung over the hills and woods behind Greyburn, staining the garden's foliage with pink and gold. The garden was large, well-kept, crisscrossed with stone and gravel paths perfect for peaceful afternoon walks. That wasn't what Cassidy wanted. Her heart was already beating fast with anticipation, knowing that soon, if only for a little while, everything would be simple again.

She'd nearly reached the edge of the garden when she knew she wasn't alone. The last person she wanted to meet now was Rowena, who would see calico and bare feet and judge Cassidy lacking with that regal, cultivated look of disdain.

But along with Rowena's scent came a half-familiar and lonely sound, dry and rasping. Cassidy hesitated, and a piece of crumpled paper blew past her feet, catching at the base of a garden shrub.

Cassidy bent to retrieve it, reflexively smoothing out the paper. There was writing on it, and words that were just like poetry. The letter was addressed to Rowena. "My Dearest," it began, and spoke of "my love for you," "great obstacles," "cruel separation," and "your brother's irrational behavior."

Before Cassidy could make out the signature, Rowena burst onto the path. Her ordinarily immaculate hair was in disarray, and her face was blotched with red.

Cassidy gaped and almost dropped the paper clenched in her hand.

The Lady Rowena Forster—refined, stylish and proper, ever-cool and condescending, member of the best London society—had been crying.

seven

"Give it back," Rowena snapped.

Still shocked by the change in Braden's sister, Cassidy complied. Rowena snatched the sheet from her hand and smoothed it out just as Cassidy had done. Her slender fingers were trembling, and tears threatened to spill from her eyes with the slightest blink. For a moment all her attention was focused on the letter, and then she seemed to realize that she was being observed. Her head jerked up, further loosening the pins in her hair. Golden curls tumbled onto her shoulders.

"How dare you read my letter," she said, without any real force, as if she spoke only out of habit. Or to protect the fragments of her shattered dignity.

To someone like Rowena, the loss of her flawless mask would be terrible. Cassidy was glad she'd never had any to lose.

"I'm sorry," she said. She meant it sincerely, and felt a genuine stab of pity. Rowena's obvious unhappiness touched her in a way the older woman's cool advice and grudging acceptance hadn't. It was something Cassidy understood. "I didn't mean to look at it."

Rowena sniffed and tried to compose her features into calm disinterest. "How much did you see?" she asked.

"That it was written to you," Cassidy admitted. "From someone who—" She paused, remembering the poetic language and sweet endearments. "Someone who loves you."

Rowena's mask crumpled again, and she turned sharply aside. "Will you tell Braden?"

Puzzled, Cassidy shook her head. "Tell him what?" she asked. "Why are you crying?"

The sound Rowena made was not quite a laugh. "Is it possible that you still don't know?" Her gaze turned inward, and when she glanced at Cassidy again there was a strange gleam in her eyes. "So Braden hasn't explained everything to you yet. How remiss of him." Her mouth curled as if she'd tasted something bitter. "And how unfair to you. Poor child."

This was the Rowena Cassidy knew, faintly mocking under her precise and soft-spoken words. But Cassidy wasn't fooled. Rowena was hurting, so much that Cassidy could feel the constriction in her own heart.

"What didn't he explain?" she asked. "What is it about the letter that you don't want him to know?"

She thought Rowena wouldn't answer, that she'd just walk away and leave her comments a mystery, her sadness unshared.

"I don't know if I can help," Cassidy said. "But I'd like to try."

Rowena seemed on the verge of laughter again, but the laugh became a stifled sob. Abruptly she tossed her head, an extravagant motion for someone so controlled, and looked at Cassidy without a hint of mockery.

"Very well," she said. "You can't help me, but perhaps . . ." She gestured for Cassidy to follow, and led her to an ornate cast-iron bench behind a turn of the path. They sat down, surrounded by the fragrance of flowers that didn't hide the feral scent of the woods, just as Rowena's lofty reserve could no longer hide emotions she didn't want to reveal.

"You came to Greyburn of your own free will," Rowena said. "Is that not so?"

"Yes." Cassidy said. "I wanted to come. To find a home. My family."

"Once, long ago, this was my home. But I did not wish to return." She clasped her hands in her lap, fingers tightening against each other. "The letter . . . was from a gentleman in London, a fine, respectable man who wishes to marry me. As I wish to marry him."

Cassidy guessed what it must be like to receive such a letter, so full of lovely phrases. To have a beau, like most ladies did. But when she tried to picture a face to go with the letter, it was Braden's that came to her. Braden, whom she couldn't imagine ever writing something like that. Feeling like that . . .

Rowena's voice slashed into her wistful thoughts. "I was not allowed that choice," she said. "Braden had already made plans for my future. I am to marry a man I've never met, a man I cannot respect. And all to serve Braden's Cause."

The Cause. Cassidy stared at Rowena. "You mean . . . he won't let you marry the man you love?"

Rowena sighed. "You are a romantic, Cassidy. Once, I was like you. Once I believed that I could be whom I chose to be. And I chose to live as a normal person, a human being, not as a beast."

A beast. She meant a *loup-garou*. A werewolf. "You don't want to be—"

"Did you know that once the Greyburn Forsters were

great county hosts?" Rowena said. "We mingled with all the best northern families. We were known in London, in the most distinguished society. We hid our curse. Not all of us wished for the 'gifts' my brother so prizes. My own great-aunt married an ordinary man."

A human. Like Cassidy's father. "So did my mother," she said softly.

Rowena gave her an earnest, almost pleading look. "Then perhaps . . . you can understand. Our cousins the Sayerses have lived free of the curse ever since my great-Aunt Grace made her choice. That is all I've ever wanted. To marry an honorable man of refinement, keep his home . . . raise children who are not half-animal."

Cassidy flinched. Less than an hour ago Braden had been declaring his contempt for humans. Now his sister spoke of the *loups-garous* as if they were monsters.

"I don't understand," she said, "how you could want to be . . . less than you are."

"Because I have no desire to take the shape of a savage and unnatural creature? One that wasn't meant to exist except as a tale to frighten children? I refuse to perpetuate—" She broke off, breathing fast. "But you want it, like Braden."

Yes. She wanted it. She wanted to know what it was like to be what her mother had been, what Braden was. She yearned for it with all her heart.

Rowena was wrong. It was a gift, the Changing. It couldn't be bad, not if Braden—

"Did he tell you of his mission?" Rowena said. "His great plan to restore the werewolf race to new glory? Yes, I see that he has. But he did not tell you everything, did he?" She looked down at her hands. "Once, I believed there was hope for him. For all of us. When Milena was here . . ."

"Milena?"

"His wife. His *late* wife." Rowena's face, if possible, grew even more bleak. "He would not have mentioned her."

Braden hadn't mentioned it. Cassidy felt a jolt of unwelcome surprise and thought back over the past few days. She'd once mistaken Rowena for his wife, but since then nothing about him, or in the words of others in London or at Greyburn, hinted that he had been married.

Milena. It was a beautiful name.

"Now he doesn't care who he hurts," Rowena said. "I am to marry an uncouth stranger who has the proper lineage, so that we can . . ." She flushed. "So that our children will be of the 'true blood.' " She mocked the words Braden had spoken so seriously. "My wishes don't matter. And neither do yours, Cassidy." Her expression hardened to something like cruelty. "He has planned your future, as well. You have walked into his trap. You wished to find a home and family, and you will have them. As *he* commands."

"I . . ." Cassidy stammered. "I can't believe—"

"Guard your heart, Cassidy Holt. Do not let it be touched. Save yourself the grief I and others have suffered."

Cassidy stood, feeling as breathless as if she still wore the imprisoning corset. "Why don't you go away?" she said recklessly. "If you're so unhappy—"

Rowena shook her head. "You don't know his power. I am a prisoner here, but there is a chance for you. Go back to America, if you can, before it is too late. Before Braden destroys you."

There were tears in Rowena's eyes again, and that more than anything convinced Cassidy that she spoke from her heart. She suffered, and she blamed Braden. But if he was responsible for her unhappiness, if he were as cruel as Rowena said . . .

Then everything Cassidy had felt from the very first moment she'd met Braden Forster, earl of Greyburn, was hopelessly mistaken.

With a whispered apology to Rowena, Cassidy turned and ran for the woods.

Isabelle heard the voices in the garden and quickly turned away, walking across the manicured lawn toward the burn.

She didn't stop to think who had reached the garden before her. She had been trying, without success, not to think at all.

Not to think of this grand house, so much like the other she remembered with such pain. Or of Lord Greyburn's arrogance and pride and easy mastery, the very essence of what she despised in the aristocracy.

Or that here she was more an outsider than ever. A pariah posing as a respectable widow, a human among werewolves. Doubly damned.

Cassidy had asked her if she wished to return to America. She had lied, as much to disguise her own cowardice as to spare the girl. How could she hope to protect Cassidy when she was here on sufferance, as the earl had made so abundantly clear before their departure from London?

But she had made a promise, to herself as much as to Cassidy. Break it now, and she would forfeit the last slivers of self-respect she had left.

She climbed the fell behind the house, breathing in England's moist evening air. In spite of her unease, all the memories of her girlhood in the country came back to her in this place: picnics in the little wood beyond the vicarage, Sundays when Papa would read from great works of literature as well as the Bible, quiet times in the evenings when all the world seemed at peace.

The world seemed deceptively peaceful now. Northumberland was very different from Surrey, but it was still the land where she'd been born. And where a part of her had died.

She sat on the rough, sheep-cropped grass near the crown of the fell. The sun was sinking to the west behind her, the last light striking off the tops of the trees in the small wooded vale below. Sheep were just visible as pale blurs against dark landscape, scattered on the surrounding fells.

Solitude was both familiar and foreign—familiar because she had long since become used to loneliness; foreign because she had almost forgotten what it was like to have a few moments of real peace.

Closing her eyes, she let the cool evening breeze caress her temples more gently than any man could have done. "Ah, Cassidy," she murmured. "If only I were stronger—"

"A trouble shared is a trouble lessened."

She started at the sound of the soft male voice and turned. Beside her sat a man . . . a man she hadn't seen or heard arrive, but who seemed very comfortably situated at her side. Instantly she assessed him, as she'd learned to do with countless clients.

To say he was oddly dressed would be an understatement of epic proportions. He wore a doublet of archaic cut, padded and quilted, shaped almost like a breastplate. The sleeves of his shirt were full and slashed to show a contrasting color underneath. His trousers were tucked into knee-length boots, and he wore leather gauntlets on his hands. Strangest of all was the peaked helmet that covered his long, iron gray hair.

"Forgive me, milady," the man said, executing a bow from his seated position. "I trust I've not disturbed ye, but 'tis not a night best spent alone."

She stiffened, instantly distrusting his meaning. But his face was serene in spite of the weathering and lines of age and sun, and she felt at once that she had no reason to be afraid.

Perhaps it was not an entirely foolish reaction. She'd met men nearly as odd in her career; such eccentrics were usually harmless. Greyburn was just down the hill; she was within shouting distance.

And she was sick to death of being afraid.

"Are you warning me of some danger, sir?" she asked, in the playful tone she often used with her clients.

"Ye'll be a stranger to the Marches, and not ken the customs of the country. 'Tis the moss-troopers I watch for, lady, and I'd not see ye harmed."

His words rolled off his tongue with the guttural Northumberland burr, curiously antiquated, and yet it was apparent to Isabelle that he was no common laborer or shepherd. His face seemed familiar under the silly helmet; she guessed him to be near fifty, firm-bodied under his clothes, relaxed and yet with a distinct air of readiness in his pose.

"Surely I need fear nothing," she said, "in the presence of so gallant a champion."

He looked at her and smiled. His smile was charming, open, devoid of deception . . . like Cassidy's, she thought. But his eyes were green, and his strong face was handsome and utterly masculine.

"Aye. And 'tisn't likely the Reivers will come so nigh Greyburn. Not when the laird's to hame."

"You mean the earl?" she asked.

"Aye." He studied her as she'd studied him. " 'Tis known all about the parish that he's browt two bonny ladies from London town." He dipped his head. "The talk of their beauty was no bairn's prattle, it seems."

She'd chosen to play along with his little game, but he spoke with such sincerity that she blushed. When had a man's compliments last touched her?

Who was he?

"My name is Isabelle Smith," she said. "I am staying at Greyburn with my young charge, Cassidy Holt, cousin to the earl of Greyburn."

"Holt?" He frowned under the narrow brim of his helmet. " 'Tis no Border surname."

"We are both from America," she said, wondering why she felt so eager to talk to a stranger. Perhaps it was because he treated her as what she was not . . . a person worthy of respect. And he was *human*, for all his oddity.

"The colonies?" he said. "A lang journey ye've had, then, lady."

His reference to the United States as "colonies" seemed all of a piece with his speech and appearance. If he was mad, it was a pleasant madness.

"Indeed," she said. "Do you live here, Mr. . . ."

"Matthias," he said.

Matthias. Isabelle's thoughts raced back to the carriage ride from Ulfington, to Quentin's talk of Greyburn and its legendary past. *"This house and these lands are filled with legends. . . . They say a ghost of one of those warriors still haunts the estate—"*

That ghost warrior was called Matthias. But this man was no spirit. He was flesh and blood.

"I tend the earl's sheep and keep watch 'gainst the Reivers," Matthias continued. "I've lived here all my life."

No ghost, then, but simply an eccentric playing the part of a legend for reasons unknown. And he was a shepherd, after all. As a girl she might have been on her dignity, knowing herself his social superior. Now such a pose was laughable.

"Do these Reivers come often, then?" she asked.

"Nae so often to these lands. They fear the wolves o' Greyburn."

The wolves of Greyburn. Did he know what the

Forsters were? Best to pretend ignorance. "I . . . don't understand."

He cocked his head. "Ye need not fear me, lady. I ken, as ye do, what manner of men the Forsters be."

"You know?"

"Aye. They're nae human, nor yet beasts, but sommat in between. And I ken you're nae one of them."

She felt an unaccustomed elation that he spoke so freely, and offered her the same freedom in return. "No," she said. "I'm not one of them."

He stretched long, booted legs out before him. " 'Tis a wonder, ye think, that wolves may raise sheep. But the wee beasties ken their masters."

The image of wolves herding sheep flashed through her mind, but she didn't laugh. "And the people here . . . do they know what the Forsters are?"

"Aye. No tenant or servant or farmer on this land ever forgets." Isabelle sensed a new tension in him. "The Forsters have held Greyburn for generations. Their secret is safe."

She could well believe it. She wasn't sure she could have told another soul what the Forsters truly were, even if she'd wanted to. And she'd never seen them Change.

But it was good to know she wasn't alone in sharing that knowledge, even with so curious a gentleman.

"How many beyond this valley guess that such beings live among us?" she asked. "Any man who spoke of it would be called mad."

"Aye," Matthias said. "But ye'll see for yerself why the • wolves o' Greyburn willna be betrayed. I hear there's an initiation this very night."

"An initiation?"

He looked at her keenly. "Mayhap ye'll have no part. The laird must see ye're to be trusted." His sweet smile returned. "Aye. I'd stake my life on it."

He rose and held out one gloved hand. She took it without hesitation. He lifted her easily, and she saw that he was not so ridiculous as she'd guessed in his antique garments. Especially not with the sword at his side.

He followed her glance and bowed deeply. "My sword is at your service, milady. If ever ye have need of me, call my name. I shall come."

There was no double entendre in his words, no hint of ridicule. He meant what he said. He was a stranger, and yet she had no doubt that he'd defend her to death against moss-troopers, Reivers or any other villain.

Perhaps even against the wolves of Greyburn.

"Thank you, sir," she said, dropping a curtsy. "I shan't forget your kindness."

"Nor I your beauty," he said. "We'll meet again."

She could feel him watching—standing guard—as she made her way down the hill. But when she reached the bottom and looked up, he'd gone as swiftly and silently as he'd come to her.

If she were one for childish fancies, she might have believed him a figment of her imagination, an illusory companion for her loneliness. But she could still feel the tingle in her hand where he'd held it in his.

And she remembered what he'd said of the Forster's secrets and tonight's "initiation." Matthias's words had been almost a warning. If this initiation had anything to do with Cassidy, she intended to learn exactly what it involved.

Meeting Matthias had reminded her that she wasn't such a coward after all. And she, it seemed, was just as mad as he was.

Grandfather's rooms were exactly as Braden had left them. Every piece of furniture, every suit of armor stood where it had the day he died, perfectly preserved by the constant attentions of servants who tended the suite like a shrine.

A shrine to the Cause.

Braden paused inside the door and listened, as he always did. Tiberius Forster was still here. He was dead, and yet his power lingered on. It was as if he'd never let go of the earldom, or leadership in the Cause.

But that was illusion. Death had loosened his grip, and his duties and responsibilities had passed on to the boy he'd groomed to replace him.

The boy. That was what Braden became, here. He had to prove himself all over again. And yet he could not stay away. Tiberius wouldn't let him.

"You will live for the Cause, as I have." If Braden had ever been in any danger of forgetting that lesson, he was reminded of it the moment he walked through these doors. He could have taken this suite, the largest in Greyburn, for his own. He hadn't even considered it.

As long as these rooms remained sacrosanct, the Cause would survive. Grandfather would see to it, even from the grave.

"Let nothing touch you, boy. Nothing and no one but the Cause. If you do, you will fail."

The voice was as real to Braden as the walls of Greyburn. It never entirely left him. Once he had allowed others to touch his heart, believing that sentiment could coexist with duty. Believing his own heirs could be born of love to carry on the Cause. He had learned three years ago that Grandfather was right.

But another voice intruded on his memories—soft and husky and fervent, as different from Grandfather's as day from night. Tiberius Forster's image was clear in his mind after all these years, but he had no picture of Cassidy Holt.

How was it possible, then, that she could trespass even here?

He'd told himself that all difficulties raised by Cassidy Holt would be solved at Greyburn, but he had been foolishly optimistic. When he'd heard her with the Roddam girl on the platform in Ulfington, he knew how easily she'd befriend anyone who offered her the slightest kindness. She was too open-hearted—still a child with no idea of what was appropriate, what her true nature required of her.

Grandfather would have taught her in a way she couldn't forget. But when Braden imagined her suffering under Tiberius Forster's harsh tutelage . . .

His mind refused the picture. Instead, it insisted upon conjuring up a face to go with that earnest young voice. Not a child's face, in spite of his assessment of her character, but one with a girl's artlessness and a woman's allure. And why did he envision a mature female's softly curved form hidden by a man's trousers and a hoyden's heedless conduct? Why did Cassidy's easy, ingenuous laugh seem to him more potent than a sophisticate's most practiced flirtation?

Why, when he was near to her, did he find it so difficult to remember the only reason she was here?

These rooms reminded him. It was all to the good if Cassidy was as he imagined. Quentin had called her lovely, and that would make it easier for him to assume his role as her mate. A strong, richly female body would serve Cassidy well in bearing children. Her open nature would make her a good mother for the next generation of Forsters—the generation that would inherit Greyburn when he and Quentin were gone.

All that remained was to tell her. He had tried to make her understand there in the Great Hall, but he'd failed. He had lost the ability to explain what he took for granted.

"You need me." He remembered how her words had shocked him—as if she saw a lack in him she thought she

could mend. Not merely his blindness, but something deeper.

As if she wanted him to need *her*.

When she had babes of her own, her unformed yearnings would be satisfied. The longer he kept her in ignorance, the more chance for misunderstanding. And yet he was reluctant to destroy even a part of her innocence, the very innocence that made her what she was.

So be it. He had become dangerously soft where Cassidy Holt was concerned; mercy was fatal to the Cause. Like the wolves in his grandfather's carving, he would surmount every barrier, defeat every enemy, conquer every weakness. . . .

Every weakness but one.

"You failed," Grandfather said. *"You failed in the one simple duty that the least of our kind could achieve. You have but one purpose left. Do not fail me again."*

Without so much as touching a carved wooden bedpost or the razor still neatly laid out beside the washstand, Braden backed out of the room. He walked to his own suite just down the corridor. At the rear of the dressing room he discarded his clothes and slipped through the hidden passageway.

Under the dim cover of twilight, Braden fled to the woods.

First he ran as human, feeling the cool wind on his bare skin, the lawn under his feet. He passed the scent of his sister, and then that of Isabelle Smith, dodging them both in his keen desire for solitude. At the woods' edge he Changed; he leaped, and when he landed again it was on four paws, four swift legs that carried him into the moist forest that cradled the burn.

This was home, as surely as the halls of Greyburn. This was the place he was most at peace, more truly himself than anywhere else in the world. He knew every inch of the wood, of the surrounding fells—every rock and tree and turn of the water's path. He remembered from his days of sight; he felt each subtle change from season to season through the pads of his feet, the thick fur that covered his body, the sensitive leather of his nose.

Greyburn's brief summer was upon them, a season of glorious life and music no human could hope to hear. Low-hanging leaves brushed his ears and muzzle, but he didn't mind his occasional encounters with new-fallen branches or other new obstacles in the landscape. Here he was undoubted master. He gloried in the bunching and flexing of muscles, the speed and grace his human form could never match.

After a time he paused at the bank of the burn to lap the cool water. A bird called, unafraid; some small animal rustled among the thickets. He found himself listening, head lifted, turning inevitably back toward the house. And *her*.

He burst into a run again, hardly aware of the direction he took. The woods settled into the hush of evening, and then grew quieter still.

He skidded to a stop, paws sliding on mossy earth. *Her* scent didn't overcome the odors of wood and water and growth and decay; it was a part of all the rest, blending and insinuating itself into the place he loved.

She was near, on the other side of the burn, and he thought that she might turn and run like any ordinary human faced with the unknown.

"Braden?"

Her feet were bare, jumping over stone and splashing in water. Cloth rustled about her legs, too loose for petticoats and stays.

"Braden?" she repeated. "I didn't know . . ." She stopped before him; her scent enfolded him as she knelt. "You're so beautiful," she whispered.

All his stern resolutions splintered in an instant, brittle twigs under his paws. He could not see her, but his wolf's senses made even those of his human form as negligible as a weak midwinter sun on the coldest day of the year. The very tips of each hair quivered, keenly aware of her nearness. He opened his mouth, and his tongue could all but taste her.

Like a poacher she'd invaded his woods, his brief peace, and slain him with gentle words more deadly than the shafts of arrows.

His lip rose from bared teeth. As a man he was armored by the Cause and years of discipline; now he was defenseless in his power, vulnerable in a form that had always meant freedom. More than speech had deserted him. He was irrational, driven, desperate with primitive hungers like to drive him mad, and it was her doing.

Go, he cried inwardly. *Go—*

But she was as deaf as he was blind. Her fingers skimmed the ruff of fur at his cheeks, drew back to his neck, plunged with hesitant wonder into the depths of his coat. She touched the wolf as she wouldn't dare touch him as a man, and yet with such innocence, unstained. . . .

And he couldn't bear it, couldn't bear the tender naïveté that made her so oblivious to every warning, to all awareness of what was fitting and what forbidden.

"Magnificent," she murmured. Her hand caressed the underside of his jaw, the space between his ears. "It's so much more than I ever dreamed." When he thought he could bear it no longer, she let him go. She rose to her feet, stepped back . . .

And began to run. With a deer's grace she sprang into motion. With a hunter's impulse, he followed. Along a narrow path beside the burn they ran, he at her heels. Then they were side by side, her feet striking earth in a steady beat, his making no sound. He could have outrun her easily, but he did not. He gave himself up to the glory once again, free of human thoughts and human fears. In the wood all was one, and they were equally children of a mother more ancient than time itself.

He was still running when he realized he was alone again.

He found himself atop the fell overlooking Greyburn, almost above the trees. A fresh wind carried Cassidy's scent from below; she was headed back toward the house. He could imagine her flushed and breathless as she reached the door, attempting to straighten her ragamuffin's dress, looking over her shoulder to see if he followed. . . .

Why she had left him he didn't know. He should be grateful. Perhaps prudence had returned to her when it abandoned him. There was nothing prudent in the elation he'd felt when they were alone together, or in the hollowness of his heart now that she was gone.

Yet all the while they ran, she hadn't Changed. Had she been too shy, too long among humans to shed her clothes in his presence without self-consciousness?

Tonight, at the ceremony, she must put aside such inhibitions. In the Great Hall, the Changing would be done for a specific purpose, rationally, with no risk of intimate contact. That, too, he should be grateful for.

The ceremony would be another essential part of Cassidy's education as a *loup-garou*. And tomorrow he would make the rest clear to her. Tomorrow the shield of duty would be firmly back in place.

When all barriers of human garments and human custom were cast aside, there was nothing left but resolve to battle the deepest instincts of the beast.

That was a battle Braden didn't dare lose again.

eight

Cassidy dashed up the stairs and into her room, closing the door behind her. She leaned against it, spreading her hands on the cool wood, until her heartbeat had slowed and she could breathe normally again.

The bathtub still waited before the fire, offering restful comfort. She stripped off the calico dress and stood naked in the center of the room, shivering even though her skin was flushed and hot.

All because of the wolf. A mighty, green-eyed gray wolf who had run by her side in the forest, whose fur had been so lush under her hands, whom she'd known the instant she saw him.

Braden.

She moved to the tub and tested the water. It had cooled, but she didn't need it to be any warmer. She sank down to her chest in the water, then lower, until her chin grazed the surface.

When she'd run to the woods, she'd expected to be alone. She hadn't counted on a wish coming true.

In the few days she'd known Braden, she'd only been able to imagine what he must be like in his other form.

She wouldn't have dared asked him to Change, as she'd asked Quentin. She had vague memories of her mother for comparison, but no recollections or imaginings could prepare her for the awesome reality.

Braden was so much more than a man, or a wolf. What he was couldn't be said in words, not even with the most exquisite poetry. Blake's Tyger couldn't begin to compare.

And *that* was what Braden expected her to be. That power, that grace, that marvelous perfection.

She looked at her own body under the water. It felt strange to her now, as if it belonged to someone else. As if she were seeing it for the first time through another person's eyes.

She touched her flat stomach, the ribs that showed a little under the skin, the curve of her hips, her breasts. Her legs were long, her waist small. Her body always did what she asked it to do.

But it didn't know how to Change.

She knew Braden wouldn't be any different when she saw him again; he'd be the same man, with the same face and the same manner. Nothing would have changed just because they'd run in the forest together, just because she'd seen him in his wolf shape and felt closer to him than ever before.

As marvelous as it had been to run by his side, to know for a few moments the rich comradeship of a shared joy and understanding—in spite of all that, something was missing. The feeling of closeness was as fleeting as a heat mirage in the desert.

Had Braden wondered why she didn't join him in the shape he wore with such assurance? Had he felt disappointment that she hadn't made that obvious crossing, jumped that last barrier?

With a cry of frustration, Cassidy ducked under the water. She stayed submerged until her lungs ached, and then came up, twisting her wet, heavy hair between her hands. She found the soap and used it mercilessly on every corner of her body, and then ducked again to rinse until she'd scrubbed herself bright as a new penny.

By the time she'd dried with the towels left on a rack by the tub, her mind was made up. As painfully embarrassing as it would be to admit the depths of her ignorance, she had to tell Braden that she must be taught how to Change. He would find out sooner or later, and then she'd seem deceitful as well as stupid.

She crouched before the fire, untangling her hair with the ivory-handled brush left for her on the dressing table. There was one good side to this; if Braden taught her, then she'd get to be with him even more. Maybe she could recapture the familiarity of their run in the woods. Maybe that was only the beginning, and when she finally learned to become a wolf . . .

Her vision snagged on the memory of a name she'd heard only once. Milena, Braden's wife.

Milena must have been *loup-garou*. She and Braden were two of a kind, able to run together as wolves with nothing to stand between them. What memories did Braden have of his wife? What was she like, and how had she died? Why did he never mention her?

More than mere curiosity urged Cassidy to find the answers. Rowena had started to talk about Milena. She was the one to ask.

Cassidy shrugged into her second-plainest dress, one she hoped wouldn't offend Rowena, and pulled her damp hair back with a piece of ribbon. Her sense of time told her that it was well past ten. The sky outside her window was too dark with clouds for stars to show, but lamps still burned in the corridor when she left her room to find Rowena's.

Rowena opened the door before she could knock. "I

thought you might come," she said. No one seeing her now would believe that she'd been weeping only an hour before. She looked Cassidy over without comment and stepped back. "Please."

The room was not unlike Cassidy's, but it was exquisitely feminine, an extension of Rowena's taste and delicacy. The object that most dominated the chamber was not the beautifully draped bed nor the highly polished dressing table with its tall framed mirror. Hanging on one wall was a life-sized portrait of a woman dressed in a striking, fur-trimmed gown. Her hair was a gold so pale as to be nearly white, and her tilted eyes were black. Fine, tapered hands rested in her lap just above the bottom edge of the painting, fingers glittering with rings. Her body was lushly curved. She was stunning, beyond any image of beauty Cassidy had seen in life.

"Milena," Rowena said. She moved to stand beside the portrait, pride and possession in her carriage. Compared to the woman in the painting, she was merely lovely, but she didn't seem to fear the comparison.

Cassidy simply stared. So this was Milena. The grace of her name didn't do her justice. Her face had a delicacy that hinted of mischief, and yet never lost its noble bearing. Cassidy knew she must have been a great lady—as great as Braden was a lord.

It was no surprise that Braden wanted to marry her.

"She came from Russia," Rowena said. "From a great family of landowners. She came to Greyburn as a stranger, but she made herself loved for the six years she was with us. She was the perfect lady."

Such a compliment from Rowena couldn't be easily earned. "You were good friends," Cassidy guessed.

"We were like sisters." Rowena looked up at the sweetly smiling face and raised a hand as if to touch the frozen fingers. "She made life at Greyburn . . . tolerable.

Her warmth, her charm, her grace—no one who saw her could fail to love her, except—" She bit her lower lip. "We hid nothing from each other."

Cassidy's mind painted a picture of two blond heads bent together, speaking in cultured voices of ladylike things. It was impossible to imagine herself in that scene. No wonder Rowena was cold to Cassidy, if Milena was her ideal.

And she'd been Braden's wife. She had been greatly loved. The picture in Cassidy's mind shifted to something quite different—salt-and-pepper hair contrasting with that pale gold like silver-gray water and leaves in autumn. Strong face and delicate one, side by side.

"How . . . did she and Braden meet?" Cassidy asked slowly.

"They met when they were very young. Her parents and my grandfather agreed that they should marry—"

"For the Cause?"

Rowena's eyes grew hooded. "Yes. But Braden was fortunate beyond all his deserts. We were all fortunate."

As much as Rowena hated arranged marriages, she didn't seem to despise this one. "Milena was *loup-garou*."

The statement had a visible effect on Rowena. She moved to the chair by the window and sat down, turned slightly away from Cassidy and the portrait. "Yes. But she understood how I felt. She was too kind and good to defy Braden, but she agreed with me. She would have put the beast behind her, except for Braden."

"Then she . . . loved him."

"She was devoted to him. She did everything possible to please him."

Cassidy gazed at the portrait, feeling a peculiar constriction in her heart. Milena sounded perfect. How could an ordinary person live up to that?

"And Braden loved her," she said.

"How could he not? She was an angel. And when he lost her . . ." Rowena looked up at Cassidy. "He hasn't spoken of her since."

So that was why Cassidy had never heard the name. Braden had been heartbroken when Milena died. Was that the reason he made himself so distant and hard—because he'd lost the love of his life?

"How did she die?"

But Rowena wasn't listening. She was staring toward the door, anguish and loathing visible in her expression before she smoothed it out to formal courtesy.

"It is late, Cassidy," she said. "You had best return to your room."

Cassidy backed toward the door, unable to stop looking at Milena. An angel. The perfect lady, yet part of the Cause. So dearly loved. Everything Cassidy wasn't.

Even closing the door on the portrait couldn't erase Milena's image from Cassidy's thoughts. She was nearly back to her room before she realized that her own door was open and a pair of burly footmen were carrying out her emptied tub.

Only one other thing had changed during her absence. On the bed lay a garment that drew Cassidy like a bee to a blossom—a robe of rich patterned fabric in red and silver, with a matching sash. It was completely unlike any of Cassidy's new gowns, more like the striking and unusual dress Milena wore in the portrait than anything else Cassidy had seen at Greyburn.

She ran her fingers over the sumptuous cloth. Impulsively, she pulled off her dress and the hastily donned undergarments and stockings and shoes. The robe settled over her like the mantle of a queen. She tied the sash and stepped in front of the mirror.

Almost, almost she could imagine herself as glorious and exotic as Milena. . . .

She heard footsteps just before the knock on the door.

"Pardon me, miss," her maid said, averting her eyes, "but I'm to tell you that you'll be wanted in the Great Hall within the hour."

In an hour it would be midnight. "What's happening in the Great Hall?"

"The ceremony, miss."

"What ceremony?"

The woman's face pinched up. "It's not my place to speak, miss." She looked so frightened that Cassidy decided not to press. "There will be no formal dinner, miss, but I can bring up anything you wish."

Cassidy sighed. She had to learn the way things were done at Greyburn, however unusual they might seem at first. "What should I wear?"

Blank-faced, the maid fetched the hairbrush from Cassidy's dressing table. "If you'd care to sit down, miss, I'll brush out your hair."

Cassidy obeyed. The maid's tension seemed to flow through the brush and into Cassidy's body, and she all but jumped when another maid brought in a tray of tea and biscuits.

She expected the maid to lay out some suitable evening dress, help her into the awful corset and button her up like a doll one more time. But the woman didn't even pin Cassidy's hair, but let it hang loose, still damp, down her back.

Then Cassidy was granted a short period of solitude, during which she crumbled the biscuits to a fine powder on the silver tray. After half an hour the maid returned and curtsied in the doorway.

"Please come with me, miss," she said.

"In this?" Cassidy said, wriggling her bare toes under the hem of the robe.

"Yes, miss."

The hairs on the back of Cassidy's neck prickled as she followed the maid into the corridor. She was very glad when they encountered Isabelle halfway to the stairs. Isabelle looked at Cassidy's clothing, or lack of it, in some surprise.

"I was just coming to see you," she said. "Has there been some difficulty with your gowns?"

"No," Cassidy said. "The maid told me to wear this." She thought of all the things she wanted to discuss with her friend and recognized that it was not the time or the place. "Something strange is happening, Isabelle."

Without a word the maid slipped away, leaving them alone. Isabelle frowned. "I'd noticed that the servants are behaving oddly," she said. "Did the maid say anything about an initiation?"

"She did talk about a ceremony. Do you know what's going on?"

"Not yet, but I should very much like to learn."

If Rowena knew, she hadn't so much as mentioned it. "I know who could tell us," Cassidy said. "If we can find Quentin . . ."

They found Quentin leaning on the balustrade at the top of the stairs, looking down into the entrance hall. Instead of his usual dapper coat, waistcoat and trousers, he wore a robe identical to Cassidy's, in the same shades of red and silver.

He straightened as they approached, and bowed. "Ah, Mrs. Smith, Cassidy. Delightful to see you again." He gave Isabelle a wry smile. "You seem a trifle confused by our peculiar apparel, Mrs. Smith. I gather you weren't invited to our quaint little ritual?"

"The maid mentioned a ceremony," Cassidy said, "but we don't know what it is."

Quentin *tsk*ed softly. "My brother seems to have some difficulty in keeping you informed, Cousin. Tonight is really for your benefit, though there are the two new servants. Wouldn't want them running about loose and unaccounted for, would we?"

"Can't you see that you're only confusing her more, Quentin?"

Rowena came out of the shadows to join them, dressed in yet another red and silver robe. Her golden hair, like Cassidy's, spilled long and loose at her back. Her face was very pale, and she wouldn't meet Cassidy's eyes. "Let her learn for herself what we truly are." She turned to Isabelle, her tone changing to frigid politeness. "Mrs. Smith, I apologize for the inconvenience. If you would be so kind as to wait in your room, I shall have refreshments sent up to you as soon as possible."

Isabelle didn't move. "I am here at Greyburn as Cassidy's friend. If something is wrong—"

"All is exactly as it should be."

Cassidy spun around. Quentin, Rowena, and Isabelle turned toward the deep, commanding voice.

Braden stopped a few steps from the top of the stairs, Aynsley just behind him. He was barefooted like Cassidy and the twins, dressed just as they were, but he seemed more imposing than ever. His heavy robe swept the stairs, splendid and barbaric, giving him the look of an ancient king.

"This is none of your concern, Mrs. Smith," he said. "You will kindly remain in your room. Aynsley, escort Mrs. Smith and then return to the Great Hall."

Isabelle might have argued with Rowena, but the earl of Greyburn was not to be disobeyed. She cast a troubled glance at Cassidy.

"Don't worry," Cassidy whispered. "I'll tell you all about it later."

Even Aynsley's usual dignity seemed shrunken as he bowed stiffly to Mrs. Smith and gestured her toward the guest wing. Braden waited until they were out of sight before he started down the stairs. Quentin went next, followed by Rowena, leaving Cassidy to bring up the rear.

The house was eerily silent. Absent was the usual coming and going of servants, the constant sense of activity just around the corner; instead, the entrance hall was empty, and the feeble lamps left much of the room in shadow.

Braden led them to the massive carved doors of the Great Hall. He drew them open, and Cassidy saw what had become of the human inhabitants of Greyburn.

They were lined up in even rows at one end of the Hall, men and women in their sober suits and uniforms, standing at attention like soldiers on parade. There were far more servants than Cassidy would have guessed, people she'd never so much as glimpsed, ranging in age from little more than children to white-haired elders. Not one of them made a sound.

Just across the room was placed a large hinged screen. Braden's valet, Telford, stood beside it, his narrow face as blank as all the others'. On every side, the walls were hung with torches, making the banners and shields and swords push out in sharp relief. The carvings of wolves and men seemed to leap and battle in the flickering light.

Braden walked slowly into the Hall and came to stand beside Telford. Quentin and Rowena drew up behind him. Aynsley slipped into the Hall and went to join the first row of servants, his movements jerky as a puppet's.

"We are gathered here," Braden said, his voice a booming echo, "to renew the bonds and pledges that have protected Greyburn since the first of my people came to this land. Tonight, we accept the vows of two who would serve this house, and promise their safekeeping as long as they live among us." He nodded to Telford, who gestured toward the foremost line of servants.

Two people stepped out of the line—a scared-looking young man and a girl Cassidy recognized as her maid in the London house. Braden went to meet them. The young man's legs nearly buckled. The maid's eyes were very wide. She glanced from side to side, as if seeking help—or escape.

"Stay where you are," Quentin said when Cassidy started forward. "You can't interfere now. Observe me and Rowena, and do exactly as we do."

Braden's voice rose over her whispered protest. "John Tobias Dodd and Kitty Wanless," he said to the two new servants, "you have chosen to serve Greyburn. You have been told the purpose of this initiation, and what is required of you both. This is your last chance to withdraw."

The young man's mouth opened and the maid closed her eyes, but neither of them spoke. Braden nodded. "Very well. You have made your choice. What you witness tonight you will never reveal to any outside these walls."

He stepped back, untied the sash at his waist, and let the robe fall to the floor. Cassidy gasped.

Clad only in torchlight, Braden faced the servants. He left them look their fill, and then he flung back his head.

And *Changed*.

It was like watching a cloud shift from one fluid shape to another through a grimy plate of glass. Dark mist wreathed Braden's nakedness, blurring the angles and edges of his body until all form was gone. The mist roiled, gathered, solidified once again into a figure undeniably inhuman.

The little maid gasped but held her place. The young man showed no reaction at all. Braden-the-wolf stared at each of them, as long and intently as if he could see into their eyes, and then stalked forward. The maid held out one trembling hand. Braden opened his jaws and closed his teeth on the fragile fingers—gently, so gently, but even Cassidy realized what the gesture meant. Braden could crush the hand, and the girl, without any effort at all. He demonstrated his power—and the consequences of disloyalty.

He released the maid's hand, unmarked, and turned to the young man. Swallowing hard, the man offered his hand. Braden repeated the ritual of dominance, and then let him go. One of the other servants had to catch the young man as he swayed and nearly fell.

Braden ignored him. He turned to his brother and sister. Quentin squeezed Cassidy's arm and stepped behind the screen.

And Cassidy understood, with sudden clarity, what was about to happen.

The door to the Great Hall was open only a crack, but that small space was just enough. Isabelle rested her cheek on the doorjamb and spied on the ceremony she'd been forbidden to attend.

She was not shocked when the earl of Greyburn turned into a wolf, though she'd almost forgotten the wonder and terror of that transformation. Edith had been her friend; Braden Forster was dangerously unpredictable, but both were of the same kind. Like Cassidy, who seemed as lost in that great ceremonial hall as she did in her gaudy robe.

But Isabelle watched with growing dread as the great gray wolf seized the hands of the two servants, one by one, in his jaws. Even when Braden released them, unharmed, Isabelle felt a sickness in the pit of her stomach that had nothing to do with ordinary fear.

This was what Matthias the shepherd meant when he'd

warned her of the initiation. And Cassidy, so naïve in the ways of her mother's people, so innocent of all arrogance and the lust to rule, was forced to participate.

"I ken it troubles ye, milady," a soft voice said at her elbow, "but there's no helpin' it. 'Tis what they are."

"Matthias!" she said, pressing to the wall. "What are you doing here?"

He was dressed as he'd been earlier that evening, ready for action, the sword at his side. For a man who was trespassing, as she was, he looked fairly unconcerned, though his stance was watchful.

"I told ye little enough on the fell, milady," he said. "I came to learn how ye fared this eve, but I see I was right. Ye were spared."

She shivered. Spared what—that bizarre ritual in the Great Hall? And if she had been subjected to it, would Matthias have come to her rescue? The very idea was absurd. She turned back to the door.

"Cassidy—Miss Holt—is in there," she said.

"Aye. Ye said she's a Forster."

Yes, God help her. But she was also Edith's daughter. "You told me that no one who knows the Greyburn secret would reveal it," she said. "Is this how they guarantee loyalty? Through terror, and threats of—" She couldn't complete the thought, imagining those brutal jaws at someone's throat.

"No threat," Matthias said, moving nearer. " 'Tis but a symbol. There is more—"

"Wait. Something's happening." She was aware of Matthias close against her at the door and felt unaccountably comforted.

The comfort was short-lived. As she watched, Braden glanced toward the waiting Forsters, and Quentin stepped behind the decorative screen in the center of the Hall. The earl's valet moved up to take Quentin's robe as he tossed it out. A moment later another wolf emerged: a beast with russet fur the color of Quentin's hair. He joined his elder brother and repeated the hand-grasping ritual with the two servants, much more quickly than Braden had done.

" 'Tis not simple fear," Matthias said into Isabelle's ear. " 'Tis the laird's will. He can speak to their minds and compel obedience. In return, they lack for nought while they live."

That nauseating sickness filled her stomach again, and she almost doubled over. Matthias caught her arm.

"He'll not use it on ye," he said. "That I vow."

With an effort she straightened. "The tenants, the laborers—does this happen to them as well?"

"Some they trust without such sureties."

"Like you?"

He smiled. "Aye. They trust me well enough." He gestured toward the door. "Take heed."

She did as he asked, just in time to observe Lady Rowena, moving like one in a dream, disappear behind the screen. Many minutes passed before she come out. When she did, it was as a beautiful wolf of pale golden color, smaller than the other two. She slunk along the ground, her ears flat, her tail low. No human voice could have announced reluctance, and unhappiness, more clearly.

She barely touched the hands of the servants, who by now seemed well beyond fright. When she was finished, all three wolves turned, as one, to Cassidy.

Isabelle knew what they expected. Cassidy's robe had a specific purpose, like theirs. Such a garment was easily discarded for the Changing. Even from across the room, Isabelle could see the girl's panic.

Cassidy had never been taught how to Change. She'd

lost her mother too young and grown up among ordinary humans. There was nothing Isabelle could do to help her.

"They gave her no warning," Isabelle said. "She can't do it."

"She canna' Change?" Matthias said. He shook his head, a look of pity crossing his face. "Poor, wee bairn."

Braden had moved away from the servants and his siblings, approaching Cassidy with an impatient, purposeful step. He made a low sound in his throat, an ominous rumble.

Cassidy clutched the robe against her chest and spun on her bare feet. One of the servants gave a muffled exclamation as she ran headlong for the door. Isabelle had just enough time to get out of the way before Cassidy plunged through, sweeping past them.

"Let her go," Matthias said when Isabelle would have followed. He drew Isabelle from the half-open door. "Best not be seen here now, milady. Becrike, there'll be fratchin' tonight, but ye canna meddle. Not with their kind."

She pulled her arm free. "If Cassidy is in trouble because she couldn't Change—"

"They'll nae hurt her," he said in a strained, flat voice. "Bide a little, my lady. I'll not abandon the bairn, nae mair than ye will."

Once again she was struck by his sincerity, though this was only the second time she'd met him. Human he might be, but he understood these Forsters and their ways. And he was allowed to come and go unhindered.

"Thank you," she said. She offered her hand. "We need friends here. Both of us."

He covered her hand with his. "We must go." Moving with swift grace in his heavy clothing, he led her to the front door and out into the night. At the side of the house he paused, lifted her hand to his lips, and kissed it with rough tenderness.

"Bide in patience, milady. You're nae alone."

He began to slip away, and she caught the edge of his doublet. "Why?" she asked. "Why are you so willing to help us?"

His eyes were warm on hers. "D'ye nae feel the connection between us, milady? We're bound together, somehow. I kent it the moment I saw ye. 'Tis a fate I'm nae willin' to escape."

And he left her with skin that throbbed where he had touched and a heart beating far too swiftly.

How as it possible that a man, and a stranger, should affect her so deeply? Cassidy was the only other person to reach her heart in many, many years. But it was undeniable that Matthias had done so, against all odds and her firm intentions.

He seemed genuinely concerned about her—and about Cassidy.

He spoke of a connection, of binding, of fate. Romantic words indeed. But what if he knew Isabelle was no "lady" at all? Would he still smile that sweet smile and promise his protection like a gallant knight content to serve with chaste respect? Or would he turn on her as a creature hopelessly soiled—or worse, look at her with eyes that saw only an object to be used?

No. There was no reason he should find out. They both played a masquerade—he out of an amiable madness, she out of necessity. Whatever Matthias's motives, they were pure. He was unlike any man she'd known. She could not afford to lose any allies, not when Cassidy was at risk.

Bide in patience, Matthias said. She would take his advice, and be ready when Cassidy needed her.

And if the time came when she must defy the earl of Greyburn for Cassidy's sake, she dared to believe that she wouldn't be alone.

.   .   .

Braden ended the initiation ceremony as he always did. He Changed back and made the final pronouncements as if nothing untoward had happened, dismissed the servants to their beds, and allowed Rowena and Quentin to return to their rooms. Not one of them, werewolf or human, dared show surprise or consternation at the dramatic turn of events.

He didn't allow himself to feel the chill of foreboding until he had dressed and retreated to the sanctuary of his library. Even then he refused to follow that chill to its source, to the unthinkable possibility wailing like a bitter wind in the back of his mind.

No other sound disturbed his solitude. But Braden found himself listening for soft footsteps, the approach of the one person at Greyburn whom he most wished, and dreaded, to meet again.

The footsteps came sooner than he anticipated, well before he was compelled to seek her out. He invited her to enter.

Cassidy hesitated in the doorway. "I'm sorry," she said.

He rose from his chair, unable to maintain his customary calm. "You ran from the ceremony," he said harshly. "Why?"

She closed the door and came farther into the room. She was, he noted, wearing one of her London gowns, armored in formality against him. Such formality offered them both a kind of protection. But she must understand, as well as he did, that there was no protection against the truth.

"I should have told you earlier," she said, almost in a whisper, "but I didn't realize that you expected—that I was supposed to know—" She faltered. "When we ran together in the forest, I wanted so badly to Change, to be a wolf like you. And when I realized you wanted me to Change during the ceremony, I . . ."

Braden came to a stop in the center of the room, every

muscle locked in place. "You can't—" he began, and his mouth refused to form the word.

The room was deathly quiet.

"My mother died before she could teach me," she said. "I . . . don't know how to Change."

Braden swayed on his feet, battered by a wave of shock. If he were human, it would have been as if she had told him she didn't know how to walk, or eat, or keep her heart beating.

Or that she had never been born.

The storm of emotion caught him unprepared. He retreated across the room, clutching at a glass-paned bookcase.

"You have . . . never Changed," he said.

"No." Her breath shuddered out. "I'm sorry. I thought . . ."

Profound emptiness followed shock, leaving him as cold as the glass under his hands. "I believed that you were one of us in every way," he said, summoning words out of the void. "You showed the signs, had all the other abilities. Your mother—"

"My mother told me I would do it someday. I thought that if I found my family, they could teach—"

"The Change cannot be taught," he said. His hands knotted into fists on the bookcase. "It is what we *are*."

From the very first, he had made a critical error. He had assumed that Cassidy was one of them in every way. Others, half-human or worse, had inherited the Change, and she was the last of the American Forsters. His devotion to the Cause had blinded him.

Unacceptable mistake. Unforgivable weakness.

"I *can* learn," Cassidy said, her voice steadfast with determination. "I've always known that I was like my mother—"

"Your father was *human*."

"And you despise humans. You . . . despise me."

A child who couldn't even Change should not have had such power to move him. Her words should not strike him like a blow beneath the ribs, driving the air from his lungs. He should be safe from the compassion that tore at his heart and awakened something very like shame.

He remembered the sense of completion he'd felt when they'd run together in the woods, something he hadn't felt since boyhood. He acknowledged his constant awareness of her unique scent of sagebrush and desert earth. And how, when he'd thought of her as Quentin's mate, his mind had refused to supply the inevitable details.

He lifted his fist from the bookcase and slammed it down again with all his strength. The glass pane shattered. Cassidy cried out. Shards drove into his flesh like needles.

"Despise you?" he whispered, and laughed, flexing his hand. Blood ran the length of his fingers.

"You've hurt yourself!" Cassidy was beside him, gently lifting his injured hand by the wrist. "I'll have to pull out the slivers, and it must be bandaged."

Her touch, so careful and sure, filled him with a strange lassitude. Her husky voice held concern, consternation, worry—for him, in spite of everything.

"*Caramba!*" she cried. "My dress is too stiff. I can't tear it. I'll call Aynsley—"

"No." Ignoring her protests, he shrugged awkwardly out of his coat and let it drop to the floor. He began to un-button his waistcoat one-handed, but Cassidy's fingers worked under his and usurped the task.

All at once the pain was gone, and he felt only her deft, callused fingers undoing the buttons of his shirt one by one. Her breath scalded his bare chest as she tugged the shirttails free of his trousers. Her hands unknowingly brushed his stomach, sending a jolt of electric sensation through his body. She was too close—working the shirt over his shoulders, sliding it down his arms, her breasts under the bodice-armor of her gown pressed to his side. . . .

She paused when his shirt was halfway off, binding his arms and leaving him unable to move. Her breathing had grown more rapid, shallow, drawing in air as if to taste it. Her hands fell.

Inescapable awareness flowed between them. Braden could feel her confusion. Except for their first meeting, when she'd so impulsively embraced him and kissed his cheek, she hadn't touched more than his hand. Except from a distance in the Great Hall, she'd never seen him less than fully dressed.

She was a girl of no experience, barely grown into her woman's body. A half-human child.

Half-human and unable to Change. And if she couldn't Change, she was no fit mate for Quentin and his pure blood. No longer suited to be the mother of Quentin's children. Useless to the Cause.

Free.

Braden struggled out of his shirt, and Cassidy took it without quite touching him. Fabric hissed as she tore the shirt into strips.

"It's not too bad," Cassidy said. She led him to a chair, awkwardness forgotten, and pushed him down. "I know a little about this from my work on the range." She fell silent and began to pull out the slivers one by one. "There are a few tiny ones I can't get out," she said. "They'll sting if we don't—"

"It's nothing," he said.

He felt her gazing at him. "All right." She wrapped his hand with the strips of cloth, deft and efficient in her movements. "There. It's not even bleeding much anymore. You said that *loups-garous* heal quickly. Whenever I was hurt, I always—" She broke off sharply.

He clenched his hand, willing it to hurt again, but

already his resilient werewolf body was repairing itself. There was so much it could repair. But not everything.

"I'm sorry," Cassidy said. "I didn't mean to fool you. I wanted . . . so much to be like you."

The smell of tears—tears he knew she must be fighting with her own undeveloped, stubborn brand of pride— made his throat tighten. He lifted his uninjured hand. His fingers skimmed her lashes and came away wet.

"I *can* learn," she said in a broken whisper. "I know I can."

"You don't understand," he said, despising himself. "The Change . . . is in the blood. When we—when our kind reach maturity, it boils in our veins and nerves and muscles, impossible to ignore, demanding release. If you've never felt the call—"

"But I *have* felt it. I can feel it now."

"Do you?" He grasped her hand with his good one and flattened his palm to hers. Her pulse pounded under his skin, and her body tensed as if she listened to faraway music. He could almost hear it himself, springing from within her, pouring from her flesh into his. Soul-music, life-music, a symphony pure and rich as the roar of ocean surf or the ancient beat of the forest's heart.

Cassidy's music had the power to make him believe that all she said was true. There was more to her than the blood she carried in her veins. When he touched her he began to believe that he, too, might have some worth beyond leadership of the Cause.

But emotion had brought him only ruin, even before he had learned the full extent of his defects. They were forever linked in his mind: passion with treachery, hope with disgrace, love with annihilation.

He pulled back, folding his injured hand against his chest. A knock rang on the library door, and it swung open.

"I beg your pardon," Quentin said. "Am I interrupting? I thought I heard something break. Not serious, I hope?"

Braden rose and made his way across the room until his foot connected with his discarded coat. He scooped it up and draped it over his shoulders. "A small accident," he said. "Nothing that need concern you."

"Of course not." Quentin strolled into the library. "I daresay the furniture has had the worst of the battle. Aynsley will be in quite a bother when he sees the carpet."

The very absurdity of Quentin's chatter worked as a restorative to Braden's shaken self-control. He was himself again.

"Sit down, Quentin," he said. "And you, Cassidy." He faced his brother. "I shall be brief. Cassidy had just informed me that she has never Changed."

"Indeed?"

Braden was in no mood for Quentin's games of airy indifference. "In spite of all precedents to the contrary, it is possible that she may be able to learn. And you shall be the one to teach her."

Quentin's chair creaked as he sat up. "I? But—"

"It's time you assumed your responsibilities, Quentin. I expect you to work with Cassidy until you have exhausted every possibility. The first delegates to the Convocation arrive within the week. She must learn to Change before that week is out."

For once Quentin was genuinely ruffled. He stood up, paced half the length of the room, and strode back again. "Why can't you teach her?"

"I have my reasons."

Quentin laughed. "I wonder if you know what they really are."

"I warn you, Quentin. Don't question me."

"For God's sake, Braden—"

"You know what this means to all of us."

"To *your* Cause—"

"Enough." Braden turned to Cassidy. "If you are one of us, you'll find what you need within yourself. You must."

Just a few hours ago he'd intended to explain her future role in the Cause in such a way that there would be no chance for misunderstanding. Now any explanations were pointless. Unless she could learn to Change.

But with Quentin as her teacher, it would be only natural that she should develop the proper bond with him, gain more . . . intimate knowledge that would ease the transition if—*when*—she proved that she had inherited her mother's ability.

Cassidy's skirts whooshed with the determination of her stride as she came to stand before Braden. "I will," she said. "I will find the way."

Braden turned his face aside. "You'll begin tomorrow. Return to your room and rest."

"I won't disappoint you," Cassidy said. "No matter what—"

"Come along, Cousin," Quentin said. "As Braden said, you do require at least a little sleep. Tomorrow morning I shall show you the stables. I think I've the perfect mount for you. You do ride? How foolish of me—of course you do. . . ." His voice, and their footsteps, faded as Quentin closed the door behind them.

Braden was alone for no more than a minute before Aynsley put in an appearance. The butler's silence telegraphed his dismay at the state of the carpet, the furniture, and his master.

"I'm all right," Braden said. "The maids can deal with this in the morning. Find Telford . . ."

"I am here, my lord." The valet could not possibly miss the state of Braden's hand, but he made no comment.

"Read to me, Telford."

"What do you wish to hear, my lord?"

"Whatever you choose." Braden sat down in his favorite chair and shut his eyes. Telford walked to the bookcase, paused, took another few steps, and opened a door. One book slid free from among the others.

Telford moved to the chair opposite Braden's and began to speak.

> *"A thing of beauty is a joy for ever:*
> *Its loveliness increases; it will never*
> *Pass into nothingness; but still will keep*
> *A bower quiet for us, and a sleep*
> *Full of sweet dreams, and health, and quiet*
> *   breathing."*

Braden stiffened and forced himself to relax again. The valet finished the poem:

> *". . . yes, in spite of all,*
> *Some shape of beauty moves away the pall*
> *From our dark spirits."*

"Keats," Braden said. "Do you believe he was right, Telford?"

"I do, my lord."

"And do you still find Miss Holt so unhandsome?"

The valet cleared his throat. "Her unique qualities appear to improve upon acquaintance, my lord.

> *"Her eyes as stars of twilight fair;*
> *Like twilight's, too, her dusky hair."*

"Surely too great a praise for such a ragamuffin," Braden said softly.

"If you'll forgive me, my lord," Telford said, "I must admit that Miss Holt is far more beautiful than I had at first surmised."

nine

Cassidy would have walked across the *Jornada del Muerto* without food or water if Braden asked, or slept on a bed of needle-spined cacti, or swum the Atlantic Ocean.

But no such simple trial was demanded of her. She had to learn how to Change within the week. And the only journey she made was on horseback, across the Greyburn lands, Quentin at her side. Quentin was to be her teacher, and she tried very hard not to wish Braden had chosen that task for himself.

The late morning was bright and sunny, with white clouds scudding across the sky and a scent of hay in the warm air. A skylark sang on the nearby moor, and rabbits darted along the path.

Quentin had obtained a pretty bay mare, Cleopatra, for her, and rode his own handsome gelding. He'd responded to her dismay at the sidesaddle by ordering the groom to replace it with a man's; it was still unlike the saddles Cassidy was accustomed to, but she could ride any horse bareback, if need be. And she was glad Quentin had suggested she wear her "fetching calico dress" rather than the tight riding habit Rowena had helped her buy in London.

Quentin was relaxed, looking for all the world as if they were out for a pleasure ride. A pack slung behind his saddle held food and a blanket—and, he'd promised with a wink, a deck of cards. Everything needed to make the day perfect.

And it would have been, under any other circumstances. Cassidy was eager to explore the countryside, to make this new land her home. She could come to love the windswept openness of rolling hills and wooded streams, moist earth and green pastures. Like the desert, this place was bursting with life, overflowing with mysteries just waiting to be revealed.

But she couldn't put her worries aside so easily. From the moment last night's ceremony had begun, the evening had been a disaster. She'd seen it coming when Quentin and Rowena Changed behind the screen. And then they'd all stared at her, waiting, and she'd felt more naked than Braden before he became a wolf.

She had tried. With all her will she tried to make herself Change like the others. If wanting were enough, she'd have done it in an instant.

She'd failed. Even Isabelle saw, and the strangely dressed man with her. Cassidy had wanted to hide in her room and pretend it had never happened. She'd wanted to return to the woods and run until she wasn't able to think about Braden's disappointment and her own disgrace.

But she couldn't run away. Not from herself, or from Braden.

So she'd gone to him, and it was much worse than she'd guessed.

Once, in New Mexico, she'd been with a *vaquero* when he was told his little girl had died of fever. The *vaquero* stood very still, as if he didn't believe, and then he'd dropped to his knees in the dirt and raged—at the world, at God, at everyone and everything within reach. Life itself had betrayed him.

Braden didn't rage or weep, but she knew he felt betrayed to the very depths of his soul.

She had failed him. Without understanding how or why, she'd failed him completely.

"Your father was human," he'd said, the words condemning her. Binding his wounds couldn't make up for her failures. But being so near to him had an unexpected effect. He seemed almost vulnerable, yet it didn't diminish his strength or his beauty. As a wolf, he'd fascinated her. When she helped him remove his shirt, she'd seen more of the man he was: the elegant contour of muscle under skin, the slope of his shoulder, the dusting of hair on his chest, the flex of tendon in his forearm, the hard flatness of his stomach. The ache of sorrow in her belly turned into feelings very different and only half-familiar, moving lower in her body.

She remembered the times at the ranch when she was driven by something alien and powerful inside herself—something the Holts didn't share. Touching Braden's hand was enough to make that energy sing in her veins. She must be close to grasping what was just out of reach, the one ability that made all the difference between being *loup-garou* and human, between being accepted or found forever wanting. . . .

"A penny for your thoughts," Quentin said. He glanced at her quizzically. "Scratch that. I think I shall offer at least a quid. I have a feeling it'll be worth it."

Cassidy sat up in the saddle and truly looked around for the first time since they'd left the Greyburn stables.

"Fine weather," Quentin continued, as if he'd set himself to cheering her up. "Northumberland is ordinarily a damp and boggy country. You seem to have brought the sun from your desert, for which I am eternally grateful."

She couldn't help smiling. Quentin's nonchalance was infectious. "Where are we going?"

"Just a nice little private place I know of," he said, prompting his mount into a canter.

Cassidy concentrated on the ride as they climbed gentle hills, jumped low stone fences and silvery burns. Quentin led her past clusters of cottages, too small to be called villages, and lonely farmhouses. Sheep scattered out of their way, and the occasional shepherd or laborer looked up from his work to watch them pass.

"How much of this belongs to Greyburn?" she asked after they'd ridden a mile or so.

"We don't own as many acres as some, but we've been here longer than most human gentry. I hear America is so vast that all of Greyburn would make a tiny fraction of one of your great ranches. Still, Braden takes his guardianship seriously. He's tended the woods, improved the soil, kept poachers out. And for all his faults, he takes good care of his tenants and laborers."

"Then the people around here—the ordinary people—aren't afraid of him?"

Quentin was silent for several moments. "You're thinking of the ceremony."

But she didn't want to think of that—not of her own embarrassment, or the disquiet she'd felt when the Forsters displayed their power to the servants.

"Greyburn is one of the main employers in this part of Northumberland," Quentin said. "People are happy to get work, and the servants always have a choice. They, and Greyburn's tenants, know that Braden will care for them as long as they remain loyal . . . and discreet." His irrepressible smile returned. "After so many years, the parish folk have heard the legends and seen things they can't explain. But they know better than to gossip." He looked keenly at Cassidy. "Braden can be quite generous when he's of a mind, though he'd never let you know it. He's a trifle obsessed, but I suppose one might be, given the burdens he has chosen to carry."

"The Cause," Cassidy stated.

"Quite. He has taken personal responsibility for saving the world's werewolves. It's a miracle he's not entirely mad."

"But you must help him. You're his brother—"

"Precisely. And since Braden has lost any talent whatsoever for enjoying himself, I've made it my life's work to compensate for his deficiency. One of the Forsters must. And Ro, despite being my twin, takes after Braden."

The mention of Rowena brought back other unsettling memories. "He expects Rowena to marry someone she doesn't love," Cassidy said.

"Ah. She told you, did she? I wondered how long it would take for her ice to crack. You have a certain way of finding chinks in armor, Cassidy Holt."

"She didn't tell me much."

"It would be a rather embarrassing topic for my prim and proper sister. It's all exceedingly medieval. Braden has plans for us—you most of all."

Anticipation and excitement shivered through her. "Tell me," she said, reining her mare to a halt. "I know I have to learn to Change. But what does he want me to do? How can I help him?"

Quentin wouldn't meet her eyes. "First you must become one of us," he said, "in every way." He sounded almost like Braden then, until he smiled and swept her a bow. "Not that I don't find you immensely appealing just as you are, my dear cousin. I don't believe you can be improved. I'm certain that you and I can find a way to make these lessons pleasant for both of us." He yawned behind his hand. "Though I'd far rather play another hand of poker. What say you? Luncheon, a bit of wine, a friendly game . . ."

He urged his horse into a sudden burst of speed, pulling well ahead of Cassidy's mare. Cleopatra gamely followed, and soon they were racing neck and neck over the broken ground of a rocky fell.

Quentin brought them to a stop beside a burn, where a copse of trees formed a sheltering hood over the bank and clumps of flowers grew among the grasses. Cracked stone thrust up here and there from the ground. Quentin tethered his mount to a tree and did the same for Cassidy's mare. He unpacked the blanket and food and laid them out between two of the stones.

"The remains of a Roman camp," he said, "from another age. Some of our ancestors were here before the conquerors came—but the conquerors are gone, and we remain." He rolled his eyes. "How dreadfully poetical of me. God forbid that I should ever aspire to become a poet. It's far too much work." He flopped down onto the grassy bank, lying flat on his back. "I trust you won't find me too ungallant if I allow you to help yourself to Cook's luncheon."

Absurd as he was, Cassidy couldn't help but enjoy his company. He made the world seem a little ridiculous, and all fears as insubstantial as the wispy clouds overhead. She reached for a slice of cold chicken.

"Good. I do like a woman who eats." He leaned up on his elbow long enough to pull a flask from under his coat. "Would you care for some brandy, Cousin?"

Cassidy caught a whiff of the stuff and wrinkled her noise. "No, thank you."

"Then I suppose I shall be forced to drink in solitude." He took a deep swallow, wiped his mouth, and lay down again, humming tunelessly.

"Rowena told me something else," Cassidy said. "She said that Braden was married."

Quentin choked and sat up. His face was slightly flushed. "It's hardly a secret."

"I saw Milena's portrait," Cassidy said wistfully. "She was so perfect. Rowena told me how much everyone loved her."

"Oh, yes. She had every man, woman, and child at Greyburn in her thrall while she was alive."

"How long has it been since she—"

"Departed this mortal coil, so to speak? Three years."

Only three years. "But no one ever talks about her," Cassidy said. "Not even Braden."

Quentin gazed up at the drifting clouds. "It is a difficult subject."

"They didn't have any children?"

Quentin's face twisted and just as quickly smoothed out again. "No—though Braden wanted them badly enough, for the Cause."

Only for the Cause? "How . . . how did she die?" Cassidy asked.

He took another drink from the flask. "An accident." With a sharp motion he capped the flask and plucked up a blade of grass. "She fell."

The short, clipped phrases were completely unlike Quentin. "I'm sorry," she said, swallowing a slice of bread that had turned to dust on her tongue. "Braden must have suffered very much."

"Yes." He jammed the blade of grass into his mouth.

For some reason Quentin did not want to talk about Milena. Had her death been so terrible a loss that everyone at Greyburn still mourned her—Braden most of all? Another cruel sacrifice added to the ruin of his sight . . .

Troubled, she abandoned her meal and went to Cleopatra, uncoiling the rope she'd hung from her saddle. She shaped a lasso, twirling it in air. The familiar motion calmed her.

"Nicely done," Quentin commented. "I presume you learned that skill in New Mexico. Where did you come by the rope?"

"I picked it up on the docks when we first arrived in England," she said. "I guess this must look funny, here."

"I find it fascinating."

She ducked her head. "Did Braden become blind before or after Milena died?"

Quentin bit the stem of his grass in two and tossed it away. "What a morbid conversation, my dear." He rolled to his side. "You have no cause to even think about Milena. You, little cousin, outshine her as the sun does a candle."

He had a peculiar light in his spice-colored eyes. Cassidy put the rope away and began to pack the remains of lunch.

"Let's not waste our breath discussing Milena, or Braden," Quentin said, coming to his knees. "Not when we can talk about you."

It was pointless trying to keep Quentin on a subject he wanted to avoid. "We came here so that I could learn how to Change. Maybe we should start—"

"Relax. We've plenty of time." He inched his way closer. "Has anyone ever told you that your lips are like rose petals? Or is that too obvious?"

"No one's ever said anything like that to me."

"What? No suitors? No lovers in America?"

Lovers—like Lancelot and Guinevere, or Tristan and Isolde. There'd been times when she imagined herself among them.

"You deserve admirers," he murmured. "A hundred dashing gallants at your feet. I don't believe you know your own loveliness." He reached out, cupped her chin in his hand. "So unaware of your own . . . desirability."

Cassidy shivered, less at his touch than at the odd note in his voice. She wanted to get up, but Quentin held her trapped with hand, gaze, and words.

"All feminine," he said, stroking her cheek. "All woman under that unpolished exterior and charming inexperience. Braden is blind indeed."

She was mute, fascinated by the new, almost frightening things he said to her. "Braden—"

"I don't believe you've ever been kissed," he said, smiling a different kind of smile than she'd ever seen on his face. "Well, well. Braden did send me out here to teach you. One lesson is as good as another. I knew there would be some compensations."

Before she understood, he leaned forward, pulled her toward him, and covered her lips with his.

In the next few seconds a thousand sensations and thoughts rushed through her mind and body. The heat of Quentin's mouth, the feather-lightness of the contact, the throbbing of her heart and the blood in her veins. But beyond that was the absence of something essential that should have been part of what he did. A warmth, a oneness—like what she'd felt with Braden in the woods, and when he'd talked of the Change and touched her hand. . . .

Braden. She closed her eyes and imagined Braden with her now, Braden's scent, Braden's lips.

"Braden," she whispered.

An ominous growl answered. Quentin drew back without haste and glanced toward the noise. Cassidy touched her mouth and did the same.

The wolf was a scant few feet away, head lowered, ears and tail erect, gray and black and white fur bristling along his spine. His gaze was fixed on Quentin, who scooted back on his knees and threw his hands up in the air with a sheepish grin.

"Easy, Brother. I'm not exactly poaching—you did say I was to teach—"

The wolf snarled, and Quentin wisely shut his mouth. Then the wolf crouched, teeth still bared, and began to blur.

When the dark mist evaporated, Braden crouched in the wolf's place. He was scowling, ominous—and undeniably naked.

Braden stood, Cassidy gasped, and Quentin fell back onto the grass.

"Let the lessons begin," Quentin said.

Braden had told himself there was excellent justification for following Quentin and Cassidy on their morning ride. For all his talk of Quentin's responsibility, Braden knew his brother too well. A leopard doesn't change his spots, nor a wolf the color of his coat.

Now it was brutally apparent how Quentin regarded the task set for him. His words to Cassidy had given warning of his intentions, and then there was the unmistakable sound of lips meeting, lingering. . . .

Braden fought back the anger that kindled in his chest. It was not reasonable. If Quentin found Cassidy attractive enough—if Cassidy was willing . . .

He didn't complete the thought. He was too aware of Cassidy's rough breathing, the heightened intensity of her scent, the lush fragrance of her womanhood.

Of arousal.

He turned on Quentin, hands clenched. "Is this how you planned to teach her?"

Quentin lolled in the grass, assuming the posture of submission. "But Brother," he said with a parody of humility, "after our several conversations, I was under the distinct impression that you wished me to—"

"Go." Braden advanced on his brother, and Quentin scrambled up from the ground. "It is clear that I cannot trust you to complete the work I set for you. If not for your blood—" He bared his teeth. "Go."

Quentin obeyed with satisfying alacrity. Leather creaked, the gelding snorted, and then there was only the sound of retreating hoofbeats.

A bird gave a hesitant chirp among the branches overhead. Cassidy didn't stir. Braden became acutely aware of the warm breeze on his bare skin, and of a tension every bit as tangible. He had learned to feel stares the way others saw them.

Cassidy was staring. He was naked from the Change, but Cassidy didn't turn away with the shock of a gently bred English girl. Among his own kind he ordinarily had no concern for modesty, but at the moment his body was not in a cooperative state. It, too, was bent on betraying him.

In the library last night he'd been at least half-dressed, with some measure of safety. Now there was none. He was envisioning Quentin's kiss and Cassidy's response, reliving his own irrational reaction—and imagining himself in Quentin's place. His own body taunted him and evaded his control as if he were merely human.

"Oh, my," Cassidy said.

Braden dropped into a crouch in the grass. "Mount your horse. I'll lead you back to Greyburn."

"But I came here to learn to Change. You sent Quentin away."

"He was—he has no discipline. I had hoped he would improve, but—"

"Then you must teach me." Her voice dropped low. "You, Braden."

That simple statement held him imprisoned like the jaws of a trap. If he agreed, he would be her mentor, her guide, helping her to reach inside herself to a place even she had never found. He would be close to her body and spirit, all barriers dissolved. And in the midst of that unwanted intimacy, he must be as insensible as stone to her nearness, her scent, her fresh simplicity and raw honesty.

If he met this challenge, everything that came after would be child's play. And he would know he was still worthy of some small part of his Grandfather's charge.

"Very well," he said. "Remain here until I return." He Changed before she could reply and ran for the nearest cache of clothing, concealed in the hollowed fork of a low tree. He Changed again, and dressed in the shirt, trousers and boots, much like those left in many hidden places around the estate.

She was still waiting when he returned on foot. Her mare snorted and pawed the grass, tack jingling.

"Mount up," he said.

"You haven't got a horse," she said. "We can share—"

"I'll run," he said. "Come." He started off ahead of her, settling into the even, loping stride he could maintain for miles even in human form. She kept her horse at a steady pace, always at his side or just behind.

Before, when they'd run together, it had been as wolf and woman. Now they were both human, yet he was just as conscious of her nearness. He focused his thoughts on the path ahead, the small obstacles he could anticipate and those new ones he might encounter, the invisible cushion of space around him that acted as shield and warning.

When her horse entered that space, he could almost hear Cassidy's thoughts. Her excitement, her hope, her yearning overwhelmed him, and then the mare fell behind and he was left to gather his shattered concentration.

It was not to Greyburn itself that he led her, but the woods beyond. They welcomed him with the promise of peace, but he could not relax his guard. By the side of the burn he stopped, and Cassidy dismounted. He slapped the mare's rump, sending her back to the stables.

Cassidy sat down on the bank. He heard her boots thump on the ground as she took them off one by one; water chortled at the touch of her toes.

"I love it here," she said. "I knew I would the first time I saw it."

He resisted the longing to kneel beside her and taste the crystal sweetness of the water. "Then you have a great advantage," he said. "That is the first thing you must understand. You are part of all this—the trees, the earth, the water. The Change is merely an extension of that understanding. Our people are born to the Change as the ash is made to lose its leaves in autumn and bud in spring. There is nothing I can teach you that is not already within yourself."

"I knew that," she said. "Even on the ranch. But I could never find it."

"You must." He listened to the play of the burn, seeking his own calm in its tranquil melody. "You must eliminate every barrier that stands between you and the essence of life."

She rose. "How? Please—tell me how."

"First . . ." Deliberately he turned his back to her. "Remove your clothing. All of it."

Her hesitation was brief. She knew he could not see her, and she'd been bold enough when he stood naked after the Change. She had nothing to fear.

But he could not shut off his senses. He heard the rustle of her skirt, the slide of buttons from buttonholes, the swish of fabric skimming shoulders, arms, hips, legs. She wore few layers to discard. He scent dizzied him as she removed the last of her garments and let them fall to the earth.

"I'm finished," she said. Her voice was very small, as if she expected him to find her wanting. Did she think he would inspect her for flaws like a farmer buying a ewe, even if he could see?

His treacherous imagination broke the bonds of discipline once again. His mind's eye provided what his outer vision could not: a picture of sleek, clean limbs; long legs woman-soft yet muscled from running; taut stomach and waist; full, firm young breasts peaked by rosy nipples; strong shoulders and shapely arms; slender neck beneath an open, earnest face.

A lovely face. A sleek body graceful even in awkwardness. Telford had declared himself wrong in his first judgment of Cassidy's appearance. Quentin found her attractive. But the mere thought of Quentin seeing her now—or Telford, or any other male, human or *loup-garou*—brought an involuntary growl to Braden's throat.

"Braden?"

He braced himself and turned to her. "Good," he said. "Close your eyes. Imagine your feet sinking into the ground like the roots of a tree. Feel your blood beat in harmony with the rhythms of the earth. Hear the song of life and let it guide you."

She caught her breath. "The song . . . I can't quite hear—"

"Last night you said that you could *feel* it. Look for it again. Look deeper than ever before."

"Last night . . . you held my hand."

There was nothing seductive in her request, yet it was all he could do to grant this one little thing she asked of him. He extended his hand, and she took it.

Her body went very still. Her skin conducted the intensity of her effort through his flesh like an electric shock. Strong, slender fingers tightened in a desperate grip.

"I feel it . . . in you," she whispered.

The last thing he wanted was that she should reach into the part of himself that defined his being, his soul, his very existence. No one but Milena had ever invaded that private sanctum, and *she* had barred its doors for all time.

But Cassidy could not fail to notice the growing heat of his skin, the pounding of his pulse, the primeval passion that lay a hairsbreadth from the essence of the Change.

"You will not find what you seek in me," he said.

"But I can . . . almost . . . so close—"

"Feel the earth under your feet, the life around you," he urged. "Hear the water and the wind. There is no separation between you and every other living thing. The division is imaginary."

"Even between you and me?"

That was the contradiction he could not, would not explain—how the restraints within himself belied everything he told her: to let go, to free the wolf, to surrender to passion. Passion warred with duty and control, yet both were essential to the Cause—the passion to mate and the control to do so logically and with full awareness of the consequences.

Essential to every part of the Cause but himself. He was the exception. Duty alone was his existence.

"Forget me," he said roughly. "Can't you feel nature within you? The water of the burn flows in your veins; fires deep beneath the earth rise up to consume you. . . ."

"Yes . . . oh, yes."

"You can command it with your will. You can draw the power through your body and desire yourself to Change—"

"Yes. I want it. I want it so much."

Braden's blood thickened in his veins and pooled in his loins. He hissed between his teeth. "Make it come, Cassidy."

"It's coming. Oh . . . Please. Don't let me go. When you touch me . . . I—" She swayed, began to fall. He caught her, his hands clasping her waist. She leaned into him, gasping. Her erect nipples grazed his chest, and the scent of her womanhood encircled him like ethereal bonds.

She was on the brink, balanced on the edge. And so was he.

He lifted her in his arms and found her lips.

ten

B raden's kiss was nothing like Quentin's.
It was nothing like Cassidy had imagined a kiss
would be, a mere touching of mouth to mouth. This one
left her breathless and amazed and exhilarated. It raged
through her blood the way he'd said the Change would
do, sent heat surging into parts of her body she'd only begun to discover.

She'd been afraid when she undressed, though she
knew he couldn't see her—afraid she could never match
his perfection, or Milena's. Her first glimpse of his nakedness had inspired awe and a host of other feelings she
couldn't name. He was a poem made flesh. Her body
had seemed ordinary compared to his, a poor and fragile
thing, only half-alive.

Now his potency poured into her like a cry of triumph,
and she was beautiful. As beautiful as Milena.

Braden kissed her, and she smoldered; she caught fire;
she burned to ashes and was born again. He initiated her
into a mystery she couldn't wait to possess.

Her hands sought and found the broad, muscular

planes of his back, drawing him nearer even as she clung to him for support. His lips urged hers apart, and she willingly obeyed. When his tongue slipped inside her mouth, she welcomed the invasion and yearned to take him into every part of herself.

This was magic. This was what he'd been trying to explain. This was the song of life, the one she'd been waiting so long to hear, the only song that mattered.

Until now she'd been asleep. She'd been walking in a kind of dream world, not understanding what she was looking for. The Change from human to wolf was only one small piece of the puzzle. Braden kissed her, and she knew she was transformed beyond her wildest fantasies.

Still it wasn't enough. Something was missing. Her body ached, and Braden was the only one who could make the aching stop. His strong hands slid down her back like cool water on parched earth. His palms settled on her hips, molding her to his body as if he, too, wanted more than he could speak in words.

She urged him to find the answers for both of them. He would know what to do. He was sure and experienced in the ways of the world: A lord. A leader. A Tyger. She took his hand and guided it to her breast, crying aloud as his finger touched her taut nipple. Wetness gathered between her legs. In the unfathomable center of her being, a new Cassidy struggled to emerge, awaiting the key that would unlock her cage.

Braden was the key. He had told her to eliminate every barrier between herself and the world, but the layers of his clothing still separated them. When he held her hand, she had a glimpse of Braden's soul. When he kissed her, she stood on the brink of rebirth. When their bodies touched, skin to skin, and nothing kept them apart . . .

Her fingers worked the top button of his shirt.

"Braden," she murmured against his lips. "Show me. Please—"

His response was all the more shocking for its silence. He thrust her at arm's length, his mouth so rigid that it seemed impossible that those lips could have been caressing her with such tenderness.

"Get dressed," he said. His voice shook, and when he walked away he stumbled over a root and righted himself like a man too long without water in the *Jornada*.

Cassidy's legs chose that moment to give out. She dropped in a boneless heap to the moist earth. Her body was a quivering knot of conflicting sensations, every one of them beyond her control. It was as if she had been ready to dive into an endless, mystical ocean of enlightenment, and someone had yanked her back at the last minute. She still yearned for the ocean, but there was no returning to that perfect instant of readiness.

And Braden was gone. His behavior confused her most of all. He had *wanted* to kiss her. Wanted *her*.

She tested that word, that idea in her mind. He had been angry when Quentin kissed her. And when Quentin kissed her, she had imagined Braden in his place.

The most secret parts of her body were throbbing with a need grown almost intolerable. She had felt it before, with Braden, but never so strongly. It was a kind of change in herself that was tied to the Change Braden wanted her to discover. The two belonged together. She hadn't known the words to explain what seemed so simple; she didn't think she'd ever find the right way to say it.

She'd been so near to *showing* Braden, but he hadn't given her the chance. If he had, how would it have ended? Her mind didn't know, but her body did. Her body would have done everything right.

A chill penetrated Cassidy's happiness. Only three years ago, Braden's wife had died. When he held Cassidy in his arms, was he thinking of Milena? Was her memory too unbearable, the ideal she set so much higher than anything Cassidy could ever hope to match?

If she could only Change. She had to make Braden proud of her, so he wouldn't think of Milena. If he still grieved for her, Cassidy would find a way to help him.

Strangely weary, she lay beside the burn in the woods and let the pulse of the earth's heartbeat lull her into sleep. She roused at the snapping of a twig and sat up before she was fully awake.

She knew immediately that the intruder wasn't Braden, or Quentin, or any of the people at Greyburn she had met. He stepped out of the shadows, and at last she recognized him: the young man who had been initiated at last night's ceremony. Then he'd been afraid, wild-eyed, shaking; she'd felt sorry for him, and for the maid who shared his ordeal.

He didn't look afraid anymore. She could see that he was only a little older than she was, his new footman's livery already stained, his gait unsteady as he started toward her.

"Wha's this?" he said. "A fairy maid?"

Cassidy became aware of several things all at once: that her dress was still in a heap several feet away, that the new footman's expression was anything but friendly, and that he stank like the stuff Quentin had offered her during their brief picnic. A half-empty bottle was clenched in his fist.

He was drunk, and she was quite naked. She scrambled for her clothes just as the footman staggered forward again.

"Lov'ly," he muttered. "Jus' what I need."

Cassidy knew she wasn't in any danger. She could outrun him easily. But there was a hostility in his eyes that belied his drawl, and she felt dirty when he looked at her. Braden made her feel beautiful; the footman's gaze branded her as an object, not a person. An object for which he had some malignant purpose.

"You're the new footman," she said, reaching for her dress. "I don't know why you're in the woods, but I think you should go back to Greyburn, before—"

"C'mon, hinnie," the footman drawled. "Le's have some fun."

Cassidy scooped her dress in front of her chest. "I don't think the earl would like it," she said pointedly. "I won't tell him, if you go back."

"Go back?" He laughed. "Aye . . . they wan' me to go back . . . to serve them . . ." He made a frantic gesture with his bottle, and his eyes narrowed on her. "But ye're waitin' here for me. All nice 'n ready 'n hot, wi' yer pretty tits . . ."

Cassidy stepped back with the dress in her arms. Her foot splashed into the burn, she lost her balance, and the footman lunged at her.

Instinct replaced thought. Cassidy struck out with both hands, shoving the footman violently. He fell sideways and tumbled to the ground, his head striking a stone. The bottle went flying.

When the footman pushed himself up again, blood flowed freely from a cut above one eyebrow. He felt his forehead and his mouth drew up in a misshapen snarl of rage.

"Ye bitch," he said. "Ye're like the others—the devil's whore, a hound o' Satan. Ye and yer kind ha' cursed the land. But I . . . I ken the truth. All the rest ha' fallen to the evil one." Blood streaked his face like a gory mask. "I'll tell—I'll stop ye all—" He clutched his head between his hands as if in torment.

"You're hurt," Cassidy said, feeling sudden pity. His

odd behavior wasn't just from drunkenness or the cut on his head. She remembered his terror at the ceremony; it was as if something had gone wrong there.

"Let me get help," she said.

"Stay back," he hissed, though she hadn't moved toward him. He pushed to his feet and scurried for his discarded bottle. "Stay away, or I'll kill ye."

Cassidy raised both hands, palm out, and backed away. "I'm leaving," she said. She wanted to dress, but if she did it here she'd be defenseless. The footman glared after her wildly as she continued to retreat. Only after she'd put the burn and a layer of trees between them did she dare to stop and pull her dress over her head.

Braden had told her that the servants at Greyburn were loyal, and she'd witnessed the initiation that ensured such loyalty. She knew there were things about the ceremony she still didn't understand, things she didn't like—but it was clear that this footman hadn't learned whatever he was supposed to have learned.

Or was it because she hadn't Changed into a wolf, and so he didn't recognize her as one of the Forsters? Either way, he was dangerous as much to himself as anyone else. She'd seen drunken men turn violent before. She would have to tell someone—

A stunning pain slammed into the back of her head. She glimpsed the twisted face of the footman one last time, and then slid into nothingness.

Isabelle had to use every ounce of her courage to defy the earl of Greyburn and stay by Cassidy's side when he brought the injured girl back to the house that evening. He had found her in the wood, half-dressed and bloodied, and the entire household collectively held its breath as he carried her up the stairs.

The earl was a formidable opponent at any time, but he was positively savage with Cassidy so limp and quiet in his arms. He looked for all the world as if he would rend anyone who approached with his bare teeth and fingers, including Quentin—bereft of words for once—and a pale Lady Rowena.

Isabelle had been very, very careful.

"Cassidy needs a woman's care," she said. "I've seen such injuries in America. Let me examine her."

At first he had been ready to send for a doctor, until she'd assured him that the bump didn't seem serious. If Cassidy woke soon they had little reason for concern. "And I know that your people heal very quickly," she added. "I can do what must be done."

She had guessed correctly that he would prefer to avoid bringing a human physician to Greyburn, and he was forced to agree. But he never left Cassidy's side, not from the moment he laid her down in her bed and ordered a bevy of servants to bring hot water and cloths and blankets, nor for a single instant of Isabelle's careful tending. He was there when Cassidy began to stir with a soft groan and shake of her damp hair.

"Isabelle?" she said drowsily.

Isabelle let out a deep sigh. "You're fine, Cassidy. You were hit on the head, but it's not a bad injury. Now that you're awake . . ."

Cassidy's heavy-lidded gaze found the earl. "Braden?"

He knelt beside the bed, and Isabelle watched as he touched Cassidy's forehead with surprising tenderness, careful to avoid the bandage. "I found you in the wood," he said. "I brought you back. Who did this to you?"

Cassidy reached from under the blanket and felt for Braden's hand. He took it, though Isabelle caught his nearly imperceptible flinch. "There was something . . .

wrong with him," Cassidy said. Isabelle put a glass of water to her lips. She drank thirstily and smiled at Isabelle.

"Who?" Braden demanded, his voice like thunder. "Who hurt you?"

She tried to shake her head again, and winced. "The new footman. The . . . one at the ceremony. He was *loco*. He didn't know—"

But Braden wasn't listening. "John Dodd," he said. "What did he do?"

Cassidy squirmed in the bed. "He . . . said funny things. Something about devils. I—" She flushed. "I hurt him first, when he came too close."

"Did he touch you?"

"He didn't get the chance. I . . . think he threw a rock at me when I wasn't looking."

Braden dropped Cassidy's hand and shot to his feet. Every muscle in his neck and jaw stood out in relief. "Quentin."

His brother, who had been waiting in the background, stepped up beside him. "It doesn't seem possible—"

"Remember Telford," Braden said. "There are always a few who can resist—or whose minds are too weak." He bared his teeth. "If he dared to attack Cassidy—"

"Perhaps he didn't recognize her as one of us?"

"It doesn't matter. You know what must be done."

Cassidy tried to sit up, resisting Isabelle's admonitions to stay quiet. "I told you—he was *loco*. He was drinking out of a bottle. I don't think he even knew . . ."

"He is dangerous, Cassidy. Not only to you, but to all of us." He spoke every word with a studied calm that couldn't hide a deadly ferocity. "You will rest here, with Mrs. Smith. The human will not harm you again."

"What are you going to do?" Cassidy said, looking anxiously from Quentin to Braden.

Lord Greyburn loomed over Cassidy, and Isabelle felt the very edge of his power, like the outermost wake of a passing steamer rocking a rowboat. "Sleep," he said. "Sleep until we return."

Cassidy stiffened in resistance, then slowly relaxed. Her eyelids drifted shut, and her breathing settled into the easy rhythm of slumber.

"I beg your pardon, my lord." Aynsley stepped in the door and inclined his head. "I have just learned that Dodd cannot be found, and a hack has been taken from the stable."

"Then he's already running," Braden said. He turned on the butler. "Is there anything you failed to tell me about this John Dodd when you proposed him for service at Greyburn?"

"No, my lord." Aynsley was visibly shaken. "He is the eldest son of a local family, with training in smaller houses. His recommendations were impeccable, and he showed no signs of . . . I cannot understand—"

Braden dismissed Aynsley with a chop of his hand. "He can't have gone far." He returned to the bedside. "Mrs. Smith, if you wish to make yourself useful, you will see that Cassidy gets her rest and remains quietly in bed."

"Of course." Isabelle met his gaze, and, once again, found it difficult to remember that he was blind. How could a blind man's eyes hold such potency?

But he wasn't merely a man. He felt for Cassidy's face, traced her brow with his finger, brushed damp hair away from her forehead. She murmured, and he withdrew his hand.

"Look after her," he said to Isabelle, and left the room, Quentin and the butler at his heels.

Cassidy opened her eyes. "Is he gone?" she whispered.

"You weren't asleep," Isabelle said.

"I couldn't." Cassidy propped herself up on her elbows. "I felt strange when Braden told me to sleep, but I'm all right now."

If Lord Greyburn had attempted to will Cassidy's obedience in the way he'd done with the servants at the ceremony, he'd failed. That small victory gave Isabelle great satisfaction.

But he'd been right in one respect. "You should rest," she said.

Cassidy shook her head, tried to sit up, and fell back again. "Isabelle . . . I have to go with Braden."

"Out of the question. You're in no condition to go anywhere. I saw men injured in the mines—"

"I'm afraid of what Braden will do." Cassidy touched her bandage. "He was . . . very angry."

"If the man attacked you—"

"But there *was* something wrong with him, Isabelle. I could feel it. And he didn't hurt me badly. During the ceremony . . . he was afraid. Sometimes fear makes people crazy."

It was typical of Cassidy's unselfish generosity that she worried over the servant's punishment, but Isabelle didn't like the idea of Cassidy putting herself between Lord Greyburn and John Dodd. She must be distracted from any idea of chasing after Lord Greyburn. "How did you come to be in the woods alone?" she asked quickly.

Cassidy's face lost its anxious look and became soft, almost dreamy.

"I wasn't alone," she said. "Not at first. Braden took me there to teach me how to Change."

Isabelle leaned forward. "What happened after the ceremony last night?"

"You know . . . I couldn't turn into a wolf." Cassidy hung her head, pleating the edge of the blanket between her fingers. "I went to Braden afterward, to explain. He was upset. He said it comes naturally, that our people don't have to be taught. I didn't know how much it mattered . . . that I could do it."

Matthias's cryptic comment came back to Isabelle: *"Becrike, there'll be fratchin' tonight."* "Cassidy, if he was cruel to you—"

"Oh, no. But Isabelle . . . it's so important to him. I convinced him that I could learn. He told Quentin to teach me, but—" she bit her lip. "We never started the lessons. Quentin kissed me."

Isabelle sat up. "Kissed you?"

"We went out riding just before lunch, and when we stopped, Quentin kissed me. Braden must have been following us. He came as a wolf and Changed, and then he sent Quentin away."

Oh, Lord, Isabelle thought. "And . . . how did you feel, Cassidy?"

"I felt sorry for Quentin—"

"No. About Quentin's kiss."

She flushed and shrugged. "No one ever kissed me before. But—" Her gaze grew unfocused, starry-eyed, sensual in a way Isabelle could not misinterpret. "Braden took me to the woods to teach me himself. And then he kissed me, too."

A disconcerting picture crystallized in Isabelle's mind. "How did it happen?" she asked carefully.

"First he told me to undress—"

"He what?"

"To be a part of the earth and the trees and the wind, so I would be ready. *Loups-garous* have to undress to Change. But I asked him to hold my hand, because when he touched me I feel closest to . . . what he wants me to be. And when I was beginning to see, when I was almost there . . . he kissed me."

"And you enjoyed it."

"Oh, yes." She smiled dreamily. "I remember a poem: 'Once he drew with one long kiss my whole soul through . . .' "

Tennyson. Who'd have guessed that a handful of battered books, carefully preserved by a naive young romantic, could prove so dangerous? She stood up and paced across the room. "Was the earl also undressed?"

"No. But I . . . wanted Braden to touch me more. I wanted us to be closer. That was when he—" She swallowed. "That was when he left."

So the earl had some scruples after all. Isabelle had wondered what he intended for Cassidy, yet this was not in character. He had been so formal, so rigid with her. As if she were more a necessary burden than a long-lost cousin—or a woman. Whatever his flaws, Braden Forster had seemed honorable.

Some men concealed their most dangerous passions behind a facade of austerity and coldness. Was that Braden's game? Cassidy couldn't possibly know how seductive she was in her very innocence, how irresistible that would be to certain kinds of men.

And Cassidy was lovely in body and spirit. She was available and unprotected save by a lone human woman. She shouldn't need a chaperon among her own relatives.

What did Isabelle know of the earl of Greyburn's past, or his proclivities? How was she to guess how a werewolf male behaved, when she had only the openhearted Edith as an example?

Ordinary men were uncivilized enough. Aristocrats could be worst of all. What primitive, uncontrollable impulses might drive a man who was more than half beast? Was it possible that the two brothers were competing for the same girl? And where did Cassidy's ability to Change fit in?

Answers must be found, and soon. Matthias—perhaps

he would know. She turned back to Cassidy. "Were you able to Change?"

"No. But I was so near—"

Isabelle reached for Cassidy's hands. "Listen to me. I know that what happened felt wonderful to you. Your whole body felt more alive than ever before, and you didn't want it to stop. But what happened in the woods wasn't all there is between a man and a woman, Cassidy."

"I want to understand," Cassidy said. "You can tell me, Isabelle. You know so much more than I do."

"Yes," Isabelle said bitterly. "Let me tell you a story. When I was very young, even younger than you are now, I knew a man. I wanted to be with him as you want to be with Braden. I was poor and he was rich, but that didn't seem to matter. In England, you see, young, unmarried men and women of good family aren't supposed to be alone together. It's a very strict rule. But I didn't care. I believed he loved me."

"Love," Cassidy whispered.

> *"I ne'er was struck before that hour*
> *With love so sudden and so sweet."*

If only it were that simple, Isabelle thought. "When you're young, such feelings can be very confusing. They can make us believe things that aren't true. A part of me knew that I would not be allowed to marry this man, because we were from very different worlds. But I ignored my common sense. When he asked me to go away with him, alone, I did. We touched one another, Cassidy—we kissed, and—when it was over, he left me. He made me believe he cared for me, but when he had what he wanted, he pretended he had never even met me."

"Oh, Isabelle." Cassidy folded Isabelle's hands in her own and chafed them gently. "But how could he do that?

Why would he want to leave you? You're so beautiful, and so kind."

Humbled by Cassidy's faith in her, Isabelle stared at the tangled blankets. "It didn't matter. He was to marry someone else. But because I'd been alone with him, no other good man wanted me. Those rules, Cassidy. One cannot ignore them, not here. So I left England."

"And I thought you wanted to come back," Cassidy said. "I'm sorry I asked you—"

"No. Never be sorry." She managed a smile. "I'm here with you now, where I want to be. And I can tell you about these rules, so you don't make the same mistakes I did. There's such generosity in your soul, Cassidy. That is why you must be careful, and use your mind as well as your heart."

Cassidy was quiet for a long time. "Braden was married," she said. "I thought that maybe he left me because he still . . . She died in an accident."

Isabelle had heard rumors of Braden's former wife. But how he had treated her, or how she died, Isabelle didn't know.

"Married people *can* be together," Cassidy said. "If I could be good enough—"

Good God. Now she mentioned marriage. Isabelle squeezed Cassidy's fingers. "You are perfect as you are. Changing yourself to please another is a path that leads only to sorrow. Do not do anything unless you know it is right for you. You may not get another chance to decide."

"But I can choose what's right for me."

Isabelle wished she could bring herself to lie. "Yes, Cassidy. The choice must be yours."

Cassidy pushed at her blankets. "Then I should go with Braden."

So much for distracting the girl. "Never forget that Lord Greyburn has great power. He ordered you to stay here. If you go after them, your very disobedience may inspire Lord Greyburn to act more harshly." Isabelle braced herself to be cruel. "Do not deceive yourself, Cassidy. You are not strong enough to defy him. You are not his match."

Cassidy's determined expression faltered. She lay back on the pillows. "No," she said, closing her eyes. But that stubborn tenacity remained in the set of her mouth, and Isabelle could imagine the words that went unspoken:

"Not yet."

eleven

For three days Braden and Quentin remained away from Greyburn, and no one could—or would—tell Cassidy when they were to return.

The house had fallen under a pall of silence since John Dodd's disappearance. The servants didn't respond when Cassidy tried to talk to them; they did their duties with anonymous efficiency. Rowena, as usual, kept entirely to her own rooms after venturing from seclusion to inquire about Cassidy's health.

No one at Greyburn seemed to care how Cassidy spent her time. She could eat when she wished and wander the grounds at will, and she had plenty to occupy her thoughts.

There were two things she couldn't forget, no matter how far away Braden went. Again and again she relived those moments in the forest: how he'd held her, kissed her.

And she remembered what Isabelle had told her the night Braden left: *"You are not his match."*

She knew why she was not—because she couldn't Change. Rowena made much of Milena's perfection; *she* hadn't lacked the true werewolf nature. And Braden had loved Milena.

Isabelle said that changing yourself to please someone else was the wrong thing to do. But if Cassidy could
turn into a wolf, Braden would have to see her differently.
He would listen to her and stop pushing her away—
let her into that lonely place he didn't want anyone to
touch.

He would let her help him.

That hope sent her out early each morning to the
woods, where she'd been so close to finding what she
lacked. For hours she struggled to recapture the sensations
she'd felt with Braden, that standing-on-the-edge-of-a-
mesa feeling at once so frightening and exciting. She ran
the length of the burn and back again, imagining herself
on four swift paws with the wind singing in her fur.

Each afternoon she returned unsuccessful, no nearer
her aim. And each afternoon, on the fell by the wood, she
saw Isabelle meeting with the man in the odd clothing.

He was another puzzle Cassidy had yet to solve. She'd
seen him in the house only once, after the ceremony, but
Isabelle obviously knew him well. After Isabelle's story of
her unhappy past, it seemed strange that she'd go alone to
see any man. But Isabelle didn't speak of him, and Cassidy
was sure she believed the meetings were secret.

Cassidy would have kept that secret. But on the third
afternoon of Braden's absence, while she was returning
from another failed attempt to Change, she saw them together at the edge of the wood.

They were laughing. Cassidy realized how seldom she'd
seen Isabelle laugh. She had her hand on the man's arm,
and their heads were bent together as if they were shutting
out the rest of the world.

Cassidy was preparing to take another path back to the
house when they looked up and saw her. Isabelle dropped
her hand from the man's arm and put several feet of distance between them. The man gestured broadly, and

began to walk in Cassidy's direction. Isabelle gathered up her skirts and ran to catch up.

"Cassidy!" she said as they came near. "I didn't realize you were about." She was flustered, but her unease didn't hide the flush of her cheeks or the brightness of her eyes or the way she glanced at the man with the sword who stopped beside her. "I . . . would like you to meet Matthias, a shepherd of Greyburn." She coughed delicately behind her gloved hand. "Matthias, this is my dear friend, Miss Cassidy Holt."

Cassidy remembered Quentin mentioning that name on the journey to Greyburn. Something about a legend of Greyburn, and a ghost . . .

She dipped a curtsy. "I'm glad to meet you, Matthias."

Matthias swept her a bow. "Milady Cassidy, 'tis an honor. I've heard much of ye, all of it bonny. Welcome to Greyburn."

"Thank you, but you don't have to call me 'my lady.' I'm just Cassidy." She returned his smile. "Have you lived her long, Matthias?"

"Oh, aye." He gave an exaggerated wink. "I'm as auld as the hills themselves, and just as set in my ways."

Cassidy studied him carefully. He was every bit as odd as he'd looked in the hall after the ceremony—like someone who had stepped right out of a poem, with his shiny breastplate and helmet and sword. He didn't resemble any shepherd she'd ever seen, but his scent was familiar, as if it were a permanent part of the land around them. He was older than Isabelle, yet his smile was boyish, and he glanced at her as if they shared some special knowledge.

"You're not really a ghost, are you?" she asked.

He laughed. Isabelle blushed. "There are no ghosts, Cassidy," she said.

But if he wasn't a ghost, he was definitely a man—and

Isabelle had been alone with him. She had been so adamant about the rules between men and women.

Those rules said that unmarried men and women weren't supposed to be alone together. Maybe the rules no longer applied to her. It certainly looked as though they enjoyed each other's company. In spite of her blushes, Isabelle had moved next to him again; their hands were almost touching.

"No other good man wanted me," Isabelle had said. But Matthias was a good man, Cassidy was certain. And Isabelle glowed. As much as she tried to hide it, she was happy. Happy to be with this very peculiar shepherd. It was as if two people who didn't quite fit in had found each other, and never wanted to be apart again as long as they lived.

All at once Cassidy realized what came into her mind when she saw Matthias and Isabelle together. It was that afternoon in the woods when Cassidy was alone with Braden: the confusing and remarkable emotions, the heightened sensations, the tingling all through her body, the joy.

That was what Isabelle felt with Matthias. But he wouldn't run from her, as Braden had from Cassidy. Matthias *wanted* to kiss Isabelle. And she wanted him.

Cassidy turned away, dazed by the new awareness that had come with Braden's kiss. "I have to get back to the house," she said. "Pleased to meet you, Matthias."

She didn't wait for his answering bow, but started off immediately. Yet she must have been focused on them even as she left them behind, for she heard their low-voiced conversation.

"So that's the lass," Matthias said. "I ken why ye're so fond o' her. But ye've no need to fash yerself over her with the laird, of that I'm certain."

"Because she keeps her spirits up no matter what Lord Greyburn does, or how much he changes toward her from moment to moment?" Isabelle returned. "She wants to please him, but she doesn't grasp the consequences. She's far too innocent—"

"And is there aught amiss wi' innocence, my bonny?" he said. "There's hidden strength in the lass. Ye said yerself that she didna' let the villain's sculduddery upset her. She is a proper match for the laird."

"I'd rather take her away from England than see—" She broke off. "He's a bitter, angry man, Matthias. And he's not human. Not like you."

"There you're wrong, my bonny. We're nae so different as a' that.'

"No, Matthias. You are nothing like Braden Forster. He hides too many secrets, and I fear to learn the answers. There's only one man in the world I can trust."

Cassidy crouched behind a rise and looked back. Matthias held Isabelle against him, and her arms were about his waist.

Her thoughts turning over what she had heard, Cassidy slipped back into the house and up to her room.

Matthias had said she was a proper match for the laird. Isabelle had called Braden bitter and angry, but if she'd watched him in the woods . . . if she'd seen the blood dripping from his hand after he'd plunged it through the glass in the library . . .

Isabelle had told Cassidy not to let anyone choose for her. Cassidy was beginning to recognize the power of choice, of making decisions that could change everything—and not only for herself.

If she had the courage and the wisdom to make the right ones.

She'd no sooner stripped off her dress and begun to wash up at the basin when a maid tapped on the door.

"The Lady Rowena wishes to inform you that guests have arrived," the maid said, "and she asks you to dress and come down to the drawing room for tea."

Guests. The only guests Braden awaited were members of the Convocation, the delegates who would meet to discuss the Cause and the survival of *loups-garous* all over the world. But Braden wasn't here. Rowena was taking charge, and that didn't seem at all like her, when she hated her werewolf heritage so much.

Cassidy finished washing up and accepted the maid's help to dress in one of her nicest tea gowns. She hurried downstairs and met Quentin on the way to the drawing room.

"Quentin, you're back!" she said. "Where is Braden?"

"He sent me on ahead—I imagine he'll be along any time now. We haven't yet caught the footman. The man seems to have vanished into thin air."

Cassidy's stomach danced a jittery little *ranchera*. The footman was gone. Braden would be home soon, and she longed to see him—but she still wasn't ready.

"Will you allow me to escort you to the drawing room?" Quentin said.

It was the first time she and Quentin had been alone together since the interrupted Changing lesson. The memory of his kiss, and its aftermath, was fresh in her mind. "About what happened—" she began. "I like you, Quentin. I want us to be friends. I hope nothing has changed."

He seemed almost to blush. "I quite understand. Think no more of it. I'm sure we've both had other things on our minds."

Cassidy sighed with relief. The kiss obviously hadn't meant anything to Quentin, just as she suspected. "I was told that we have guests," she said. "Are they here for the Convocation?"

"Hardly." Quentin strolled down the hall at a deliberately

slow pace. "Lord Leebrook and Lady Beatrice are unexpected arrivals—the descendants of my great-aunt Grace, who chose to live as humans among humans. Braden considers them personae non grata at Greyburn; luckily he's not here."

"They chose to live as humans?"

"Quite. My great-aunt Grace married a human marquess, and they raised their children to ignore their werewolf blood and abilities. Lady Beatrice, Grace's widowed daughter, has been hosting Rowena in London for the past several Seasons. Rowena and Lady Beatrice's niece, Lady Alice, made the social rounds together. It was part of Rowena's bargain with Braden." He buffed his fingernails on his immaculate jacket. "Ro's been trying to get out of the bargain ever since. She wants to live like the Sayerses, and marry a human."

"That was why Braden went to London to bring her back here," Cassidy said.

"And now the Sayerses have arrived at just the right moment. They are very much on her side. I discern Ro's devious mind at work."

"Devious" was not a word Cassidy would have used for Rowena, but there was still too much she didn't know about Braden's sister. She wondered what would happen if Braden returned in the middle of this visit.

She prepared herself to brave the haughty stares of more well-bred, well-dressed aristocrats cast in Rowena's mold, but when she and Quentin arrived at the drawing room, only Isabelle was present. She threw Cassidy a half-apologetic, half-pleading look, and returned to gazing at her folded hands.

This wasn't the time to discuss Matthias. Cassidy would certainly keep Isabelle's secret. She sat as close to Isabelle as she could, while Quentin wandered about the room in apparent boredom.

They were all fidgeting by the time the next guest arrived. Quentin looked up first, and let out a low oath.

The man was instantly familiar in spite of his change of clothing, and Cassidy stifled a gasp. Isabelle was last to see him. She sat very still and very erect in her chair, making not a sound.

He was Matthias, but a Matthias utterly unlike the one Cassidy had met just hours before. Instead of antique armor, he wore a coat, trousers, and waistcoat that were crumpled, patched, and worn—and, Cassidy guessed, unfashionable. No helmet covered his long gray hair. He glanced about the room, his movements somehow lacking the easy confidence he'd shown outside. It was almost as if he weren't completely there.

His glance fell on Cassidy, and he smiled hesitantly. "Good aftern-noon," he said. "Quentin. And—" He looked at Isabelle, who continued to stare at him expressionlessly.

"Uncle Matthew," Quentin said. "What are you doing here?"

Matthew. Not Matthias. Was Cassidy's mind playing tricks? Could there be two men who looked so much alike?

But they smelled the same, and no fine suit could cover the scent of hay and bracken and sheep.

"Ladies, I don't believe you've met my uncle, Matthew Forster." Quentin said. He made introductions with a laziness that didn't quite disguise a keen interest in the reactions of each of the participants.

His uncle, a shepherd? But if he was a Greyburn Forster, he couldn't be human. Cassidy was too mystified to do more than murmur a greeting. Isabelle rose stiffly. She didn't offer her hand to the newcomer.

"Mr. Forster," she said. "I wonder that we have not met before. Do you reside far from Greyburn?"

Matthias . . . Matthew . . . gazed at the toes of his

scuffed shoes. "Not . . . f-far, Mrs. Smith. Just over the fell." His voice was slightly hoarse and halting, as if he were seeking the right words.

"And what brings you to Greyburn today, Uncle?" Quentin asked, his gaze sliding from Isabelle to Matthew and back again. "We so seldom have the pleasure."

"I could not be so r-remiss as to . . . ignore my nephew's guests," Matthew said. "Especially when they bring such b-beauty to our distant northern lands."

Isabelle raised her chin like a queen regarding her humblest subject. "Perhaps you have met a shepherd, by the name of Matthias?"

He went still as a rabbit scenting a coyote. "Yes. I know of him."

"Then perhaps you'll be so kind as to tell him that in spite of his kind offer to guide me about the estate, I will have no need of his services."

Matthew jerked back. "He . . . he . . ." He drew a handkerchief from his pocket and dabbed his forehead. "Forgive me. I—"

He was unable to finish his sentence. There was a small commotion at the drawing room door, and a procession entered, led by Rowena. She was followed by a middle-aged woman and a young lady close to Cassidy's age, both perfectly poised in their tasteful gowns. Aynsley and a footman brought up the rear with trays of tea and biscuits.

Rowena paused when she saw Matthew, frowned, and quickly regained her composure. She was about to begin introductions all around when the last guest walked through the door, a tall, thin man with graying hair and a long face.

"Ah, Lord Leebrook," Rowena said. "I am so glad you are able to join us—"

A whole host of peculiar things seemed to happen in rapid succession. Isabelle's attention snapped away from

Matthew and fixed on Lord Leebrook. He looked back at her, and his sallow skin paled even further.

"Isabelle," he cried in a choked voice. The stout older woman, Lady Beatrice, let out a gasp.

Isabelle stood up, swayed, and stumbled from her chair. Matthew reached for her as if to steady her, and then stared in bewilderment as she fled the room through the French doors leading to the garden.

Lady Beatrice sagged in her chair. "Is it possible? That woman, here—"

Lord Leebrook opened his mouth several times, turned on his heel, and left the room by the opposite door.

"What has happened?" Rowena said, rushing to Lady Beatrice's side. "Aynsley, bring water and sal volatile at once—"

"No." Lady Beatrice sat up, her sagging face drawn in lines of affront. "You cannot have realized, my dear Rowena, that this creature you have harbored under your roof is—" She fanned herself violently. "Oh, my poor child, you have been deceived. She is no better than a common trollop."

Cassidy hesitated only a moment longer, and then ran off in search of Isabelle.

The game was up.

Isabelle ran blindly for the hills, to the place she had almost come to think of as sanctuary—an enchanted realm of happiness and companionship she'd believed she could never have again.

But there was no such sanctuary, no such companionship. It was all as much a lie as her own masquerade. Her body still felt weak with reaction to the double shocks: recognizing that Matthias was a Forster, and meeting Percy Sayers again.

No. Not Percy Sayers. He was Lord Leebrook now, a

marquess, untroubled by the brief scandal that had shattered the reputation of a vicar's lowly daughter.

Isabelle laughed and staggered halfway up the hill, her skirts catching at her legs. What supreme irony that Percy Sayers should be of the Forster blood. How fitting that she had come to the one great house in England where she was most likely to meet the author of her ruination. It was a circumstance for which she had never prepared herself.

The damage was done. Soon all of them would know. Lady Beatrice would see to that; she had been the one who had most influenced Percy to discard Isabelle like a soiled neckcloth.

And she *was* soiled. Soiled beyond redemption. How could she have forgotten that?

And how had she dared to trust any man again? She deserved Matthias's betrayal. He must have thought it a great joke to play the part of eccentric gallant to a poor widow. Lord Leebrook had stolen his thunder in the drawing room, but he could not have timed it more perfectly to destroy Isabelle's brief flirtation with happiness.

She stopped at the crest of the hill, winded and nauseated. Someone had followed her. She tried to move, but her legs had lost all their strength.

Matthew Forster bounded up the hill like a great lumbering hound, coattails flapping. Her heart still insisted upon doubling its beat when he approached, and she cursed it for yet another betrayal.

He was Matthew, not Matthias. Not her gentle knight. He was not even human.

But he wasn't laughing as he reached her, nor was there condescension or contempt in his green eyes. "Mrs. . . . Mrs. S-smith," he said. "I beg . . . your pardon. I should have explained—"

"What?" she said. "That your little masquerade was all

in fun? Well, I cannot chide you, Mr. Forster. I, too, have been exposed as a fraud."

His gaze dropped to the ground between his feet. "M-Matthias told me of you. But he c-can't be here today. So I came."

She stared at him. One of them was surely mad, and she was all too much aware of her own sanity. "But you are—"

"Your friend, Mrs. Smith. I w-wish to be."

She set aside her own misery and tried to make sense of his words. She knew he was Matthias; she had been too much with men not to be sure of that. This was no matter of identical twins.

But if he was Matthias, why did he refer to someone separate from himself? His patterns of speech, his demeanor, even the way he held his body were completely different from Matthias's. He was not playing a joke on her now—or, if he was, he was the greatest actor in history.

She had thought Matthias a little crazy with his fantasies of Reivers and border battles. This was something else entirely. Could one man be two people at once and not even know it?

"May I sit d-down?" Matthew asked.

Isabelle was beyond despair or incredulity. She gestured to the grass, and he sat, loose-limbed and clumsy.

"Thank you," he said. He pushed a hank of untidy iron gray hair away from his forehead. "You see, I first f-found Matthias when I was very much in n-need of a friend. He once kept me from . . . a t-terrible mistake when I w-was in disgrace. I know what it is to b-be an outsider."

"An outsider," Isabelle repeated.

"Yes. Y-years ago, I w-was to marry a woman chosen for me by m-my father, Tiberius, who was earl then. You came with Miss H-Holt, so you know h-how we Forsters do such things."

"That is one thing I do not know."

"T-Tiberius started the tradition of arranged m-marriages among us—among all the werewolves, to s-save our kind. He called his plan the C-Cause." He gave the word unmistakable emphasis.

Isabelle labored to absorb his explanation. The topic of arranged marriages made her think of Braden's former wife. Had that, too, been arranged? She had been unable to learn anything more of importance about Milena, not even from the most loose-tongued servants—which was not saying much, at Greyburn.

"The Cause," she echoed.

"Y-yes. My marriage was to be p-part of it." He laughed shortly. "But it was called off, because I was not g-good enough. My blood was not pure. I could . . . couldn't Change."

Isabelle opened her eyes. "You could not become a wolf?"

"No." He ducked his head. "I f-failed. I was of no use to the Cause. My f-father did not wish me to be n-near him. So I have lived away from Greyburn ever since. M-Matthias was m-my only friend. He stopped me, w-when I would have k—" He flushed. "He m-made me see the reason to go on living."

Good Lord. Isabelle put the puzzle together in her mind. Matthew Forster was like Cassidy, unable to Change into a wolf, and it had led him into a profound despair— profound enough to make life unbearable.

Then Matthias had appeared. A man at peace with himself, eccentric and solitary but happy to be so. A man with the resilience to find joy in life, who had nothing to prove to the *loups-garous* of Greyburn.

When they'd first met, Matthias had told her: *"Ye need not fear me, Lady. I ken, as ye do, what manner of men the Forsters be. But you're nae one of them."*

Matthew Forster *was* one of them, and yet outcast. And so Matthew Forster had become someone else. Someone human . . . and unafraid. Was that so very different from what she herself had done?

He *was* Matthias. Sitting here with him now felt almost the same as when she and Matthias shared quiet moments overlooking the peaceful valley and grazing sheep, in perfect harmony with each other, needing nothing and no one else in the world.

She shivered in the afternoon sunlight. If Cassidy was not able to Change, would she suffer the same fate as Braden's uncle: outcast, unwanted, discarded?

"I know a-about Miss Holt," Matthew said, as if he had guessed her thoughts. "My nephew Braden is . . . very much like Tiberius. He is devoted to my f-father's Cause." He met Isabelle's gaze. "Matthias . . . knew I would w-want to help, if I could."

You couldn't even face your own problems, Isabelle cried mutely. *How can you help her?* But Matthias had been her ally. She couldn't afford to reject Matthew, for Cassidy's sake.

"I will be leaving Greyburn," she said tonelessly. "Cassidy will need someone to watch over her. If you—"

"Leaving Greyburn?" He struggled to his feet. "Why?"

Didn't he know? Wouldn't Percy or Beatrice have made it abundantly clear, the instant Isabelle fled the drawing room?

"Because," she said. "I am a whore, Mr. Forster. A fallen woman. If not for Lord Leebrook, you might never have known. I returned to England for Cassidy's sake, but I will not be permitted to remain in a respectable house."

He shook his head. "What n-nonsense, Mrs. Smith," he said. "You are no—"

"But I am." She stood up, not bothering to brush the grass and earth from her dress. "I lay with Percy Sayers when I was little more than a child. He left me and married a woman of his own class. I went to America and turned to the only occupation for which I was fitted. It is only because I knew Cassidy's mother that I am here now." She laughed. "What would Matthias say to that, Mr. Forster?"

Matthew looked about as if he'd lost something he couldn't quiet recall. "I . . . d-don't—"

"You need not pretend civility, Mr. Forster," she said. "But I shall ask you to keep your promise to help Cassidy however you may. You—and Matthias."

He cast her a glance of bewilderment and pain. Isabelle looked away, and saw another figure mounting the hill . . . Cassidy, climbing as fast as her narrow skirts would allow.

Without another word, Matthew left. Cassidy barely slowed as he passed her.

"Isabelle!" she called. "Isabelle, wait—"

She forced herself to stand very still as Cassidy flung her arms about her waist. "You shouldn't have come," she said. "The others—they will think . . . I am no fit companion for you now, Cassidy. I never was."

Cassidy grabbed her hand and refused to let it go. "I don't understand what's going on, Isabelle. All I know is that when you saw Lord Leebrook, you ran. And then . . . that woman called you names—"

"With good reason." *Oh, that I could have spared you this.* "Do you remember the story I told you about my youth?"

"Yes, but—"

"Lord Leebrook was the man I loved. The man who scorned me. It was because of him that I left England."

Cassidy pressed Isabelle's hand to her face. "It must have hurt, to see him again—"

Still so innocent. "Yes, but not in the way you think, my dear. I never thought to meet him at Greyburn. But now that he is here, everyone will know." She caught her breath. "When he and I were together, I was disgraced. The rules marked me as a . . . no better than a woman who sleeps with men for money, even though I'd been with no one else. I was unfit for respectable men, good men."

"But those rules," Cassidy said fiercely. "They were for Lord Leebrook, too—"

"No. Not in our society. The woman must remain pure. Untouched—" She saw Cassidy's confusion. "You lived on a farm, Cassidy. Do you . . . know how men and woman create children?"

"Is that what you did with Lord Leebrook?"

"Yes. Because I believed I loved him. Because he asked that of me, and I could not refuse, no matter the consequences."

"But if it's what men and women do when they love each other," Cassidy said, "how could it be wrong?"

Isabelle mourned silently. "It is not always done out of real love, Cassidy. And only a woman can bear children. A man must know the children she bears are his alone. Without marriage, children have no name. That is why the rules were made. I didn't have a child, but it didn't matter. I was ruined in the eyes of society."

"It doesn't make any sense. Why should they hate you now? It ended so many years ago."

"But it didn't," Isabelle said. She freed her hand. "When you came to find me in San Francisco . . . Cassidy, I gave myself to men. For money. When I first went to America, I didn't know what else to do, or how to survive. I had no useful skills but the one Lord Leebrook had taught me. For a while, after I met your mother, I gave it up. But in the end, I went back to the life I had made for myself." She smiled bitterly. "You see, men will pay good money to be with a woman. Men, like bulls and stallions, are driven by powerful instincts that must be served, whether they are married or not. There are always women like me who will accommodate them—for a price. Love is not part of that price."

Very pale, Cassidy gazed at her. "Lord Leebrook knew what would happen when he . . . did that with you," she said. "It's not your fault. I don't care what you did in San Francisco." She gripped Isabelle's arms. "You're my friend, Isabelle. That will never change."

Tears slipped from Isabelle's control. "I can't help you now, Cassidy. My presence here will only bring you harm."

"I'll talk to Braden," Cassidy said. There was a peculiar, obstinate certainty in her voice that Isabelle had seldom heard before. She pushed a rumpled handkerchief into Isabelle's hand. "He won't make you leave."

What made the girl think she could sway Lord Greyburn? Simply because he'd kissed her?

Isabelle studied Cassidy's flushed, determined face, and realized that it had undergone a metamorphosis that had begun the moment they arrived in England.

Was it the face of a girl awakening to full womanhood—the face of a woman in love?

If Isabelle left now, she wouldn't see that final blossoming. And she would have no chance of protecting the fragile petals that could be crushed by masculine arrogance.

By Braden and his *Cause.*

"I still need you, Isabelle," Cassidy said. "Promise me you'll stay."

Promises were deadly. Isabelle was afraid: of humiliation and scorn, of the softness that had grown in her since she'd met Cassidy and Matthias. Yet she could almost believe that Cassidy would protect *her*, as she once thought to protect a naive girl.

"If it's possible," she said softly, "I shall try."

twelve

"S he cannot stay."

Rowena sat on the edge of the chair in the library, her voice eloquent with distaste and civilized affront. Braden could imagine her back ramrod-straight, the slight curl of her lip and the hauteur within her hooded eyes.

For the past three days, nothing had gone as planned. He and Quentin had failed even to locate the treacherous John Dodd, let alone capture him. All of Braden's resolve and lupine tracking skills hadn't been enough to bring the man to justice.

And during those three futile days of hunting across the countryside, Braden had been unable to put Cassidy out of his mind. She haunted him, waking and sleeping: her eager innocence in his arms, the taste of her lips and the sleek strength of her body, her fortitude after the footman's attack.

He should have been entirely focused on the final preparations for the Convocation, with all such distractions behind him.

Instead, this morning he'd returned to chaos.

"You have explained," he said, his back to Rowena,

"that Mrs. Smith is not the respectable woman she has pretended to be. What you have not explained is why the Sayerses were here in the first place."

"They are family, Braden, whatever you may believe. I had the right to ask them—"

He swung on her. "You invited them because you still believe they are allies who can help you escape your duty. It's as well they've gone, or I would have sent them away myself."

"It wasn't they who should have left," she said, rising. "It was that woman—"

"You may regard Beatrice as a second mother, and Alice as your sister, but they turned their backs on us and everything our grandfather fought for. Forget any hope of assistance from that quarter."

Her frustration and defiance was a living presence between them. "As you stated, they are gone," she said. "But that woman is still here. I demand—"

"You demand?" He smiled, and she fell silent. "I suggest that you rephrase your request, Rowena."

"You are a tyrant," she whispered. "Very well, I request that you ask that woman to leave as soon as possible. She is no fit guest in this house. She must have fooled Cassidy as she did the rest of us."

Yes, Isabelle Smith had fooled them all. She had broken all the rules of decent society, and she was Cassidy's companion. . . .

The library door swung open. Cassidy strode into the room, stretching her skirts to their widest limits in her haste.

"Braden, you're—" She checked when she saw Rowena. "Braden, I have to talk to you. It's about Isabelle. . . ."

Braden lost the thread of her words as he labored to compose himself, struggled not to breathe in Cassidy's scent or let her nearness remind him of their sharing in the wood.

"I do not believe I requested your presence, Cassidy," he said, interrupting her.

"I had to see you—"

"If you are to remain, please sit down and be quiet."

"Whatever Rowena's told you—"

"*Sit . . . down.*"

Skirts rustled and hissed contentiously. She sat down hard.

"Rowena has told me everything," he said grimly. "Did you know about Isabelle Smith's past?"

"I didn't know until today," she said. "It doesn't matter to me. Isabelle is my friend." She lifted her chin. "You can't make her leave. She's had enough trouble—"

"My dear cousin," Rowena said. "Surely you realize that such a woman is no fit companion for any respectable lady. She corrupted a man about to be married, brought embarrassment upon a good family, and was quite rightly cast out of society—"

"Enough," Braden said. "I have already made my decision. As soon as it can be arranged, a carriage will take Mrs. Smith to the train station, and accommodations will be made for her elsewhere until she can make plans to leave the country."

Cassidy stood up. "Why? You aren't even giving her a chance. I thought you would—" Her voice turned toward Rowena. "Why do you hate her so much? You hate being a werewolf. You judge Isabelle the way you think other people would judge you if they knew what you were. Does that really make you happy?"

Rowena's stunned silence was the only answer she made before she swept from the room. The door shut with an angry thump.

"You speak very freely, Cassidy," Braden said coldly. "I believe Mrs. Smith has already done you harm by her presence here. She's proven herself unworthy—"

"Because she broke the rules of your society?" Cassidy said. "Isabelle explained all about those rules. You told me that humans aren't as good as we are, but even you follow the rules they make. And you . . . in the woods, we broke the rules, too, didn't we?"

She caught him without a ready answer, springing her trap with neat ingenuity. His first instinct was to subdue her with his greater size and stronger will, dominate her with his body in the ancient manner wolf and werewolf shared alike.

But he didn't dare get so close to her. "We obey the rules that preserve our people," he said. "Humans are flawed even in their mating. *We* mate for life, Cassidy. That, too, makes us superior."

Even as he spoke, he knew he lied. Milena taunted him from the grave—Milena, who was the true equal of Isabelle Smith.

"Then werewolves are never wrong," Cassidy said. "They never make mistakes."

Did even Cassidy dare to mock him? "I will not justify myself or my decisions to you."

"But you won't tell me anything," she said. He could hear her, feel her coming toward him. "Isabelle hasn't done you any harm." Suddenly she was touching him; coldness turned to blazing heat, resentment to hunger. She overwhelmed his every thought, every intention.

"Why are you so angry, Braden?" she asked. "You want everyone to believe you don't care about hurting people, but all the time you're hurting, too."

He grabbed her arms. "You know nothing of me," he snapped. "You're an ignorant, half-human child. You can't even Change—"

"You haven't given me the chance. Just like you won't give Isabelle the chance." She pulled away. "It isn't fair."

"*No.*" He jerked her nearer, feeling her heartbeat through her bodice and his waistcoat. "It is seldom fair."

She stiffened, and then her body went boneless against him, sinking into his hold. Her arms below his grip bent so that her hands lay flat against his ribs.

"Why do you make this wall around yourself?" she whispered. "I spent most of my life alone, wishing for someone to share with. But you have your family. You have . . ." She broke off, settling her cheek on his chest. His heart slammed a frantic drumbeat. "You lost someone you loved. I know what that's like. We aren't very different at all." His grip on her loosened, and she took the lapels of his coat in her hands. "Give us both another chance."

He didn't know quite how it happened; one moment she was speaking, and the next she was pressing her lips to his. The first kiss had been an exploration; this was deliberate action. Cassidy knew what she was doing. She had learned from his single lesson. Her lips parted, inviting him to do the same. He groaned and caught her around the waist, deepening the kiss, taking control of it.

There was no point in denying it any longer. He was profoundly, dangerously attracted to her, in every way— not only to her freshness and unaffected honesty, to her simple courage, but to her woman's body with its mane of hair and lush curves, the face under his fingertips both stubborn and lovely.

He couldn't view her as an abstract, a carefully placed game piece in the great Cause. She was less than he'd hoped, and yet she had become more than he'd ever anticipated. It wasn't her strict obedience he wanted now, or her susceptibility to his power and authority. But he did *want*. Oh, yes. He wanted very badly.

If he let this continue, it wouldn't stop until he had

that firm young body naked in his arms again. And he wouldn't have the strength to walk away, as he had in the wood.

If he took her, she would be ruined for Quentin, or for any other worthy mate. *He* was not worthy. Passion had blinded him before. His lust would betray the Cause, not further it.

He drew back abruptly. She murmured a protest. "Braden—"

"I will speak to Mrs. Smith," he said. "I will give her the chance you wish. Will that satisfy you?"

"Isabelle? Yes." Her breath shaped a sigh. "I knew you would—"

"Go. Send her to me."

He made it a dismissal she couldn't contest. If she chose to interpret this as a victory, he would let her so believe. It was better than the alternative.

And Mrs. Smith might yet serve a purpose.

"Thank you," Cassidy said quietly. Her step was a little unsteady as she made her way to the door.

He sat down heavily in the chair and tried to regain the cool detachment that had once been so easy for him.

Isabelle was fully prepared to be ejected from the house when she saw Lord Greyburn's face. No other man she'd known in her long years of experience could project so much anger and menace with such a lack of expression.

But that stony face didn't mean he couldn't feel. No, indeed. She tried to remember that as she walked into the room and stood before him. He did not invite her to sit.

"I am permitting you to stay at Greyburn, for Cassidy's sake," he said without preamble. "You will conduct your-self with complete propriety while you remain. I will see that your things are transferred to a room in the family wing. When my guests arrive, you will remain confined to that wing alone. Is that clear?"

"Abundantly," she said.

"I'll brook no insolence from you, Mrs. Smith," he said, "if that is indeed your name. I know what you are. Your position here is precarious at best. If I learn your unchaste habits have in any way affected my cousin—"

"*My* habits?" she said, outrage overcoming caution. "Cassidy told me how you kissed her." She caught his flinch because she was watching for it. "Yes, I know men, Lord Greyburn. And I know when a man wants a woman, the way you want Cassidy."

"You dare to suggest—"

"I suggest that you have encouraged Cassidy to believe that she is falling in love with you—though she has only the barest notion of what she feels. I suggest that your motives are no more pure than those of any man who would use a woman as I was used."

For a moment she half believed that he would turn into a wolf right there before her, Change and leap on her and tear the life from her body. His growl—there was no other word for the sound he made—seemed to shake the very floor beneath her feet. She closed her eyes and stood her ground until she heard him move away.

"You measure everything by your own taint," he said. "You see evil where there is only—" He stopped himself. "My sister was correct in her judgment of you."

She laughed a little wildly, knowing she had nothing left to lose. "I know of your Cause. Perhaps it was originally your intention to control her through her attachment to you. Men fool themselves so easily. What was it that Burns said? 'The best laid schemes o' mice an' men gang aft a-gley.' Surely that applies even to werewolves."

The earl surprised her by sitting in his chair and casually stretching out his legs, as if their conversation were all informal civility.

"You wish to know my plans for Cassidy?" he said. "Perhaps it will set your mind at ease to know that I never intended her for myself." His words were heavy with sarcasm. "She is destined to aid our Cause by marrying my brother."

Her mind went blank. "Quentin? But—"

"It was settled on the evening she arrived at the London house," he said. "Cassidy is strong and healthy and can bear many children in the service of our people. She will remain within the family, and have everything she will need or want for the rest of her life."

Reason flooded back, and with it a righteous anger that renewed the old hatred. "So Cassidy is to be a brood mare to keep your line pure."

"It is no different from the arranged marriages made between great human families," he said, "and to a far more noble end. What would have become of her without us? Do you wish your own fate on Cassidy, Mrs. Smith? Discarded, despised, belonging nowhere?"

She sucked in her breath. "You Forsters have great skill in twisting everything to your own advantage," she said, "especially the vulnerabilities of those you would rule. I am no match for you, Lord Greyburn. And yet I wonder why you have not been so frank with Cassidy herself. Why do you fear to tell her what you've told me?"

"She required time to adjust, to become one of us—"

"I heard of another Forster who did not live up to your expectations and was cast out as worthless. Cassidy has not been able to Change into a wolf, has she? If she fails, will you exile her as well?"

The earl of Greyburn was very still. "This conversation

is at an end, Mrs. Smith. Be prepared to move to your new quarters within the hour."

In spite of all her boldness, she'd achieved nothing. Her defiance was as useless as pride. She walked slowly to his chair and bowed her head. "I beg you, Lord Greyburn. Don't hurt her."

He stood, forcing her to step back. "You have but one part to play at Greyburn," he said, "and that is to discourage Cassidy from believing I have any personal regard for her. It should be no difficulty in light of your obvious antipathy for me." His voice was utterly flat. "She will be cared for. You have my word."

"The word of a Forster."

"*My* word, Mrs. Smith. Do not confuse me with Lord Leebrook or his kind. He disgraced himself as much as he ever did you. It will not happen again."

Such an admission must have cost him much. He lifted his head and turned toward the door. "You are dismissed, Mrs. Smith. I have business to attend to. Remember what I've said."

The door swung open before she could reply or retreat. Quentin walked in, agitation plain in his movements.

"Mrs. Smith," he said with a distracted glance. "I beg your pardon, but I must speak to my brother—"

She studied him, armed with the knowledge that Cassidy was meant to be his wife. He was a kind enough man; he alone of his siblings didn't look upon Isabelle as if she were a whore.

But he did not love Cassidy, of that Isabelle was certain. Nor did she love him—if Cassidy had more than the faintest grasp of what love entailed.

All men, human or otherwise, were fools.

"Thank you, Mr. Forster," she said to Quentin. "I was just leaving."

•   •   •

"You wanted me to inform you as soon as the first guests entered Greyburn land," Quentin said when he and Braden were alone.

Braden struggled to wrench his thoughts from Isabelle and her accusations. It wasn't easy; she and Cassidy had chosen the worst possible time to rattle the very foundations of the world he had built.

In telling Isabelle of his plans for Quentin and Cassidy, he'd removed any possibility of further misunderstanding. But he had taken a grave risk. Cassidy had yet to prove she could Change, and if she married Quentin lacking that proof, Quentin's heritage might be wasted.

But he had to put such worries aside. Now he must bend all his concentration to the gathering that was about to begin. He'd sent Quentin out to watch for the arrival of the Convocation delegates; his return meant that the first guests would be here in less than an hour.

Not for a single moment could he allow any of the delegates to sense weakness in him or any of the Forsters—physical, mental, or emotional. The Forster blood must be strong, invulnerable. Cassidy would be kept apart from the other *loups-garous*, so that they never had the opportunity to guess that she was not fully one of them.

As for Rowena . . . her selected American mate would claim her at this very Convocation. Soon enough she'd learn what it was to submit to her proper destiny.

He turned to Quentin, who waited in silence for his recognition. "Well?"

"The first guests are approaching Greyburn," Quentin said. There was a strain in his voice that was more than the fatigue of a long run and Change. "The German and Hungarian delegates, and one of the Spaniards. But—Braden, there's someone we didn't expect."

Braden felt a chill of premonition. "Boroskov," he said.

"Yes." Quentin walked across the room and flopped into a chair. "Stefan, Fedor, and a woman I don't recognize. I knew damned well that you didn't invite them—"

"No." Braden rang for Aynsley. When the butler appeared, Braden asked him to send for Telford, Mrs. Fairbairn, and the head groom. He instructed each personally, impressing upon them the urgency of the situation, and dismissed them. He turned to Quentin.

"There can be only one reason why Milena's brothers have come to Greyburn."

Quentin had procured himself a drink, which he inhaled with great concentration. "Indeed," he said.

"If there was ever a time we must be united, it is now. Should we fail, should we show any sign of weakness, Milena's kin will do their best to destroy all we've worked for."

"The Cause, you mean."

"Do you think they'll stop with the Cause?" He turned toward the window, as if he could see the approaching threat. "When I last met Stefan, he cursed me. I knew the matter was not resolved, but he and Fedor were chastened enough to return to Russia without a fight. Evidently they have found courage—or hatred—enough to challenge me."

"I don't suppose," Quentin said softly, "that they're here to make peace?"

"Peace? I'd accept no peace with their perverted blood. You deceive yourself, Quentin. If they can, they'll kill me and take control of the Convocation. Can you doubt the outcome?"

Quentin shifted uncomfortably. "Did they know three years ago that you were—"

"Blind? No. I concealed it then, at the time of Milena's

death. Now—" He smiled, almost wishing for one of Quentin's poisonous libations. "They'll know soon enough. When they arrive, we will meet them with indifference and shall force them to make the first move."

"Let me take the challenge," Quentin said suddenly. "Stefan is—"

"I know what Stefan is." He felt a rush of gratitude that Quentin, who abhorred violence, had offered to take his place.

"You know the rules Tiberius worked to establish," he said. "He is head of his family, I of mine. He may challenge me for leadership of the Convocation—and because of what he is, he won't stop until he destroys the Cause and the Forster line. That includes Rowena, Quentin. And Cassidy."

Quentin's face had gone as serious as Braden could wish. "I'll speak to Rowena. She'll understand the need for a united front."

And so she should. Whatever her loathing of the marriage arranged for her, she knew that her fate would be far worse if left to Stefan.

Stefan would never settle for anything less than full challenge. Blind or not, Braden was prepared. He had always been prepared, worked to harden his body and hone his remaining senses—and now he was eager for the inevitable duel.

To fight for one's life was easy. No conflicting emotions, no inconvenient complications. As a wolf in battle, Braden would know only the need to protect what was his and defeat his enemy. His heart would beat and his blood would flow to the ancient rhythms of the earth, unblemished by the pollution of man.

Rowena and Quentin were both at his side, poised and serene, when the first carriages arrived bearing the German and Hungarian delegates. The Spaniard came behind the Germans, a flamboyant young man who was succeeding his father as delegate to the Convocation.

The Russians delayed their appearance until well after the delegates were settled in their rooms in the guest wing. A light dinner had been sent to each chamber, and the guests had just gathered for the first informal assembly in the drawing room when the Russian's elegant carriage pulled up in the drive. Leaving Rowena to entertain the guests, Braden took Quentin to meet his enemies at the front steps.

Count Stefan Boroskov languidly descended from the carriage, aided by what sounded like a large retinue of servants scurrying to and fro. Braden could no longer see the Russian, but he remembered how much Stefan resembled Milena—more than resembled her, with his white-blond hair skimming his shoulders and his dandy's clothing obscenely expensive and hinting of eastern exoticism.

He was exactly like his sister in his elegance, his sophistication, his frightening beauty. His laughing, malicious gaze was a mirror image of hers, steeped in years of hedonism and every vice known to man.

Or *loup-garou.*

"Ah," Stefan said in accented English, strolling forward. "How pleasant to see you again, Lord Greyburn. We parted under such . . . unfortunate circumstances. Our invitation to this gathering must have gone astray somewhere between England and Russia. Naturally we did not wish to miss the first Convocation since our mutual loss."

If Stefan expected a welcome, he was to be sorely disappointed. Braden pinpointed the direction of Stefan's voice and stared, unblinking, careful not to reveal a single thought or emotion.

"You have come a long way, Count," he said. "I fear

that you may find this Convocation of little interest to your family."

"Indeed? And yet here I have a marriageable brother—you do remember Fedor, do you not? And my cousin Tasya, who begged to come." Braden heard the other two Russians move to join the count. He identified Fedor's scent; the woman was a stranger. Braden nodded to her, immediately aware that she was afraid. Neither Fedor nor Tasya spoke.

"Your brother I recall from years ago, before he joined the army," Stefan said. "Quentin, I believe? You've become quite a man, I see." His voice turned toward Braden again. "Have you a mate selected for the Honorable Quentin Forster, Lord Greyburn? Perhaps I may even suggest our Tasya?"

"This is not the time or place for such a discussion," Braden said.

"Of course. I trust we are not the last to arrive?"

"Our guests are in the drawing room, and the other delegates will arrive over the next two days. The Convocation will not begin until all are assembled. You're likely to find the amenities at Greyburn . . . not at all to your taste, Count Boroskov."

"Not to my taste? I disagree. There are so many wholesome pastimes to pursue in your pleasant English countryside." His words alone seemed to foul his surroundings with the promise of debauchery. "If nothing else, there will be the charming company of your sister, Lady Rowena. She is not yet wed, I hear, though somewhat . . . shall we say, overripe?"

So it began—Stefan's first attempt to provoke Braden into anger. But Braden wouldn't give the Russian that much advantage. As long as he remained unshakably in control, he held the upper hand as his grandfather's heir and leader of the Convocation. It was a primal game of thrust and parry born long before man used edged weapons in battle—just as deadly, but played as much with the mind and will as with tooth and claw.

"I hear you've a new addition to the family," Stefan continued. "An American cousin—lovely and inexperienced, I'm told, but delectable. Cassidy . . . most unusual. I am eager to make her acquaintance."

Braden stopped himself from taking the Russian's bait. If Stefan knew of Cassidy, he had been watching the Forsters for many days—possibly in London as well as at Greyburn.

"Miss Holt," Braden said carefully, "is in seclusion. She will not take part in this Convocation."

"A pity. I shall hope that changes before this meeting is over. And now, if you will be so kind, we should like to be shown our rooms."

The only alternative to acquiescence was open challenge. Braden gestured to Aynsley, who was ready with footmen to assist the Russian servants with the Boroskov's luggage. The Russians didn't travel light, and though the days of serfs were past, the count delighted in a large retinue of obsequious human underlings.

Braden had arranged to put the Russians in a suite of rooms as far as possible from the other guests—and from the family wing. Well-placed footmen would report immediately if either Stefan or his brother ventured where they should not go. Braden himself escorted the Russians up to their suite, Quentin at his side for good measure. Beyond such precautions, there was little to do but wait.

But Stefan, it seemed, had no interest in waiting. After a brief inspection of his suite, he made clear that he and his relatives wished to join the other guests as soon as possible. "Rest can come later," he said. "It has been long since we walked among our own kind beyond the borders of Russia. I do not intend to miss a moment of this delightful company. Come, Tasya; Fedor will see to the servants."

The small hairs stood erect along the back of Braden's neck as he and Quentin led the two Russians to the drawing room. Instinctively he listened for the sound of Cassidy's voice, or the drift of her unique scent—anything that would betray her presence. But she was safe in her room, with Telford himself guarding her door, and Stefan descended the stairs without showing undue interest in the family wing.

Stefan Boroskov would not touch the tip of Cassidy's smallest finger unless it was over Braden's shattered body.

thirteen

Cassidy lassoed the chair by the fireplace for the hundredth time, pulled the noose tight and let the rope fall, listening once again for the distant voices and music echoing up from the drawing room.

Since the first werewolf guests had arrived at Greyburn several hours ago, she'd been a virtual prisoner. She hadn't spoken to or seen Braden after their last conversation in the library; he'd conveyed his "wishes" that she remain in her room via Telford, who still lingered in the corridor outside like a jailer. Even Isabelle was confined to her new room down the corridor, permitted to stay only on condition of complete isolation from the *loups-garous* at Greyburn.

From her window facing the drive, Cassidy had watched the third set of guests arrive—the pale-haired man, his darker male companion, and the not-young, not-old woman accompanying them. Though Cassidy hadn't been able to hear the brief conversation between Braden and the newcomers, she'd known immediately that something was very wrong. The stance of Braden's body, the way the pale-haired man looked at him . . . the blatant hostility sent shivers racing up her spine. She'd almost flung open the window and shouted to Braden to watch out for the attack she was sure must come at any moment.

But she hadn't. Braden would not have thanked her. He didn't want her among the delegates. He had agreed to give Isabelle a chance, but not her. She still wasn't part of his Cause.

Cassidy gathered up the rope and twisted it in her fingers. It gave her too-long idle hands an occupation, practicing knots and roping inoffensive pieces of furniture while her mind went over and over the events of the past two days.

In New Mexico, she'd been good at some things, like working cattle and tracking. At Greyburn, it seemed that no matter how hard she tried, she did everything wrong. Especially where Braden was concerned.

She couldn't Change, but she'd been sure that learning was only a matter of time—and being with Braden. When he returned to Greyburn, she'd wanted so badly to re-create the perfect union they'd shared in the woods. *That* was how it was meant to be.

But Braden wasn't a hero out of a romantic poem or a paragon far above all uncertainty and loneliness. He was hurting, and yet he rejected any help. His words pushed her away, but his body urged her into his arms.

Isabelle's explanations about men and their instincts kept running through Cassidy's mind like a herd of stampeding cattle. She'd asked Cassidy if she knew how men and women made children. Until she met Braden, that subject had been very cloudy to Cassidy, something that didn't have much to do with her life.

Suddenly feeling very warm, Cassidy tossed the rope on the bed and went to the washstand to splash water on her face.

If not for Braden's kisses, she might still not understand. They had made her feel light as air and hot as fire all at once. Men had wanted Isabelle enough to pay her to do more than kiss them—and not for babies. *That* . . . what Isabelle had talked about . . . was what might have happened if Braden hadn't left her in the woods.

Isabelle had said it didn't always have to do with love. But the first time, she *had* been in love. Lord Leebrook had ruined it for her, ever after, and she'd been blamed.

The rules of society made little sense to Cassidy, and the meaning of "love" was still a muddle of tangled emotions and lines of poetry.

Cassidy went to the small shelf that held her few books brought from America. She thumbed through them one by one. The answers were there, if she could only interpret them. She found a poem by Coleridge:

> *All thoughts, all passions, all delights*
> *Whatever stirs this mortal frame,*
> *All are but ministers of Love,*
> *And feed his sacred flame.*

Braden's kisses were delights. Love meant wanting to be with someone all the time, in every way.

Cassidy stared at her damp face in the mirror above the washstand. Braden had said that *loups-garous* mated for life. If two werewolves shared that with each other, they would stay together. Forever.

Milena was dead. Braden had never mentioned her. But it seemed, more and more, that Milena was still here at Greyburn. And Cassidy wasn't a true *loup-garou*.

But she wasn't going to give up. Not now. There had to be a way. . . .

"Cassidy?"

Isabelle's voice, muffled but recognizable, came through the door. Cassidy dried her face and answered, offering Isabelle the chair near the fireplace.

"I'm glad you came," she said. "I've been trapped here since noon."

"Yes. We are both exiles, are we not?" Isabelle spoke lightly, but her gaze was very grave and steady. Sadness hung about her like an invisible veil, and Cassidy knew its cause. It wasn't just because nearly everyone at Greyburn despised her. She had lost a person very dear to her, whether he went by the name of Matthew or Matthias. He'd left Isabelle on the hill, and he hadn't been back since.

"I know how difficult it's been for you," Cassidy said, kneeling beside the chair. "I should never have asked you to stay—"

"No. There is a reason for my being here, if only because I know so much more of life." She cupped Cassidy's chin. "I must not let you go on in ignorance of the plans the earl has for you."

Cassidy's heart jumped. "Rowena and Quentin told me about Braden's plans, but they didn't explain—"

"I doubt they would dare." She sighed. "Cassidy, you deserve to know that Braden has already settled your future as part of his Cause. He is using arranged marriages to save the werewolf race from dying out—"

"I know. Braden wants Rowena to marry a man she's never even met. It isn't right—"

"No, it is not. Lord Greyburn intends that you should be simply another pawn in his strategy. His plans for you, Cassidy—" She lowered her gaze.

Cassidy closed her eyes and held her breath.

"He has decided that you are to marry his brother, Quentin."

"Marry . . . *Quentin?*"

"I believe the earl intended this all along," Isabelle said quietly. "He determined that his breeding program will best be served when you and Quentin produce children. You will remain safely within the family, but are not too nearly related to the Forsters to create . . . difficulties." She shuddered. "Oh, Cassidy, would that I could have spared you this."

Cassidy sat down on the edge of the bed, numbly coiling the rope between her fingers. She'd been worried that Braden didn't consider her truly a werewolf or part of his Cause—and now Isabelle said that he expected her to . . . wanted her for . . .

Quentin. A man Cassidy liked. A brother. Not someone whose kiss could make music in her blood and send lightning shooting from her head to her toes.

"Why Quentin?" she demanded. "Why not . . ."

Isabelle's eyes were filled with pity. "I don't know. The earl did not choose to share his reasons with me."

Nor had he shared them with Cassidy. He could have explained countless times, and had chosen not to. Instead, he'd begun to make her imagine, hope, believe in things she hadn't known were possible until he came into her life.

But Braden didn't want her.

Pain shot up Cassidy's arm, and she realized she had wrapped the rope so tightly around it that she'd nearly cut off the flow of blood. Her teeth were clenched, and her heart pounded. Of all the new feelings Braden inspired, this was the one that scared her most.

Anger. She tasted the emotion cautiously, like an unfamiliar seasoning. She was *angry* at Braden, in a way she'd never been before.

In New Mexico, she had become used to her place as an unwanted orphan. Her aunt and uncle, in spite of their indifference and Aunt Harriet's small cruelties, could never upset her for long. She could lose herself in work or in her books. And there'd always been the knowledge that her life would be so much better someday, if she could only be patient.

At Greyburn it was different. Little by little, like a rattlesnake waking up to the sun, unfamiliar anger uncoiled from some hidden place inside. She hadn't recognized it at first, but now she knew. She'd been *angry* with the rules that made Isabelle suffer, *angry* with Lord Leebrook, *angry* with Rowena. In the library, she had even dared to challenge Braden's decision about Isabelle.

This anger was strongest of all. Personal. Scorching as the desert on a summer afternoon. The more she tried to wish it away, the stronger it became. It was a wild animal trapped behind her ribs, frantic and formidable, trying to claw its way out.

"Cassidy." Someone touched her arm. She sprang up from the bed, and Isabelle recoiled.

"I'm sorry," Isabelle said, hugging herself. "If only I'd known—"

"I *am* a foolish child," Cassidy said. The words came out clipped and short and hard, like Braden's so often were. Now she knew why they sounded that way. "You and Rowena tried to warn me, but I didn't understand."

"How could you?" Isabelle said. "Men were born to deceive women, and use them. It's in their blood, human or otherwise."

A fresh burst of music came up from the drawing room. Cassidy marched to the door and put her ear to the wood, then opened it a crack. Telford was gone.

Milena's perfect features filled her mind. What would she have done now? Rowena said she was obedient and good. Maybe that was why Braden loved her. But being good hadn't helped Cassidy.

Her mouth formed a crooked smile that felt strange on her face.

"I'm not waiting in this room for other people to decide my future," she said. "If I am part of Braden's Cause, I should be with the others. I'm going to go down, Isabelle."

Isabelle stood up and smoothed her dark skirts. "A few days ago I might have discouraged you from such rebellion, Cassidy," she said. "But not today. Not anymore." She went to the wardrobe and drew out Cassidy's best evening dress. "Let me help you don your armor."

When Isabelle was finished with her, Cassidy knew she was as ready as she'd ever be to face the guests she was forbidden to meet. Isabelle opened the door and pronounced the way clear, then kissed Cassidy's cheek and wished her good luck.

There were servants in the corridor and by the staircase, but no sign of Telford. Cassidy could have used stealth to cross the house, but she chose to walk tall and bold, impelled by the anger that smoldered low and steady in her chest. Several of the footmen she passed seemed about to speak or move to stop her, but she looked at them and they fell silent, exactly as if she'd been Braden himself.

That was a power she knew was wrong, and they had no reason to fear her. But she took the advantage she was offered. She reached the drawing room in a matter of minutes. Aynsley, who waited just outside the doors with maids and footmen, glanced at her in some trepidation but didn't block her way.

Tension struck her like a tangible force the moment she entered the drawing room. She paused just inside the doorway, disoriented by the heavy sense of mingled ill will, anxiety, and wariness. No one noticed her, and she was able to make a quick assessment of the people gathered there.

Braden was far across the room and his back was to

her, but she knew from his posture that he was waiting—waiting and watching for something to happen, and not something good. Danger was in every line of his body under the perfectly cut evening clothes.

Except for Braden's stance and the pall of apprehension in the air, the gathering would have seemed like an ordinary party of acquaintances. Rowena sat at the piano, playing a lively melody as if nothing were wrong. Quentin stood beside her, turning the pages of the music. There were seven other people in the room: three women and four men, one of whom was speaking to Braden. One couple was dancing to Rowena's music. Another man and woman stood off to themselves, and the remaining couple sat at the chairs grouped next to the piano. All of them wore neutral or pleasant expressions, and every single one was a mask.

What were they trying to conceal?

She raised her chin and stepped into the room.

Quentin, at least, had seen her. He left the piano and strode to her side.

"Cassidy," he whispered, taking her arm. "It wasn't such a good idea for you to come down this evening."

She pulled her arm from his grasp. "Don't you think I have a right to know what's going on?"

His gaze swept over her as if he were seeing a stranger. "As a matter of fact, I do. But it's far more complicated than you can possibly—"

"Understand? How do you know when you won't give me a chance—or tell me the truth?" She stared at him, and he was the first to look away. "Will you tell me the truth, Quentin?"

He looked up, the corner of his mouth twisted into a wry smile. "I'll do my best, but there won't be much time for explanations."

"Something is about to happen, isn't it?" she said. "I can feel it. What's wrong?"

With a quick glance around the room, he drew her close to the wall. "What you sense is only to be expected whenever so many werewolves of different families gather together," he said. "It is natural among us to defend our territory and challenge those who would trespass. These assemblies are relatively new among our kind. We've learned to set aside instinct in favor of civilization—and survival." His smile was openly mocking now. "If we had not, there would be none of us left to further Braden's Cause."

The Cause. Always the Cause. She took in a deep breath of the stifling air and shook her head. "There's more to it than that. I—"

But Quentin had stepped aside to make way for another. Braden claimed Cassidy's hand and looped it through his elbow, pinning her fingers to his sleeve.

For just an instant his expression promised terrible retribution for her disobedience. But the man to whom he'd been speaking was only a step behind him, and Braden's dispassionate mask slipped quickly back into place.

The stranger was dark-haired, mustachioed, and handsome, with sharp features and tanned skin. He looked from Cassidy to Braden, one eyebrow arched.

"May I be permitted an introduction?" he asked.

"Miss Holt," Braden said with stiff formality, "may I present Don Alarico Julian Del Fiero, delegate from the premier *loup-garou* family of Spain. Don Alarico, this is my cousin from America, Miss Cassidy Holt."

"Miss Holt," Don Alarico said, bowing with a flourish. "I am enchanted."

Cassidy curtsyed. *"Buenos noches, señor. Qué te parece Inglaterra?"*

He laughed with delight. "You speak my language! *Como no voy a amar a Inglaterra estando usted aqui, señorita?* Lord Greyburn, how is it that I did not know of your delightful cousin?"

"I grew up in New Mexico," Cassidy said. "I—"

"Miss Holt arrived in England only a short while ago," Braden said. He managed to pull Cassidy still closer to his side. "Her parents are dead, and she has become one of our family."

"And an ornament she is, indeed," the Spaniard said. "Nuevo Mexico must weep to have lost her." He looked at Cassidy with open appreciation.

"Have you ever been to New Mexico?" she asked Don Alarico. "It's beautiful here, but sometimes I miss the desert."

The Spaniard nodded. "*Yo comprendo.* I have not yet been to your country, but in Spain—" He broke off and cocked his head. "Ah, the music. Perfect for dancing."

The music had changed, from something soft and unobtrusive to a light waltz. Rowena, at the piano, had a fixed smile on her face. The seated man and woman were now on their feet, positioned for dancing.

"With your permission, Lord Greyburn?" Del Fiero said. "*Señorita,* may I have the honor of this dance?"

Cassidy flushed. "I'm sorry, *señor.* I never learned how."

"Then perhaps I shall teach you," he said. "I have no doubt that you shall be *magnífica.*" He held out his hand.

Braden maneuvered Cassidy so that she was behind him. "Forgive me, Don Alarico, but I claim this dance."

The Spaniard stared at Braden, gave a brief bow, and backed away. "Of course, my lord. I shall be patient."

Before Cassidy could react, Braden swept her into his arms. It wasn't quite an embrace; he held her a little apart from himself, placing her left hand on his shoulder and putting his right arm around her waist. Then, in time to the music, he began to move—guiding her in the kind of graceful motions she'd only glimpsed through the windows of her aunt's drawing room.

She knew she was clumsy. The snug gown didn't make learning any easier, and she hadn't dismissed her anger at Braden. But the music created a kind of magic, and Braden was gazing down at her with an intensity that made his blindness seem unimportant. His fingers curled around her waist were very warm and strong, his clasp of her other hand possessive. Two other couples shared the center of the room, but Cassidy barely noticed.

Braden swept her about the floor, and she nearly forgot the tension, her resolve to seek answers, even the outrage that had brought her downstairs in the first place. The music, the dance took her to another world. It was like the woods, when she and Braden were in such perfect accord for a few precious moments. Braden's face was near hers, its severity gentled by the melody; his lips were slightly parted, and she could have sworn that he, too, had almost forgotten they weren't alone.

Didn't he realize that this place out of time was where they both belonged? Didn't it seem as right to him as it did to her? Was it possible that he didn't feel these quivers of hot and cold, this reckless need to press every part of her body against every part of his, with nothing in between?

There was only one way to find out. She had to speak to him, now, before he found a way to dismiss her again.

She was considering how to shift the direction of their circling so that they would move toward the drawing room door when another stranger stepped into their path. Immediately, before she could think it through, Cassidy understood that the source of all the tension, all the ill will in the room, was here.

Here, in *this* man, who smiled beautifully but without any of the Spaniard's sincerity. His hair was long and pale and flowed about his shoulders like an angel's. His skin, too, was pale, his face held unearthly charm, and his eyes glittered silver in the lamplight.

He looked unmistakably like the portrait of Milena.

"So this is the mysterious Miss Holt, of whom I've heard so much," he said. "And you keep her from us, Lord Greyburn. You must share such a treasure with your guests, or we may believe you are lacking in hospitality."

Braden's hand was crushing Cassidy's. "My hospitality is limitless . . . for my guests. Miss Holt was just on her way back to her room."

"But she hardly looks in need of a rest. Indeed, she appears quite . . . ripe for the pleasures of our assembly." He looked Cassidy up and down in a way very different from Del Fiero's courteous appreciation. "Since your guardian seems unwilling to introduce us, I shall take the liberty myself. I am Stefan, Count Boroskov, of Russia."

Abruptly the piano fell mute. The two other couples trailed to a halt. Cassidy saw every face in the room turn toward Braden and Stefan. Rowena stood up from the bench, hands braced above the keyboard. Quentin took a step forward and stopped again.

"So quiet, Miss Holt?" Boroskov said. "That is not what I've heard of you. I appreciate the refreshing candor of the Americans. It makes them so . . . unrestrained." His silver eyes skimmed over her again, and she knew that somehow he was imagining her without her clothes, naked and vulnerable.

What would have been wonderful with Braden was somehow shameful and dirty with Boroskov. She met the Russian's stare. "I only talk when I have something to say."

Boroskov laughed. "A bit of spirit, as well. Excellent.

She might be even more interesting to bed than I'd hoped, eh, Greyburn?"

"Silence," Braden snarled. "Keep your damned mouth—"

"But aren't we all here for that very purpose?" Boroskov said, a sneer in his voice. "To mate and perpetuate the species?" He snatched Cassidy's free hand. "Getting Miss Holt with child would be a most pleasurable experiment. Give her to one of us. I assure you that we know how to satisfy our females."

Braden pulled Cassidy's hand from Boroskov's grip and thrust her behind him. She landed in Quentin's arms. Braden spun to confront the Russian, teeth bared.

Cassidy struggled in Quentin's grip. The men had been locking horns over her, but she knew she was only an excuse—an excuse for the battle both obviously wanted.

"Rowena, please escort the ladies outside," Braden said.

His sister hesitated, then stepped away from the piano. "Ladies, if you will be so good as to accompany me to the garden."

The three women guests glanced at one another, at Cassidy, and at Rowena. The smallest one, with mouse brown hair, joined Rowena at the piano, followed by a tall, blond woman of middle age. The third woman, younger and dark, stood firm.

"We have a right to witness," she said in a heavy accent.

"You will be kept informed," Braden said. "Now, go."

The woman cast him a narrow-eyed look, but obeyed. Rowena took Cassidy's arm. "We must go outside," she said.

Cassidy held her ground. "Why?"

"Do not make things worse than they already are," Rowena whispered. "There is still a chance . . ." She broke off and, with surprising strength, tugged Cassidy toward the garden doors. The other ladies followed.

"Miss Holt," Boroskov called after them, "I am certain

we shall get to know each other better very soon. Much, much better."

Only Rowena's grip kept Cassidy moving. The tension among the women was every bit as acute as it had been within the drawing room.

"Rowena, tell me what's going on," Cassidy demanded when they were gathered outside. "They're about to fight, aren't they?"

"You can do nothing to interfere," Rowena said. Her voice was ragged and harsh with loathing. "This is what comes of the beast in us." She walked away and stood alone, arms wrapped about her ribs.

"Miss Holt."

The woman who spoke was the small, brown-haired guests who'd been first to go to Rowena. Cassidy recognized her accent; it was exactly the same as Boroskov's. Immediately she went on her guard.

But the Russian woman seemed both anxious and afraid, glancing over her shoulder toward the doors as if she expected attack. "My name is Tasya," she said. "I am Count Boroskov's cousin. Please, there is something I must tell you. A life is at stake. I did not know who else to approach." She looked toward Rowena and shuddered. "You must know, since you are to be Lord Greyburn's mate."

Cassidy opened her mouth to contradict the Russian woman, but Tasya was still speaking with undeniable urgency.

"This is my only chance," she said. "My cousins will stop me if they know." She caught timidly at Cassidy's sleeve. "You must help to save Lord Greyburn's son."

fourteen

Every man in the room knew what was to come.

Braden had allowed himself to believe that Boroskov would be more subtle. He'd been prepared to watch the Russian every minute until he made his first move—for days, perhaps, even until the very end of the Convocation.

His judgment had been badly flawed. The waiting was at an end almost before it began. Boroskov was impatient. But so was Braden. The Russian's insult to Cassidy was an outrage that could not be allowed to pass unchallenged.

Braden struggled to master his mindless fury. When Boroskov spoke to Cassidy, *of* her, as if she were a mere object of lust, his self-control had almost snapped. Every primitive impulse demanded that he attack the Russian without warning, oblivious to Tiberius's careful rules of challenge.

Such a lunatic action would have ended in disaster. He needed the icy dispassion that came of absolute focus on survival. If he failed to uphold his leadership now, he would lose it. The Cause would be damaged irrevocably.

His weakness would be an open invitation to any other *loup-garou* who wished to break his dominance.

No other werewolf would get the chance. His blindness was a disadvantage, but he must defeat the Russian nevertheless. Nothing else was acceptable. It wasn't a matter of saving his own life—that alone was of little value.

But the Cause was at stake. The Cause—and Cassidy's fate. Boroskov had not been making idle threats. If he won, he would use Cassidy for his own vile pleasures. He would see that Rowena suffered as well. Quentin, too, would die attempting to avenge his brother.

It could not happen. No one else would ever touch Cassidy. . . .

He shook himself and faced Boroskov. The ritual must proceed correctly, step by step. To kill one of their own kind was a grave matter among the *loups-garous*, and this would be a battle to the death.

The room was deathly silent.

"Why have you come here, Boroskov?" he asked.

The Russian laughed softly. "You know, Greyburn. We have both known since I arrived. My brother and I have waited long enough for our vengeance." His voice swept the assembly. "Hear me. This hypocrite married my sister for the sake of his precious Cause, but he could not prove himself a mate worthy of her. When in his insane jealousy he sought to enslave her like a serf, she asked to be released from their mating. He refused. He held her here like a prisoner until she was compelled to escape. She died in the attempt." He turned back to Braden. "Where are your heirs, Greyburn? Where is proof of the purity of your blood and the reason for Milena's pain and suffering?"

Braden felt the others look at him, begin to wonder and question. Yet he would not lie, even now.

"You have not done what you demand of the rest of us," Stefan said. "You are not fit to lead." He snapped his fingers. "You will learn how easy it is to smash the very Cause that destroyed my sister."

"Nothing can bring down the Cause," Braden said. "Least of all you."

"Ah, but you are wrong. You are the only one who cares enough to keep it alive. There will be no more grand Convocations when you are dead."

"You will not succeed," Don Alarico said, stepping forward. "I—"

Even lacking the benefit of sight, Braden knew what happened then. The Russian blood was hardy; that was why Grandfather chose to blend it with the Forsters'. Del Fiero retreated and didn't speak again.

Braden broke the silence. "Do you challenge me, Boroskov?"

"Will you bow to me, Greyburn? If you do, I may spare your life. You are only half a man, after all. I almost pity you." He sighed. "Yes, if you abase yourself to me and swear allegiance, I may allow your sister to leave Greyburn unmolested. I will end this Convocation without unnecessary violence. But Miss Holt . . . she will be my prize."

"Never."

"Then I challenge you, Lord Greyburn. By the very laws your grandfather established, I claim the right to lead this Convocation. By the most ancient of laws, I claim all that is yours."

"I accept your challenge, Count Boroskov. By the laws of the Convocation, and in the ancient ways of our people, I will defeat you." He addressed the others calmly. "There is no reason to delay. We will gather in at the edge of the wood behind Greyburn, in fifteen minutes—"

"Alone," Boroskov said. "You and me, Greyburn. No one else."

"We have the right to witness," the Hungarian delegate said, as his wife had earlier. "You cannot prevent us, Russian."

Again Boroskov laughed. "Very well. You may all watch Greyburn die at my feet."

He strode from the room. The others spoke in hushed voices, mingling alarm and relief.

"Quentin," Braden said, drawing his brother to the side of the room. "See to Rowena and Cassidy. Take them away from Greyburn—as far as you can."

"The Hungarian was correct," Quentin said, utterly serious. "The ladies have just as much right to witness the challenge as we do."

"Rowena will not want that right, and Cassidy won't know of it."

"You expect me to leave you now?" Quentin said. "Braden—"

Braden gripped Quentin's arms and gave him a shake, merciless in his urgency. "Do as I tell you, brother. Keep them away. Whatever happens here, keep them safe."

Quentin let out a long breath. "And the other women?"

"Let them come." He turned his back on his brother, trusting that Quentin would obey. Quentin knew the consequences of Braden's failure; he, too, would want to protect Cassidy and Rowena. And if he were gone, he could not challenge Boroskov himself.

Braden waited until he heard the garden doors close behind Quentin, and faced the guests. "Gentlemen," he said. "I shall see you in fifteen minutes."

"If your brother is not to be your second, I offer my services," Don Alarico said at his shoulder. "It will be my honor."

"Very well, *señor*. Thank you." Del Fiero left the room. The other delegates followed. Braden stood alone, composing himself for the coming fight.

He found Aynsley just outside the drawing room, smelling of fear. In a few words Braden related what the butler did not already know or guess. Aynsley would make certain that no humans came near the circle of challenge; Braden told him to find Telford and order the valet to wait for his master's return. When this was over, Telford would hear about his dereliction of duty in guarding Cassidy from Boroskov's obscene influence.

Fifteen minutes later, Braden walked to the edge of the wood. The scent of violence was already thick in the night air; he identified the Hungarian and German women, as well as all the male guests. Cassidy, Rowena, Quentin, and the Russian woman were absent—and so was Fedor, Stefan's brother. The hairs lifted on the back of Braden's neck.

Stefan waited for him in the center of the circle formed by the delegates. Hatred and malice poured from the Russian like noxious gases from a disease-ridden swamp. His power was tangible: raw, corrupt power of the most rabid kind.

Threats were redundant now. Words meant nothing. This was the heart of the werewolf nature, the savage soul that had never been civilized. It understood only action and the will to survive at any cost.

It was the *human* half that hated.

Braden began to undress. He heard Stefan follow suit. The witnesses made no sound but that of their breathing.

When he was naked, Braden Changed. As always, he gloried in his body's transformation. Muscle and bone shifted painlessly, shaking free of human restraints. In a handful of seconds he crouched ready as a wolf, blind as before but possessed of keener senses than he owned in human shape. Every scent had color, every sound a texture.

And everything became simple, clean, clear. He put the witnesses from his thoughts and gathered himself for the charge. As challenged, he was permitted the first attack.

But Boroskov broke the rules. Because Braden was ready for such a betrayal, the impact of the Russian's body was not as devastating as his enemy had hoped. They tumbled onto the ground, each thrashing for the superior position, teeth bared and ears flat.

Braden let the wolf take complete possession of his mind as well as his body. He forgot that he had ever had the sense of sight. His ears and nose and supple body, and the sixth-sense unique to the werewolf kind, were developed to their maximum capacity. Unerringly his jaws found Boroskov's upper foreleg and bit down. Boroskov howled with pain.

It was only the first feint in a long and desperate contest. For Boroskov, too, was powerful, and his depravity was unbounded by any regard for ethics. He gave free rein to his hatred, and in his very recklessness he was a deadly foe. Had Braden been able to see, his own discipline would have given him the ultimate advantage. Now, they were equal.

The battle was ruthless and without mercy on either side, no quarter asked or given. Braden was thrown to the ground again and again, only to fight his way up to meet Boroskov's razor fangs. Blood flowed and claws scrabbled for purchase on torn earth. The numerous small wounds that pierced his body under the heavy pelt went disregarded, as Boroskov ignored his own. Only the rare snarl broke the eerie, relentless silence.

But the damage inflicted became more severe, and exhaustion took its toll. Boroskov used his blindness against him with greater and greater frequency. Blood matted Braden's fur and made Boroskov's slick in his grasp. Muscles strained to their limits. Braden called on deeper reserves of energy to keep himself on his feet.

And then he made a mistake. For one disastrous instant, all his senses failed him. He miscalculated Boroskov's position, lunged at empty air, and suddenly the Russian was at his throat, pinning him down under fourteen stone of bone and muscle and malevolence. Teeth ground into Braden's flesh, piercing, rending.

Cassidy. Choking for air, Braden felt her as if she were standing beside him, lending him her courage and strength. Inwardly, he howled. All her courage would mean nothing if Boroskov won. She would become his plaything, her innocence debauched, her body broken. . . .

With a final burst of energy, Braden erupted upward, flinging Boroskov aside like a mantle of dead autumn leaves. He pounded the Russian down with his full weight, straddled him, snapped for the life-pulse beating hot under the werewolf's jaw.

The booming crack of a gunshot exploded close to Braden's ear, and he lost his grip. Voices cried out. A body slammed into his—not Boroskov's, but another. *Fedor.* Fedor, who had been missing all this time. Fedor in wolf form, treacherously joining his brother.

The witnesses could or would not interfere. Fedor was fresh, unwounded. With his brother beside him, he charged again. Braden fell. The odds were against him now, and death watched at his shoulder. Exhaustion and pain betrayed him as surely as his enemies. He clawed at the very edge of the pit.

Fangs ground into his throat. The world went blacker than any blindness could make it.

Cassidy, he cried soundlessly.

She answered. She was there, in truth, her scent and

her unmistakable spirit. He was unable to warn her away; he made one last effort to swim up out of oblivion.

One moment Stefan's fangs were ready to sever his windpipe, and the next the Russian was gone, yelping in shock. A commotion of shouts and scurrying bodies descended around him. He gasped for breath, aware only that Fedor and Stefan were no longer killing him . . . and that Cassidy was somewhere near, her presence a triumphant melody.

"Wait," a familiar voice commanded. Quentin. "Telford, please—"

Telford, too, was there, and all the delegates, and Rowena. Quentin had disobeyed. He hadn't taken the women to safety.

"Braden," Quentin said, his hand settling gently on Braden's side. "Can you hear me?"

Unconsciousness was very near, and with it total helplessness. Miraculously, he was alive, and his enemies had been temporarily subdued. But if he did not Change swiftly, he would be trapped in wolf form until his wounds fully healed, unable to speak or lead.

There was a considerable risk in Changing now. If he waited, he could heal naturally and Change when he recovered. If he Changed while badly wounded, weak as he was, he could exhaust the last of his life's energy, and die in the process. He would either heal himself in one great effort through the miracle of the transformation—or forfeit his own life.

He chose. He was vaguely aware of Quentin's oath as he compelled his body to become human again. This time it was no easy metamorphosis. Every cell protested; his bones and muscles and flesh screamed in agony.

But when it was over, he was alive. His body was whole, but he was as feeble as a day-old pup.

"Where . . . is Cassidy?" he demanded.

"You idiot, Braden—you could have killed yourself just now." He swallowed audibly. "Cassidy's safe. She's the one who saved you."

Braden tried and failed to lift himself from the ground. Quentin supported him onto his knees. "I told you to take her—" He coughed. "How?"

Quentin understood. "When I went into the garden, she was gone, and so was the Russian woman. I collected Rowena and went looking for her. I found her with Telford at the last moment, but she refused to come with me. I would have had to use force to stop her, and even then I don't think I would have succeeded. She was a veritable tigress. She *knew* what was about to happen. She ran to her room and came out with a rope, and then beat us all here."

He laughed with an edge of bitterness. "Lucky for you, for all of us. The gunshot you heard . . . that was John Dodd, Braden. Firing at you." He acknowledged Braden's shock with a snort. "Yes, Dodd. He came out of nowhere. There was another man with him, similarly armed. They turned on us, giving Fedor the distraction he required to emerge from hiding and attack. Del Fiero was wounded trying to help you—and then Cassidy dashed in and roped Stefan by the hind legs."

Dazed, Braden tried to picture the scene. "Cassidy . . . roped Stefan?"

"Like a contrary bit of beefsteak on the hoof. I believe they call it a 'lasso.' Most entertaining. She pulled him off you, giving us the chance to overcome the humans and catch Fedor."

"Don Alarico is injured?"

"He was—but before we could help him, he disappeared. We haven't seen him since. Oh, there's no doubt that he was on our side, but he's most definitely gone. We took Stefan and Fedor prisoner; they're in hand, now. So is Dodd. The other man escaped. Everyone else has returned to the house."

"Dodd," Braden said. "The Russians must have got to him, before the ceremony. Turned him to their will, against us—"

"They tried to turn me as well," another voice said. Telford knelt beside them. "Forgive me, my lord. I failed to guard Miss Holt. I left for a few moments to investigate suspicious activity in the guest wing, and Fedor accosted me. He revealed Stefan's plans to tamper with the challenge. He intended to compel me to betray you. I had to let him believe he succeeded." Telford cleared his throat. "He would not let me go until he was certain I would do as he ordered, and by then Miss Holt was gone. I was too late to warn you."

That explained Telford's uncharacteristic dereliction of duty. "They obviously found others to obey them," Braden said. "I'm grateful that there are some humans who cannot be influenced."

"Nevertheless," Telford said stiffly, "I failed—"

"The failure was mine. I should have known they would attempt this."

"It's over now," Quentin said. "You need rest."

Braden swayed on his knees. "See that Dodd and the Russians are securely held, Quentin. I'll deal with them as soon as I—" Only Quentin's grip kept him from falling. "Bring my clothes, Telford."

The valet moved off, and Braden concentrated on keeping himself conscious long enough to get dressed and back to the house.

"Help me up," he ordered Quentin. "See that Cassidy . . ."

His command was never completed. Strong, slender arms wrapped around his chest; the sweet scent of Cassidy's hair filled his nostrils. Her lips moved in the hollow of his shoulder, and tears wet his skin.

"You're all right," she said. "Thank God."

"I couldn't restrain her any longer," Rowena said. "Braden?"

But he had no attention to spare for his sister. Cassidy's hands were flying over his body, touching him everywhere as if she had to convince herself that he was whole. Braden had no strength, and no desire, to repel her. Her touch was healing as nothing else in the world could be.

"I'm all right," he said, stroking her hair. "All right."

Quentin took his arm and lifted him to his feet. Cassidy supported him on the other side, chattering out a steady stream of soothing words like the rush of crystal-clear burn.

If ever he'd needed all his resolve, it was now. The Cause was still dangerously fragile. A single misstep could shatter it.

He had put off settling Cassidy's future. Today proved that he could wait no longer.

"Lord Greyburn will see you now, Miss Holt."

Cassidy jerked up in the chair Telford had brought her, blinking the sleep from her eyes. The hallway outside Braden's room was dim, but she knew it was early afternoon. Braden had been recovering in his suite for more than eighteen hours; to Cassidy, the wait was endless. She was completely unaware of what had been happening at Greyburn since the duel.

She looked at Telford's gaunt and weary face. The valet hadn't slept, either, and his usually immaculate clothing was creased and smudged. "He's still all right?" she asked.

"Yes. Miss Holt—" He stopped and shook his head. "Please go in."

She wanted to ask Telford a host of questions; he alone had been tending to Braden since the fight. She'd hardly even had a chance to talk to the valet. He was like Braden's shadow, imposingly reserved, appearing when he was needed and then vanishing back into the woodwork.

If he'd wished to speak to her, he'd since thought better of it. He held the door open for her with a slight bow. Cassidy stepped into the darkened room.

She'd never been in Braden's suite before. The door opened into a sitting room; a bed was just visible in the adjoining chamber. It was immense, set in a richly carved frame and hung with tapestried curtains. Yet, in spite of its grandeur, there was something intimate about it. It was the place where Braden slept. He lay there at night, perhaps dreaming, as she did, of not being alone. . . .

"Telford said you wished to speak to me," he said behind her. "I have only a short time to spare you."

Braden sat in a chair beside the window fully dressed in coat and trousers, an untouched meal on a small table beside him, his face and shoulders bathed in sunlight. Cassidy hurried to him and pulled up short a foot from his chair.

"You weren't hurt," she said. "Quentin told me you healed yourself—"

"I am perfectly well."

She wanted to fling herself on him, hold him tight, kiss his mouth and his hands, whisper how glad she was that he was safe and alive. Last night's anger had made her bold, but that anger deserted her when Braden nearly lost his life. She stood where she was, drinking him in with all her senses.

"You saved my life," he said.

"It was luck," she said. "I had the rope in my room. I

couldn't find anything else. When the other wolf attacked you, I . . . didn't think. I just lassoed him."

He stood up and turned his back to her. "While John Dodd held a gun on you."

"All I knew was that you were in trouble. I saw a chance, and I took it. I wasn't afraid."

Something smashed violently to the floor; Cassidy flinched as the remains of a teacup and saucer scattered across the polished wood beneath the table. Braden's arm snapped back to his side; he held himself rigid, yet Cassidy could see his trembling.

"You weren't afraid," he said. "Yet this is the second time you could have died while in my charge." His fist flexed, open and closed, open and closed. "*I* am responsible."

His voice was laced with self-disgust, and she knew he was ashamed. Ashamed because he thought he should have protected her and made everyone else do exactly as he wished and won a battle against treacherous enemies, all without any help.

He thought he should be perfect. Never make mistakes. Never need anyone or anything.

"You were the one who was hurt," she said. "Do you think the rest of us would just stand by and watch while you—"

He swung about. "It was a challenge," he said. "Your interference was acceptable only because Stefan was first to break the rules."

"So if they hadn't cheated, the others would have let Stefan kill you?"

"If I was too weak to defeat him. If I proved myself unfit. It is our way."

"The *loup-garou* way," she said, hearing the voice that came from that angry new part of herself.

He turned his head aside sharply. "They had the right

to challenge me for leadership and forfeited it. They are disgraced, and their challenge is void. But the Cause has suffered—"

"The Cause," she said. She sat down on the cool floor, among the shards of china cup and saucer. "It only seems to bring sadness. To everyone." She picked up a sliver of saucer and turned it in her fingers. "I know why the Russians challenged you. When you sent us out to the garden, Stefan's cousin Tasya came to me. She told me everything." Braden started. "She wasn't part of what they were planning, but she needed to talk to someone. She chose me. I know that the fight was about your wife—Milena, their sister."

"And what else did you learn?"

"That the marriage was arranged by your grandfather. Milena was beautiful, and everyone at Greyburn loved her. Rowena called her an angel."

"Rowena," he said, a catch in his voice.

"Tasya didn't talk much about it. She only said that Milena wasn't completely happy here. And Milena's brothers blamed you for her accident." She swallowed. "How did she die?"

"She fell," he said. "During a storm."

"I'm sorry. It must have been awful for you."

He said nothing. Cassidy imagined his grief, losing Milena and then being blamed for her accident. Another thing he couldn't control. But there'd been at least one thing he could have changed.

"Tasya told me that you were supposed to have children, but it wasn't until you'd been married for years that she—" Cassidy flushed, caught in a whirlwind of emotion at the thought of Braden with another woman, making children. "Tasya told me about your son."

"My . . . son?" he whispered.

"Mikhail. The one you sent away."

Braden stepped back until his shoulders touched the window. His face was paper white. He didn't speak again for a long, long time.

"It's true, then," Cassidy said. "I didn't want to believe it. Why, Braden?" The sliver of broken saucer cut into her hand. "How could you send your own child away?"

He stared into emptiness. "I could not raise him . . . after Milena was gone."

Milena's portrait flashed into Cassidy's mind. Had his grief been so unspeakable that he couldn't bear to have a constant reminder of his loss? But that was no excuse for making the boy an orphan. No one should do that on purpose.

"So you sent him to Milena's family, in Russia—"

He twitched as if in shock. "I did not send him to Russia. I arranged a decent home for him, in Scotland—"

"But he's living with Stefan's family. Tasya takes care of him. She came to warn you, but she was afraid of Stefan."

Braden's reaction hit her like a physical blow. "I sent him to Scotland. It's impossible—"

"He's there—and Tasya says he's in trouble." The shard of saucer dropped from her hand, and she clenched her fingers to stop the bleeding. "I know that Stefan and Fedor are bad people. I felt a wrongness in Stefan, even before he tried to kill you. I knew he wanted to hurt you." She grimaced at the memory. "Tasya called them evil. She told me . . . some of the things they do on their estate in Russia. Terrible things to the humans who live on their land. They want Mikhail to be like them. Tasya says that if Mikhail stays with them, he'll turn out the same."

Braden turned to the window, his hands braced on the sill. "It is too late," he whispered.

"For what? He's only a little boy. Tasya has tried to raise him herself, but Stefan is taking him away from her. If Mikhail has people like Stefan teaching him—" She jumped to her feet. "Tasya can't stop them from hurting Mikhail. She came here to ask for your help. You're the only one who can."

Braden was like stone. "You don't understand."

"He's your son. You *can't* abandon him. I know what it's like to live with people who don't really care what happens to you. If I ever had a child—" She broke off, overwhelmed by the thought of making a baby and all that went with it. The things Isabelle had spoken of.

She wanted those things. Being with someone because she couldn't imagine life without him. Marrying. Having children she could love, the way she'd been loved so long ago.

And she wanted the same for Braden. For him, and for a little boy she'd never met.

For *all* of them.

"You're his father," she said. "He's *loup-garou*. Isn't he a part of your Cause?" She pounded the table with her fist. The tea tray jumped. Anger flowed through her, cleansing and bright. "You're forcing Rowena to marry a stranger, and you had to fight the Russians—all because of the Cause. But you won't bring your own son back."

"He is not—" He leaned his forehead against the window. "I have my reasons. Do not ask more than I can give."

"You won't even accept it when someone wants to give to *you*," she said. "I know you plan for me to marry Quentin. Is that because of Milena, too? Do you want me to go away, like Mikhail?"

Outside the window, a cloud passed over the sun. Braden was shrouded in shadow.

"I will not mate again," he said.

Because *loups-garous* mated for life? That was what he'd told her. But that wasn't the whole reason.

"Is it me?" she asked.

"Please . . . go."

It had become almost easy to disobey him. She touched his rigid back. "You have so much," she said. "Not only your family, and this house, but . . . so much strength. You know who you are. What are you afraid of?"

"You presume too much."

She brushed her hand the length of his arm, wishing that she could melt into him with her entire body, and feel him melt into her.

"Only because I finally know what *I* want," she said. "I want to belong here, Braden. I want to be part of everything that matters to you. I want you to—" Desperately she pulled a quote from memory, hoping it would be enough.

> *"I would I could adopt your will,*
> *   See with your eyes, and set my heart*
> *Beating by yours, and drink my fill*
> *   At your soul's springs,—your part, my part*
> *In life, for good or ill."*

He turned slowly. "Only for ill, Cassidy. You cannot see with my eyes. Not ever."

"But you can see with mine."

"My soul's spring is dry. You'll die of thirst."

"I've crossed the desert before. I can go a long time without water."

He stared at her. She'd never seen tears in his eyes, but if ever he could weep, it would be now. Yearning shone like light from his face. He looked like the boy he must have been long ago, still young enough to be crushed by a word or devastated by a single mistake.

Or trusting enough to love with all his heart.

"Let me try, Braden," she said. "Let me find the trail for both of us."

His fingers pressed into her arms. His lips parted. She closed her eyes and lifted her face.

From somewhere deep in the heart of the house, someone screamed.

fifteen

It was the scream that saved him.

Braden thrust Cassidy back and strode for the door. She was only a step behind.

"What is it?" she said anxiously. "Who—"

"John Dodd."

"The footman? Where is he?"

"In the Great Hall," he said, "awaiting questioning. I told you that I have business to attend to."

She caught his arm. "You're punishing him—"

"Not yet." He shook her off, sensing Telford nearby. "Since John Dodd attacked you first, you have the right to observe. Otherwise you may return to your room."

He strode ahead again. She picked up her skirts and ran after him. "But the Russians—"

"I will deal with them soon enough."

"You mean kill them?"

He didn't answer. He had resolved to finish matters with Cassidy today, as soon as he was fully recovered, and she'd outmaneuvered him once again.

She actually claimed to love him. Let her witness what

was to come, she and her too-tender heart, and then repeat those claims to his face.

A second scream echoed through the house as they approached the high carved doors to the Great Hall. Any outsider might suspect that the footman was undergoing the most hideous torture.

But he was quite unharmed. Braden had ordered him, somewhat bruised but whole, bound in the Great Hall before the massive mantelpiece. His screams were those of terror, and the madness of a mind twisted by evil.

Only Quentin waited for Braden in the Hall. Not one of the delegates had asked to observe; this was Lord Greyburn's concern alone. One of his own servants had betrayed him. There would be no interference—neither from werewolf nor ignorant human law.

"Untie him," Braden said as he approached the prisoner.

Quentin moved to obey. Braden heard and smelled Dodd's fear, his mindless frenzy, but he felt no pity. When Dodd was free and scrambled to escape, Braden blocked the man effortlessly and stopped him with a thought.

Resistance was strong. Stefan had already made the footman his unquestioning tool. But the human would not leave this house until his mind was purged of every idea or direction it had received from the Russian renegades— whatever the cost to his sanity.

The intoxication of battle returned to Braden in all its primitive force. He gave his rage full mastery, remembering Cassidy's danger, the Russian's deadly perfidy, his own unforgivable errors in judgment. He advanced on Dodd with head low and teeth bared.

"Please . . . please don't kill me," the footman whimpered. They were the first rational words out of his mouth since his capture. They left Braden unmoved. Dodd was no longer facing a lone, naked girl, or armed with a gun and the Russian's false courage. He was in the presence of inevitable retribution.

Braden focused his will on Dodd's mind like a shaft of scalding white light.

"Come to me, John Dodd," he said.

The footman gave a high, thin cry.

"Come," he said, and at last the footman began to move, scraping the stone floor with every step. Braden felt the savage satisfaction of complete mastery, of knowing he could bend this man to his will as he could nearly every other human. He waited until the footman collapsed at his feet like a puppet with snapped strings.

Braden stood over him, snared in a web of fully human passions. He wanted to punish. He wanted revenge. There were older, more barbaric ways of dealing with disloyal human servants. Ways that entailed no risk of further treachery.

Grandfather had longed for those ancient days, when more than a human's thoughts were erased. It would be easy to break this man's mind—or his neck.

So easy.

"Braden!" Cassidy cried, suddenly beside him.

"Quentin," he said. "Hold her back." He bent to grab Dodd's collar. "Let her watch . . . and learn."

"What are you going to do?" Cassidy said. "Quentin—"

"Explain, Quentin," Braden said. "You have the more facile tongue. Tell her."

Quentin hesitated. "You witnessed the ceremony, Cassidy. The earls of Greyburn use it to . . . ensure the loyalty of their servants."

"You did something to John Dodd and the maid," Cassidy said.

"It's a skill among our kind," Quentin said. "Many of us, like Braden, can focus our will to command the obedience of humans. It's a sort of mesmerism, a mental control. We use the ceremony to . . . suggest to our servants that they remain faithful and not disclose the unusual attributes of their masters."

Braden felt Cassidy's gaze like an accusation. "Then that's what you meant when you said they would never betray you," she said. "You *make* them loyal."

"It sometimes fails," Quentin said. "My brother is careful about the servants he approves, but mistakes can be made. There are those who can resist. Others . . . unfortunately, some human minds can't tolerate the intrusion, or the knowledge of what we are. Such men can go quite mad."

"Then that's why he attacked me—"

"No," Braden said. "The Russians turned him. They got to him before the ceremony." Dodd choked as Braden twisted his collar. "They created a human weapon to use against us. He attacked you and betrayed me. He can never again be trusted. I will wipe his mind of any knowledge of Greyburn and what we are."

"But it's wrong." He heard Cassidy pull free of Quentin. He snatched Dodd away. "It's *wrong* to do that to anyone. How do you know he didn't go crazy because you and the Russians hurt his mind? He was *loco* . . . he talked about devils. He didn't know what he was doing."

"It makes no difference."

"If you hurt him again, aren't you the same as the Russians?"

Dodd gasped for breath, and Braden loosened his stranglehold. "It is for our survival. If the world learned what we are—"

"Isabelle knows," she said. "My father knew. They didn't betray my mother." Her voice took on the fierce ring of absolute conviction. "You don't even *try* to trust people. I can't believe your way is the only way. I won't."

Braden stood very still. How was it possible that her disapproval tore at him like the teeth and claws of an unexpected enemy? When had she transformed herself from a child who would serve a specific purpose in the Cause to a woman whose only certain role was to shatter his peace and drive him to acts of madness?

If Tiberius were here, he'd cut her down to size with a single word.

Yet even as Braden burned with anger and incongruous shame, his body was alert to her nearness, her scent, the tiniest of her movements. He wanted to touch her again. She distracted him from duty and necessity and the vow he'd made to himself since Milena's death.

He let Dodd fall limp to the floor and swung around to face her. "Would you have me release him, to attack you again? To kill you?"

"I'm not afraid. He needs—"

"*Enough.* Either you are one of us, Cassidy Holt, or you are not." Lost in despair and bitter regret, Braden turned his will on her. "Leave me," he growled. *"Go."*

It was as if he slammed into an unseen wall. Her natural defenses were so high that he was repelled instantly.

She made a low sound of shock. "What did you do?"

Appalled, he couldn't answer. He had done the unpardonable. Contemptible. Forbidden by unwritten *loup-garou* law.

"You tried to . . . go into my mind," Cassidy whispered.

The denial came instantly to his lips and stopped there. He could see Cassidy in his mind more clearly than ever before: her stubborn face, her bold stance, the mutinous flash of her eyes. He could not only see her, but he could feel her. Feel her . . . power, her will.

How could she be half-human? She was unconscious of whatever power she possessed, but the knowledge, the aptitude, was there, waiting for release.

Had she come close to that release in the woods, before he left her? Her words, her little gasps of excitement, had awakened a desire in him that overcame his restraint. She was like a young virgin in her marriage bed, eager and frightened at once—a girl whose inexperience masked embers that would burst into flame at the right man's touch.

The Change was like the act of love between a man and a woman. The consummation, the completion, the ecstasy. Had she trembled on the brink, awaiting the final cue from him?

"I think I understand," Cassidy said, her words unsteady. "You blamed Isabelle for giving in to Lord Leebrook, but he's part of your family. A werewolf, even though he doesn't live like one. He could have forced Isabelle to . . . be with him, the way you make the servants obey you. The way you just tried to—" She backed away. "If becoming a werewolf means hurting people, I don't want to be one."

"The decision is not yours to make. I brought you to Greyburn for a single purpose—"

"Then I won't stay at Greyburn."

"If you are so certain of what you wish, Cousin, I will not stop you."

Perhaps she expected him to admit he was wrong, order her to stay, make some absurd declaration of devotion. She didn't move for several agonizing seconds. Then she walked out—not in a flurry of skirts and hurried footsteps, but with a remote dignity that chilled his already icy heart.

"You're a fool, Braden," Quentin said. "It's time someone showed you just how much a fool you are." He turned on his heel and followed Cassidy.

Braden listened to John Dodd's shallow breathing as the man waited, beyond terror, for the determination of his fate.

In that moment, Braden and John Dodd were all but brothers.

Braden didn't come after her.

Once she was beyond the carved doors, Cassidy ran. She crossed the entrance hall and took the stairs to the landing two at a time.

"I won't stay at Greyburn." She'd flung that threat out recklessly, scarcely aware of what she was saying.

But Braden hadn't come after her—not even for the sake of his Cause. *"I will not stop you,"* he said. There'd been only blank indifference in his expression, his voice, his posture; no rejection could have been more complete.

And the way he'd treated the footman appalled her. She couldn't get that image out of her mind: Braden dangling the man from one hand, like half-dead prey in a puma's claws. He was filled with rage, and he turned it on someone who couldn't fight back.

He'd even exiled his own son.

Nothing could reach Braden—not anger, or kindness, or pleading—not even love. She had gambled and lost.

Her ankle twisted as she missed one of the stairs in her haste. A narrow, long-fingered hand caught her at the elbow.

"Miss Holt," Telford said. "May I help you to your room?"

Startled, she looked into the valet's grave brown eyes. His detached concern cut through her misery.

"I'm . . . all right, Telford," she said.

"I beg leave to doubt that, Miss Holt," he said. "May I have a word with you?"

She remembered how Telford had seemed ready to speak before she'd gone in to see Braden in his suite. He had certainly never initiated a conversation with her before.

But many things had occurred lately that hadn't happened before. Especially not to Cassidy.

"I know you're troubled about the earl, Miss Holt," he said. "I know about John Dodd, and I wish to explain . . . if you would be so good as to hear me out."

Something in his face urged her to listen. She sensed in him an absolute loyalty to Braden completely different from the obedience of the other Greyburn servants. *He* was not afraid.

"I have been with Lord Greyburn for many years, Miss Holt," he said. "Since before his accident."

She leaned heavily against the nearest wall. "His accident? When he became blind?"

"Yes. I assisted him with the initial adjustments to his injury. Reading, correspondence, attire. But he is a remarkable man. He has requested my services for such matters less and less, and—" He gave her a strange, penetrating look. "I believe, now that you are here, he may soon not require them at all."

Cassidy stared at her feet. "What is it you wanted to tell me?"

"You must know, Miss Holt, that the footman John Dodd was influenced by Count Boroskov. Perhaps you are not aware that the count also attempted to suborn me, to turn me against you and the earl."

"You, too?"

"That is why I failed to guard you, and was able to return only just in time to warn you of the challenge. In so doing, I put you in some peril, Miss Holt. For that I apologize. But I did believe that you could help the earl. I still believe so."

She bit her lip to stop a stinging denial. "How did you escape what happened to John Dodd?"

"I am somewhat resistant to the *loup-garou* power," he

said softly. "Lord Greyburn learned this early in my employment, but he chose to trust me without the addition of such protective measures as he must utilize with the other servants."

"The ceremony," she said.

"Indeed. Lord Greyburn could have discharged me, but I was in . . . somewhat dire personal circumstances at the time. I had served in the finest houses in Britain, but my arrogant mistakes had brought me to ruin. Lord Greyburn set his own concerns aside for my sake. In essence, he saved my life."

So, after all his implacable insistence on compelling the loyalty of his humans, his cruelty to John Dodd, Braden *was* capable of letting someone close to him . . . out of simple trust and compassion. The same trust and compassion humans had to use with one another.

Why was it so hard for Braden to risk his trust again?

"I found a place at Greyburn," Telford said. "I was given a second chance. I believe in second chances, Miss Holt." He looked away. "When you first came to London, I was not certain you belonged here. I made the mistake of judging you based upon the most shallow of considerations."

"Maybe you were right," Cassidy said.

"No, Miss Holt. I have no doubt whatsoever that I was quite wrong." He plucked at his collar as if he could straighten its drooping edges. "Lord Greyburn is not the easiest man to comprehend. But I believe you have made a change in him, Miss Holt. I believe he . . . values you greatly."

Cassidy's heart gave a lurch. Surely, of anyone else in the world, Telford would know what Braden thought. What he wanted.

But he didn't seem to value his brother, his sister, even his own son. And still he hadn't come after her.

"I'll . . . think about what you said, Telford," she whispered. "I'm very tired. I'll go to my room now—"

He bowed. "If you require anything at all, Miss Holt—"

"Thank you." She made her way to her room, slipped inside the door, and closed it. She pressed her cheek to the wood, struggling to clear her thoughts.

How could she think clearly when she felt even less anchored than a twig carried along an endless wash in a flash flood? What was true, and what false? Whom could she trust?

Hinges creaked somewhere behind her. She turned to see Quentin walk through a door in the far wall that hadn't been there a moment before.

"Did I startle you?" Quentin asked, dusting off his trousers. "I suppose Braden failed to tell you that all the family rooms—except Rowena's, of course—have these convenient little private exits." He gave the hidden door a push, and it sank back into the wall, so artfully concealed that the edges looked like part of the wallpaper decoration. "Very useful when one wants a midnight run."

Cassidy put her back to the door. "Why are you here, Quentin?"

"To see you." She saw that his skin was flushed under his shock of auburn hair, and his smile was strained. "There's something I must show you."

"Please. Not now."

"But there is no better moment." He came to her and traced her cheek with his finger. "Tears, Cassidy? Then you need what I have to offer. You deserve to know the truth."

She commanded her eyes to dry and met Quentin's gaze. He didn't look or act like a man eager to marry her. But that had all been Braden's idea, from the beginning.

"What truth?"

"About my brother. The truth he'll never let you see."

Quentin knew. He'd guessed just how desperate she was to understand Braden Forster.

He wasn't the only one. Telford, Isabelle, Rowena—they all knew. For the first time in her life she was ashamed that she couldn't hide her feelings.

She made her face into a mask, like Braden's. "What about John Dodd?"

"I understand your concern, but I think you'll find a solution to that problem as well. If you come with me now."

"Where?"

"I'll tell you on the way. It's some distance from here. We'll take my phaeton." He moved past her to open the door and looked up and down the corridor. "Come—there's no time to lose."

And what, after all, had *she* to lose?

For once, Quentin seemed to be in a hurry. Instead of leading her out the door, he closed it again and took her to the hidden passageway. With a touch at a specific point, he activated a nearly invisible latch, and the door swung open again.

Immediately inside the door was a narrow stone staircase, damp and smelly. Cassidy followed him down the stairs and a long, cramped corridor to another door. They emerged at the back of the house, behind a concealing shrub. The afternoon was abnormally still; no guests wandered about the gardens or took tea on the lawn, though Cassidy knew that more delegates had arrived for the Convocation. She was glad she didn't have to meet any of them.

A carriage—small and built for speed—was waiting in the lane beside the laundry and wash house building. There was no coachman or footmen in attendance. Quentin himself handed her into the carriage and took the reins.

He started off at a swift pace out to the main drive, almost as if he were expecting pursuit. After they had driven a good mile from Greyburn, he relaxed.

"Now can you tell me where we're going?" she asked.

He threw her a reckless grin. "I believe it's safe enough. I suppose you know that Braden intends for you to marry me."

She stared straight ahead. "Yes."

"Well, I wasn't too keen on the idea at first—I'm not the marrying sort—but I've changed my mind. I think we shall rub along tolerably well together. I've decided there's no reason to put it off any longer."

"What?"

"Don't fight it, Cassidy. We're both the captives of fate and the Cause." He laughed and patted his coat pocket. "I've a special license prepared. With no further adieu, I'm carrying you off to the altar."

Cassidy was already poised to jump off the moving carriage when Quentin caught the gathered fabric at the top of her skirt and hauled her back into her seat.

"Come, now," Quentin said, chuckling. "You can't claim I'm so very unappealing!" He clucked to the horse and urged him to greater speed. "Is marriage to me truly a fate worse than death?"

Cassidy took hold of her panic and braced herself against the carriage's rock and sway. "You surprised me," she said. "And you lied. You said you wanted to show me something about Braden—"

"Because I was rather concerned that you might refuse to come, otherwise. I have some idea of what's occurred between the two of you. In fact, that's what gave me the idea that we ought to get on with this, before more damage is done."

Damage. Did he mean to her, to Braden, or to himself?

He'd only flirted with her, tried to kiss her once and never followed up on the attempt. "I don't know what you're talking about," she said, mimicking Rowena's cool, cultured tones. "Quentin, this is ridiculous."

"Is it?" He laughed. "To misquote Napoleon the first, let's hope that it's but a step from the ridiculous to the sublime."

"But you don't want to marry me. It was Braden's idea, not yours—"

"Yes, and for once it was a good one. You haven't seen yourself lately in the mirror, sweetheart. There are some compensations to marriage, you know."

She knew what he meant. But there was only one man in the world she wanted to touch her that way. And he could not be touched.

"Take me back, Quentin," she said, clenching her fingers on the edge of her seat as the carriage bumped along the lane. They were already nearing the edge of Greyburn land, and soon they'd be past the places she recognized. "I can't marry you."

"Why not?" He arched a brow at her. "I may even be falling in love with you. In any case, I promise that I'll not be as indifferent as my brother."

"He's not—" *Indifferent.* He was right, wasn't he?

"You're unhappy, Cassidy, and it's his doing. You're too plucky to admit it, just as Rowena won't let anyone see how miserable she is. Stiff upper lip, and all that. But you're too honest to lie." All humor left his expression. "Admit the truth. Braden is a cold, cruel, and calculating bastard who doesn't care about anything but his Cause. You're just another piece on his game board, like the rest of us. Oh, he may lapse from time to time, but any heart he once had is withered and dead."

Cassidy lifted her face against the wind. "Because of Milena."

Quentin gave her a sideways glance. "Ah, Cassidy. He's no good for you. Once you admit that, you're free."

She could admit it to Quentin, and satisfy him. She could even try to convince herself. But she couldn't pretend hard enough to marry him . . . *be* with him, and have his children.

"Do you really care about me, Quentin?"

"Of course."

"Then take me to the train station. I'm going back to America."

"To America? Now?"

"Yes."

"Oh-ho. I misjudged you after all. You're running away." He saluted her. "We're a better match than I'd hoped. A fine pair of cowards. Or didn't you know that about me, Cassidy? I'll do anything to avoid a fight." He clucked sadly. "You've never really been tested before this, have you? You find yourself at the line of battle, facing your first real defeat, and you turn tail. What a jolly life we shall have together, forever running away."

Alarmed beyond thought, Cassidy lunged sideways and snatched the reins from Quentin's hands. The horse broke into an uneven gallop as if she'd struck it a cruel blow, veering off to the edge of the road.

"Cassidy," Quentin said, "watch out for—"

The carriage bumped over a large stone at the side of the road and shot into the air. Cassidy's skirt caught on some part of the vehicle and tore halfway to her waist. She nearly tumbled from her seat, struggling to keep the phaeton upright. By the time she turned to check on Quentin, the place beside her was empty. He had vanished.

She pulled the carriage to a stop and jumped to the ground. "Quentin! Where are you?"

The horse threw up its head, half reared in its harness,

and bolted down the road. Cassidy stared after it, wondering if she were dreaming.

But the thunder of hoofbeats continued to echo in her ears, coming closer instead of retreating. She was shaking her head to clear it when a huge, dark horse pulled up beside her, kicking up dust in a choking cloud.

The rider dismounted in a blur of motion.

"Cassidy," he cried hoarsely. He wore only a shirt open at the collar, plain trousers, and boots. His expression was one she'd seen only once or twice before: neither cold nor aloof nor angry, but wild. He was wolf and man all at once. He felt her body and found the torn edge of her skirt.

"Quentin!" he roared. The roar became a howl, a wolf's howl, mournful and yet potent with challenge.

But Quentin had disappeared, his scent already fading. Braden stood with his head lifted, nostrils flaring, and when he turned back to her the wildness had transformed him into a stranger.

Without a word, without another sound, he swept her up into his arms.

sixteen

The black horse needed no guidance. It seemed an extension of its master, obeying some silent command as Braden tossed Cassidy sideways into the saddle. With remarkable agility he vaulted over the horse's rump, mounting behind Cassidy, and locked his arm around her waist.

Then the horse began to run. Cassidy clutched at the heavy mane, but Braden's arm held her as surely as if she were bound to the animal's back with the strongest rope.

The twin drumming of the horse's hooves and her own heartbeat filled her ears. Wind lashed her face and pulled her hair loose from its pins. The horse's muscled shoulders flexed beneath her. Braden's breath scalded the nape of her neck. Everything was sensation, and she was paralyzed in its embrace.

In Braden's embrace. She knew why he'd come. He was stealing her back from Quentin, reclaiming her, taking her for his own. She was as certain of that as she was of the sun sinking in the west: his intent shouted from every line and angle of his face and body.

Elation and fear suffused her heart in equal measure. She wanted this, and she dreaded it. She'd gone with Quentin still appalled by Braden's ruthlessness, angry and hurt and despairing, and yet her feelings had not changed. Quentin himself had convinced her of that. His harshest condemnation of his brother had only sparked the one realization she couldn't hope to resist.

And Braden had come after her. No apologies, no words of explanation, only action as relentless as ever before.

They flew toward Greyburn, over the fells and haughs and burns, avoiding the roads and tended park. Always the horse seemed to know his rider's unspoken will. They took a wide arc around the great house itself, skirting even the familiar woods. When Braden drew his mount to a halt at last, it was before a small, neat cottage at the foot of a hill. The place was deserted save for the sheep on the upper slope behind.

Braden jumped from the horse's back and reached for her. Cassidy slid down, half tripping over her torn skirts. Braden caught her.

"Where are we?" she asked.

He simply scooped her up in his arms and carried her to the cottage threshold. He kicked at the door with one booted foot, and it swung open.

Inside it was warm and pleasant and plainly furnished. There was no need for a fire, but the fireplace had been made ready for one. There were two chairs and a rough-hewn table and cupboards against the wall. A clean but tattered blanket divided off one end of the single room.

Almost at once Cassidy recognized the scent of the place: it was Matthias's. Matthew's. Faint and several days old, but distinct. This must be his cottage.

Braden set Cassidy down in one of the chairs and strode

back to the door. He slammed it closed and barricaded it with his body as if he expected her to try to escape.

"You left with Quentin," he said. "Why?"

A week ago she would have done nearly anything to win his favor. But now her blood was high and her body sizzled with anticipation, and she was ready to fight back.

"Why did you come after *me*?"

He stared at her, silent. She started toward the door, and he moved just enough to block her way.

Cassidy's pulse throbbed in her ears. He truly would not let her go if she tried to escape. The new, still-foreign anger told her to resist, that he had no right to impose his will on her yet again.

But she was tingling with excitement, moist and aching in the secret places of her body. She didn't want to escape.

"Why?" she repeated.

Braden's scent was stronger now, as if a new element had been added. "Can't you guess?" he said. "Or are you still too much a child?"

"I'm not a—"

He caught her face between his hands and kissed her. It was different from both times before, hard-edged and rough. She reveled in it.

"Do you want me, Cassidy?"

Her mouth was too dry to form words. Slowly she took his hand and raised it to her breast. It felt good, better than good, to feel his touch there. "See how fast my heart is beating," she whispered. "Braden, can you—"

He gave her no chance to finish. He lifted her again and carried her behind the blanket hung at the end of the room.

Behind it was a bed, as simple as the other furnishings but equally neat and clean. Braden laid her down on it.

Cassidy knew what was about to happen. Isabelle had tried to explain, but her body already understood. This was what had begun with the kiss in the woods, a union free of shame and sadness. A man and woman alone together in spite of all the rules.

Almost before she could settle on the bed, Braden's fingers were working at the buttons at the front of her bodice. "You liked what happened between us in the woods," he said, breathing fast.

"Yes."

A button snapped from her bodice and bounced onto the coverlet. "There is something I must do, Cassidy. I can't wait any longer. I've tried—"

She covered his mouth with her fingers. "I want to learn," she said. "I want you to teach me."

Without further hesitation he tore open the front of her bodice in a shower of buttons. He pushed the stiff edges to either side, exposing her chemise.

"No stays," he said gruffly.

"I was waiting outside your door for hours," she said. "I couldn't bear it that—"

He stopped her words with another rough kiss while his fingers undid the buttons at the top of her chemise. Cool air washed over her chest, and then he was pushing the soft cloth down, beneath her breasts, lifting them so that they were supported by the bunched fabric.

Instinctively she arched up, offering herself to him. She wanted him to touch her breasts, and more, but she didn't know how to say the words.

She didn't have to. His hands found her, caressed her, molded to her shape. The sensation was indescribable. Her nipples hardened into aching peaks.

A groan rumbled from his throat. He sought her mouth again, urging her lips apart and meeting her tongue with his. He cupped her breasts on either side. He tested their weight in his hands and stroked her nipples with his fingertips.

"Braden," she sighed. It was already more than she'd ever imagined, but it wasn't enough.

As if he'd read her thoughts, he bent over her and took her nipple in his mouth.

She gasped and clutched at the back of his shirt. She hadn't known that her breasts were so gloriously sensitive. He used his tongue and lips in ways that made her cry out in joy. Each time she did, he held her tighter and stroked her with greater urgency, as if the sounds she made excited him.

Reaching up, she tried to kiss his chest above the open collar, to return some of the pleasure he'd given her. But he pushed her back, gently but firmly, and gathered the hem of her skirts in his hands. His fingers slid beneath, up to the edge of her drawers, and then ran down the length of her calf. Her entire body hummed with each caress. Her drawers were becoming damp, drawing all sensation to the part of her that ached most. The drawers were made to be open in that very place.

If he were to touch her *there* . . .

But he withdrew and took her hand in his. She watched his expression as he guided her hand to the top of his thighs. He was very hard there, and she remembered how he'd looked when she first saw him naked.

"Like bulls and stallions," Isabelle said. But Cassidy had thought Braden far more beautiful. She made a cup of her hand and pressed it to him.

This time he was the one to gasp. His eyes were closed, and she knew she gave him pleasure. She moved her fingers gently, tracing the firm length under the fabric of his trousers.

He grabbed her wrist. "This is what happens when a man wants a woman," he said raggedly.

"Does that mean that . . . when Quentin kissed me, and you came to find us—you wanted me then?"

His laugh was little more than a growl. "Do you understand what happens when a man and woman lie together?"

"I . . . lived on a ranch," she said awkwardly. She didn't dare tell him what Isabelle had tried to explain. And so much had been left unsaid. "I want to do it, Braden."

It didn't take long for her to discover the fastenings of his trousers, but she didn't get the chance to undo them. Braden was too quick. Her fingers grazed warm, smooth flesh, and then he bore her back onto the bed with his body. She felt the full impact of his size and strength as he braced himself over her and kissed her. He started with her lips, and then moved to her chin, her cheeks, her forehead, her ears. His lips and tongue worked magic in the hollow of her throat and the sensitive place where her neck and shoulders joined.

At last he returned to her breasts, tasting and suckling, drawing a response from deep in her belly. He drew her skirts above her waist and parted the open inner edges of her drawers.

The air was very cool where she was most warm and damp. She felt completely exposed, more naked than if he'd removed her gown and shoes and stockings. His fingers brushed the insides of her thighs, low at first, then higher. Nearer to the place where all her need was centered.

Then, without warning, he touched her . . . there. She thought that if she made a sound, she would howl. Or weep with joy.

"You're ready, Cassidy," Braden said, his voice husky and raw. "Completely ready for me." He drew his finger through the tight curls that shielded her, down into the cleft where she was most tender. Her senses seemed to burst with delight.

"Oh," she said. "It's—" She struggled, but she didn't know the words to describe what his touch did to her. Her body grew taut as a rope attached to a wild mustang, as fluent as water.

Braden's hands fumbled between them, and his knees worked her legs apart. She felt a new pressure in her secret place, a column of firm flesh sliding against her thigh.

"Cassidy," he said hoarsely. "What I'm about to do will hurt, at first. But I can't stop—"

"I don't want you to stop." The moisture between her legs had become a flood, and she felt like a yucca blossom opening its petals to the sun, waiting for the bee to drink her nectar.

His hand found her again. He stroked, sliding between her petals. The heaviness of his breathing shook them both. He was leading her to some place she'd never been—the top of the highest mountain, the shore of the widest river. She pulsed with the rhythm of his heartbeat. Pulsed, and throbbed, and poised for the great leap. . . .

But Braden wasn't finished. He repositioned himself, pushed down, found her center, and slipped within.

She felt a stretching, and vague discomfort that she hardly noticed. All her senses were focused on one part of her body. He was inside her—not all of him, but enough that she knew how it would be when he went the rest of the way.

This was what Isabelle had tried to tell her about—having a man become part of you. But not just any man. She wanted Braden to possess her completely, now and forever.

She arched up. "Now, Braden," she gasped. "Come inside me. Now—"

.   .   .

Her invitation was more erotic than the blandishments of the most experienced courtesan. Braden could not have stopped if he tried.

Nor could he hold back. He thrust with one deep stroke, sundering her single barrier to pleasure. Her thighs encircled his hips, and she pushed up into him, urging him on. No discomfort, no fear, only eagerness that was unbearably seductive in its very innocence and absence of shame.

Milena had been an exquisitely practiced lover. Cassidy was blessed with a natural talent that outshone Milena's a thousand times over.

And *he* possessed her. He was the first, and the last. He, alone, made himself part of her. With triumphant exaltation he rode her supple young body, driven to the brink of her cries of pleasure. Somehow he held himself back. He arched to suckle her nipples in time to his thrusts, intoxicated by the taste of her, the feel of her, the rich scent of her arousal: the hot core of her womanhood tight around him, the hard tips of her breasts, the slender sturdiness of her legs about his waist, and the arms holding him against her.

"Braden," she gasped. "Something is about to happen—"

"Let it come," he urged, slowing and deepening each thrust. "Let it take you. Cassidy—"

Her body convulsed beneath him. She cried out in wonder and surprise, her legs drawing him closer.

He couldn't wait. He didn't have to. He stiffened, losing all thought in sheer pleasure. With one final thrust, he let himself find release.

When the shuddering ecstasy had passed, he lifted himself away from her. Her hands flexed on his back as if she wanted it all over again.

"That was—" she began. "I . . . didn't know—"

He silenced her with a kiss. Her skin was damp, her hair tangled, but he could feel her smile, the heavy-lidded contentment of a woman well pleasured and sated.

And he'd called her a girl, a child. She was so much a woman that he thought he could take her again in a matter of minutes. Already he was stirring.

But his first, violent desire had left him, and he could think clearly again. He rolled her into the curve of his arm, entwining her fingers with his.

He knew what he had done. Perhaps it had been inevitable, from the time he'd touched her nakedness in the wood. Perhaps long before that.

But only today had his reason deserted him entirely. Not when Cassidy all but declared her love, nor afterward when she defied him over the footman and threatened to leave. Even then he'd been able to keep his head. He had been returning John Dodd to confinement, unable to concentrate on what still must be done, when Telford brought him word that Quentin had been seen driving off with her.

Braden never clearly understood what came over him. It was wolf and yet not wolf, for he had never thought to Change. Somehow he found himself in the stable saddling his fastest mount, ignoring the attempts of the groom to help.

He rode recklessly, trusting Kinmont Willie to carry him past the obstacles he couldn't see. He followed scent alone until he found the carriage, and Cassidy.

Quentin had disappeared. There was no one to remind Braden of duty or necessity. He touched Cassidy, and he was lost. Lost beyond recovery.

His vows to take no second mate, to dispense with passion, to devote all his energies to leadership of the Cause and accept that he would never beget *loup-garou* heirs . . . all that was abolished by this one act.

His grand scheme for Cassidy and Quentin was finished forever. He had failed again, just as his grandfather had failed in his plans for him and Milena. But Grandfather would never have blamed himself. *He* knew who was at fault.

Traitor, he would say now. *Weakling.* He would refuse to see any mitigating circumstances.

But Braden saw them. By all the standards of the *loup-garou* and of the Cause, Cassidy was imperfect. She could not Change. And he was yet more deeply flawed, a far greater disappointment to his grandfather's mission.

Perhaps in the realm of deepest instinct he had known that they were alike. That they belonged together. The wolf had conquered the man and his logic, no matter how hard he had tried to control it.

It seemed impossible to believe that he had actually considered letting her go.

He stroked her shoulder, struggling with the long-unfamiliar tenderness and awe that held him as surely as her body had done. Was it possible, in spite of everything, that passion and caring would not destroy what remained of his value to the Cause? Could he dare to trust his heart again—and trust a woman with that heart? Could he guard Cassidy from the difficulties life with him must inevitably bring? Could he trust himself?

Perhaps that was the lesson Cassidy was trying to teach him—that there was something in himself worth trusting.

Now she lay beside him, soft and warm. She'd given herself to him like the most precious gift, the only one she had to bestow. And she would be loyal with all her soul. She would never betray him.

He felt . . . content. It was more than satiety after years of abstinence. More than the satisfaction of possession.

But some things hadn't changed. Some facts remained unassailable, and no wishing would make them otherwise.

"Braden?" Cassidy splayed her fingers on his chest, drawing close.

He allowed himself to savor the thick softness of her hair tumbled about her shoulders. She nuzzled his chest. "I'm so happy," she said.

If he could have made her happy for eternity, he would have given his life, his soul—everything but the Cause—to make it so. But one thought nagged at his contentment.

"Why did you go away with Quentin?"

She made a face. "He said he had something to show me."

"*Show* you?"

"Something about you. But he wasn't telling the truth." Her mouth quirked at the corner. "He said you wanted me to marry him, after all—"

"Did you wish to?"

She sat up and glared at him. "That is a very silly question," she said. "I like Quentin. I consider him a friend. But I couldn't marry him."

Braden closed his eyes. "He's so much a coward that he left you alone—"

"I wasn't hurt. It wasn't his fault. He was only doing what he thought you expected him to do."

And just what had Quentin intended? Had it been marriage, or something far more devious?

"What made you change your mind?" she asked softly.

He could not misunderstand her. But his feelings were still too unexplored, too raw for explanations. He had yet to face all the consequences of his reckless actions. And he was already thinking how fragile this moment was, how quickly it would be gone. Duty still awaited him at Greyburn. More delegates arrived each day, and soon all would be present. He must be ready to formally welcome the guests and open the Convocation.

Undeterred by his silence, Cassidy spoke again. "What are you going to do about the footman, and the Russians?"

He'd been a fool to think she'd let that matter go. One thing was certain. There wouldn't be time enough to properly deal with either problem before the Convocation.

"And Mikhail," Cassidy persisted, arms folded across her breasts. "Did you think about what I said?"

His shame at breaking his resolve regarding Cassidy was nothing compared to what he felt when he thought of Mikhail. When he'd sent the boy away he'd been but a newborn babe, irredeemably marked by the tragedy of Milena's death and the revelations that came with it.

Yes, he'd had his reasons. Good reasons, he had believed then. He could neither bear to look upon the boy nor trust himself. But Boroskov had stolen the child and somehow silenced his foster parents. Now the child was in Russia, where Braden would never have allowed him to go.

It had been a long, long time since he'd felt any emotion too strong to endure. Until Cassidy came, he'd learned to eliminate almost all the risks of feeling.

But he was naked now, and the cause of that nakedness was also the cure for his pain.

He turned on his side, rolling Cassidy onto her back. He kissed her before she could ask another difficult question. She wriggled beneath him.

"Do you think I could take my clothes off this time?" she asked.

He laughed, and the sound surprised even him. Her bodice was already torn open, and her chemise was easily removed. He set about relieving her of skirt, petticoat, stockings and shoes, and then her drawers. She tried to help him at first and then, her breathing unsteady, let him finish alone.

At last she was naked. He could not see her, but his

sense of touch more than made up for the failure of his eyes. He ran his hands over her body, from delicate toes to thick hair and every part in between. She was as he'd imagined: generously curved yet taut with muscle from hard work and constant activity, soft and strong at once.

He was about to follow the path of his hands with his lips when she stopped him.

"I want to see _you_," she said. "I want to feel your body."

Without waiting for his response, she sat up on her knees and reached for his shirt. She worked each button free slowly, lingering, as if she were unwrapping a much-anticipated gift. His heart seemed to stutter with each button undone. It raced when she pushed the shirt back over her shoulders and spread her palm against the center of his chest.

"You are so wonderful," she said. She stroked the hair on his chest as once she'd stroked his wolf's pelt. She traced all the contours of his muscles, so unlike the shape of her own. She touched his nipples. He was momentarily certain that he would never breathe again.

She closed the space between them and pressed herself to his chest. Her breasts fit perfectly into the slight hollow under his ribs; she kissed the base of his neck where his pulse beat so strongly. She rubbed the flat plane of his belly, then lower still.

The first time she'd touched him there, it had been through a layer of sturdy cloth. Now he was flagrantly erect, and her fingers wrapped around him unerringly, fearlessly.

"So smooth," she murmured. "Like warm silk." Her fingers explored its contours, from the base to the tip. Braden flung back his head, clenching his teeth.

She withdrew abruptly. "Am I hurting you? I'm sorry if I—"

"No," he bit out.

"But your face—you're in pain."

He laughed a little wildly. "Not pain," he said. He groaned. "Cassidy—"

"I only want to make you feel the way I did," she said, and reached for him again.

He burst into motion, stripping off his trousers with no regard for their future state. He took Cassidy by the shoulders and lifted her up and back, laying her across the bed. He poised over her, head to toe. His chest grazed her nipples. He ached with the need to bury himself in her without any preliminaries, but for once he would not be so selfish.

She returned his kiss with unbridled enthusiasm. He indulged in her sweet lips and then worked his way down her supple body. Her breasts, firm and full, filled his hands. Her nipples grew hard at the touch of his tongue. Her little cries made the anticipation nearly intolerable, yet he couldn't get enough of them.

Her chest rose and fell rapidly as he caressed her stomach and her rounded hips. The lush scent of her arousal intoxicated him. He teased her curls, kissed the inside of her thighs, drowned in her fragrance.

Cassidy knew no guilt, no maidenly modesty. She moaned as he touched his tongue to her delicate femininity. He took the first taste, then another, deeper still. He stroked her, opening up the flushed, damp petals. Nestled between was the tiny bud, her most guarded secret; he drew it into his mouth and suckled it as he had her nipples.

Her thighs parted and her body arched against his. Her nectar flowed over his lips. He tested the way with his tongue, and she arched upward again, begging him wordlessly. She tugged at his shoulders, pulling him up, and in.

She was just as hot and tight the second time as the first, but now there was no barrier to breach. Tilting her head back into the pillows, she gasped in rhythm to his thrusts. It had never been like this with Milena. Never. Cassidy was unique. She was the impossible combination of innocence and erotic passion, simplicity and mystery.

And she was his.

Once more he led her to the brink before he allowed himself release. Her unabashed joy in her completion made him lose control. He filled her, was cradled within her afterward in profound peace.

"It's time to return," he said at last, raising himself but unwilling yet to be parted from her.

She sighed. "So soon?"

"Yes. There are arrangements to be made."

"Arrangements?"

"I must obtain a special license for our marriage as soon as—"

"Marriage?"

"Did you think I'd take you and not provide the honorable protection of marriage?"

She flung herself up, legs locked around his waist and arms at his neck. "Oh, Braden—"

"It must be a private ceremony. The Convocation makes anything else impracticable."

"But no one ever has to know that we broke the rules. I'm glad we did." She kissed him and leaned back. "I knew," she said softly. "I knew this was right. The way it had to be."

He lifted her away and touched her face. "There is one thing I ask of you, Cassidy. As my wife, you must be prepared to obey me—and never question my work for the Cause."

She was quiet for a full minute before she spoke. "I understand."

The last remaining tightness left his chest. "I'll bring water for you to wash."

He used the few minutes apart from her to clear his thoughts, and then allowed himself the luxury of feeling, free of regret or censure. Cassidy hummed some lilting American tune under her breath as she dipped a cloth into the bucket of water and washed herself, completely unaware of the erotic allure of her ablutions. She radiated a pure exultation that humbled him.

She humbled him.

Half of her skirt was torn, but she did the best she could with it. He found his own clothes and dressed as well. Kinmont Willie was cropping the grass just outside the cottage; Braden collected his reins in one hand and Cassidy's fingers in the other. Greyburn was just over the fell.

"You must stay here for a short while, Cassidy," he said. "I'll bring you fresh clothing. It will be best if we return separately to Greyburn."

Her hand slipped from his with obvious reluctance. "Until we're married," she said.

"Until then." He cupped her face in his hands. "All will be well." He kissed her again and swung up into the saddle, choosing an indirect approach to Greyburn. Any of the *loups-garous* he encountered would know what he'd been doing—and with whom. The scent was unmistakable. Marriage would be the formal seal placed on their mating.

As he neared the house the early evening wind shifted, carrying with it another scent. Telford. He met the valet at the edge of the garden and dismounted.

"My lord," Telford said, a little breathlessly. "I have

a telegram for you from London, and a note from the Honorable Quentin Forster."

Braden composed his expression into the stern, unbending visage of the Lord of Greyburn and leader of the Convocation. "Read them, Telford."

"The telegraph is from London. If I may paraphrase . . . Lord Leebrook sends the message that the Honorable Matthew Forster has appeared at Leebrook House. He has apparently—ah—challenged Lord Leebrook to a duel. With swords."

Braden resisted the urge to snatch the telegram from Telford's hand. "Uncle Matthew? In London?"

"It appears so, my lord."

Braden had believed, when he took Cassidy to Matthew's cottage, that the old eccentric had gone off to live in the hills as he so often did. But Matthew hadn't truly been away from Greyburn lands. He was half-mad, if harmless, running about dressed as a seventeenth-century Reiver. Braden would not have believed that he'd use his antique sword in earnest. Duels were a thing of the past.

Matthew lived in the past.

"Why would he challenge Leebrook? He's hardly met the man."

"I fear the reason may not be far to seek, my lord. I have observed that Mr. Forster—in his antique guise— has been keeping company with Mrs. Smith on occasion. Or was, before the incident of two days ago."

"Keeping company?"

"I believe it was quite proper, my lord. Mr. Forster was in the drawing room when Lord Leebrook and Mrs. Smith were . . . reintroduced. He followed Mrs. Smith from the room. It seems possible that he wished to defend her honor."

A whore's honor. "You see everything, Telford."

"Had I thought trouble would come of this, my lord, I

would have spoken earlier, but I did not wish to bother you. Lord Leebrook asks that you collect the Honorable Matthew Forster as soon as possible, or he shall feel the need to make other arrangements."

Braden bared his teeth. "Read Quentin's note."

"The Honorable Quentin Forster says—" He paused, his embarrassment almost tangible. " 'My dear elder brother, I trust that by now you have come to your senses, and Cassidy is under your protection. Knowing you as I do, I felt you would be sure to want this.' " Paper rustled. "My Lord, Mr. Forster has enclosed what appears to be a marriage license made out in your name—and Miss Holt's."

An astonished laugh caught in Braden's throat. Of course. He didn't even wonder how Quentin had managed the license, or how he'd orchestrated events so smoothly and with such certainty of results. It had all been a game to him; his talent for games was extraordinary.

Braden's immediate reaction was to thrash his younger brother within an inch of his life.

But thrashing would have to wait. He had an errand for Quentin in London.

"Thank you, Telford," he said. "Kindly inform me when my brother returns. You may assure him that I won't demand his head—yet."

"Understood, my lord."

"Oh, and Telford . . . wish me luck. I am going to be married."

The little country church was nearly deserted. Dim morning sunlight tinted the stained-glass windows, and the only witnesses to the ceremony were the curate, the parish clerk, and Telford, who stood slightly behind Braden.

Cassidy had no attendants. Last night Braden had returned to the cottage driving a small carriage laden with food, one of Cassidy's simplest dresses along with a coat and a change of shoes and stockings, and additional blankets. In his pocket was a special marriage license, and he explained that they would be married first thing in the morning. They had shared a meal of bread, cheese, and fruit, and afterward Braden spread the blankets on the floor beside Matthew's narrow bed. He remained there while Cassidy slept restlessly in the cot, wishing Braden would join her.

But it was as if the marriage license kept Braden from touching her again. At dawn they rose and dressed, Braden in a dark blue frock coat and white waistcoat, and he went ahead to speak to the curate who would marry them. He returned with Telford, and the three drove to the church, reaching its doors just at eight o'clock.

Now the brief ceremony was finished, and a ring sparkled on Cassidy's finger. A handful of curious countryfolk had entered the church with the final vows, but Braden ignored them. He seemed unaware of anyone but Cassidy, and she could hardly believe any of it was real.

"Till death us do part," he had promised her. And she had promised the same. Mated for life, in the church and in the way of the *loups-garous*.

They signed the parish register, and Cassidy wrote her own name for the last time: Cassidy Holt. Her hand was a little unsteady on the pen. From now on she was Cassidy Forster, Lady Greyburn.

Braden's wife.

She didn't mind that there was no wedding breakfast, or girls her own age to be envious. She had everything she'd ever wanted. Braden kissed her, and the world spun so fast that she swayed in his arms.

At the church doors she found Telford waiting and took his hand. "Thank you," she said. "Thank you for what you said to me yesterday."

"I am gratified that I was able to be of some assistance, my lady," he said, bowing over her hand. "May your life together be long and joyous."

"Oh, it will, Telford." She gazed at her new husband, who was having a last word with the curate. "It can't possibly be anything else."

seventeen

I t's true, Isabelle," Cassidy said, her face alight with a
new and unmistakable happiness. "Braden and I are
married."

Isabelle sat down on the edge of her bed, fighting dizzi-
ness. "Married?"

"I'm actually the countess of Greyburn, can you believe it? It sounds ridiculous."

Ridiculous. Isabelle composed herself and thought back
over the past two days. The house was swarming with
loups-garous; she'd been strictly confined to her room, and
Cassidy hadn't come to see her even once since the earl
was wounded in the duel.

But wherever there were servants, there were very few
secrets, even in a household such as Greyburn. Isabelle
knew that Cassidy had argued with Lord Greyburn since
his recovery, and that she had subsequently run off . . .
with the Honorable Quentin Forster.

If that hadn't been alarming enough, she'd soon heard
that the earl had gone after the pair in a veritable frenzy.
And then she'd received the anonymous note, slipped under her door.

Now . . . now it was too late to warn Cassidy. Nothing could have prepared Isabelle for the denouement of this drama.

"I'm sorry you couldn't have been there," Cassidy said, oblivious to her dismay. "It was in a very small church, and Braden didn't want—oh, Isabelle!" She hugged Isabelle and bounced down beside her. "It doesn't seem real. But I knew it was right, the moment we—" She stopped grinning quite so broadly. "I know what you were talking about, now. What men and women do together. Only it's so much more than I dreamed."

"You and Braden—Lord Greyburn—"

"Yes. Before we got married. But you don't have to worry, Isabelle—the rules are safe now."

Not worry. Isabelle covered her eyes with her hand. She'd seen the desire in Greyburn's face . . . but she'd never have guessed it would come to this. She'd worried that Cassidy would be taken advantage of or pressured into a marriage she didn't want. Now she was bound to the earl for the rest of her life.

It was better than being used and abandoned or cast out. But there would be years and years for regret and disillusionment, with a man like Braden Forster.

Perhaps even terrible danger.

She fingered the note in her pocket. Why had it come to her, of all people? How much truth was in it? Surely some, for it tallied with her own suspicions. But how much should Cassidy be told? Didn't she deserve some warning if the worst were true?

"Aren't you going to wish me happy?" Cassidy asked.

Isabelle kissed her cheek. "Always. Happiness is what you deserve above all things." *And that is why I must tell you. Forgive me.* "Cassidy, I received a letter this afternoon . . . I don't know who wrote it, but it pertains to you, and you ought to be made aware of its contents."

"A letter?"

"About Lord Greyburn." She crumpled the paper, still inside her pocket. There certainly was no need for Cassidy to read the note itself. "It's about his previous wife."

"Milena?"

"Yes. I do not know how much truth is in it, but . . . Cassidy, it claims that Lord Greyburn . . . caused Milena's death."

Cassidy showed no signs of surprise. "I know," she said. "Tasya, Stefan's cousin, said that the Boroskovs blamed him for it. Braden told me himself that she died in an accident—she fell, during a storm. And she—" Her expression grew remote. "It was an accident."

If only it were so simple. "The note also says that Lord Greyburn's . . . love for Milena was a kind of sickness. That he held Milena prisoner here for months, cut off from the outside world, while she was with child. That he was so jealous that he refused to let anyone see her. When she was very near to her time, she escaped, and the earl hunted her down. She fell from a height during the confrontation—the note suggests that she was pushed. When she was brought back to Greyburn, badly injured, her . . . child was stillborn."

Pale and tight-lipped, Cassidy stared at her. "That isn't true."

"I'm sorry. I thought it best that you knew what others were saying of the earl. If Lord Greyburn did any of these things—"

"He didn't." She stood up and walked rigidly across the room. "You don't know him, Isabelle. He did love Milena—" She closed her eyes. "I can't change that. But the rest . . . I don't believe any of it."

Isabelle sighed and covered her eyes. She'd done her duty, but she'd be damned before she made Cassidy suffer any more than necessary. "Perhaps the note is nothing but a malicious trick by one of the Boroskovs or their people." But she couldn't drive away the notion that there was some kernel of truth behind the missive. If ever she'd planned to leave Greyburn, it was quite impossible now.

"Oh, Isabelle." Cassidy knelt beside the bed. "Braden hasn't treated you very well, and maybe you have good reasons not to like him. But I *know* him. He's not what you think."

Isabelle felt perilously close to weeping. "My dear," she whispered, taking Cassidy's hands. "All I want is for you to be happy."

"I know. You've been such a good friend." Cassidy kissed the back of Isabelle's hand. "Trust me, Isabelle. I'm grown up now."

"Yes. And I have no right to interfere."

Cassidy rested her forehead on Isabelle's knee. "Everything would be perfect, if only you could be as happy as I am."

To that Isabelle had no answer. Matthew was gone. She was still isolated and alone here at Greyburn, but she dared not leave, as long as Lord Greyburn's character remained in question. She doubted she would ever be sure of it.

Yet Cassidy had become a woman in every way. She'd chosen her own destiny. Isabelle had no doubt that she'd gone willingly into this marriage. She'd caught the earl herself.

Was it possible that this improbable union might work? Could Cassidy's innocence, unsullied by her knowledge of sex, remain her strength?

Cassidy was fully capable of loving the earl with everything inside her, even to denying his faults. But was he able to return that love? Was he driven only by desire, or duty to some inner code?

If there was any justice in the world, perhaps Cassidy had changed him. If Cassidy could enjoy a full and happy life, then Isabelle had no regrets.

She smiled. "Don't worry about me, my dear. I muddle along very nicely just as I am. I'm only sorry you couldn't have had a proper wedding with all the trimmings."

"I didn't need it. Everything is perfect just as it is."

But all was far from perfect. Though Cassidy moved into Lord Greyburn's suite and everyone in the house was informed of the great event, it was almost as if nothing had happened. There was no party or celebration or wedding feast, not even among the servants. Cassidy didn't seem to mind or even notice, but Isabelle was troubled. It became clear that Lord Greyburn did not expect Cassidy to take on the duties of a countess or the wife of a peer—that, in fact, he didn't even want her involved with the Convocation.

Quentin reappeared the day after the marriage and was sent off again immediately on some errand for his elder brother. The Convocation officially began the next day. Delegates had arrived not only from Spain, Germany, and Prussia, but from France, Portugal, Greece, Italy, the Slavic countries, Canada, the Scandinavian nations, and even exotic India and Japan. In appearance the guests were human, but Isabelle had learned the dangers that came with this strange gathering, and was glad enough to remain in seclusion for the two weeks of the meeting.

Cassidy, too, was kept in virtual isolation. She told Isabelle calmly that Braden felt she wasn't ready to face such a large assembly of *loups-garous*; she seemed to accept his judgment.

But her resignation was strained, as if she were making a supreme effort not to rebel. Isabelle understood; Cassidy wanted to keep what she had, this illusion of belonging to someone, at all costs. For once in her life she was truly deceiving herself, and Isabelle could not help her.

For his part, Braden was wholly absorbed in managing the business of the Convocation. He had little attention to spare for his new wife. Isabelle had learned enough of these *loups-garous* that she knew he had to guard his position of dominance, which had been so recently tested. The others looked to his leadership; he oversaw the decisions made with regard to marriage and alliance, all designed to preserve their kind from extinction.

Often, during the next two weeks, while the werewolves met in the Great Hall and servants crept about like ghosts, Cassidy came to spend her time in Isabelle's room. They would talk or read; Cassidy even tried her hand at embroidery, though she'd never learned the fine art of it. Such domestic pursuits were not Cassidy's forte, nor should they be.

But at night, when the day's meetings were ended, Cassidy would fly back to the suite she shared with her husband, bursting with anticipation and pride and love.

Isabelle had no doubt that their physical relations were excellent. She was an expert in all matters pertaining to the act of love; she recognized a satisfied person, male or female. She seldom saw the earl, but Cassidy was no shrinking bride raised to dread a husband's attentions. She retained that aura of wonder that came with sexual knowledge before it was tempered by time and disappointment. Or betrayal.

God forbid that was *all* she and the earl shared.

Days passed, and then the two weeks of the Convocation were nearly up. The guests would be returning to their homes, new marriage contracts signed and ties between families cemented for another five years. Isabelle sensed Cassidy's excitement; at last she'd have her husband to herself.

On the morning the remaining delegates were preparing to leave Greyburn, Isabelle watched from her window, which, like Cassidy's old room, overlooked the drive and park stretching out in front of the great house. Two carriages were drawn up before the door; Greyburn footmen loaded baggage and assisted men and women into the vehicles. The departing guests might have been the French delegates, or perhaps the Italians. All of their personal servants had entered the rearmost and more humble of the two carriages, and the coachmen were just whipping up the horses, when there was a sudden commotion.

The earl of Greyburn burst onto the scene from within the house, plainly furious. Footmen scattered out of his way as he strode up to the delegate's carriage. There was a brief and hurried conversation, and then the earl moved to the rear vehicle.

The carriage door opened. Braden summoned a footman and waited while the man helped one of the delegate's maids to descend. She was not the subject of Braden's wrath. A second maid emerged, and then a third, each one ignored in turn.

It was the fourth, her face shielded by a hooded cloak, who earned the earl's full attention. He caught her arm with one hand and pushed back her hood with the other.

Lady Rowena stared at him, stiff with defiance. From behind her window, Isabelle could hear the muffled hum of raised voices. The earl shook his sister none too gently.

Then Cassidy arrived. She flew to Rowena's side. She, too, spoke to Braden, and her countenance was both pleading and mutinous.

The earl turned to his wife and said something that made her flush and drop her gaze. Then he gave Rowena a command, and after a moment, trembling, she obeyed and walked with futile dignity back into the house.

After a last exchange between the earl and the dele-gates, the maids reentered their carriage and the party was off. Isabelle left the window and sat in the comfortable chair near the fireplace, listening carefully. She heard doors slam, voices echoing in the entrance hall—and then silence.

Cassidy came to Isabelle's room soon enough. She closed the door and marched to the window to gaze down at the empty drive.

"You saw what happened," she said.

Isabelle rose and joined her. "I saw, but I couldn't hear. Do you wish to talk about it?"

Cassidy whirled about and paced the length of the room. "You know that Rowena is to marry an American she's never met," she said. "The man was supposed to come to this meeting, but he didn't appear. So when the French delegates left, she tried to escape."

"Dressed, I gather, as one of their maids."

Cassidy paused by the washstand and pushed the heavy, loose hair from her face. "Yes. I don't know how she got them to take her . . . but Braden found out. He caught her. They argued."

Isabelle knew that the conflict was far more hazardous than a mere argument. Was it a reflection of what had happened between Milena and the earl—if indeed her desperate attempt to escape Greyburn, while heavy with child, was a real event and not some fabrication of a mali-cious enemy?

"You came to Rowena's defense," Isabelle murmured.

"I know what it's like to be expected to marry someone you don't love. Sometimes I'm not sure Rowena likes me, but she's so unhappy. I can see what the Cause has done to people. It isn't right."

And you believe you can alter what isn't right, Isabelle

thought. Was Rowena only the second prisoner held against her will by Lord Greyburn? Would Cassidy become another?

"But the earl didn't listen to you," Isabelle said.

"No." Cassidy sat down on the bed and hugged herself. "When we came inside and Rowena went to her room, he reminded me that I'm his wife now, and I have to obey him. I must never stand against him where the Cause is concerned." She looked up. "I don't think I can do that, Isabelle."

Yet there was a time, not very long ago, Isabelle thought, *when you wouldn't have dared openly defy him. Is the earl beginning to realize what you're becoming?*

Perhaps Milena had disagreed with Lord Greyburn. Perhaps she, too, had defied him. If Cassidy pushed Braden to the edge of his tolerance . . .

"I know that Braden is wrong about this," Cassidy said. "About Rowena. I think she'd do anything to get away. Anything."

Isabelle found sympathy in her heart for Rowena in spite of that lady's cold condemnation. They would never be friends, but they were both women. They'd both been used by men, in one way or another.

"There's little you can do, Cassidy," she said. "It is a matter between the earl and his sister."

Cassidy plucked at a fold of Isabelle's counterpane and crushed it between her fingers. "It was so good with Braden, Isabelle. I thought we finally understood each other. I thought he would listen to me."

How difficult those first lessons are, Isabelle thought. *Would I could have spared you them.* "Men and women are different, Cassidy—human or otherwise. There are always misunderstandings, difficulties—"

"I don't know why. I'm so happy, to be married to Braden. Knowing we'll always be together. But I can't pretend that everyone else is as happy as I am. You, Rowena, even John Dodd and the other servants—how can I just ignore what's going on around me?"

"You can't solve all the world's problems," Isabelle said. "I am responsible for my own fate. Rowena is responsible for hers. That is the way of the world."

Cassidy popped up from the bed. "I may not know much about the world, but I can't stop saying what I feel. Even Braden can't tell me what to think." A stubbornness that was almost anger flashed across her face. "Not when it means doing something wrong. Isabelle—I look in the mirror now, and I see someone I never knew before. For the first time in my life, I'm sure of who I am and where I belong."

"That is a great gift indeed," Isabelle said, her throat aching with pride and sorrow.

"You told me once not to change myself for anyone. Not even for Braden. You were right, Isabelle." Her expression softened. "If he loves me, he won't shut me out."

If he loves me. Cassidy couldn't hide the yearning in that phrase. She believed the earl loved her, but Isabelle knew he hadn't given Cassidy the gift of those words.

In the end, words meant nothing. Isabelle had once been assured of love, only to have it end in betrayal.

And the earl had loved his first wife. She was dead.

"Now that the Convocation is over, Braden will have time for me again," Cassidy said. "I'll make him see through my eyes." She gave Isabelle a quick hug. "Thank you, Isabelle."

She left the room filled with new hope and faith that her confidence alone would sweep all difficulties from her path.

Isabelle resumed her seat by the fireplace and sank deep into the upholstery. *I did tell you not to change for anyone, Cassidy. But you have changed—for yourself. You have become a strong person in your own right. And maybe that is something the Lord of Greyburn can never accept.*

She drew the crumpled letter from her pocket and read it again. If any of those neatly written words held truth, Cassidy's happiness could not last.

Quentin returned with Uncle Matthew just after the final delegates had left Greyburn, as unrepentant as ever for his tardiness.

Braden saved the admonishments. Quentin's presence at the Convocation would have been useful, but hardly essential. His future, now that Cassidy was otherwise occupied, had yet to be determined, but several prospective mates were under serious consideration. He hadn't dodged his fate, only postponed it.

Quentin claimed he'd searched high and low for Uncle Matthew, who hadn't been so good as to wait at Leebrook House to be fetched home. But Lord Leebrook wasn't harmed, and Matthew, it seemed, had also returned unscathed from his peculiar adventure. He'd since fled back to the fells—one less complication to be dealt with.

That left Rowena—and Cassidy.

"I am sorry I missed the happy event," Quentin said, feigning relaxation as he sat opposite Braden in the library. "Though I hear it was a very private ceremony. Anxious to get past the preliminaries, were you?"

He was deliberately goading Braden, as if he wished to be punished for his impudence. But the anger Braden had felt earlier was gone. He had none to spare for his foolish younger brother and no desire to rise to Quentin's bait.

"I do thank you for one thing, Quentin," he said. "Your irresponsibility demonstrated how little you were suited to Cassidy." He showed his teeth. "If she'd been hurt—"

"But she wasn't. She's a remarkably resilient little thing,

as strong as any of us." He clucked. "Come now, Braden—even you can't believe I'd have left without making sure of that. I just didn't care to be present when you arrived on the scene."

"In that you were wise. I'll be certain to provide you with a mate who is up to all your tricks."

Quentin yawned. "What a dull subject. I understand you've put poor Ro through the mill—"

"She tried to escape."

"Our sister would be so much more clever if she weren't concerned with such minor matters as reputation."

"You don't deceive me, Quentin. I suggest that you do not even consider helping her."

"It would take far too much effort." The leather of his boots creaked as he recrossed his legs. "And how is married life, Braden? With Cassidy, I mean?"

"She has much to learn," he said stiffly, "but I have every confidence that with proper guidance, she'll be of great help to me in the Cause."

"Wonderful. All you could ask for."

Quentin's voice was heavy with sarcasm, but Braden didn't let it touch him. "Yes. All I require in my wife—honesty, loyalty, and obedience."

"And what do you suppose she requires, Braden? A magnificent home? Fine dresses? A wealthy family?"

"I shall do my best to make her happy."

"Another duty on your shoulders, brother. I don't envy you." He sighed. "Has she . . . mentioned children?"

Braden froze.

"You haven't told her, have you?"

"You're undoubtedly tired from your journey," Braden said, rising. "And I have estate business that's been waiting since the Convocation began. You may go."

Quentin paused at the door. "If you're not careful, brother, you'll find enough business, related to the Cause and otherwise, to keep you from ever knowing your wife. And I don't think she'll consent to remain in your shadow."

Braden went riding soon afterward, Telford and his estate manager beside him, to inventory repairs and alterations needed on Greyburn lands before the coming of winter. He visited tenants and listened to Telford's description of the state of cottages and fences, roads and pastures. As always, the laborers and shepherds and farmers were mute in his presence, awed and intimidated. They spoke freely only when he delegated his human companions to deal with the people who lived under his patronage.

It would have been another story had he taken Cassidy. She'd naturally make the tenants feel at ease; she wouldn't know how to play the aristocratic countess. She'd see herself as little different from these ordinary folk. How could they fail to love her?

But she would go too far. She always did. She'd let the formalities lapse beyond recovery, and make the humans forget their place. Like the Greyburn servants, they had everything they could want or need. He wouldn't let them have Cassidy as well.

Only when he was certain that she recognized her limits, accepted her station as his wife—then he might permit her to go with him on his rounds. When he was sure of her. When the last of his doubts were laid to rest.

That night, as always, he took her to their bed. It was the one time in the day they were absolutely alone, the only hours when they didn't depend on inadequate words to communicate. And he never stopped wanting her.

But tonight he must tell her the truth he'd withheld. The part of the truth she must know.

He expected this morning's argument over Rowena to create a strain between them. Cassidy's usual flood of cheerful, inconsequential chatter and questions about his day was replaced by a pensive silence as she sat in bed waiting for him to undress.

Sulking, perhaps, or more likely preparing to renew her arguments. She'd proven that she had a woman's passion, but even that hadn't altered her nature. Quentin had warned him that he might never know Cassidy. Quentin was wrong.

He knew her as she was—an innocent who still saw the world through rose-colored glasses. He'd sworn to himself a thousand times that she had to learn the harshness of reality, but now—standing beside the bed and listening to her steady breathing—he admitted that he, too, had been wrong.

Because he would fight to keep her just as she was tonight, awaiting him in his bed, vibrant and alive. Yes, he'd teach her what she must know as his wife. She'd accept the necessities of life among the *loups-garous*. But he would also continue to protect her from anything that could taint the guileless and unsophisticated simplicity that made her what she was. That made it possible for him to trust her.

Let her have her small, harmless rebellions. They couldn't hurt him.

She would not become another Milena.

He lay down beside her and kissed her lips. Her arms looped about his neck.

"Braden—"

He knew how to counter her unspoken debate. He slid his tongue inside her mouth and teased her until she forgot all about disagreements and opened herself to him. As always, her passion was utterly uninhibited, filled with little cries and sighs and moans that made him hot and hard in seconds and gave him no relief.

His bed—their bed—was far larger than the pallet in

Matthew's cottage. There was room enough for every sort of sensual game, if Cassidy had been of Milena's bent. But she needed no such exotic diversions.

She already knew how to drive him to near madness with her simplest touch. Her very boldness was the most potent of aphrodisiacs. But tonight, she used her slender strength to roll him onto his back, and she braced herself over him, hair sweeping across his face.

It was not merely seduction. He felt it as an attempt at dominance, and his immediate instinct was to throw her off. He had to resist the need to use his greater weight to roll her beneath him and teach her who was master.

But Cassidy began to kiss him, and his struggles vanished in waves of pleasure. Her kisses fell like gentle rain on his brow, his eyelids, his cheekbones, his chin. If she mastered him this one time in love play, it was by means he had no will to resist.

She made him *feel*. Sight was unnecessary. Cassidy made him forget he'd ever possessed that sense, that he was less than whole, perfect, without it. His entire body took the place of his eyes.

Taking obvious delight in his reactions, Cassidy worked her way down the column of his neck and licked the hollow below his collarbone. She rubbed her cheeks and hair across his chest, all but purring. Her slightly callused palms made light circles on his belly, each circle lower than the one before.

His nerves sang with anticipation of the most intimate touch, but again she surprised him. Surprise was far too faint a word. Her mouth closed over him, and he nearly shot up from the bed.

Milena had done that often, and well. He hadn't expected it of Cassidy. But her explorations were filled as much with curiosity and wonder as with the wish to please him. She made the private caress her own. He held himself still on the bed, fighting to keep from taking her then and there.

But she wasn't done with surprises. She moved above him, straddling him with her thighs to either side of his, and cupped his face in her hands.

"Is it all right . . . if we try it this way?" she asked.

He bit off a mildly mad laugh. "Yes," he whispered. "Yes."

She needed no further encouragement. Her moist heat eased down to enfold him, and she braced her hands on his shoulders. He moved, urging her into the same rhythm. He massaged her breasts, felt the tension in her arms and back as she rode him. She was strong, and beautiful, and he had nothing to fear.

It was a strange thought, and it fled his mind instantly. Cassidy leaned over, brushing her nipples across his chest and veiling him in a curtain of her thick hair.

He couldn't hold back. He lost himself, but she followed an instant later, breathing a deep sigh of fulfillment against his mouth.

"That was nice," she said, "Wasn't it?"

He pulled her flat atop him and kissed away the perspiration on her brow. "More than nice," he said, and meant it.

She nestled her head in the curve of his shoulder. "There must be . . . lots of ways we haven't tried yet."

How could she fail to notice that his body was readying itself for another experiment? "Perhaps," he murmured, nuzzling her neck. This was the time to explain, when they were both content with the lassitude of repletion. "Cassidy—"

"I hope we can make a baby," she said, her voice muffled. "Our baby. I'd like that, Braden."

His throat grew very tight. "We've only just married."

"I know . . . that's what you always planned, for me and

Quentin. But I want one, with you. Your child." She stroked his chest. "I still have a lot to learn, but—"

"Cassidy." He gripped her arms. "I owe you the truth about myself."

"Braden—if it's about Mikhail—"

"It is, but not in the way you think. Mikhail . . . is not my son."

She sat up. "Not your son?"

"I will never be a father. I am . . . incapable of siring a child, Cassidy. Do you understand?"

Her breath stopped for too many heartbeats. "But . . . Mikhail—"

"He was Milena's child," he said roughly. "Not mine." Bile was acrid in his mouth. "A human did what I could not."

"A human?"

"Milena and I were together for almost six years. In all that time, the only child she carried was another man's. Do you know what a bastard is?"

"It means that the child's mother and father weren't married."

She knew that much more of life than he expected. "Yes. Milena was still married to me when she had the human's baby."

He could almost hear Cassidy absorbing what he had said, working through the implications.

"Then that's really why you sent Mikhail away," she whispered. "And Milena . . . *didn't* love you."

There were a hundred things he could have said then, but he kept his teeth locked over them. Milena was gone. She couldn't touch him anymore.

Cassidy was the one who still must suffer.

"Do you see now, Cassidy? In six years I could not father a child. You and I . . . will never have one."

He waited, a sickness in his gut, for Cassidy to react, for the shock and denial. It wasn't like her to weep, or take her pain out on others—but he had deceived her again. She'd had a right to know this about him before he married her. After all his talk of bloodlines and offspring to carry on the werewolf kind, she would have anticipated children of their union.

And she wanted them. Wanted *his* child.

"Oh, Braden," she said. "I'm so sorry." She collapsed onto him, wrapping her arms around him as far as she could reach. "That was what you were supposed to do, wasn't it? Have children with Milena, for the Cause. And you couldn't." She kissed his temple. "All the pain you must have felt. The sadness, knowing—and then Milena—" She hugged him fiercely. "I wouldn't leave you, Braden. Not for that, or for anything."

The knot in his throat made it impossible to answer, even if he could think of a response. How had he come to deserve this child-woman, with her heart as big as the sky above the fells? He had not, and did not. The feelings rose up behind his ribs, crowding his lungs so that he could scarcely breathe. He grabbed at the first rational thought that came into his mind.

"Now you realize why it's so important that Quentin and Rowena do as they must," he said. "For our family. For our blood. For our kind."

She was very quiet. For a while she remained where she was, holding him, silent.

"There's still Mikhail," she said at last. "In spite of everything, he's half *loup-garou*, like me. He's just a little boy, no matter what his mother did."

And surely an innocent at heart. Like Cassidy. Was it possible he could be saved?

"I can be his mother, Braden. We can make him ours."

Ours. Cassidy would make a wonderful mother. Of all people in the world, she could help her mate face the consequences of what he had done three years ago.

"I'll consider it," he said.

She kissed him, and he could feel the warmth of her gaze. "Braden, I love you. I love you so much."

He was grateful then that he couldn't see what lay in her eyes. Her words alone were more than he could endure. He wished them unspoken, knowing that Cassidy bared her heart as she bared her body, and hoped for him to do the same.

He desired her. He trusted her above all others, human or werewolf. She brought a new contentment into his life that he never thought to find again.

But what she asked opened up a great, dark void inside him, frightening in its ungovernable power. Yes, she made him feel—too much. Too deeply. He lost all objectivity, all coherence when she was near. His human intellect counted for nothing against the wolf's feral spirit that claimed her as mate. Even the Cause became unimportant.

It was too much as it had been with Milena, all over again.

And yet it was nothing like that time of madness, that destructive passion. He had forgotten that desire could be something other than malignant. Cassidy reminded him with her gentleness.

There must be a balance between emotion and duty. There must be some chance of redemption for himself outside of the bitter vows he'd sworn upon Milena's death.

He'd been proven flawed in every way that mattered: sterile, incapable of reliable judgment, apt to lose his reason completely when he allowed himself to care about anything but the Cause. He did nothing by half measures, and therein lay the danger.

Cassidy saw worth in him. She saw someone to love. Could he dare to love in return without sacrificing either her or the Cause?

If there was a way, he must find it or be driven mad by the two warring halves of his soul.

Cassidy herself had suggested a possible means, a symbol of hope for them both. He could not give Cassidy a child of his body, but he could help fill the void he had made and undo some part of the wrong his rage had perpetrated.

Mikhail must be brought back to Greyburn. All at once Braden saw how it could be done. But there were still no guarantees.

"Cassidy," he said, keeping all emotion from his voice, "I must go away for a while . . . a fortnight or two, perhaps."

"Go away?" The bed bounced as she jumped up. "The Convocation just ended!"

He was not prepared to give her the real reasons he had to leave, not when they might raise her hopes too high. "I have business on the Continent that cannot wait."

"But I thought that we could finally be together—"

"My duties have not disappeared because I married you, Cassidy. I am still responsible for this estate, my family's interests, and the Cause. And the Russians must be dealt with." He swung his feet over the bed. "You won't lack for whatever you need here at Greyburn. You have a home now."

"My home is with you."

He patted her hand. "I'll see to it that Mrs. Fairbairn and Aynsley make themselves available to show you the workings of Greyburn in greater detail and suggest appropriate activities. You'll have plenty to keep you busy."

"The way Rowena's busy? Locked up in her room, waiting for someone else to decide—"

"We will not discuss Rowena. I have explained how it must be." He turned to give her a perfunctory kiss on the forehead, deliberately cooling his lust. "Go to sleep, Cassidy."

"Where are you going?"

"For a run in the wood."

"I'll come with you."

"No." It was a blunt command. He had to be by himself, out of this maelstrom of emotion. "Don't wait up for me."

He heard the bedsprings creak as she lay down, tugging the sheets up over her shoulders. The urge to join her was strong, but he resisted it.

"Sleep well, Cassidy," he said. He passed soundlessly through the hidden doorway at the back of the room and gave himself up to the night.

But the sheer joy of the Change, the freedom of running as a wolf, the vibrant scents and sounds of the wood were no longer enough. There was an empty space at his side that only one woman in the world could fill.

Cassidy was still asleep when he left for Dover.

eighteen

I beg your pardon, Lady Greyburn."

It was several moments before Cassidy realized that the voice was addressing her. Since her marriage to Braden, she'd never become used to the title. It didn't mean anything—not to her or to anyone else at Greyburn.

She turned from the drawing room windows to face Telford in the doorway. Lord Greyburn had not been in residence for nearly four weeks, and his wife's authority was limited. Not that Cassidy wanted to rule the servants, or take on the duties Mrs. Fairbairn carried out so well, let alone play great lady among the human tenants she had yet to meet. She wouldn't know how if she tried.

But she might as well have been back at the ranch in New Mexico, avoided and ignored. "Lady Greyburn" was unable to assist those who most needed her help.

"Have you been feeling better this morning, my lady?" Telford said. "If you wish me to send for a physician—"

"No. It's nothing, really." Cassidy rubbed her waist through the snug bodice of her morning gown. Lately it seemed that she woke up early every day with the feeling that she was about to lose her last meal, even when there wasn't much in her stomach. And she'd lost her appetite for many things she used to like.

Werewolves could heal themselves of almost everything, it seemed, yet she couldn't cure an upset stomach. Maybe it was her human blood.

"Very well, Lady Greyburn," Telford said, his mouth twisting with disapproval. "I wished to report on Lady Rowena, as you requested. She has sent back the soup and bread you took to her. I fear it remains untouched."

Cassidy bent her head and sighed. "I'll speak with her again, Telford."

The valet bowed and slipped out of the room. Since Braden's departure, he'd been the only servant Cassidy could speak to as an equal. He was the one who kept her informed of Quentin's wild cavorting about the country— adventures that kept him away from Greyburn six days out of every seven. Telford seemed to find Quentin's activities harmless, but Cassidy sensed something frantic about Quentin on his rare visits home, as if he were trying to game and drink and flirt his way one step ahead of some sadness he couldn't acknowledge.

For the past two weeks, he hadn't come home at all.

Isabelle had grown as quiet and withdrawn as a shadow. It was as if she'd accepted the judgment of society in naming her a whore and outcast; all the fight had gone out of her. She hadn't spoken Matthew's name, nor had Cassidy seen the odd man in either of his identities, though she'd searched the fells time and again.

The footman, John Dodd, had also disappeared, his fate unknown. Mikhail was still in the hands of the Russians.

But Rowena's case was worst of all.

Cassidy climbed the stairs to the family wing. As always, there were footmen placed here and there along the landing and near Rowena's room. They were her jailers. Cassidy didn't know how humans could stop a werewolf if she wanted to leave, but obviously Rowena believed they could. The men showed Cassidy formal respect but remained at their posts like soldiers.

Cassidy didn't bother to knock on Rowena's door.

Rowena sat in a chair by the window in a starkly plain dress, her hair up and her back straight, a desolate figure surrounded by furnishings of feminine elegance and beauty. At first glance she looked the same as always, until one noticed the hollows under her eyes and cheekbones, the pallor of her skin. Until it became clear that the black dress she wore was almost too large, because she was attempting to slowly starve herself.

There hadn't been a formal family meal at Greyburn since before the Convocation, and Rowena remained alone in her suite day and night. Cassidy had discovered Rowena's purpose by accident when she'd caught a maid in the hallway, removing an untouched tray of food from Rowena's room. A little careful questioning revealed the disturbing truth: Lady Rowena hadn't eaten at all since the earl left Greyburn.

Braden wasn't there to bully his sister into eating, and none of the servants would dare. Quentin couldn't be located. Rowena had chosen the perfect time to protest her fate in the only way she knew how.

And she was silent. She starved herself of words as much as nourishment. Every day for the past two weeks Cassidy had tried to coax Rowena into eating, and every day she'd left defeated.

How long could a werewolf survive without food—even a werewolf who didn't want to be one?

Cassidy sat down in the chair opposite her sister-in-law's. "This can't go on, Rowena," she said.

Hands resting passively in her lap, Rowena didn't answer. She continued to gaze out at the park, watching summer rain spatter against the glass.

Cassidy stood up and planted herself in front of the window. "Do you really plan to kill yourself? I didn't know that was something proper English ladies did."

Rowena's eyes met hers. "Leave me alone," she said, her voice hoarse from disuse.

Hunger hadn't robbed Rowena of her aristocratic temperament. She was determined to control her life, and she wasn't about to let an American country bumpkin interfere.

But Cassidy had had enough of Forster obstinacy and her own feelings of helplessness. She missed Braden with an abiding ache in her chest that had spread to fill her stomach as well. She needed him—and she'd dared to believe he needed her.

But he was gone. The brief notes and telegrams he sent on his travels were filled with light trivia about this country and that, none specific enough to tell her where he was or how long he would be gone. She was a little cheered that they also contained restrained words of affection, though only she might have interpreted them so.

Still, they gave her no clue about her purpose at Greyburn. She couldn't be a mother. She was useless to the Cause. Loving Braden should have been enough. Six weeks ago, it had been.

Six weeks ago, perfect happiness had seemed right around the corner. Now she felt more cut off than she'd been in New Mexico from all the things and people who should have mattered most.

That was going to change.

"I'm sorry," she said, "but I can't leave you alone or let

you starve. Maybe you don't much like me, Rowena, but you're family. That means something to me, even if it doesn't to you."

Rowena stared at her as if she were a two-headed calf. "You truly haven't learned. If you expect domestic loyalty, love, and tranquillity, you have married into the wrong family."

"I think I've learned that . . . sometimes we have to make things happen ourselves, instead of waiting for them to come to us."

Rowena rested her head on the back of her chair. "You defended me to Braden when I last attempted to follow that advice. I have not forgotten."

"Then let me help you now."

"Have you heard from Quentin?"

"No."

"Then there is nothing you can do." She looked at Cassidy without hope. "He was to return two weeks ago and help me escape from Greyburn while Braden is gone. He has not come."

Cassidy let out a slow breath and sat down in her chair. So Rowena hadn't just given up after the first attempt—and her twin brother was prepared to assist her in spite of the inevitable consequences. Quentin had done a very good job of hiding his intentions. He'd never interfered between Braden and Rowena before, at least not in Cassidy's presence.

But he was Rowena's twin, and it made sense that they would be close, even if both concealed that closeness along with their plan for her escape.

For reasons unknown, Quentin hadn't come as promised. Rowena's last chance was gone. She was desperately unhappy and afraid—desperate enough to choose the only kind of release she saw still open to her. . . .

No. If no one else at Greyburn needed Cassidy, Rowena Forster did. Not just words, but actions. Someone had to care that much.

She clenched her fingers around the armrests of her chair and leaned forward. "You said Quentin was going to help you escape. How?"

"He did not share all his plans with me. I only know he was to provide a suitable distraction for the servants who guard me, and we were to take a ship at Liverpool, to America—"

"America?"

Rowena's mouth formed the ghost of a smile. "It is the last place Braden would ever search for me."

That was true enough. Rowena had made clear her distaste for things American, including her prospective mate.

"And what would you do, in America?" Cassidy asked. "Will you meet the man you love?"

"No. That is over." Rowena closed her eyes. "It no longer matters."

"It might if I help you in Quentin's place."

Pale brown eyes snapped open again. "You?"

"I'm the only one who can."

"You are Braden's wife now," Rowena said bitterly. "You saw how he reacted before. Don't you know what will happen if you interfere again?"

For a moment Cassidy thought of Isabelle's note and wondered if Rowena had sent it. She would have an excuse to criticize Braden if Milena, whom she'd loved so much, had also been kept prisoner by her brother.

But Rowena had said that Braden loved Milena. She'd never suggested anything else. She didn't know about Mikhail, and hadn't spoken of a stillborn child.

How could she go on admiring Milena if she knew that Braden's wife had been unfaithful to him? Or did she think he deserved it? If she believed that Braden had actually pushed—

There was no truth to that letter. None.

"Is that why you didn't ask for my help," Cassidy said, "because you were worried about *me*?"

Rowena glanced away. "You cannot stand against him, Cassidy."

"Not against *him*. I love him. But if I have to choose between his Cause and saving your life—I don't see how I can do anything else."

Rowena put her hands to her face. After a long silence, she raised her head. Her eyes were moist. "He married you," she murmured, "even though you cannot Change. If anyone in the world can make him understand . . ."

If he loves me, Cassidy had told Isabelle, *he won't shut me out. He* will *listen.* "Then it's settled." Cassidy rose and paced across the decorative carpet to Rowena's bed. "I don't know how Quentin planned to distract the servants—I've seen the ones watching you."

"Braden has willed them to lose all respect for me," Rowena said. "They will lay hands on me to prevent my escape, and I will not fight them."

"Then . . . you'll have to get out in the only way they'll never suspect. As a wolf."

Rowena tried to stand, lost her balance, and clutched at the chair for support. "No."

"I know how much you hate it, but if it's for the last time—you'll have to, Rowena."

Looking pale and ill, Rowena fell back into her chair. "What you ask . . . They will know me, even as a wolf—"

"Because of your color. But what if I darken your fur with ashes, so that you look like Braden? At night, no human will be able to tell the difference."

"How will I leave the house?"

"Through the secret passageway in our room. I've seen

Braden use it, and I know how it works. I'll think of some good reason to get you to our suite. I don't think the servants will say no to me."

Rowena shuddered. "I cannot go to Liverpool, as . . . a beast."

"You won't have to. We'll make a bundle of clothes and other things you'll need, and . . ." Cassidy thought rapidly. "I'll get a carriage to meet you away from the house. There must be a train—"

"And who will drive this carriage, if we can trust none of the servants?"

"I will. I can handle horses. I'll drive you to the station, and—"

"I believe that I have a better alternative."

Cassidy and Rowena turned as one toward the door. Isabelle stepped into the room and shut the door carefully behind her.

"I beg your pardon for coming to your room uninvited, Lady Rowena, but Telford said I might find Cassidy here." She met Cassidy's gaze. "It appears that my timing was impeccable."

Rowena's body stiffened as if she would stand, but her weakness got the better of her. "Mrs. Smith—"

"I know what you have been discussing, Lady Rowena. I have been expecting something of the kind." She made no attempt to come farther into the room, but stood very still near the door, palms pressed flat to her skirt as if to prevent it from touching anything that belonged to Rowena. "I believe that I can be of service to you"—she glanced at Cassidy—"if I may speak with Lady Rowena alone for a few moments."

It was the first time in weeks that these two women had been in the same room together. Maybe there could be a kind of acceptance between them at last.

And maybe Isabelle, like Cassidy, was hungry to be needed.

"I'll wait outside the door," she said, "and make sure you aren't interrupted."

She left them alone, and tried to keep her thoughts too busy to dwell on the fear that what she was about to do could never be undone.

The first thing Isabelle had seen when she entered Rowena's room was the portrait of Milena. She took it in with a single glance and instantly perceived why this dead woman was the center of so much turmoil.

But if Milena were part of the current problem, she was but a peripheral one. She would have to wait.

Isabelle leaned against the door and wished she could be anywhere but here, in this tasteful and expensively decorated room so well suited for the sister of a peer of the realm. She felt crushed by the weight of society's judgment, contained in the arrogant, proper figure of the young woman seated by the window.

Proper still, perhaps, but no longer quite so arrogant. Lady Rowena had been forced to suffer, had watched her private dreams and wishes trampled by a man who had no concern for her happiness.

How different were the fine lady and fallen woman now?

"Lady Rowena," Isabelle said, "I'm sure you understand that it is impossible that Cassidy should accompany you to Liverpool."

Rowena did not quite meet her eyes. Was she offended at the whore's outrageous effrontery—or was she wretched enough to accept aid wherever she could find it?

"I realize that you and Cassidy have not been close," Isabelle continued, hardening her voice. "You did not want her for a sister-in-law, but what's done is done. I ask you to consider her future here at Greyburn, long after you are gone——"

"I have considered it, Mrs. Smith." She looked up. "From the very first day Cassidy spent with us in London, I saw that Braden felt something for her that could not easily be dismissed. When we arrived at Greyburn, I told her about his previous wife." Her delicate throat trembled. "I made Cassidy believe that Braden loved Milena, that she was so perfect that no one could ever take her place. I believed the latter, Mrs. Smith, but not the former."

"Lord Greyburn didn't love her?"

"No. Perhaps once he was infatuated with her, but that passed, and all that remained was lust and possession. A male animal's domination of its mate. I deceived Cassidy to protect her. I hoped she would lose heart and stay away from Braden."

Isabelle held her gaze. "Was it you who sent me the letter?"

"I sent you nothing," Rowena said with a return of her cool dignity. "I tell you this now so that you can help Cassidy if she requires it."

"Is it true, then—that Lord Greyburn was jealous and kept Milena here, isolated—"

"Yes. It was an arranged marriage. They never had much in common. She tried everything to please him, but by nature she preferred being among people who could laugh and find joy in life—just as she brought joy to us at Greyburn. She delighted in society and the Season. But Braden wished to remain here with his Cause. That was all he ever cared for. He came to despise her because she had not given him a child for the Cause." Her eyes glittered as if with tears. "For a while he allowed her to return to London every Season, but the last year of their marriage, he—went mad. In his sickness, he believed that every man she spoke to was her lover, and he was determined to punish her. He brought her back, just as he did me, and kept her prisoner. While she was confined at Greyburn, he . . . got her with child. Milena could not bear the thought of letting her babe be brought up here, without love or happiness. She begged me to help her escape. But I was too much a coward to defy my brother."

Isabelle felt ill. The letter's claims hadn't been wholly false, then. "And her death?"

Rowena flinched at the blunt question. "She contrived to leave, in spite of Braden's ploys. He went after her during a terrible storm. He brought her back, injured and unconscious. She never fully became herself again. Her child died."

"I see," Isabelle murmured. "Thank you for telling me this, Lady Rowena."

Rowena's pale brown eyes were the only spots of color in a proud, handsome, brittle face. "I wished you to know. If Braden finds out that Cassidy helped me escape, the consequences . . ."

The consequences. There was no telling what Lord Greyburn might do if he had any reason at all to doubt Cassidy's loyalty. Lying now served Rowena no purpose. Even if Lord Greyburn hadn't pushed his wife, her death was his responsibility. He had treated her cruelly, accused her of the very sins society had pinned on Isabelle, perhaps even compelled her to submit to his lust.

Once Isabelle had sensed that Braden was a man who hid great passions beneath a cold exterior. Those passions were more dangerous than ever she'd suspected.

"I have no doubt that Cassidy offered her help freely," Isabelle said. "Once I would have thought this a child's impulsive action, but she has grown and changed in the past months. To dissuade her would be difficult." She took several steps into the room and stopped, fighting her own agitation. "Even though Cassidy knows Braden will be angry, her faith outweighs her reason. She has already heard . . . some of what you've told me, yet she loves Lord Greyburn, and because she can only love with all her heart and soul, she believes that alone will protect her."

"It cannot." Rowena glanced away. "Not with Braden."

Isabelle shivered at the dull finality of the words. "Then we must both protect her from becoming involved any more than necessary. I will go with you to Liverpool."

They stared at each other. Isabelle smiled unevenly. "I know how you feel about me, Lady Rowena. But I also know that as a respectable young woman, you will not wish to travel alone. I fancy myself a rather good actress . . . no one outside Greyburn is likely to suspect my true identity."

Rowena turned to the window, her profile pinched in the rain-filtered light. "I grant," she said, "that you are most talented."

"And you're afraid that my talents will rub off on you." Isabelle laughed. "You already feel soiled by your inhuman abilities, which Cassidy would sacrifice anything to gain. Well, Lady Rowena, if my assistance is so repellent, you may still take the coward's way out and kill yourself. Whatever my faults, and my mere humanity, that was the one recourse I never considered."

With a sharp indrawn breath, Rowena jerked around in her chair. The hectic flush of her skin paled to white. Her mouth opened and closed again. Little by little her aristocratic mask lost all its sharp edges. It seemed to crumple as Isabelle watched.

"You are right," Rowena whispered. She covered her eyes. "I would be . . . grateful for your assistance."

Pride was a difficult medicine to swallow. Rowena's gratitude was strained, but genuine. *And did you wish to feel triumphant at such a victory?* Isabelle asked herself. *Do you feel superior now? Have you not both sacrificed honor for survival?*

"We cannot expect any of the servants to accompany us," Rowena said. "Someone must drive the carriage to the station."

"I shall think of something. I suggest you set aside the minimum of what you will require for the journey, and restore your strength by eating what you can."

Rowena looked up. "Braden may return at any time—"

"Then we must be prepared to act upon a moment's notice." She had turned to leave when Rowena's voice stopped her.

"You don't care about me," she said. "Why are you doing this?"

"For Cassidy's sake. There is little enough Lord Greyburn can do to me." At the door she hesitated and turned back. "And because . . . I believe, in the end, that we must be free to shape our own destinies."

She fled the room with relief and found Cassidy waiting as promised. If the footmen stationed in the corridor were disturbed by all this coming and going, they gave no sign.

"I believe Lady Rowena will consent to eat now," Isabelle said. "Would you see to that, and help her select what she'll need for the journey? I must make my own preparations."

"Then you are going with her?"

Isabelle touched Cassidy's cheek. "Only as far as Liverpool. There is business here I must attend to."

She hurried off before Cassidy could ask questions or witness her tears. There was one more hurdle to face, if she were to see that Cassidy remained out of this imbroglio as much as possible. It was the one gift Isabelle could be sure might do some good.

And it meant that she, too, must swallow her pride and forget everything but Cassidy's welfare.

She changed into a skirt suitable for walking, left the house through the rear garden doors and climbed the fell rising from the park. She'd never actually been to Matthias's cottage, but she'd seen it from the top of the fell, nestled in a tiny valley below. She knew that Matthias—no, she must think of him as Matthew, now—had returned to Greyburn after an unexplained absence.

No. Not unexplained. He'd left because of her. Because he hadn't been able to accept the truth of her transgressions.

But he'd seemed well disposed toward Cassidy, in both his incarnations. At heart, he was a kind man. And he was relatively free of the machinations of the Forster clan. If anyone at Greyburn would help, he might.

Isabelle descended the other side of the fell, scraping together her courage. Beg she would not—but everything short of that, for Cassidy.

She didn't know who to expect when she knocked on the door. Would a man in quaint armor answer, or the stranger she'd last seen under such humiliating circumstances?

The unlocked door swung open to an empty room. He wasn't there. Mingled relief and panic weakened her knees.

"Mrs. Smith," a hoarse voice called behind her.

She turned, hand at her throat. The man who greeted her from the yard was dressed in worn and somewhat shabby clothing, but it was the attire of a well-bred man of the nineteenth century, not a Border Reiver of the seventeenth.

Matthew.

She straightened and met his gaze. So long since she'd seen him, and yet he was as achingly handsome as before. Iron gray hair flowed about his shoulders, unfashionably long. His face was weathered and lined with some new sadness. His eyes . . .

His eyes swept over her and clouded with emotion.

"Isabelle," he said. He took a step forward, paused, tugged at the collar of his frayed shirt. "It's b-been—I didn't expect—"

"Where is Matthias?" she asked suddenly.

"Gone," he said. "I'm sorry. If you . . . came to find him, I f-fear . . . He is gone."

Isabelle flinched at the strangely final ring of the words. He spoke as if Matthias were dead. And yet he stood before her, in his other form, very much alive. "Mr. Forster, I know you have little wish to see me now. Nevertheless, I have come to ask you—"

He plunged forward in an ardent dash, one hand held out in supplication. "I failed you, Isabelle."

She stared with incomprehension at his flushed face. "I do not understand—"

"No. They wouldn't have t-told you, would they?" He laughed under his breath. "Matthias was the one who proposed it. He said that . . . one of us m-must go to London to challenge Leebrook and defend your honor."

"What?"

"He could not be permitted to . . . insult you as he did. But Matthias . . . could n-not go to London. I went in his place. And I failed."

Isabelle was very much in need of a place to sit down. As if he anticipated her thoughts, Matthew rushed to take her arm and lead her inside the cottage. He seated her at a plain chair beside an equally plain table.

"You . . . challenged Lord Leebrook?" she asked faintly.

"Matthias gave me his sword. I traveled to London . . . but it was all a d-debacle." He leaned heavily on the table. "Leebrook would not accept my challenge. They thought me m-mad. The earl sent my nephew Quentin to fetch me home."

Isabelle resisted the urge to gather Matthew's bent head against her breast. "Then . . . *that* was why you left Greyburn?"

A blaze of fierce pride crossed Matthew's face. "Aye. I'd have made that b-bastard Leebrook pay—" He broke off, and when he looked at Isabelle it was with a bitter sadness. "But he didn't pay for his crimes. And I . . . am ashamed."

The world had turned upside down. Matthew, ashamed, for failing to defend her nonexistent honor? It was the sort of mad scheme an old-fashioned hero would invent—a man like Matthias, bred to another, less enlightened age.

But *Matthew* had gone to London—Matthew, who for so many years had hidden himself away in loneliness and sorrow.

"No," she said softly. She dared to touch Matthew's hand. "You have nothing to be ashamed of."

He sighed and bent his chin to his chest. "It was when I was in London . . . that I knew I w-would never need Matthias again."

"Where has he gone?"

The light in Matthew's eyes was unlike any she'd seen there before. She realized that his stutter was much reduced, and he spoke with an echo of Matthias's calm assurance. "When I came home to Greyburn, he wasn't here. We both knew that he wasn't n-needed anymore."

She searched his face, wondering if she understood him. "Why?"

"Because I had come to . . ." He turned his hand to

clasp Isabelle's. "I told you part of a s-story before . . . about how Matthias rescued me from despair. You m-must have thought me mad indeed, Isabelle. But I knew all along that I was Matthias, and he myself. It was my way of p-pretending the real world no longer existed. I drew into my own dreams of raids and Reivers. I lost myself in an ancient l-legend of a guardian of Greyburn. It gave me purpose, no matter how illusory, and I could b-become someone strong and sure. I let my family believe I was m-merely a harmless eccentric. I preferred my fantasy to my family's contempt."

He tightened his grip. "You see, I wished to know you from the first t-time I saw you walking the fell. But only Matthias had the courage to approach. So I let that part of me c-court you, in the only way I knew how."

She lifted his hand to her cheek. "Oh, Matthew. How lonely you must have been—"

"I never realized it, until I met you. And when I saw young Cassidy's bravery, d-despite the very inabilities that would make her outcast, as I was—I was shamed by my cowardice. When Leebrook insulted you, I went after him." He dropped his gaze. "I have been just as much a c-coward in failing to seek you out and admit that I could not defend you. Can you forgive me?"

"But I was the one who deceived you," she said. "How can you ignore what I—"

He put a finger to her lips. "Once, long ago, there might have been another Isabelle, who was forced by circumstance and a man's d-dishonor to fight for her survival. Is she here now?"

How she longed to say no. "Yes, Matthew," she said, withdrawing her hand from his. "She is a part of me. I cannot disavow her choices."

"But now, here, today . . . you have n-new choices to

make." He recaptured her hand. "I shall be a coward no longer. I must know. Is it only M-matthias whom you . . ." His tan skin reddened. "Have I hope, Isabelle?"

"Hope?" she whispered.

"When I returned, I feared I had lost you. I knew it was Matthias you cared for. Now he is gone, and p-perhaps I am a poor second." Even as he spoke, his eyes watched her with longing.

Isabelle's heart hammered beneath her ribs. "But you *are* Matthias."

"He will always be a part of me." His fingers caressed hers. "But he was a role I played, a phantom. I have something b-better than fantasies to live for, now."

Yes. Matthias's peace was there, in Matthew's face, in his voice. The anguish and remorse to which Matthew had referred seemed to disappear, taking hers along with it.

"I love you, Isabelle," he said.

She closed her eyes. This was a dream. Matthew and Matthias spoke to her with one voice, united—of love. Love with its eyes wide open. No tricks, no deception, no remorse.

He gathered both her hands in his and knelt beside her. "Can you love me, Isabelle? As I am?"

She rested her forehead against his shoulder. "Oh, Matthew . . . give me time. This is not something I expected to happen. Ever again."

"Of course." He stroked her hair. "It takes time to learn to t-trust again. And a man can live a very long while on hope, my bonny, dear one."

She looked into his kindly eyes. "Matthew . . . I came to find you for a reason. It cannot wait." Putting her own confusion aside, she explained how Cassidy planned to help Rowena, and her own part in the venture.

"But we need someone to drive us to the station," she said. "I did not know who else I could turn to."

"You came to *me*. And I will help." He rose, pulling her up with him. "You . . . w-wish to accompany Rowena to America?"

"No. I'd planned to leave Greyburn—but certain circumstances have changed in the past little while." She backed away from Matthew. "We cannot ask the grooms to prepare the carriage, nor can we hide our roles in this."

"I understand." He held her gaze but made no attempt to follow her to the door. "I have some s-skill with horses. I can do what is necessary."

"Then come to the stables an hour before dawn tomorrow morning. We must take the carriage to meet Rowena a safe distance from the house."

"I shall be there."

Isabelle left the cottage and climbed the fell, refusing to look back. She'd expected this meeting to be humiliating and painful, but all her predictions proved false. She had one night to make a decision that would determine her future: to give her heart and her trust to a man she barely knew, well aware that in England she would never be able to forget her past—

Or to put any hope of love forever behind her.

She'd spoken to Cassidy of choices, believing her own made and settled long ago. It seemed that one was never too old to be a fool.

The dawn was wreathed in heavy mist that carried the hint of approaching autumn. The carriage horses stamped, blowing steam from their nostrils; Isabelle pulled her shawl about her shoulders and stared at the blurred silhouettes of a copse of trees just to the west. Toward Greyburn.

Matthew perched on the coachman's seat, loosely holding the reins. He whistled softly.

"Someone's coming," he said. But there was no further warning before a wolf, mottled black and gray, emerged from the mist.

It stopped to crouch several feet before Isabelle and shook its coat vigorously. Black ash flew from its fur, leaving it dullish white.

A white wolf. She'd seen this wolf before, when she spied on the ceremony in the Great Hall, but it was something quite different to be so close to Rowena Forster in her alternate shape. In its way, the wolf was just as elegant and beautiful as the woman, but it was also unmistakably more. *She* was unmistakably dangerous.

Rowena met Isabelle's gaze with eyes slightly more yellow than those she possessed as a human. Isabelle felt the challenge in that gaze, and shivered. But Rowena despised herself at this moment more than she could possibly resent the whore whose help she so badly needed.

Isabelle returned to the carriage and pulled out the folded blanket she'd brought along with Rowena's smallest trunks. She shook it out and held it wide between herself and the wolf.

As if the surrounding mist obeyed Rowena's commands, it gathered about her and wrapped her in a cocoon made of air. Within that cocoon, she Changed. Isabelle blinked, and a woman stood before her, pale and naked and distressingly thin.

Quickly Isabelle offered the blanket, and Rowena snatched it from her. The wolf's boldness was gone; Rowena wrapped the blanket over her bowed head and hurried to the carriage.

As agreed, Matthew slipped away to grant his niece the privacy she required to don the simple traveling dress Isabelle had brought. But there was still no sign of Cassidy.

For a moment Isabelle dared hope that Cassidy had found the good sense to remain at the house.

But the muffled sound of hoofbeats quickly laid that hope to rest. A horse and rider, moving at a brisk trot, appeared where the narrow country lane vanished into the haze. Cassidy wore her calico and rode astride, hair damp and loose like a heavy mane at her back.

She dismounted with a soft word to the horse and glanced at the carriage. Her skin was unusually pale and there were dark hollows under her eyes, as if she hadn't slept. Isabelle doubted that any of them had.

"It worked," Cassidy said. "No one stopped me when I invited Rowena to my room last night. By the time the servants start wondering where she is this morning, it'll be too late." She grimaced. "The grooms and stable hands are still hunting down the horses I let loose. I didn't like doing that, Isabelle. If it weren't for Rowena—"

"It was necessary," Isabelle said. The last thing Cassidy needed was more guilt on top of the consequences she had yet to face—even if she didn't appreciate how great they might be. The truths that Rowena had revealed must remain hidden until Isabelle returned and had time to explain as gently as possible. "You've done your part, Cassidy. You can go back now—"

"Not yet." She gazed at Isabelle, eyes moist, and rested her cheek on the horse's neck. "I would have been here sooner, but I haven't been feeling well. I had to wait a few minutes before I could ride."

Instinctively Isabelle felt Cassidy's forehead. She wasn't the sort to complain about minor discomforts, and Isabelle had never seen her sick except after the footman's attack. "How are you ill?"

"My stomach. Sometimes early in the morning, I have to—" She swallowed, paling further. "Excuse me." She pushed the horse's reins into Isabelle's hand and ran to the nearest clump of shrubbery. Isabelle heard the sounds of dry heaving, and then Cassidy returned, moving slowly and stiffly.

"I'm sorry," she said. "This hasn't happened to me before."

Illumination came to Isabelle like a shaft of sunlight through the mist. She did a quick mental calculation. "How long have you been feeling this way?"

"Not long. Do you know what's wrong with me?"

Isabelle looked for somewhere to sit. Rowena was still occupied behind a makeshift screen made of blankets tied up against the carriage, and Matthew hadn't yet returned. She led Cassidy to a clump of small boulders and pushed her down.

"Cassidy . . . sometimes these troubles are not a sign of illness at all. There is a very real chance that you may be with child."

Mere sunlight would be shamed by the brilliance of Cassidy's face. "You mean . . . a baby . . ." She began to rise and just as suddenly sank back down again. The light left her eyes. "It can't happen, Isabelle."

"Can't?" That brief, stunning bliss convinced Isabelle that Cassidy wanted a child. Her condition could only be an asset in her husband's eyes, a protection against his wrath. What else could be wrong? "I know I should have discussed this with you much earlier, but—"

"Braden can't have children," Cassidy said. "He explained it to me just before he left."

Isabelle blinked. Braden had told Cassidy something that directly contradicted what both the letter and Rowena claimed—that Milena gave birth to a stillborn child. Was this another deception by the earl of Greyburn? What could he gain by lying? He wanted children for his Cause.

Unless it was that he didn't want children who were

less than full *loup-garou*. Cassidy's children. Even so, he would find it difficult to prevent their conception without the use of chancy protection. Cassidy would be sure to catch on.

Cassidy folded her arms across her stomach. "If only . . ."

Isabelle knelt awkwardly. "Oh, my dear."

"Don't worry about me. It hurts Braden even more."

Naturally she would think of him before herself. Isabelle brushed off her skirt and hid her anger and disgust behind a veneer of calm. "Nevertheless, you are obviously not well. We shall take you back to Greyburn before we continue to the station."

"No." Cassidy stood up and looked past Isabelle. "Rowena. You're ready to go?"

Rowena came to join them. "Are you well, Cassidy?"

"I'm fine. And you?"

"I am free," Rowena said. In spite of her haggard appearance, she smiled with greater warmth than Isabelle had ever seen in her. She looked . . . *human*.

"It is thanks to you"—Rowena included Isabelle in her gaze—"to you both that I will never again be forced to endure the beast. I owe you my life. I shall not forget your kindness."

Cassidy stepped forward and gave Rowena one of her impulsive hugs. "I wish we could have known each other better," she said. "I hope you'll find what you're looking for in America."

"And I hope and pray that you shall find your happiness here," Rowena said. But her gaze met Isabelle's over the top of Cassidy's head, and her gaze was sad.

"If you wish to cross Greyburn land before full light, we must leave soon," Matthew said behind them.

Rowena nodded. "I shall wait in the carriage," she said. She clasped Cassidy's hand one last time and left her alone with Isabelle.

Cassidy struck right to the point. "What about you and Matthew, Isabelle?" she asked.

Evading that piercing insight was impossible. "I don't know," she said. She found herself unable to meet Cassidy's gaze. "I never expected—"

"To love someone again?" Cassidy smiled wistfully. "I needed you, but I didn't stop to think that you needed someone, too." She grew serious. "Matthew is a good man. I think you can trust him, Isabelle."

Ah, but you trust far too easily. I am not like you. Yet Isabelle felt her heart expand, as if someone had removed a weight from behind her ribs.

Cassidy embraced her and stepped back. "Take care, Isabelle. Come back safely." Her smile hovered between sadness and brave determination. "You've done so much for me. I didn't know anything about life when we came to England—but I have learned one thing, Isabelle. Love is worth fighting for."

nineteen

Two miles to go.

Only two short miles remained of the journey back to Greyburn, and as the hired carriage neared the border of his land, Braden was aware of a new, poignant happiness at the smells and sounds of home.

Because of Cassidy. His *wife*—new, miraculous thought that was—who awaited his return, whom he had never stopped thinking about during these long weeks apart. Cassidy's scent was still too distant, but he found himself leaning into the window, stretching his senses for the first hint of her unique essence borne on the wind.

He missed her now as he had every day of his absence. Acceptance of that need had been difficult. Always before he'd traveled alone, with only Telford as companion. He had denied any loneliness or desire for companionship, proud of his self-sufficiency.

Pride. How thoroughly his pride had suffered at Cassidy's hands. And yet he remembered her in that place the blindness couldn't touch—joyful, welcoming, loyal in her devotion—and his heart filled and overflowed with answering exaltation.

During his journey to Russia and all that followed, he had begun to feel his doubts and fears turn insubstantial as shadows. If his separation from Cassidy had been a test, it had given him the beginnings of an answer.

His emotions could be trusted, not rejected. He would *make* it work. He would forget the past. He would remain true to the Cause and to Cassidy, whatever else he must sacrifice. Cassidy would become a part of the Cause, his partner, inseparable from it in his heart.

With an effort he settled back in the seat and turned his attention to the other occupants of the carriage. He knew the boy was watching him. He'd felt those eyes—Milena's eyes—gazing with steady concentration ever since they'd left Russia, and every mile by train, ship, and carriage from the continent to England. On this last stretch of the journey between Ulfington station and Greyburn, Braden was fully aware of what he had done.

And of Milena's son, come at last to Greyburn.

The agreement with the Russians had been reached easily enough. Braden had allowed Stefan and Fedor to return to Russia unharmed in exchange for a hostage from their house—Milena's only son, Mikhail. He hadn't been foolish enough to let the brothers believe that he wanted the child for any other purpose than as insurance for their good conduct. By the time they realized that no amount of such behavior would win him back, the boy would be established at Greyburn.

Braden had expected to find an infant hellion at the Boroskov estates, a creature he might have cause to regret bringing back to England. Instead, Tasya Boroskova had timidly introduced him to a three-year-old boy who barely spoke and maintained an oddly mature dignity in his wiry little body. Braden knew then that he would not be leaving alone.

More, he wanted the boy. Cassidy's instincts had been right. Healing lay in this act of reconciliation, for both orphaned child and remorseful guardian.

But Mikhail Boroskov's self-possession was almost frightening. He hadn't wept when he'd said good-bye to the woman who'd raised him. He had come without resistance, obeyed Braden and the nurse hired in London, and been in every respect ideally behaved. In every way the opposite of his mother.

He would be Cassidy's son.

And Braden's.

He felt an unexpected protectiveness, a wolf's need to shield the young and helpless. But there was more to it than that, and more than guilt and repentance. It was as if Mikhail were flesh of his flesh.

That could not be so, but he could refuse to let it make a difference. He had done his best to treat Mikhail kindly, though he felt awkward in his attempts. Perhaps the boy felt just as confused, and that was the reason for his shyness and steady gaze. He was, after all, half *loup-garou*.

He had been raised with Tasya's love, but he had also spent his first three years as part of a family steeped in viciousness and cruelty. There was about him something closed off, sleeping, waiting—waiting for the one soul that could reach out to his.

Cassidy, who had broken down Braden's walls with headstrong persistence and quiet faith.

Cassidy, his wife. His . . .

The word stayed locked in his mind.

The carriage clattered through the wide gates that opened into Greyburn's park. Mikhail's nurse, a middle-aged woman named Betsy, gave a low gasp of appreciation. Braden knew he'd have to see to the woman's initiation himself; she seemed respectful and submissive enough, so he could leave that matter undone for a day or two—until the boy adjusted, and he knew all would be well.

They drove up to a quiet house as yet unprepared for their arrival. Some servant would have noted their approach; shortly a gaggle of footmen would dash out and Aynsley would proffer his formal greeting, but Braden was glad for a few moments of peace.

He stepped out of the door opened by the coachman and turned back for the boy. Mikhail crouched on his seat beside the nurse, silent as always.

"Come, child," Braden said. "This is your new home."

Perhaps the nurse gave him a push, or the child couldn't break the habit of obedience. He slid forward and allowed Braden to lift him to the ground. He clutched Braden's hand, and Braden let himself pull the boy close.

"You'll soon be used to it," he said gruffly. "We've horses here, and room to run."

He felt the boy looking up at him. Waiting. Perhaps hoping beneath that stillness. Braden had the sudden urge to take Mikhail to Cassidy at once, just so he could feel and hear her delight at the surprise he'd brought her.

"There is someone you'll meet soon," he told the boy, giving his hand a squeeze. "Someone you'll like very much. But first the nurse will take you to your room, where you can rest."

Mikhail's hand was pried from Braden's only with the greatest persistence by the nurse, who fussed and chattered at the boy all the while. Aynsley arrived, his movements less assured than usual. Braden gave instructions for the boy's installment in the long-unused nursery.

Telford hurried down the stairs. "Welcome home, my lord," he said. Braden almost would have called his tone uneasy.

"You've handled the matter of Dodd as I instructed?"

"Yes, my lord. All is in readiness."

"Excellent. You may depart when you're ready." He gripped Telford's shoulder. "I appreciate your efforts. I will make it worth your while."

"It is my pleasure, my lord." Telford backed away and strode off, leaving Braden with a sense of something not quite right.

But that was the old Braden's pessimism, the voice he was determined to forget. He was home. He turned from the bustling footmen and followed the urgent dictates of his heart.

Cassidy waited for him in the entrance hall just within the door. She was very quiet. She didn't run to him or fling herself into his arms. Her stillness made her seem years older than her age—or perhaps it was his time away that made him imagine a new dignity. Had she learned to be a lady in six weeks?

Not his Cassidy. She could not change. He wouldn't let her. His desire came immediately, and with it the image of his wife naked in his arms, taking him into her supple body and whispering words he hardly dared believe were real.

"Cassidy," he said, his voice husky with feelings unspoken. "I'm home."

"Yes," she said. Only that, as if they'd been married and indifferent to each other for decades. He heard her draw a shuddering breath. "I have something to tell you, before—"

He wished then that she were incapable of speech as he was of sight. He stalked up to her and swept her into his arms, becoming whole the instant he felt her heart beating against his own.

Home. This was home as it had never been; this was

life, and promise, and happiness. He found her mouth and kissed her, thoughts racing ahead to the most efficient way of reaching their room and relieving her of her clothing. The dress was tight and corseted, one of Rowena's selections. He hated it.

"Cassidy," he murmured, kissing her hair and wishing it loose from the pins that secured it. He couldn't hold that thick mass in his hands until they were alone upstairs. He wanted to stroke her skin and taste the nectar of her body, take her to ecstasy again and again. From this moment on he'd never be alone. . . .

Her body went stiff and unresponsive in his arms. "You have to know, Braden," she said. "We need to talk about it now."

Smarting and perplexed, he released her and stepped back. "I'm delighted that you missed me so very much, my dear wife. What more could I ask after such a long journey?"

"I am glad that you're back. More than glad. Without you—Oh, Braden—" She touched his arm, and he shook her off.

"Since it seems so urgent that you speak to me, please do so. I'm certain that we both have more important matters awaiting our attention."

He didn't require visual clues to recognize her frustration—or her deep unease.

Something was wrong. Something bad enough that she couldn't bear to greet him with the love she had professed so eagerly before.

But she didn't want to displease him. She was a new bride in a world still strange to her. Doubtless she'd committed some minor faux pas with the servants or a similar transgression that would seem far worse to her than to him. She was awkward and gauche by English standards, young and brash by any.

He curved his mouth into a smile and held out his hand. "Forgive me, Cassidy. I'm merely tired from the journey. Where is Quentin?"

"Quentin . . . hasn't been here in a month," she said. "I don't know where he is."

A hum of alarm moved along Braden's nerves. He hadn't been present to keep Quentin's excesses in check; the boy could be anywhere, in any sort of trouble. But he'd be damned before he let Quentin's absence mar his homecoming.

"Don't be concerned," he told Cassidy. "I'll track him down soon enough. I trust Rowena is well—I shall speak to her shortly. I have a surprise for you—"

"Braden . . . Rowena is gone."

Cassidy's voice was soft and serious, but she might as well have shouted. Braden snapped erect, head up, testing the air.

Rowena's scent was stale, days old. Braden strode for the staircase and took the stairs two at a time, ignoring his occasional stumbles. He reached Rowena's room and found the door unlocked.

The room was vacant. Rowena had been gone long enough that even her scent was fading.

Cassidy came up behind him, moving with steps light and hesitant. "She left two weeks ago."

He swung on her. "How? How did she get away?"

His heart counted out nearly a score of beats before she answered. "I helped her," she said.

The declaration hung between them like a dying cry. Braden found himself unable to breathe.

"I had to," Cassidy said. "She was hurting too much. She would have let herself die before . . ." She lifted her chin. "It was something I had to do, Braden. Please understand."

Numbness sapped all sensation from his body before

he could feel or react. He simply stood where he was, absorbing her confession.

He imagined Rowena in her room, driving herself to hysteria in her hatred for what she was. Convincing herself that death was the only escape.

Pity came unwanted out of nowhere—pity and regret and sorrow for the sister who'd once loved him. Another sacrifice to the Cause. But the sacrifice was necessary. No one life could outweigh the survival of a race.

Rowena knew that. And so did Cassidy, yet she had betrayed him in deliberate defiance of the basic requirements he'd laid down for their marriage—her absolute loyalty to and acceptance of the Cause and its necessities.

Betrayal. His stomach and throat twisted as if a torturer had bound him in bands of iron. He struggled to find any explanation that might absolve her.

"Quentin," he said hoarsely. "Quentin was behind this—"

"Rowena hasn't heard from Quentin."

Not Quentin. But Rowena was his twin. She hid cunning behind propriety, feral instinct beneath a veneer of human normality. If she'd been desperate enough . . .

"How did Rowena convince you?" he demanded. "She must have tricked you. Taken advantage of your natural kindness—"

"She didn't take advantage of me, Braden."

"Rowena has the werewolf powers," he said. "She could have used them—"

"I helped her of my own free will," Cassidy said. She moved toward him, stopped again. "I know how you feel about the Cause. I know what you told me, and I never wanted to disobey you." He heard her suck in air as if she, too, found it difficult to breathe. "But it was wrong, Braden. Wrong to keep her prisoner. If only there'd been some other way—"

He ignored her attempt at explanation. It was all his heart could do to keep beating when the claws of despair had torn it from his chest.

Cassidy. His naive, innocent Cassidy had deluded him into believing that she was different from anyone else he'd ever known. Artless, guileless, steadfast. Milena's opposite, without even a trace of Rowena's bitterness or Quentin's blithe irresponsibility. Someone with whom he might relax his control for an hour, or a day. Someone impervious to treachery.

He would never have believed her capable of this. He had left for a few weeks, and even that was too long to hold her devotion. She *knew* what Rowena meant to the Cause. She had known from the start that the Cause was his life.

And she asked for his *understanding*.

He felt his way to Rowena's bed and curled his fingers around the carved bedpost, pressing until he felt the designs imprinted on his flesh. "Do you know what you've done?"

"Yes." No apology. "I know. But—"

"Where has she gone?"

"To a place where she can live her own life," Cassidy said, and he wondered distantly how she could speak so calmly of disaster. Of the undoing of his careful plans, the trust given him by Tiberius so many years ago.

And the destruction of his hope. The stupid, gullible hope that Cassidy was what Milena could never be: the other half of himself.

His . . . love.

He released the bedpost and turned toward her again. "You will tell me where she's gone," he said in a voice bereft of expression. "I'll bring her back."

"I can't," she said. "I promised Rowena. She has a right to find her own happiness, just as I have. With you."

The irony of her words filled him with scathing amusement. "You should have given more consideration to your happiness before you helped her. Do you think you can withstand my will if I choose to use it?"

"But you won't," she said softly. "I know you won't."

Was she so certain of him—so sure he'd accept her faithlessness simply because he'd married her? Because they'd shared a bed and a few hours of passion?

Milena had been that sure of him, confident that he'd never open his eyes to her infidelity or take action against her, no matter how flagrant her licentiousness. She'd used his love for her against him time and again, and laughed at his metaphorical blindness.

How she must have laughed, even from beyond the grave, when metaphor became reality and plunged the earl of Greyburn into perpetual darkness.

But he'd learned to adapt. His other senses had grown keener, his intuition sharper. In all but one respect.

His strongest defenses had not been enough to keep Cassidy from invading his heart. And breaking it all over again.

What a fool he had been to give her the power to hurt him.

The lightless void behind his eyes seemed to take on colors he still remembered, scarlet flame and blood red that pulsed to the rhythm of unreasoning rage—rage to drive out the pain. He grasped her wrist.

"You were *happy* with me," he snarled mockingly. "Do you know why I married you? Because we're both useless to the Cause and the werewolf blood. You cannot Change, and I could not waste Quentin's blood on marriage to such as you. I am sterile. I took responsibility for you, and in all honor I could not disown you when you proved more human than *loup-garou*. What more convenient solution than that we should marry?"

He felt shock run through her body. "But . . . in the wood . . ." she stammered. "When you came after me and Quentin . . ."

He knew what he was doing to her, doing to himself. He wanted her to feel his hurt, even as he was deeply ashamed of his weakness. Contradictory emotions tore him apart, and he couldn't stop the words of rage and pain that burst from him like fatal venom.

"I wanted you," he said. "Yes, Cassidy, I desired your young, untouched body. You were eager and willing and ripe for the plucking. As my wife, you would be mine to bed whenever I wished, all proprieties satisfied. Surely you didn't think it had anything to do with love?"

The blow left Cassidy breathless and shattered, as if Braden had struck her to the ground with fists rather than words.

Words meant as weapons. True words, for she knew with one glance at his anguished face that he was not lying.

She'd prepared herself for his anger, his rebukes, even punishment for disobedience. All those things she would accept as her due, because she'd made her choice.

But not *this*.

He'd wanted her. Wanted her body, the way men wanted Isabelle and paid for her services. But *he* obeyed at least some of the rules of human society—and he believed in duty. So he married her—not for love, or even friendship, but because she was worthless to his Cause. Of no use for anything but to relieve his needs in his bed, doing just what he told her to do for the rest of their lives, believing as he believed.

Only she was not his shadow, bound to agree with everything he thought was right and wrong. She'd acted on her conscience, knowing he would disapprove, confident that he would forgive because he loved her. He had never said it, but she had been so certain, so absolutely sure.

She remembered Isabelle's voice, relating a story she could not accept: of a love that had changed and become jealousy, of imprisonment and tragedy. And Braden's part in Milena's death.

"It's because of Milena, isn't it?" she said, choking on the words. "You loved her too much, and then she—"

"*Loved* her?" He laughed. "Is that what you thought? Rowena would not have told you that. She always believed I hated my wife."

But Rowena *had* told her, if not in so many words. The real truth lay in Braden's face.

"You hated Milena," she whispered. "Because of what she did with that other man—"

"She was my mate in the Cause. Nothing more. She failed to serve her purpose."

"But you . . . desired her."

"She was beautiful," he said, hard as stone. "She could awaken lust in any man."

Lust. Lust was all he'd ever felt, for Milena or his new wife.

"And you were jealous," Cassidy said. "You kept her prisoner, like Rowena—"

"Yes." He let Cassidy go. "I kept her here, to serve the Cause. She would not accept my authority. She—" He turned his head.

"Why did she go to that other man?" Cassidy said.

But she knew the answer to that question. *"He made her life a misery,"* Isabelle had said, reading from the letter. Without any hope of love from her husband, was she so wrong to seek it elsewhere? If he could not give her children, denying her even that small happiness . . .

"You didn't love Milena," she said. "Everyone else

loved her, but you couldn't. And if you couldn't love someone like her, you could never love me."

Some last, fading hope within her waited in mute desperation for a single word, a single motion from him that would prove her wrong. But Braden remained completely immobile, neither looking toward her nor touching her. And so he answered.

She'd made a terrible mistake.

She felt as if a veil were lifted from her eyes, letting her see clearly for the first time—see Braden as he truly was, and herself as she had always been. Foolish, stupid, wanting so badly to belong and to be loved that she ignored the realities that Isabelle had tried to teach her.

She backed away from Braden, choking on unshed tears. She might have gone on for years fooling herself, living in her own childish dreams. She'd always seen the possibilities and the doors opening one by one before her, not the limitations and the high stone walls people— werewolf or human—built to make their world seem safe.

The Cause was Braden's unassailable barricade, made not only to protect himself but to trap and hold and crush anyone within his grasp. He wouldn't even look inside those walls to see who or what he destroyed.

Her Tyger turned on her with teeth and claws bared to devour faith and love and everything she had become.

"Now you know," Braden said, allowing her no respite. "You deceived me as well, Lady Greyburn. Your apparent innocence hides a natural skill for duplicity that I failed to recognize. It seems that I was the naive one." He gave her a smile grotesque in its desolation. "Our marriage cannot be undone. You have my name, my wealth, and my protection. Seek your happiness elsewhere, Cassidy. You shall never find it with me."

Slowly, deliberately, he turned his back on her, as if mere blindness was not enough to remove her from his notice. It was more than dismissal; it was elimination. She felt the finality of it, like a massive gate slamming shut and sealed into place. For him, she had ceased to exist.

Her legs wobbled, threatening to give way. A flash flood of pain washed through her, tearing at the foundations of her very being. There was nothing left. Braden had withdrawn to a place she could not follow, and with him he took her future and herself.

She fell into an endless pit, a place unimaginable in its darkness. She lived the torment that Isabelle had known all her life, the anguish that had nearly driven Rowena to suicide and Milena to another man and eventual death.

This was agony. This was hopelessness. She'd been only half-awake before, blind to true despair. The price for seeing clearly, for growing up, was too high. She would do anything to return to blindness, to her old, childish life of gullible belief and unenlightened loneliness.

But there was no going back. Either she let herself be destroyed, or she must find another way. A new way . . .

From the deepest center of her body, from that very place Braden had awakened with his touch, a violent rage roared up to drive out the shock and suffering. She'd begun to acknowledge her own anger before, but this was to the earlier emotion as a wildfire to a candle flame. Cassidy was born anew, stretching limbs and muscles and tendons like a panther rising hungry from long slumber.

The liberation of her rage released feelings she hadn't known she possessed. She hated Braden in that moment. Hate pulled her out of the pit as he would not, and with it came the will to fight back.

She had lied to Isabelle: Braden's love was *not* worth fighting for, not at the price of her soul. She didn't need anyone, least of all Braden Forster. *He* was not worth the struggle.

She was free, strong, powerful in ways Braden could

not guess and she was only beginning to comprehend. To live here without love would be surrender, and she would never surrender again. Not to despair, and not to the earl of Greyburn.

"I am not your sister, and I am not Milena," she said to Braden, fists clenched and head high. "I'm not Lady Greyburn. I am Cassidy Holt. Once I thought loving you was all that mattered. You were everything I wished I could become—noble and strong and sure of yourself. I pretended that there were good reasons that you treated people the way you did—the servants, Isabelle, Rowena, even Quentin. I made myself believe that you could learn to care about something besides the Cause."

His back was rigid, unyielding, but she knew he heard every word. "I was wrong," she said. "I read about love in poems, but I didn't understand what it really was. Now I know you don't have it inside you. And I don't want what little you're willing to give."

Heady triumph carried her beyond all common sense. She wanted to hurt Braden, and keep on hurting him. "I'm not afraid of breaking the rules anymore, Lord Greyburn. You will never imprison me. I am Cassidy Holt. And I'm free."

Heedless of the rich fabric of her gown, she tore at the buttons of her bodice, scattering them like seeds on the carpet. All her mother's werewolf strength came to her service as she ripped the heavy cloth from her body. Shoes flew across the room. Her petticoat tumbled in shreds about her feet. The corset came apart with a snapping of laces, and she stood clad only in chemise and drawers. Her skin tingled at the caress of cool air.

Free.

Her mind went blank of all thoughts, her heart seared clean of emotion. She let instinct take her as once she'd let Braden possess her body and heart. It drove her to the door and out into the corridor, down the stairs at a dead run and to the entrance hall. She caught a glimpse of a footman's startled face just before she flung open the heavy front door and plunged into the cloudy afternoon.

There might have been others who saw her, fleeing wild as a lunatic in her underclothes, but they meant nothing to her. The landscape passed by in a blur of shape and color. She ran without destination or purpose, away from Greyburn, over the park and the fells and past copses of trees and low stone fences.

All the world was reduced to the pounding of her heart and the burning air in her lungs and the rhythm of running feet. There came a moment when even the scant clothes she wore weighed her down like chains; she paused just long enough to tear them off.

Naked, she leaped, and as she began to fall she felt a new abyss open beneath her. She twisted sideways to avoid it, and her body *Changed*.

Like water flowing from river to sea, like the gentle shift of seasons, like a chrysalis turning into a butterfly, she made the transition with ease and joy. Two legs became four. She hit solid ground again, graceful and sure. Wind rushed through the lush blackness of her coat. All of life opened up to her: every sound was music, every scent intoxicating.

She was wolf, she was magnificent, she was one with all of nature.

She was *loup-garou*. She was whole, and free, and she would never need anything, or anyone, again.

An hour passed, perhaps two, before Braden emerged from the dark citadel of his own mind and found Cassidy gone.

He listened for her. The house was as silent as a tomb.

They were all gone, now. All he heard was the uneven pop of raindrops on the window.

Braden moved mechanically to the door, his foot catching on cloth. The remnants of Cassidy's garments, scattered about the room in testament to her final rebellion.

"I made myself believe that you could learn to care about something besides the Cause. I even believed I could love you."

He kicked her torn petticoat out of his way and walked, as carefully as a crippled old man, down the corridor of the family wing. Not even a housemaid troubled his solitude. He passed by Cassidy's room with only the slightest stumble and paused at the door to Isabelle Smith's chamber.

Like the rebuke of a tenacious ghost, Isabelle's accusations came back to haunt him. No disdain for her humanity, or her shame, could shield him from them now.

". . . your motives are no more pure than those of any man who would use a woman as I was used. . . . You Forsters have great skill in twisting everything to your own advantage, especially the vulnerabilities of those you would rule. If Cassidy fails, will you exile her as well?"

How clairvoyant those words have been. He *had* cast her out, as surely as if she'd been a human servant guilty of betrayal. He'd done it with a few cruel phrases, destroying the last of her innocence and the fragile shield of her self-deception.

What else had Isabelle said? " *'The best laid schemes o' mice an' men gang aft a-gley.'* "

Braden Forster was neither mice nor man, but he found little consolation in that fact.

He left Mrs. Smith's door and passed several others that led to vacant, long-unused rooms. Quentin's door stood half-ajar just beyond them. His brother's scent was even fainter than Rowena's had been. The place had an air of desertion; Braden knew with a sudden certainty that Quentin would not be returning any time soon. He, like Rowena, had fled Greyburn.

One betrayal upon another. Desertion. Loneliness more profound than any Braden thought he had mastered.

He had driven them away.

He wandered aimlessly about the room, making no attempt to avoid the unfamiliar furniture. His body hardly felt the bruising impact of each obstacle he struck.

In the end his nose led him to the locked cabinet in the corner. The stench of Quentin's liquor, his poison, was unmistakable. Braden tore the door off its hinges and pulled the bottles out one by one. He opened the window and raised the first bottle high.

"If you're not careful," Quentin's voice mocked him, *"you'll find enough business, related to the Cause and otherwise, to keep you from ever knowing your wife. And I don't think she'll consent to remain in your shadow."*

He let his arm drop and the bottle slip from his fingers. He leaned on the sill, sucking in lungfuls of rain-washed air.

It had been storming the day he lost his sight. The day he lost everything but the Cause.

He knelt beside the window and felt for the discarded bottle. It fit surprisingly well under his arm. He found crystal glasses on a shelf in the same cabinet, and took one along with the bottle. He closed Quentin's door firmly behind him as he left.

His destination was the room at the end of the corridor. The door to Grandfather's suite was heavy and carved like the woodwork in the Great Hall. Its very appearance had intimidated Braden as a young child, when he'd equated it with lectures and punishment.

He was far beyond fear now.

Everything was the same as it had been when he'd visited the room two months ago. As it would always be. He walked to the bed and placed his hand on the velvet bedspread. Tiberius Forster had breathed his last in that great, medieval bed, a tyrant to the bitter end. A tyrant who knew his Cause was safe in the hands of the grandson he'd made into a mirror image of himself.

There'd been a day, long ago, when Tiberius called Braden into this room. The final day of the Convocation where Braden first met Milena.

"Quentin is only worth to me whatever children he can sire," Tiberius said. *"Rowena is the same."* How well Braden had taken that lesson to heart, that philosophy as his own.

He sat down on the edge of the bed. That distantly remembered boy woke within him, feeling greatly daring for the sacrilege. He set the bottle and glass on the coverlet and poured carelessly, letting the brandy slop over the rim of the glass to splash his trousers.

The taste was as poisonous as the scent, but he downed the stuff in one swallow. He felt Grandfather's stare, full of disgust and scorn for the flawed weakling he was.

"You will not betray me in the end."

No. He'd betray everything and everyone else, but never Tiberius Forster and his Cause.

"By the time I'm finished with you, you will have no other purpose. You will live for the Cause. Nothing else will matter. . . ."

Braden replenished the glass and emptied it as quickly as the first. His body was a hollow vessel filling with honeyed warmth. The nectar of forgetfulness. What had Quentin been trying to forget? The duty Braden forced on him?

He raised the empty glass to his absent brother. "But you've won, haven't you? I won't go chasing after you. I'm done. I'm done with—"

"You will not betray me," Grandfather roared.

Braden hurled the glass to the ground and heard it shatter on bare wood. He stumbled to the perfectly preserved suits of armor and slammed into the nearest. Metal clattered and screeched. He pushed, and it fell with a cry almost like that of a man dying in battle. In rapid succession Braden toppled the others, until the floor was strewn with the dismembered limbs and torsos of once-proud warriors.

Breathing hard, he laughed. How brave he'd proven himself when Tiberius wasn't here to witness his petty insurrection. He tripped and staggered his way back across the room and snatched the half-empty bottle from the bed.

Telford was waiting for him just outside the door.

"My lord," he said softly. "May I be of service?"

Braden bared his teeth. "What are you doing here?"

"The wagon is ready to depart, my lord."

"Then go. Go."

"Perhaps it's an inconvenient time—"

"I don't need you, Telford." He leaned his head against the door. "She's gone."

The non sequitur spilled out all unexpected, as if the liquor had loosened his tongue. Telford would already know. Everyone at Greyburn would know by now.

"If you see her—" *No.* He wouldn't ask. He wouldn't beg. "Go."

Telford backed away as if he were in the presence of royalty—or a viciously unpredictable beast. When the valet was gone, Braden walked back to his room— the room he'd shared with Cassidy—and sat down in the chair by the window. He couldn't see the light, but he knew it was growing late. The smell of rain leaked through the glass. Cassidy's scent overlaid that and everything else in the room. He tried to wipe it out with the taste of liquor, drunk straight from the bottle.

When that bottle was empty, he went back to Quentin's room and found another, discarded on the floor with the rest. Sound and scent and touch had begun to merge in his mind, becoming a great blur of sensation. He made his way with exaggerated care down the corridor, down the stairs, to the front doors while startled servants scurried out of his way like mice.

The rain fell in torrents, hard enough to pierce his numbness. He walked into the drive and beyond, where the lawn was drenched and soft under his feet. Just like before. Fresh water ran into his upturned mouth, diluting the taste of alcohol.

Cassidy's voice whispered between the raindrops. *"I read about love in poems, but I didn't understand what it really was. Now I know you don't have it inside you."*

Braden reached out as if she were there before him, as if he could . . . what? Compel her to admit she was wrong? Punish her for leaving him?

With every breath he took she slipped farther and farther beyond his reach. He could not even create an image of her in his mind. He'd never seen Cassidy—his second wife, who had left him just like the first. The face that came to him was exquisitely beautiful and fair-haired and cruel.

The last face he'd ever seen, on a night exactly like this.

The first thunder rumbled, and he went rigid, as if he'd been struck by lightning. Terror bled into him like rain scalded by fire. Quentin's poison worked its way through his veins, penetrating his heart and mind, mingling with subtler poisons that Braden had buried and nearly forgotten. Time itself tangled until past and future had no meaning. His wet clothing clung to his body like bindings meant to strangle and suffocate.

"I don't want what you're willing to give." Someone had said that to him. Someone who had claimed to love him. But it was a lie. She was a lie, a dream, a false hope of happiness.

He let go all control and let hatred take him. It possessed him utterly, red-eyed with the need to wreak vengeance, to punish, to destroy. It was the beast that had been waiting to escape all these years, kept chained by duty, by fear, by unbearable guilt.

Something, someone had broken its chains at last.

"You can't hold me," she said, laughing cruelly. *"I'll be free of you forever—"*

Pain slammed into his chest. Her blow shattered what was left of his heart. He roared, ignoring the agony that clawed through him as he Changed.

The bottle rolled onto the grass, spilling liquid like lifeblood into the thirsty earth.

twenty

The black wolf ran. She tested her new shape to its limits, oblivious of her destination. The rain blinded her, but she had little need of sight. Broad paws skidded in mud and rolled on loose stone, but her balance was uncannily perfect. Human needs, human concerns, human weaknesses were cast aside like the naked woman's body she had worn hours or years ago. Time ceased to have meaning.

She had no enemies and no equals. She sensed smaller animals cowering around her, acknowledging her supremacy. Flocks of sheep, bunched up against the weather, scattered and fled. Her only foe was exhaustion, and she fought that as long as she could, until muscles and nerves and laboring heart and lungs rebelled.

She fell in an unknown place beside a muddy road. Her body shifted back to human without her consent, recognizing her weariness better than she did herself.

In human form she remembered all that had happened before the miracle. The protection of anger was gone, melted away during the headlong, reckless flight. In the wake of her triumph was misery as black as the wolf's pelt.

She'd proven her werewolf blood . . . too late. Fury and despair and sorrow had driven her across that final barrier as love and happiness could not. She had found her whole self at last.

But she couldn't go back. Braden had married her because she lacked the werewolf ability to Change, and because he was sterile. He'd proven himself incapable of accepting or giving love. The Cause had taken the place of his soul.

What would he say now that she had Changed, knowing that he'd robbed his own Cause of her blood? What punishment that knowledge would be. What agony. She wanted to weep.

It was all too late.

The rain had lessened, falling in a light mist that matched Cassidy's listlessness. Too spent to do more than crawl, she lay still where she was among the saturated bracken and grass. She willed the escape of sleep, but even that had deserted her. Her senses felt raw, as if every nerve in her body were pierced with cactus thorns. Her eyes stung with unshed tears.

This was what it felt like to be completely alone. Even at the ranch, it had never been like this. Anger and hatred were vicious, fickle companions. Love was no better. Belonging was an illusion. Braden had given her something precious, and then pitilessly taken it away. Better never to have had it at all, to have never known even the possibility of real happiness.

If she was to be alone forever, without love, she had to become strong again—not the strength of ignorance, but of survival. A wolf's strength. A woman's strength. She withdrew far inside herself, shut off her senses, and made her mind a gray place of nothingness.

But something was waiting for her in that place. *Someone.* A presence, a spark of light, part of her body and yet not. She wrapped her arms around her belly as the knowledge seeped into her.

She wasn't alone. Another soul shared this space with her. Another . . . person. Unformed, indistinct, but there. Resting in her womb.

She was going to have a baby.

Cassidy pressed her face to the sodden grass and laughed until only dry sobs emerged from her throat. She was *loup-garou*. She was going to have a baby—Braden's child. Braden had been wrong about both things, and it was too late.

Braden's child.

She hugged herself, cradling the precious burden she could not yet feel with her outward senses. Isabelle said the sickness came with being with child. She would gladly have gone through it a hundred times to keep this gift.

Braden hadn't left her with nothing of himself. She had what he would not willingly give up, if he knew. But he wouldn't know. She wouldn't surrender her baby to a man who couldn't love. A ruthless, coldhearted, bitter man who would only regard their child as another token in the Cause.

No. She shouted inner defiance toward Greyburn. *This baby is mine. It will be loved, and wanted for itself, and it will never be alone. Do you hear me, Braden Forster? It will be loved.*

She bent low, rocking on her knees, until the tears stopped. Gradually she heard what she'd ignored before: the clop of horse's hooves, drawing ever nearer. Not the violent drumming of a galloping steed, but the steady pace of a draft horse.

She hadn't realized how close to the road she had come to rest, or on whose land. She peered over the screen of bracken.

It was a wagon, well made but modest, carrying a

driver and three passengers. She almost sank down into hiding again before she recognized the man who held the reins.

Telford was no longer dressed in his usual spotless, formal attire. He wore a tweed coat, practical trousers and boots, and a cap on his head. The simple clothing made him seem very ordinary.

In the end, Telford had been a friend to her, even if he'd been wrong about Braden. The wish to speak to him once more engulfed her with yearning. She'd deliberately kept him ignorant of the plans to help Rowena escape, but of course he'd learned immediately afterward. She knew he had not judged her for her act, that he worried about her even though they never discussed Rowena's disappearance.

And he was the only part of Greyburn she'd ever see again.

But she had no clothes, and no explanations she was willing to give. She stayed where she was, and the wagon was nearly past when she saw the face of one of the men in the back of the wagon.

That face was very different from the last time she'd seen it. In Greyburn's Great Hall, it had been frozen in terror and bereft of hope. Now John Dodd the footman—human, traitor, and pawn of the Russian werewolves—was sitting comfortably beside an older woman, smiling as if he hadn't a care in the world.

Cassidy stepped onto the soggy road before she knew what she was doing. Someone in the wagon gasped. Telford turned in his seat, checked the horses, set the brake, and jumped down.

"Countess!" he said, snatching a loose blanket from the back of the wagon with hardly a glance at its staring occupants. He hurried toward her and, averting his gaze, wrapped its damp folds around her. "What are you doing here?"

He knew better than to ask why she was naked—but he also knew she wasn't supposed to be able to Change. "It's a long story, Telford," she said wearily. She looked at John Dodd, who gazed at her without recognition or hostility or fear. "Why are you here, with him?"

"Lord Greyburn released him." Telford's thin face was very grave. "I know you judged the earl harshly for his treatment of Dodd. But he would never have done him permanent injury." He lowered his voice. "Sadly, the man's experiences . . . damaged his mind. The Russians would have taken little care to preserve it beyond its use to them. Lord Greyburn believes he will heal in time, with rest and proper care."

Cassidy remembered Braden's fury with the footman. How could he have gone from such violence to concern for a mere human? "Who are the other people?" she asked.

"Dodd's family—the mother and sister and brother he was supporting. Lord Greyburn has made arrangements so that neither Dodd nor his family will ever want for anything as long as they live. He's given them a fine farm in Yorkshire, and a regular income—even a doctor's care until Dodd has sufficiently recovered."

"Even after . . . what he did?" she said.

"Even so, my lady." He studied her face. "He asked me to see them to their new home. I suspect that upon my return, I shall be looking for a new position. He will not require my services any longer."

"You're wrong. He'll need you, if he needs anyone. I've left Greyburn."

No surprise showed in his expression. "Lord Greyburn spoke little to me before our departure, but I knew—" He stopped and sighed. "My lady, I tried to explain to you, once—"

"I remember. You said you believed that I'd made a change in him. But I know more about what he was like before I came." She shook her head. "I thought he . . . cared enough to understand what I had to do. And I *had* to do it, Telford." She pulled the blanket tight about her shoulders and stared at her bare toes. "But he told me that he married me for convenience. He didn't know what else to do with me, because I wasn't any good for his Cause." She laughed. "I actually thought he could love me."

"But you love him."

She wanted to deny it with all the newfound anger and power and independence she'd found within herself, but even now she didn't know how to lie. "Yes," she whispered. "But it doesn't make any difference." She met Telford's gaze. "I'm going to have a baby."

His skin flushed bright red. "You are—"

"Braden told me he wasn't able to sire children. But he did."

Telford paced several steps away and back again. "Do you know what this would mean to him?"

She spread her hand across her stomach under the blanket. "I want my baby to be loved, Telford."

The people in the wagon were very quiet, watching. A bird called from the nearest tree. Telford passed his hand across his face and closed his eyes.

"You think him incapable of such emotion, my lady. He is not. In the past—"

"I know all about Milena. He didn't even love her. She was just someone to make children for the Cause."

Telford opened his eyes and held her gaze. "Lord Greyburn lets you, and everyone else, believe that, Countess. To admit the truth would be to accept that he made mistakes, that he was weak. Weak enough to be human.

Whatever he may say, my lady, the *loups-garous* are partly human, and for him that means unacceptable frailty and imperfection."

"But why?"

"His grandfather, the former earl of Greyburn, drummed it into him from childhood. Tiberius Forster was not a kind man. He despised humans, and those *loups-garous* who chose to live as human, including his own sister. He ruled Greyburn with an iron fist and molded his grandson in his own image, to be his heir in the Cause. The current earl learned through cruel discipline that duty to the Cause supplanted all other interests.

"But when he was promised to marry Milena, he fell in love with her. In spite of his grandfather, he dared to think that he could pursue both duty and happiness. She was very alluring, very accomplished in flirtation. In the beginning, she seemed to want Lord Greyburn as much as he wanted her."

"Rowena called her an angel—"

Telford laughed, startling Cassidy. "Ah, yes. She was an expert in deception, even of her fellow werewolves. Rowena fell for her performance completely. Milena led everyone at Greyburn, and in London, to believe that she was a paragon—even Braden, at first. He was still an innocent then, in his way. Of course she hid her true nature to the outside world, but she was quick enough to use her abilities to get what she wanted."

Cassidy tried to reconcile Telford's description with the face in the portrait, and with Rowena's passionate praise. Where lay the truth?

She was quick enough to use her abilities. . . . Rowena had been desperate for someone with whom to share her feelings and fears, another woman to be her close confidante. "Do you mean that Milena used her powers to make people see her the way she wanted them to?"

"It is against *loup-garou* law for one werewolf to use his or her will against another. But she would not have hesitated to do so." His mouth twisted. "It didn't matter that the earl loved her to distraction. He would have given up anything but the Cause to make her happy. But she cared nothing for the Cause, and quickly grew bored with her husband. He was too bound by duty and lived too quietly. She was devoted to the gaiety and pleasure of London, and she spent as much time away from Greyburn as possible, among human society. He begged her to return, but she refused."

Braden, begging? It seemed impossible. "He became jealous," she said. "He made her come back—"

"Only after she had taken one human lover after another. She hid that as well, but she was in every respect no better than a prostitu— Pardon me, my lady."

A prostitute, he meant. Like Isabelle. "She was with other men, even though she was married," Cassidy said.

"With every man she could seduce, and that was a simple matter for her. She even approached—" Telford caught his breath and went on. "Yet she mocked the earl because after five years he had not . . . fathered children for his Cause. He blamed himself for that failure. I think he came to believe that was why she left him. It was easier to take the blame than recognize the truth."

Cassidy remembered Braden's self-contempt when he'd revealed his sterility. Milena had been all these terrible things, and he'd still blamed himself?

She touched her stomach gently. "But he was wrong, Telford. My baby—"

"Yes. But he loved her, and so it was necessary for him to pretend. To do otherwise would lay his faults bare to his own eyes. He would be no more than a pathetic cuckold, unfit to lead his fellow werewolves or follow in his grandfather's footsteps. He would be forced to surrender all promise of love or happiness. So he deliberately blinded himself to her infidelities, and to her wild and reckless behavior in London. Until the time came when even he was compelled to admit the truth."

"What happened?" Cassidy asked, feeling ill.

"Milena's final lover was a libertine of scandalous reputation, a former officer in the royal army. Milena had become less and less discreet in her amours, and at last she committed an act which—suffice it to say that Lord Greyburn could no longer ignore it. Lord Greyburn traveled to London and brought her back by force. No one would argue with his right, but Milena had convinced all London that he was a tyrant who mistreated her and drove her away with his cruelties. Human society pitied her, but he was an object of scorn. To the *loups-garous*, he'd shown weakness by allowing her to cuckold him so blatantly, defy him so openly in direct contradiction of his own Cause. He had to prove all over again that he was fit to be their leader."

Cassidy tried to imagine Braden allowing anyone to treat him the way Milena had. He must have loved her greatly—and she'd betrayed him. She'd hurt him and his standing among the werewolves. The betrayal would be devastating beyond endurance, for Braden couldn't separate himself from the Cause. He was worth nothing to himself without it.

"Lord Greyburn learned not long after her return that she was with child." Telford said. "He believed that it was his. But she demanded that he set her free, and when he refused, she told him that the child was her human lover's." Telford's voice dropped very low. "The revelation drove the earl half-mad, yet even then he did not punish her. Milena convinced all Greyburn, even his own sister, that he was tormenting and abusing his wife while she carried *his* child. The earl would say or do nothing to refute her stories. It was his only way of proving himself strong and unassailable, to let himself seem ruthless and unfeeling."

So that was why Rowena feared her brother, and his plans for her, so deeply. She had learned to hate her brother because of Milena's lies. And he hadn't even tried to change her mind.

"Lord Greyburn watched his wife growing with her lover's child, and she never let him forget it. Then, very near her time, her lover came in secret to set her free. Lord Greyburn pursued them across country. The lovers managed to get as far south as Hadrian's Wall before the earl discovered them."

"The accident that blinded him," Cassidy said with a flash of insight. "That was when it happened—"

"Yes." But Telford's flow of words stopped like a spring gone suddenly dry.

"How?" Cassidy asked, her throat very tight.

"Only two people know, my lady—the earl and his brother. I learned the rest from Quentin Forster afterward."

"But Quentin told me he was out of the country."

"Nevertheless, he was there. He alone witnessed a part of what happened that stormy night, and he would not speak of anything beyond what I have told you. But the earl did not regain his vision.

"Milena was injured when he brought her back. She didn't survive more than a handful of days."

Because she'd "fallen." But had it truly been an accident?

"Milena survived long enough to bring her child into the world, but she died soon after."

"Mikhail," Cassidy whispered.

"The earl had no wish to keep Milena's child. He told the Boroskovs and the household at Greyburn that the babe was dead, and secretly sent it to be raised by a good family in Scotland. But the Boroskovs must have learned the truth, and stole the child away to Russia. Lord Greyburn never knew."

Cassidy sat down on the road, heedless of the mire and stones. Now she realized why Braden couldn't tolerate any disagreement or hint of rebellion from those under him or any vulnerability in himself. Now she knew why he'd acted as he had toward Rowena, John Dodd—even Isabelle, who reminded him of a wife who'd given herself to many men. Why he hadn't wanted Mikhail.

And why he cut himself off from any possibility of loving again.

Yet he'd shown mercy to Dodd—he'd gone out of his way to help the former footman. He'd allowed Isabelle to stay, when he must have despised her. And he'd promised to consider bringing Mikhail back to Greyburn.

But Milena had died, and no one but Braden and Quentin knew how.

"Do you think," she said, "do you believe that Braden could have . . . that he did something to . . ." She couldn't finish, but Telford understood.

"I do not know, my lady," he said grimly. "I do not know. But when the rumors started, spread perhaps by Milena's lover, he refused to speak against them."

And so he'd been judged, and found guilty.

"Thank you," she said softly, looking up at Telford. "Thank you for telling me." She glanced at the wagon. "You shouldn't keep them waiting any longer."

"I do not like leaving you here alone, my lady," he said.

It was typical of Telford that he didn't speak of her returning to Greyburn. He respected her, as she respected him. He trusted her to make her own decisions, her own choices.

But his concern was real. She felt a rush of warmth for him, and got to her feet.

"You don't have to worry about me. I can Change now, Telford. I'm *loup-garou*."

He nodded without surprise. "You have always had a great power, Cassidy Holt. I didn't perceive it at first, but only the blind could fail to see it in you now." He bowed. "I will not say good-bye. I believe that we shall meet again."

She swallowed and impulsively took his hand. First Quentin and Rowena, and now Telford, walking out of her life. She would not think of Braden.

Telford clasped her hand in a firm grip. "I once read a poem that I have never forgotten." He began to recite:

> *"Say not the struggle naught availeth,*
> *The labor and the wounds are vain,*
> *The enemy faints not, nor faileth,*
> *And as things have been they remain. . . .*
> *And not by eastern windows only,*
> *When daylight comes, comes in the light;*
> *In front the sun climbs slow, how slowly!*
> *But westward, look, the land is bright!"*

He squeezed her hand again and released it, turning toward the wagon.

Cassidy stayed at the side of the road until the wagon had vanished around the nearest bend. Long after the last vibrations of the horse's footfalls were gone from the earth, she remained where she was, a prisoner of her heart.

She willed some certainty to return, the confidence that had come to her as a wolf, the freedom from want or care. But those things had abandoned her as surely as the people she'd come to love.

No, not abandoned. They had made their choices, and she had made hers. With a strange clarity, she could look back and see each decision as it happened. She hadn't regretted a single one, or questioned that it was right.

Because she hadn't known better. The world had seemed simple, when it wasn't simple at all. Isabelle had tried to teach her that, but it was the sort of thing you had to learn for yourself.

As Cassidy had learned.

She had chosen to come to England, hoping to find herself and a purpose and a place to belong. She'd chosen to give herself to Braden, loving him. Ignorant as she was then, her motives had been worthy.

But not for the third choice, to defy him and help Rowena. She'd felt so noble, and told herself that she could face Braden's displeasure.

Now she saw, with painful understanding, that it hadn't been just for Rowena. She'd believed enough of Isabelle's letter and Rowena's tales to feel justified in defying her husband. Braden had left her alone at Greyburn after their marriage, and she'd wanted . . . *wanted* to hurt him. Wanted him to feel as lost as she did, even though she hadn't let herself see how she really felt inside.

She'd wanted him to feel as . . . forsaken and alone as she did, because what she'd found with Braden wasn't the poetic dream she expected.

She'd succeeded too well. She did have power over him; she had become like Milena. No better than Milena. She made the past come alive for him again, to drown whatever trust and affection he might have felt for the girl he'd married.

But she wasn't a girl any longer. She was a woman. She would have children of her own. And that meant she had to live with her choices, the way Isabelle did. Accept the consequences of what she'd done instead of running away from them.

If Braden had caused Milena's death, he lived with that

guilt every day. Or perhaps—perhaps he kept himself from feeling anything, to protect himself from an emotion too horrible to bear.

He held himself bound in chains of his own making, as if, with a single lapse, he might fly to pieces like the glass he'd broken in the library. His blindness was another way to keep people, and the threat of love, always beyond reach.

The consequences of love were hard to bear. She couldn't stop loving Braden, whatever he said or did. But had she the power to make him face himself? Could she live with a man who might have . . .

She closed her eyes, sensing the child they'd made together. It was as much Braden's as hers. To let him go on believing that he would never have children . . . If she wanted to punish him, there could be no better way.

Perhaps Braden deserved punishment, but not from her. She had no right.

Slowly she let the blanket fall in a heap at her feet. She flung back her head, drinking in the moist scents of twilight and fading summer. The land was on its way to the season of sleep and stillness, of death awaiting rebirth. Her child would be born when the world was just awakening again. To hope.

She'd come to England with little more than hope and innocence; it was as if part of her had been asleep. Now she was awake to the pain of wisdom, and anger, and fear. She was afraid as she'd never been in her life. Afraid of Braden. Afraid for her child. Afraid of herself and what she was becoming.

Of what she might never become, might never have if she went back.

It was the most important choice she'd ever make.

As she'd done once upon a time in the desert of New

Mexico, she let her turbulent emotions find their voice. She howled, drawing on the wolf within her, and summoned up the Change.

From the north, and Greyburn, another voice harsh with rage and sorrow answered her cry.

twenty-one

The wolf's howl came out of the mist like a trumpet of war, and he answered the unspoken challenge, crouched atop a high fell as the rain renewed its assault upon the earth.

His humanity had been left far behind. He couldn't remember when he'd Changed or what had driven him to it. He knew only that he hunted and that what he sought must not be allowed to escape him.

Not what he hunted, but *who*. The faint howl sounded but once, and it filled him with fury.

She, who had betrayed him, was running. She thought herself his equal. She thought she could defy him with impunity.

She was wrong.

He burst into a run, scraping wet soil with his claws and shaking the rain from his pelt with every bounding stride. Breath sawed in his throat and whistled between his teeth. He knew how to find her now, after hours of searching. He would outrun her, because his fury made a machine of his body, a burning coal of his heart.

Images chased through his mind like stoats after rabbits. His futile trust in her. His repeated efforts to make her happy. The last time he'd lain with her—the hope, the tentative happiness, her whispered promises—all empty, all lies. They all laughed at him, at his failures. Only one thing would make them respect him again.

The sacrifice must be made, for the sake of the Cause.

The heavy rain had no power to distract him, nor the slick ground to slow him. Her scent was a beacon growing ever nearer. It was almost as if she were standing still. Waiting.

He called her name, and it emerged as a roar. He smelled the dampness of her fur. He plunged through a screen of bracken and felt her presence like the memory of sunlight seen in a prism of water.

Beautiful. Beautiful, and deceitful, and his enemy.

With a great leap he closed the distance between them and knocked her from her feet. At the last moment he held back, using only a small fraction of his strength.

He pinned her down, jaws wide about her neck. Her fur brushed his face, soft and fragrant. She didn't struggle. She lay beneath him, throat bared, utterly still.

A voice, a human voice, shouted in his head. He tried to shut it out. *Enemy.* She was his enemy. . . .

"Do you know what you are, Braden Forster? A fool. A weakling and a fool. And you though I ever had any love for you?"

Each word drove like a stake through his heart. She'd beaten him. She reveled in his defeat and humiliation. He must have revenge. He readied himself to snap his jaws and crush flesh and bone.

But he couldn't move. Couldn't hurt her, just as before. And as he hesitated, the very substance of her body seemed to melt from beneath him, shifting, flowing with the rain until smooth, bare skin replaced fur.

Milena. He bared his teeth, helpless to do more, unable even to weep. Milena—

"*You are nothing to me. I despise you.*" She laughed. "*You hoped for children. Well, now you have one. But he isn't yours. He is half-human—*"

"Braden!" someone cried.

Wrong. The voice was wrong, husky and warm.

Cassidy. But that was impossible. He had hunted a wolf and found a woman.

Fingers caught in his fur, but not to push him away. They pulled him closer, until every drop of rain was infused with her scent.

Wrong scent. Wrong voice. Not Milena, fleeing with her lover. It was Cassidy he'd come hunting, Cassidy who'd left him. But Cassidy couldn't Change.

Cassidy. Milena. They became one in his mind, flaunting treachery, mocking his clemency. His weakness. His unforgivable flaws.

"Braden," she said again, this woman he had loved. "You don't have to force me to return. I was coming back. We're going to have a child. *Our* child, Braden—"

He tilted his head back and howled. His body Changed, casting off its wolf shape with unnatural frenzy. Rain slicked his hair to his head and cascaded from his skin, unable to cool the inferno in his heart.

"You . . . lie," he cried. "Not my child. You'll . . . never lie to me again."

Her fingers spread across his face. "It's me, Braden. I've never lied to you—"

He made himself deaf to her pleas as he was blind to her lovely, deceiving beauty. He would stop her, once and for all. He hated her. He would shatter her mind, as she had destroyed all he lived for.

He focused on the very essence of her spirit, gathered

up his power and his will and loosed them like a pack eager for the kill.

It was like leaping headfirst into the sun. Agony such as he had never known slashed through his body, its hellish core centered within his mind. Her counterattack was deadly, and he knew that she was killing *him*.

He tried to contain that burning and felt it char through every bond he had created. He tried to break it as he would command the mind of a deceitful human. *You are mine,* he cried. *Mine!*

But her will was a weapon he had no strength to turn aside. She held him helpless like a gasping fish in a net, and all the while she laughed as her mental blows beat him down.

He was losing. Milena had proven herself his master. He was unworthy of the Cause, too flawed to survive.

So be it. Let her destroy him. Let the sacrifice be his life.

He bared himself to the inferno and let it take him. He tumbled into the crucible. But as he stood on the brink of oblivion the agony ceased, and the light became a brilliance that healed instead of killed.

Cassidy's brilliance, unmistakable, pure at its very heart.

And he could *see*. He saw himself, crouched on the ground, his face contorted with pain and hatred. Then he was swept away on a tide of memory, and it was Quentin's face that filled his mind: Quentin, ever laughing but with a deep and unbearable sadness behind the facade of jovial indifference. Quentin, whose fear was not of his brother but of something within himself. And Braden had been too obsessed to see.

Quentin's face faded, and Rowena's took its place. His stately and arrogant sister, who, like her twin, hurt inside.

She hated her werewolf nature, yet a part of her wanted to be convinced that it was not an abomination, but a release. She would have turned to Braden if she could, but he had refused to listen. He had made her into a tool of the Cause and kept her at a distance, like Quentin, because of his own dread of weakness. And so she had turned to Milena.

Isabelle came next, a woman loyal to a girl she'd brought to England, recognizing the earl of Greyburn as a man who cared for nothing and no one but his own desires. A woman who endured humiliation and exposure to help another, a woman of undoubted courage, who saw Braden as he truly was.

And Uncle Matthew, a gentle soul forsaken by his family, driven mad by the Cause because no Forster would be his advocate.

Telford, whose loyalty knew no limits, a gift far greater than anything his master deserved.

A human girl, one Emily Roddam, who saw in him a monstrous legend come to life when he treated her with the contempt he held for all her kind.

John Dodd followed, and Aynsley, and a succession of servants afraid to meet his eyes. Afraid of his power, even while they paid the price for security and employment, their minds violated as Milena had violated his.

Illumination penetrated the hidden corners of his being, and the mad rage and hatred within him splintered into a thousand shards of radiance.

The light set him free.

He slammed back into his body as if he'd been soaring high above the earth.

Cassidy was there, sprawled on the ground where he had thrown her down. Not Milena. Never Milena. It had all been an illusion.

With a shaking hand he wiped hair from his face. He

had come out of the madness stripped clean, like tarnished silver brought to a high gloss in one swift motion. He felt the brand of Cassidy's brilliant soul emblazoned on his own. He could *see* her, not with his eyes, but with a part of himself so nearly forgotten that it no longer had a name.

He could see the whole truth for the first time in his life: the terrible price of the Cause, Grandfather's expectations, Milena's betrayal. The rage he'd hidden for years, fearing to let it loose, pretending cold disinterest in the feelings of others. The searing knowledge of his unforgivable mistake in loving and daring to hope for happiness. The guilt, knowing he had brought about Milena's death.

He had killed her. In his terror, blinded and in unendurable pain, he had found enough strength to use his body to push her away. Push her with such violence that she fell, and kept falling, until she lay at the bottom of a cliff, and he'd felt his way down to discover her limp and broken, barely alive. . . .

"Braden," Cassidy said. "Can you hear me?"

He came back to the present and crawled to her, lifting her in his arms. She freed herself and stepped away.

She knew. She knew was he was, and couldn't bear it.

"You thought I was Milena," she said softly.

He remembered attacking her, bent on murder. All that suppressed fury turned against the wrong woman, a woman who deserved so much more than he could ever give.

"I could have . . . killed you," he said.

"No, Braden. I felt you come into my mind, but you couldn't hurt me."

Insane laughter welled up in him. Milena had turned the tables on him and overwhelmed his will with her own. And Cassidy had the ability to rebuff him as if he were bereft of any power at all.

"I know how Milena betrayed you," Cassidy said. "Her face was the last thing you ever saw. She was the one who blinded you."

Yes. Her unleashed will had done damage to his body as well as his mind. It had attacked some part of his brain, burned out his vision in an instant.

Only Quentin knew the truth: Quentin, who'd followed him that stormy night and observed the climax of the tragedy. In his delirium of loss and guilt, Braden had confided the whole to his brother and then sworn him to silence. He let the world believe what he knew to be the truth.

He had caused Milena's death. And blindness was his deserved punishment. Punishment for mistakes that could never be rectified.

"Braden." Cassidy touched his arm, and he felt her quiet power. "I saw what Milena did to you. She went into your mind and tried to destroy it."

As Braden had invaded the minds of so many servants, had once tried to do to Cassidy. He was the same as Milena.

"Milena was a cruel person," Cassidy said. "She fooled everyone. And you fooled everyone, too."

All but this girl, who saw so keenly into his most hidden heart.

Suddenly he knew how he had come to see Quentin, Rowena, Isabelle, Matthew, all the others so clearly. He'd seen through Cassidy's eyes. For the time their minds had been linked, he saw them as she did. Saw what he'd done to them.

"It was never over for you," she said. Her hand slid up to his shoulder, a gesture of comfort that might have come from a sister. "You couldn't completely admit your hatred for Milena, the same way you couldn't admit your guilt. And you did love her, so much that you couldn't see what she was until it was too late. Love for you was a curse.

"So you tried to make yourself stop feeling anything. You carried those scars every day, with your blindness. And when I left . . . it was like Milena's betrayal all over again. Everything you tried to hide came out when you found me."

The rage, the shame, the madness. All over again.

"And was I justified, Cassidy?" he said harshly. "Do you pardon all my sins, including murder?"

Her hand tightened, fingers digging into his wet skin. "You didn't mean to. I was there, with you. I saw through your eyes. The things you remember are all tangled up, but I saw it the way it really happened.

"It was storming. You found her with her lover, near a great wall on a cliff. You could have killed him easily, but you didn't. He ran off, and Milena pretended to surrender. You didn't hurt her, Braden, even though you were very angry. She attacked your mind when you believed she'd given up. You struggled with her, and while you were fighting to survive, you used the last of your strength to push her away. But you were both at the edge of a cliff, and she fell."

"I pushed her," he said.

"But you didn't know. It was instinct, Braden. Afterward you tried to save her. You gave her the best care possible."

Why did she make excuses for him? She'd claimed to love him, and he refused to believe. He dared not believe.

"I was responsible," he said. "I refused to see. At the end, I did hate her."

"Because you loved her so much. You made mistakes, but you were only part of it, Braden. Only a small part."

She could forgive. Yet he had been incapable of forgiving her for caring more about people than his Cause.

"I understand why you came after me, and why you thought I was Milena. It seemed like another betrayal. I didn't think about how much it would hurt you." She let her hand fall. "I hope you can forgive me. And I hope you can learn to forgive yourself."

He stared at her, blind but able to see her as she truly was. She could feel the pain of others and take it upon herself, no matter what the consequences. It was her greatest gift and most terrible liability. She had changed: naïveté had given way to enlightenment, innocence to experience, hesitance to certainty. He had thought those changes a threat to him, to his frozen heart and his carefully constructed life. He had fought to keep her out.

He might as well have tried to dam the English Channel. It was no longer possible to hide from himself. He forced the confession out of hiding, giving it shape in his mind.

Love.

He . . . loved . . . Cassidy Holt.

Somewhere in the region of his heart a wall crumbled, like the ancient fortifications this land knew so well. He opened his mouth to give the thought voice. To tell her. To beg her to return to him.

But he did not deserve her. He could still hurt her without even realizing it. That bright core of inner strength was not invulnerable. With time and enough neglect it could be worn down, lose its luster, become a cold shard of dull metal at the center of that lovely body. He'd proven himself unstable and fatally flawed. He could still destroy what he had finally learned to love.

The words slipped out of his reach. He shuddered if he had just stepped back from the edge of a precipice. Cassidy must never know his true feelings. She'd broken away; let her find her own path. She had the nerve and the will and the heart.

"You were right, Cassidy," he said tonelessly. "About

Rowena, and Isabelle, the servants. And about me." He turned his face toward Greyburn. "I will not interfere with your freedom again. You are my wife; that will be difficult to change in England. But I will provide you with whatever you require to live wherever you choose, even in America. I can find you decent rooms in Ulfington, while my lawyer draws up papers—"

"I don't want your money," she said. "I wasn't running when you found me, Braden. I was coming back."

For a moment hope was an aching knot in his chest. Coming back, to him, because she—

He turned to her, hardening his expression into indifference. "Don't make the mistake of believing that I yearn for companionship because I have suffered so *greatly*. I am accustomed to being alone. You require a different kind of life—"

"What kind of life? The kind Quentin has? The kind Rowena wanted?" Her hair slapped at him as she shook her head. "No. I'm no fine lady, and I'm not a helpless child. I can take care of myself. I could live out here alone, if I had to, and not need anything else. You see, I've learned how to Change."

At first he didn't understand the full meaning of her words. But then he remembered lush fur brushing his, a sleek female shape and delicate muzzle. . . .

"No," he said sharply. "It was my madness—"

"It happened while I was running away from Greyburn," she said. "I can Change, Braden. I'm *loup-garou*."

All at once he felt the electric tingle of the Change— not his own, but hers. It hummed through the ground and up into his body, a palpable charge that raised the hair on the back of his neck.

And then he felt her press against his hand.

"Cassidy," he said. His fingers closed to grasp the thick

fur circling her neck, but she danced out of his reach. Another sizzling current, a few half-swallowed breaths, and she stood beside him, a woman once again.

She was *loup-garou*, and the full irony of it hit him like a blow in the belly. He himself that betrayed the Cause when it was the last thing he'd tried to preserve.

He sank to his knees in the mud. The greatest punishment of all was knowing how he'd deceived himself.

He heard her knees hit the ground beside him. "Now you know that I can be with you in every way," she said. "Do you still want me to go?"

After all this, she still waited for his judgment, as if he had the right to make the decision for both of him. "Would you come back when the only thing that's changed is the proof of your blood?" he asked, driven to test her and hating himself for it.

She was silent while returning rain blew in fitful gusts between them. "Some things have changed, Braden. But not everything. Not the most important thing." She leaned so close that he could feel her breath on his cheek. "I made my choice long ago. I wanted to be with you. I wanted to marry you."

"Duty," he said bitterly. "I will not hold you to what you promised in ignorance. You owe me nothing."

"If I had to do it all over again, I wouldn't choose any differently. Maybe for a little while I hated you. I'd never felt that way before. But you were the one who made me feel all those things for the first time in my life, and . . . I found out that hate just isn't much use.

"I love you, Braden. I know you don't love me, but maybe in time . . ."

"Would you share me with the Cause, Cassidy?" he demanded mercilessly. "Would you take second place to something that's caused so much pain?"

The crown of her head, wet with rain, came to rest

against his shoulder. "I would never ask you to give it up, Braden. It's too important, even if mistakes were made. Maybe neither one of us is perfect. Maybe it won't be easy, but I want to try. Unless you send me away, I'm coming home. To Greyburn, with you."

God help him. He could not fight it any longer. He could not help loving Cassidy any more than he could deny his blood. If he let her go, his soul and his strength would wither and die as surely as his vision.

She *was* his soul.

He bent to touch his forehead to hers. "Forgive me," he whispered. "I want you to come home. I want you, Cassidy." He framed her face with his hands, as if he might lose his courage if for a moment she slipped from his grasp. "I love you."

Her skin shivered under his palms. "You don't have to say that. You don't have to—"

"I love you," he repeated fiercely, and seized her mouth with his own. When she was dazed into temporary submission, he poured out the rest of it. "I always wanted you, Cassidy, even when I couldn't admit it to myself. You were like . . . clean desert air in the midst of London's choking fog. You swept through me and worked your way into my heart, and I was afraid." She tried to shake her head. "Yes," he said, "afraid. If I let you in, I thought I would lose the compromises I'd made with life to protect myself. Lose even the Cause. And I was afraid I would hurt you—yet I was glad when you couldn't Change. I took the excuse to make you mine, but I wasn't prepared to accept the consequences. I lied to myself a thousand times. And I lied to you." She drew breath to speak, and he covered her lips. "Listen to me. No more lies. I love you, Cassidy, and I can put the past behind me. You have helped me. I see my mistakes. I wronged Quentin and Rowena as I wronged you. If you can live with me, and the Cause—"

"The Cause is part of you," Cassidy said. "Part of what I love. It's worth the struggle, even if it needs to change. I want to share that with you."

He dared to imagine what life would be like with this woman, so loving and warm and strong. His mate in all ways, by his side at the next Convocation, teaching him how to rule and guide with compassion.

A thickness filled his throat. "We still cannot have children," he said. "But the boy, Mikhail—if you could be a mother to him—"

She made a bubbling sound of joy. "Yes. I want to be Mikhail's mother. But he won't have to be alone. He'll have a little brother or sister." She caught up his hand and held it to her stomach. "Our child, Braden—*our* child is growing inside me."

If it hadn't been for the exultant conviction in Cassidy's voice, he would have laughed in disbelief. But there was no denying the second, distinct kernel of light and life he sensed within Cassidy's body, a thing not of sight but mind and heart.

And *he* was there. He thrust his fingers into the mud as if he could force the world to stop spinning.

"Milena lied, Braden. I think Mikhail is your son."

His son. He'd already hurt an innocent child with no justification but his own selfish hatred, and to think that very child could be his own . . .

"How could I fail to know?" he whispered.

"Milena's mind was very strong. She could make anyone believe whatever she wanted. If she hated you, she could have stopped any babies from coming, couldn't she?"

Braden wrapped his arms about his chest. It was more than possible. Even humans had ways to avoid conceiving—but for *loups-garous* it would be even simpler.

"Mikhail," he whispered. "My son. Forgive me."

"He will," Cassidy said. "It isn't too late." She folded her arms about him. "You're going to be a father, Braden. And our children—all of them—will be loved." Suddenly she jumped to her feet, and he heard her splash unheeding in the mud. "You love me!" Rain fell lightly, laughing with her. "Don't you see? Our baby . . . he'll be something new for the Cause, because he comes from love. Maybe that's what's missing and has to be put back in. It's love that will keep our people alive. *Love.*"

Out of nowhere she spun up to him and tugged him to his feet. She pulled him into a wild dance, slipping and tripping with no regard for dignity. She swayed and began to fall, squealing, when he caught her and held her fast.

"Stop!" he commanded.

She stopped. He felt just the slightest flicker of defiance to remind him that she was his by choice, not compulsion. "What's wrong?"

"If you're to have our child, there'll be no more of this wild behavior," he said. He pulled her against him, his body quiet but his heart still dancing. "I won't lose either of you, Cassidy. I can't."

She sighed into his neck. "I can't wait until Isabelle comes back, so I can ask her more about babies. There's so much I still don't know. What *else* am I not supposed to do?"

Her resignation both relieved and touched him. "When the babe is so new, it's safe enough to Change," he said. "Your body shields the child from harm. But soon it will not be wise." He stroked her hair in apology. "You shall have to remain in human form."

"I've waited this long. I can wait a little longer."

"And I want you to rest," he said gravely. "Let the servants wait on you—"

"Do we have to have servants at all?"

He was startled into a laugh, though he should have

been well beyond surprise. "I can alter myself only so much, even for you," he said. "And Greyburn is a major employer of people in this parish. It would be cruel to dismiss them. But perhaps—" He muffled his words in the fragrant fall of her hair. "Perhaps there are better ways to deal with humans than those my grandfather taught me."

"Maybe you could learn to trust them."

"Maybe."

"No more ceremonies in the Great Hall?"

"Perhaps we can find a way to . . . improve them."

"Maybe you'll even start to like humans."

"Anything is possible. I believed you were all but human when I fell in love with you."

She pulled away, hands clasped in his. "What about Rowena and Quentin?"

Mingled regret and anger played havoc with his unbalanced emotions. "They are both very likely beyond my reach, are they not?"

"Not forever." She hugged him, stirring a comfortably definite appreciation for her physical attributes as well as her other fine qualities. "We'll see them again, some day."

When it was too late for the Cause. But Braden was able to accept the trade: love and Cassidy in exchange for the loss of two pawns in a game for which the rules must be changed. On the day they were reunited, he hoped he could greet them as a devoted elder brother and not the tyrannical shadow of Tiberius Forster.

The Cause would not die, as long as he had hope. And Cassidy at his side.

"There's something you should know about Isabelle and your uncle Matthew," Cassidy said. "They went with Rowena to Liverpool, but I think . . . when they come back, there's going to be another marriage."

He remembered what Telford had told him. Another courtship had gone on right under his nose, and he'd been oblivious. It was time for him to reach out to his uncle, welcome him back into the family. And if that meant welcoming Mrs. Smith . . .

"Isabelle always stood by you," he said. "She was a loyal friend. They shall both be welcome at Greyburn."

Cassidy stretched the length of him, wrapped her arms about his neck, and planted a warm, wet kiss on his mouth. "Oh, Braden, I'm so happy." She nuzzled his cheek. "Tell me . . . out of all the things I'm not supposed to do now, does that mean we can't—" She murmured into his ear. His body reacted as if to a shout.

"I believe that will still be acceptable," he said, sliding his hands to her waist.

"Good, because I'm not always going to obey you, Braden. If you'd said no—" She kissed him again, and he lost all sense of duty and dignity in the most wonderful way imaginable.

"Ah, Cassidy," he whispered. "I love you." He cradled her face and stroked every curve and line until he knew its shape and expression in a way more profound than mere sight could ever allow. At last he could openly mourn his blindness, but he found that he had no need.

"My love," he began softly.

> *"My love in her attire doth show her wit,*
> *   It doth so well become her:*
> *For every season she hath dressings fit,*
> *   For winter, spring, and summer.*
> *No beauty she doth miss*
> *   When all her robes are on;*
> *But Beauty's self she is*
> *   When all her robes are gone."*

He bore her back onto a blanket of bracken and rain-softened grasses, warming her with his body. She responded with all the ardor of her generous spirit, and the heat they made burned away the damp and cradled them like a bed of down. He worshipped her body, not with lust, but with love and tenderness and gratitude. Her every caress released another knot of sorrow and pain, until he felt himself truly free for the first time in his life.

He kissed her lips, her breasts, her belly and below, drawing her gently toward the peak. But she would not submit so easily. Laughing, she tumbled him onto his back and sat astride him, the veil of her hair sweeping his face in a teasing arc. And then she made love to him, guiding him inside her. They become one being, and their ecstasy when it came brought the moon from behind the clouds, blazing in victory.

But they were not content to lie in lazy satisfaction when it was over. There was yet one thing they had never done together. Before Braden could speak his wish, Cassidy was Changing, dancing about him, nipping his hands with playful jaws. His heart swelled with pride and awe.

He Changed, and they stood shoulder to shoulder, fur brushing fur. She licked his muzzle, leaped straight up in the air, and dashed away with a mischievous yip. He pursued, and when he caught her they ran in perfect tandem under the bright moon, all the way home to Greyburn.

epilogue

Greyburn, 1876

The thirteenth Convocation was without precedent. It was called but a single year after the last, when Stefan Boroskov had tried, and failed, to challenge the earl of Greyburn's leadership.

The great lawn at Greyburn, bathed in late-summer sunlight, was awash with laughing children. Whole *loup-garou* families attended this gathering, from all parts of the world. There were no more formal delegations. The Convocation had become a joyful celebration of life, and love, and hope.

Cassidy crawled out from beneath the shrubbery, the lost ball in her hands. She tossed it to the gaggle of children, who resumed their play with waves of thanks. As an afterthought, she made a vain attempt to brush off her grass-stained skirt.

"Beggin' your pardon, my lady," the nurse said, approaching from the cluster of chairs and tables set up for tea under the shade of ancient elms. "I think young Lady Angela is lookin' for her mother."

"Thank you, Betsy," Cassidy said, reaching for her daughter. The small face gazed up at her, grinning toothlessly from among the blankets, and a curled fist batted at her hand.

"Do you want some tea as well?" she said, tickling Angel's nose with her own. "I hope that milk will do."

Angela Edith Forster burbled, reaching for her mother's chin. Cassidy kissed the tiny fingers and returned to her chair to look after Angel's needs. The servants had become quite accustomed to seeing her feed her own child, with only a nod toward modesty, just as they had gradually accepted that the old formality and fear were banished from Greyburn forever.

Which didn't mean, of course, that Aynsley was any less dignified, or that the maids failed to curtsy to their earl and countess. The respect was still there, but it was a healthy respect untainted by distrust and coercion.

She watched *loup-garou* couples pass by, some already long mated, others courting. The Cause was no longer about duty and arranged marriages, but Cassidy knew that those changes, too, were for the better.

With Angel cradled in one arm, she reached for the folded letters on the small table beside her.

The first of Rowena's missives had arrived at Greyburn six months after her departure. It had been sent minus a return address, and Cassidy still didn't know where in America Rowena had settled.

She unfolded the most recent letter and smiled, still amazed at the precise, perfect handwriting. Hard facts about Rowena's life in America were scarce, as always, but one thing came through very clearly: Rowena was doing well, and she was content. Not happy, perhaps; Cassidy knew that her sister-in-law hadn't yet confronted the fears that had gripped her so strongly at Greyburn, nor made peace with her werewolf nature. But she was free, now, to make that peace when the time was right.

As for her would-be American mate, he might as well never have existed.

The letter from Quentin was likewise vague and without return address, but it assured his loved ones that he, too, was well. He had never returned to Greyburn after his final disappearance over a year ago, but now they knew that he had followed Rowena to America and was, like her, making his own life there.

With any luck, he would find healing for the pain he hid so well behind that carefree manner and laughing face.

Cassidy refolded the letters and rested her cheek on the top of Angel's downy head. She had faith that Rowena and Quentin would find their destinies, just as she had.

Isabelle had already made her own. She and Matthew had purchased from Braden a pleasant farmhouse on the edge of Greyburn land, and were happily settled into a life of domestic bliss. Matthew was fully reconciled with his family, and the couple were frequent and welcome guests at Greyburn. The legend of the ghost of Matthias was, once again, only a legend.

And, after so many years, the doors of Greyburn had been opened to human guests—Emily Roddam and her family. There would be others to come, though not at the same time as the *loups-garous*. The world wasn't quite ready for such an open meeting. But the first steps had been made.

The longest journey began with a single step. And faith.

"Mother!"

Cassidy looked up. A short little boy with madly pumping arms and legs hurled itself toward her, pale hair flying. Mikhail giggled and skidded behind Cassidy's chair, peeping around its edge.

"Father's chasing me, and I'm hiding!" he announced, unable to control his laughter.

She laughed in response, but already her pulse was leaping with anticipation and joy. It never failed, this sudden increase in her heartbeat whenever she knew Braden was coming.

He did not disappoint her. He strode across the lawn, making a broad show of searching for his son—pausing to sniff the air, cocking his head, scratching his chin in apparent puzzlement.

"Cassidy!" he called, his voice warm with affection. "Have you seen a young scamp of a lad running this way?"

"Not I," Cassidy declared.

Mikhail burst into renewed laughter. Braden stiffened like a hound on the scent and crouched low. Unable to contain himself, Mikhail darted from his hiding place, and Braden caught him in midstride, swinging the boy up on his shoulder.

"I have you, you little rascal," he said. "Shall I eat you up now, or will you spoil my dinner?"

Cassidy gazed with wonder at the two heads so close together, blond and dark. In spite of the differences in their coloring, no one could deny the resemblance between them. It had been clear to Cassidy from the first moment she saw Mikhail. Braden could not have known when he brought the boy home to England, but no one doubted that Mikhail was the earl's true son and heir.

Swinging Mikhail in a wide arc around his shoulders, Braden planted a kiss on the boy's forehead and set him down. Immediately Mikhail ran to Cassidy's side.

"Mother, can I hold Angel?"

From the moment of Angela's birth, Mikhail had been fascinated by his tiny half sister, and had swiftly become a devoted brother. Whatever life Mikhail had led in Russia, it had left no permanent mark on his sunny nature. The reserve and shyness he'd shown upon his arrival had vanished with the attention and love given him by his father and new mother. Braden had set himself to making up for his neglect of the boy, and soon they became inseparable. Mikhail worshipped the ground Braden walked upon.

Cassidy carefully extended the sleeping Angela to her brother, half supporting the baby while letting Mikhail take part of her weight. Mikhail stared at the pudgy face with something very like adoration.

"My sister," he said. "Father, come see!"

Braden came. He rested one hand on Mikhail's shoulder and the other on Cassidy's. He could not see his daughter with his own eyes, but ever since that day of reckoning when he and his mate had shared minds as well as bodies, he had learned to see through Cassidy's. He knew that Angela had his mother's raven hair and his own green eyes.

"Beautiful," he said. But he looked directly at Cassidy, a world of love and pride in his face. "How did I come to deserve so much, my darling American ragamuffin?"

She caught his hand and kissed his knuckles. Mikhail pressed closer, and Angela yawned.

"I had so much to learn," Braden said, gathering them all into his arms. "But you taught me the greatest lesson of all, my beloved Cassidy.

"The only Cause . . . is love."

author's note

Touch of the Wolf is the first of a projected trilogy of werewolf historical romances. My intention is to link these books with my previous and future contemporary werewolf novels. Eventually, I hope to have a full family tree involving the Forsters, Holts, Gévaudans, Randalls, and MacLeans, possibly stretching back even further into history.

There are countless stories to be told about these werewolf families, and, with any luck, someday I'll be able to tell all of them.

I am grateful to all those readers who have encouraged me to continue writing the paranormal romance I love so much.

A historical note: The River Ulf is fictional, located in the approximate vicinity of the North Tyne and River Rede in Northumberland.

about the author

SUSAN KRINARD graduated from the California College
of Arts and Crafts with a BFA, and worked as an artist and
freelance illustrator before turning to writing. An admirer
of both Romance and Fantasy, Susan enjoys combining
these elements in her books. Her first novel, *Prince of
Wolves,* garnered praise and broke new ground in the
genre of Paranormal Romance. She has won the Romantic Times Award for Best Contemporary Fantasy, Affaire
de Coeur's award for Best Up-and-Coming author of
Futuristic, Fantasy and Paranormal Romance, and the
PRISM award for Best Dark Paranormal in 1997.

Susan loves to get out into nature as frequently as possible, and enjoys old movies, wolves, dogs, books of every
kind, classical and New Age music, history, mythology,
the Southwest, fresh bread, and Mexican food. She bakes
a killer chocolate cake.

A native Californian, Susan lives in the San Francisco
Bay Area with her French-Canadian husband, Serge, a
very spoiled dog, and two cats.

Susan loves to hear from readers. She can be reached by
e-mail at: Skrinard@aol.com

Her web page, with quarterly newsletter, links, and
book information, can be found at:

http://members.aol.com/skrinard/

Or you can write to her at: P.O. Box 272545, Concord, CA 94527. Please include a self-addressed stamped envelope for a personal reply.

For Rowena's story, be sure to watch for the next book in Susan Krinard's spectacular werewolf trilogy . . .

Passion of the Wolf

On sale in fall 2000 from Bantam Books

"A red-hot voice in romance, Ms. Krinard continues to offer strikingly original romantic fiction for our reading pleasure."
—*Romantic Times*

"Susan Krinard . . . is the yardstick against which all other supernatural romances should be judged."
—*Affaire de Coeur*